FIC   Klein, Norma, 1938–

The swap

DATE		

© THE BAKER & TAYLOR CO.

THE SWAP

The SWAP

NORMA KLEIN

ST. MARTIN'S / MAREK · NEW YORK

Grateful acknowledgment is made to David Higham Asso-
ciates Limited for permission to reprint lines from "Curfew"
by Paul Eluard, translated by Quentin Stevenson.

Design by Mina Greenstein

Library of Congress Cataloging in Publication Data

Klein, Norma, 1938–
    The swap.

    1. Title.
PS3561.L35S96   1983   813'.54   83-3383
ISBN 0-312-77988-7

First Edition
10 9 8 7 6 5 4 3 2 1

For Norma Fox Mazer—
N to the nth power

One

From inside his office, the newly repaired air conditioner clanking in the background, Misha Edelman looked out at the teenage couple wandering around the lot where he sold used cars. Sometimes he hated them. It wasn't fair, didn't make sense, even on the grounds on which he tried to justify it—that they were wasting his time. So they wouldn't buy anything in the end? Business was slow at this time of year anyway, even slower than normal, which was slow enough. They might not even want service. It was just shopping, only no windows. What harm was there in that? Yet more and more lately he felt a rage that would rise up and settle, almost without his control, over the most unlikely objects. Just the other day he'd hurled an empty tin can at the dog down the block who only came around because he had occasionally petted it. The dog had a long, slightly paranoid face with small dark eyes and had stared at him—he'd missed, the can tumbling off into the bushes—with amazement and he, amazed also, had smiled ingratiatingly and beckoned to him to return, to forgive him. Which he did. Dogs, particularly strays, couldn't afford to harbor grievances.

In fact, occasionally a teenager bought a used car, but mainly if Daddy had money and they had some knack at fixing one up. This kid, the boy anyway, didn't look like he came from a well-heeled home—just the usual: jeans, a T-shirt, shaggy dark hair, sneakers. Were they married, already? They looked like high school kids!

The girl was staring off into space—they always did—while the boy circled the brilliant red Z-28 Camaro, squinting into the July sun at its polished surface. She was pregnant, pretty far along. Her face, to the extent Misha could see it from twenty feet away, looked stunned with heat and fatigue.

Save your money, he told the boy silently. You're going to need it. Save it for bottles and diaper services and babysitting. But of course that was exactly what the boy wouldn't want. He wanted something that had no practical purpose, something racy and quick and beautiful, something as far removed from the world of babies and diapers as he could get. Then why did you get her pregnant? Misha asked him. He had gotten into the habit, since his wife's death, of having these silent conversations with people, almost forgetting at times that they were only going on in his head. They all got pregnant, none of them used birth control, especially in a small town like this. Sex between the two of them had probably been furtive, quick; she didn't know what hit her. Misha started seeing it all in his mind, the back-seat grapplings, her phone call to the boyfriend, scared sick her parents would hear. Go out. Talk to them. What else have you got to do?

"Can I help you?"

They looked up, almost frightened, at his approach. Was the kid thinking of how to make off with the car? Not impossible. Likely, in fact. "That's a great car," the boy said, with a shy intensity.

"It's in terrific shape. A man bought it for his daughter for her sixteenth birthday. She hardly used it, never learned to drive in fact."

His brother Wolf, who had set him up in the business, thought he was crazy to tell the truth about the cars he sold. But Misha lacked the energy or passion for deceit, about either trifles or larger matters.

The boy sighed. "How much you asking?"

"Six thousand." He knew, before he said it, the precise expression of woe and disappointment that would darken the boy's face. He remembered how Wolf had once, in Holland, debated going to a fancy whorehouse, but the price, two hundred dollars (this was in the sixties), stopped him. "I figured I could get two bicycles for that!" he'd said.

"That's a lot, isn't it?" the boy asked.

"Well, like I said, it's basically a new car. It's got maybe ten thousand miles on it. I could've sold it for new."

"Yeah." He accepted this unquestioningly.

"Jed?" It was the girl. Misha looked at her. She looked impossibly young to be having a baby, hardly a teenager, even; a round, soft face, freckled, a wide mouth, and saucer-shaped hazel eyes, not pretty, but appealing. "I feel kind of—" She looked up at Misha. "Could I sit down somewhere?"

"Sure, of course." He led her back into his office while the boy continued circling the car. Maybe its value had shot up in his eyes, knowing now that it was so far beyond his reach. It was funny—all he'd done professionally in the fifty years of his life was sell cars, except for the brief stint teaching high school history from which his brother had "rescued" him several decades earlier. And yet he didn't like cars especially, couldn't even understand that expression of greed, joy, almost sexual pleasure he'd seen gleam in the eyes of so many men who came in to inquire or buy.

His office was messy, but it was at least twenty degrees cooler than the ninety-five-degree heat outside. The girl slumped against the wall. "Could I, um, sit down?"

"Sure . . . Here, come on over. It tilts back. Would that make you more comfortable?"

She sat down carefully. As she sat, her backless sandals slipped off her feet and clunked onto the floor. "It's not the heat," she said apologetically. "I don't mind the heat. It's that I'm pregnant."

"Yes, I—noticed." Some of her awkwardness was getting to him. He was ill at ease with women, even ordinarily. "Would you like a glass of water?"

She nodded gratefully and sat, motionless, till he returned.

"It's your first child?" It was pleasanter, being in here where it was cool, than having to answer questions about a car he knew that kid would never buy.

3

"Yeah." She gulped almost all of the water, and then took a deep breath. "We're not married yet," she said quickly, as though afraid he would disapprove. Did he remind her of her father, some stern parental figure, with his graying hair and bushy eyebrows? "But we're going to be. We just haven't gotten around to it yet."

Fuck that kid! He wasn't going to run out on her, was he? Is that what he needed the car for? There was something pathetic about her, accentuated by the roundness of her stomach, the very light skin. She was looking at the photos he still kept on his desk of his wife and grandson. None of his son. He'd never had a picture of him.

"Is that your baby?" she asked, reaching forward to touch the frame. "He's cute."

"Grandchild."

"Oh . . . Is it a boy?" She flushed. "You can't always tell when they're wearing yellow."

He hesitated. "He was. He was killed two years ago."

She looked horrified and hastily replaced the photo. "The baby?"

"Both of them. It was a car accident." Suddenly he wanted to escape out into the heat again, even though that expression of horror and pity was exactly what he must have wanted. Women did that to you—that appealing, sympathetic look. He tried to stifle the sense of rage at himself as he went out into the lot again. Grovelling for pity from strangers! He hated that beyond anything! Why keep the photos there? But he wanted them. They were still his life. He hadn't set up, created, or found any other.

"I think she's okay," he said to the boy.

"Yeah?"

Misha smiled, but it was forced. For some reason he hated this boy, but he felt too tired to do anything except recognize the emotion, monitor it, and control it. "I gather you're going to be a father?"

The boy's face darkened, as though he'd mentioned his failing an exam. He nodded reluctantly.

"You're both pretty young . . ."

4

"For what?" The boy was suddenly defensive, belligerent.

"For being parents . . . It's a lot of work."

The boy laughed, but mirthlessly. *"She's* the one who got pregnant," he said. He cast a quick, accusing glance at the girl in the office, who was blissfully stretched out in the reclining chair, eyes closed.

"It usually works that way," Misha said drily.

They stood in silence. "It'll work out, I guess," the boy said listlessly. He was still looking at the car. The fantasy in his mind, Misha saw as tangibly as though it were in his own, was to get in that car and drive off and never see that girl again. Can you blame him? He's seventeen at the most. But there's abortion now. Not for these kids. They never use it.

"Sure, it'll work out," Misha said with unconvincing cheerfulness. And she'll get pregnant two months later. At thirty they'll have four, maybe six. Some of them got pregnant in the hospital! He'd heard of that. They did it right in the hospital or the night they got home maybe; the next one was born nine months later.

The boy cleared his throat. "Uh, listen, I was going to ask you . . . you don't need anyone, like, to help around here? I'm pretty good with cars."

"I have someone," Misha said shortly.

"But maybe part time? You're open some evenings."

In fact, he'd had someone part time in addition to Homer, his main assistant, who did some of the body work—knocking out dents, replacing leaking radiators—but when he'd quit, Misha hadn't bothered to replace him. How was this boy going to support a wife and kid with a part-time job? "I can only pay four dollars an hour. Business is pretty slow."

"That's okay . . . If you want to try me out, free of charge, you can," the boy said, swaggering a little uncertainly. "I'm good. I took a couple of courses in high school."

"Well, listen, come around in six weeks, after Labor Day . . . we can talk about it then. Do you have a regular job?"

The boy's face became sullen. "I'm looking."

"There's not much. It's hard."

"Yeah." The boy's eyes flitted to the office again. Was he hoping that by some miracle the place would go up in flames and she would disappear? Sorry, kid. It doesn't work that way.

For the last ten years, since Wolf's death, even more since Brenda's, he'd thought of selling the lot and moving somewhere far away, to Florida or California, maybe. But he had gotten used to Wolf's doing things for him, setting him up, bailing him out, and now, with the emotional inertia that had gripped him since Brenda's death, he felt as though someone had poured concrete over him. He looked at maps, debated change, and woke up in the same bed. So he could sympathize with the boy, though their circumstances were so different. It was so easy to get locked into things, so impossible to get out. Wolf had been the opposite. Always on the move, jumping from one business deal to another, with that uncanny shrewdness about where to jump next. Even as a kid he'd had that. He was fifteen years older than Misha, but what Misha remembered best from their childhood was that crazy, lopsided grin that came over Wolf's face when he had put one over on someone. He loved it, loved the conniving, the subtle maneuvering involved. Reality was a game that you could invent as you went along, changing the rules if the old ones didn't work or got boring. He was like that with everything, even in his three marriages. He didn't want children. "You're my kid," he used to tell Misha. "I raised you, I taught you everything. That's enough." But, knowing most women wanted a family, he would say, "I'll be your first husband. You'll practice on me. When you get good at it, we'll get divorced." They all thought they could convince him otherwise, or just get pregnant by mistake. He never mentioned the vasectomy he'd had at twenty, claiming fertility tests would unman him. And, in fact, he had been the first husband three times. Only his death at fifty-four from a heart attack had prevented Alice from moving on. The others all settled down with their new spouses; they sent him Christmas cards every year, photos of their babies. The first one, Elsie, even named her son after him.

Misha and the boy walked back to the office. The girl was still sitting in the same position, her face dazed. Maybe that was just her expression, maybe it wasn't the heat or being pregnant. For the first time Misha's sympathy shifted slightly to the boy. Imagine being faced by that soft heaviness everywhere, in bed, over the kitchen table. She looked up at them with slight surprise, coming back to reality. "There's a funny sound," she said to Misha.

He nodded. "It's the air conditioner . . . I had it fixed, but something's still clunking around."

"It works okay," she said hastily, as though afraid he'd be offended. "It's just . . . I mean, it's cool."

"Listen," he found himself saying. "You don't . . . Would you kids like a bed?"

They both looked up at him in surprise.

"I have a bed at home, a double . . . I just thought maybe you'd be setting up a home. You might be able to use it. You could have it free. It's not new, but the mattress is good."

"Where will *you* sleep?" the girl asked with that worried look.

"Oh, I . . . There's a bed in another room."

"How about your wife?" the boy said, sensing something peculiar. "Does she know you're giving it away?"

"He doesn't have one," the girl said quickly.

"Oh." The boy was nonplussed, glancing at the wedding ring Misha still wore.

"Is that the bed you want *us* to have?" she asked. "The one you used to—"

Okay, don't take it. He knew she was feeling uneasy, contemplating the idea of sleeping in the bed of someone who had died. Which *was* basically why he wanted to get rid of it, though he didn't consider himself even mildly superstitious. "Listen, it was just an idea. I thought you might need some furniture."

"Yeah, we'll take it," the boy said. "Give us the address and we'll pick it up. I have a friend with a truck."

"But—" the girl started.

"He said it's a double," the boy said, exasperated. "What do you want?"

The girl looked frightened, awkward. "She died," she whispered.

"Who?"

"His wife died." She looked up at Misha. "I'm sorry." Whether for the death or for breaking a confidence was hard to say.

"What's *that* got to do with it?" The boy seemed irritated.

Misha profoundly wished he had not made the offer. "Why don't you talk about it and think it over?" he suggested, wanting only to get them out of his office.

"I *thought* it over," the boy said. "We're taking it. . . . Just give us your number, okay?"

The girl sat crushed, miserable. Misha felt caught between sharing the boy's irritation and pity for her. She wasn't getting to make a lot of decisions, probably wouldn't know how anyway.

"So, we'll be in touch," the boy said, enjoying the authority of being manly, no matter how wrong-headed. "About the job too, right?"

"Right."

He watched them walk off. They were arguing. Misha heard their conversation in his mind. The boy: "Look, it's a bed, it's free." The girl: "I just feel funny about it." "How're we going to afford all that stuff?" "I don't know." "Let's just look at it, okay?" The first of many losing battles on her part, Misha thought.

It was past five. He would close early. He valued any day that gave him an excuse to close early. On days like today, broiling days, almost anything would do. He was going to his sister-in-law's, Ardis', for dinner, but he would go home first. Outside, the dog he had hurled the can at was resting in the shade. Usually the dog spent his days chasing cars or trotting from yard to yard, always alone. Now, seeing Misha, he didn't get up, but watched him with an alert, slightly wary expression. The memory of the hurled can was tucked somewhere in his canine brain. Misha went over, bent down, and scratched him behind the ears. The dog rolled over onto his back. I know how you feel, pal. But the dog had some innate sense of limits. After being rubbed, he sat up, but didn't follow Misha to his car, just thumped his tail once or twice gratefully against the dusty ground.

At home, after showering, Misha looked at the bed. Maybe it had been a foolish offer. The couch wasn't especially comfortable. What he ought to do was move the bed to another room. But that act was connected with so many others, getting rid of Brenda's clothes, clearing things out, realigning his life somehow, that he always stopped short of even such a simple gesture. Now he just lay on the bed, naked, staring at the ceiling. He remembered a man they had known slightly, about fifteen years ago, he couldn't remember his name. The man's wife had cancer, kept having remissions but finally became terminal. When you passed him on the street, for the months before and after her death, it was as though he had a tangible aura of grief around him. He looked as if he might walk off cliffs, not seeing them, or into walls. One night Brenda had said, "But one *second* after she's dead, women'll be lining up knee deep outside his door: chorus girls, Ph.D.s." It was true that the man was handsome, a long lean face, a cloud of grayish hair. "He's not going to be interested in anyone for a long time," Misha had said, expressing what he truly felt. "Years, maybe." "Sure," she replied sarcastically. Sensing she wanted some consolation or reaffirmation, he added, "*I* wouldn't, if anything ever happened to you." She had smiled, a combination of affection and teasing. "Listen, you wouldn't even have to date! You'd just wake up married."

The accident had been almost two years ago. He was still waking up single. Would she be pleased to learn it wasn't as easy as she had thought? Pleased at what could be interpreted as his faithfulness? And yet he wasn't sure it could be called that after a death. Cowardice, more likely. Why was he giving away the bed? Not only the connection to Brenda, but because it seemed to stare at him accusingly. There should be women in it, someone new, an attempted replacement. He wasn't, maybe unfortunately, too old to abandon erotic needs. If Wolf were alive, he would have seen to it. His girlfriends would've had younger sisters, cousins. Once, when Misha had been debating having an operation for back trouble, Wolf had exploded, "Are you crazy?" and proceeded to tell a story about a friend who'd had such an operation and now, instead of the long shooting pains along his back and legs, had permanent arthritis, a belt of pain that never went away. "Do you think you can chase women that way? Hobbling around the bedroom?"

It always surprised him that his brother, who in some ways

knew him better than anyone, so frequently confused him with himself. Misha had never chased women, either literally or figuratively. Mainly, when he was young, at least, they had chased him and, occasionally, he had let himself be caught. But even to be caught you had to take some initiative, put yourself in a position where it was possible! When you were young, everyone was doing it. Now everyone he knew was married. To Wolf relationships with women had been like business deals. Marriage had been invented to heighten the delights of cheating. Whereas Misha's only such misadventure had, as he recalled it, "just happened," though he was suspicious, even in retrospect, of blaming everything on his own passivity. Passivity had its own forms of wiliness—he knew that well enough.

It had not even been that long ago, the summer Brenda had gone to Michigan to stay with Seth and Celia, his son and daughter-in-law, to await the birth of their first child. Brenda had had several miscarriages, one before Seth's birth, two after. Hence, perhaps, her hovering over Seth, which at times had seemed to Misha excessive and to which he attributed, perhaps unfairly, the whiny weakness of his son's character. She had wanted to be there, to give Celia "moral support," though when they had first gotten married, she had claimed Celia wasn't "up to Seth's level," educationally at least, having never gone to college. He had felt forlorn, neglected, abandoned, despite the twice-a-week phone calls to announce how the nine-and-a-half-months-pregnant mother-to-be was progressing.

The woman in his office, his bookkeeper, Sophie, had been a widow, a young one, early or mid-thirties. She had no kids, had taken the job shortly after her husband's death. Misha knew little of her beyond the fact that she was waging a desperate struggle to give up smoking. The first six months on the job she was continually wreathed in smoke, stamping out one cigarette after another in the turtle-shaped ashtray he kept on his desk. When once he made a few gently reproving comments about it being bad for her health, she gasped, "Oh, it's terrible! My husband died of lung cancer; everyone in my *family* died of cancer! It's so *dumb.*" That summer, she told him, she was going to a hypnotist to cure herself.

He offered to drive her there, and then waited—it was early evening—to take her home. She came out looking grim. "I don't think it's going to work, I don't think I'm the type." For the last month she had carried several large packs of banana-flavored bubble gum with her and tried earnestly to munch on it whenever the need for a cigarette arose, roughly every five to ten minutes. "But don't you think I deserve *something?*" she said suddenly, stuffing in another piece of gum. "He just died, like that! We were happy, I mean, really. I'm not just saying that." Misha found himself patting her clumsily on the shoulder. "Of course you deserve something," he said.

From a conversation like that on a sultry, slow summer evening to her bed was a short and not painful progression. She was so happy to have him there! Her delight, the force with which she wound herself around him, squeezing her eyes shut, her delicate hums of pleasure, made him appear to himself more like some kind of savior than a predator. Afterward she lay there, snuggling against him wistfully. "It's hard not being married," she sighed. "You know?" "I guess I've been married more or less forever," he confessed, "but I know what you mean." "I'm not, like, a nymphomaniac, at *all,"* she said, as though such a suspicion might be lurking in his mind. "I don't even—I mean, sex isn't such a huge thing in my life. But you miss it when you don't have it. When you *have* it, you don't even think about it. But all of a sudden it's gone." He stayed to change the filter of her air conditioner and from then on drove her twice a week to her hypnotist and waited outside to take her home. *She* seemed more worried about his being married than he was. She had spoken often to Brenda on the phone. "Your wife sounds like such a nice person," she said. "She is," he admitted. "Very." "I'm not the kind of person who does this," she frequently assured him. "I just—I don't know." "I'm not either," he offered lamely. "That makes me feel better," she said. Her kisses always smelled fragrant and edible, a mixture of the banana-flavored gum and the clove-scented perfume she sprayed on after showering. She fixed him clumsy meals, mainly take-out food from delis, saved from the weekend.

The day Brenda came home, the day before actually, he came

into the office where she sat bent over the accounts. "My wife is home," he said, unable to think of a more graceful introduction. She jumped up nervously. "Should I get another job?" she said. "Should I start looking?" She seemed ready to bolt out the door that second. "No, no, I just meant—" Sophie wouldn't let him finish. "Oh yeah, no, listen, I understand. I'll start looking tomorrow . . . I was going to move to Alaska anyway. My brother lives there. He says there're a lot of men. He thinks maybe I could find somebody." She looked so plaintive and uncertain that he hugged her. "You'll find somebody," he promised her. "I guarantee it."

Had she? Of course. How not? She hadn't been a knockout, her two teeth protruded a little in the front, giving her a slightly chipmunklike smile. But everything else, as he recalled it, had been lovely, in place, in working order. Now, when he, supposedly, could have used a Sophie—not that he thought they were easy to come by—he had no bookkeeper. Business was so slow that he did the accounts himself.

He got dressed and drove to his sister-in-law's. On the way he got stuck behind a woman driver who drove so much the way Brenda had that he felt a stab of pain mixed with exasperation. They were at an intersection and she hesitated for a full minute over making a turn, looking in both directions for oncoming traffic (there was none) before lurching onto the highway. Probably she, like Brenda, had gotten a license late in life. Brenda had learned to drive at thirty-six when she'd taken a teaching job that was forty miles away from their house. The school where she'd taught in Auburn had let her go and this was the only one she could find, after a six-month search. He'd worried about winter traffic. Winters could be severe here. Often it began snowing in November and continued till May. Easter Sunday was almost always frosty; forsythias bloomed with frost on their branches.

He was glad, in a peculiar way, that it was not Seth who had been driving when the accident occurred. Even though, from the reports, it had not been an accident that they could have avoided— the other driver was drunk and smashed right into them, losing his own life as well. But if it had been Seth driving, he felt he would

12

have had to harbor, even after his son's death, an extra grudge—their relationship had been difficult enough in life. It had been July. Seth, Celia, and the baby, Noah, were visiting, staying with them for a week before going on to visit some friends in Vermont. Celia was off shopping. Brenda had set off at midday, driving Seth and Noah to a local mall to get the baby a new pair of sneakers.

Stop! But when he was driving, he couldn't help thinking of it. Every car that wove slightly on the road seemed to him a potential drunk driver who, no matter whom he killed, would, at best, get a weekend in jail, his license returned in a couple of weeks. Every woman driver, especially if she looked anxious peering over the wheel, was Brenda. Every baby, especially held in someone's lap, was Noah, ready to be smashed out a half-open window and hurtled onto a cement road. He had never liked cars, but now he felt there was something almost immoral in selling them. He felt, though he knew this was an illusion, that he could tell which of his customers were going to go out, get drunk, and kill someone. It was like selling guns. Slow down, pal. He tried mentally putting a hand on his own shouder. Relax. It's the end of the day. You're going for dinner. Cars are cars. *Anything* can be lethal.

They always ate early at Ardis' because her husband, Simon, ran a newspaper delivery business and had to get up at three-thirty every morning. He went to bed promptly at eight. "She *always* marries schlemiels," Brenda used to say. "And she could have any-one!" The last was perhaps a sisterly overstatement. But it was true. His sister-in-law, his wife's twin sister, was attractive, in a different way from Brenda, but undeniably attractive. They were technically identical, and had in their relationship all the intense closeness and competitiveness born of that, but to him they merely looked like sisters, or cousins at best. He remembered a photo Brenda had once shown him of the two of them in a crib together at eleven months. Both had the same mop of black curls, the same number of teeth, but where Brenda was sitting quietly, inspecting a rope of rubber teething beads with a gentle kind of bemused introspectiveness, Ardis was hanging over the edge, waving, ready to fall head first, but clearly not caring, a madcap gleam in her eye.

That difference had shown not only in their personalities as adults, but in what they did with the same physical attributes. Brenda had remained slender, while Ardis had a "weight problem," which never got out of hand, but which always plagued her and made her look bustier; her blouses were always bought optimistically, when she was slim. They both had pierced ears—a way for their parents to tell them apart as children—but Brenda, as an adult, usually forgot to wear any earrings or wore small pearls that screwed directly into her earlobe. Ardis' were gypsy gold hoops, dangling fish, something that caught your eye provocatively. And where Brenda had decided to let her hair go gray—though it had been hardly gray at all at the time of her death, at forty-three—Ardis claimed she would go to her grave a brunette. "Does it mean I'm not a feminist?" she asked them. "No," they assured her.

Ardis had been married once before, though Brenda claimed you couldn't really count the marriage at eighteen to a fellow student in high school who'd died from being hit on the head with a surf board before he was old enough to vote. "A total loser," Brenda described him. "He read comic books!" "But he was gorgeous," Ardis would sigh. For years Simon's business ventures were more like hobbies than successful financial transactions. Wily, resilient Ardis supported the family, getting jobs in all of the half-dozen cities they lived in for periods of two or three years, simultaneously raising their two daughters. She was a computer programmer, but had, over the years, risen in position and salary to Data Base Administrator, Technical Assistant, and now was second in command at a small firm in Syracuse. "They all sound like things out of *Star Wars,*" Brenda wailed. "Can you understand what she does, sweetie?"

"To some extent." His sister-in-law wasn't brilliant, but she had a tough, bouncy energy that reminded him of Wolf's. Her rise in the world of commerce didn't surprise him.

"So, how's business?" Simon asked as they sat down.

"Slow."

Their entire relationship over the years had scarcely gotten beyond that exchange. Stoop-shouldered, frail, Simon barely talked. There was no special family tension, but Misha always felt Ardis was waiting eagerly for Simon to get up at eight and say, as he always did, "I hate to leave you good people, but I've put in a pretty hard day."

"So, how's business?" Misha mimicked with a fond smile after Simon had vanished. Before Brenda's death Ardis had always regaled the two of them with all her adventures with men. They were funny stories. She would assure them that her extramarital escapades had nothing at all to do with Simon, was no reflection on their marriage. Brenda swore this was true. "She just likes men, she likes sex. It's really terrific. I mean, she's honest about it." There had been, at times, a mournful envy on his wife's part. "She did it with a black man in a van," she exclaimed one afternoon. "He came up to her after a business meeting and said, 'Do you fool around?' and he had this van. With rock music in the background!" To Misha, Ardis' attitude toward men was unique, among the women he'd known anyway. She had a cheerful, common-sense sensuality. There were men she worked with whom she'd never been to bed with and never intended to. But sometimes she'd go into their offices, she said, and neck for half an hour. He'd never known anyone but teenagers still "necked."

With him, of course, there was a flirtatiousness that was heightened now. She knew he saw no one, knew he found her attractive, knew the bond through Brenda made things both impossible and likely in ways which so far had been a stand-off. Why was he here? Not just for a free meal, but because it was a relationship he didn't have to *create*. It existed already, they were already fond of each other. He didn't have to try to not mention Brenda or feel awkward when she came into the conversation. In a sense she *was* there, with them, all the time.

"I'm bushed," Ardis confessed, kicking her shoes off. They had moved from the kitchen into the living room. "I just got back from Phoenix last night." She grinned. "But I had a good time."

"With who?"

"A lawyer, kind of . . . more Bren's type than mine in looks, actually. Dark, nicely dressed, kind of arrogant. Not conceited, but arrogant."

He laughed. "What's the difference?"

15

"I don't know . . . He was just, you know, the way men do, telling me all his credentials, his wife earns sixty thousand a year, he earns twice as much, kind of coming on too much. But the plane was stalled, and we were bantering back and forth." She looked dreamy. "I love bantering! Simon never banters. I mean, you can't divorce someone for not being able to banter, but I like it. Listen, you want more coffee?"

"Sure, thanks, if there's any left." He could, had their relationship been different, have felt excluded when she related these adventures, but instead he felt some kind of vicarious enjoyment, whether the men sounded at all like him or not.

"So, we got to the hotel and I kind of waited around while he signed in, but he didn't turn to me or anything and it was four in the morning. I figured what the heck: no show. I went to my room and about two minutes later the phone rang! He said, 'Do you want to get together tomorrow night?' I said sure."

Misha sipped the coffee. "Didn't you have to work during the day?"

"Yeah, but that ended at five. What else was I going to do in Phoenix?"

"So, how was it?"

She wrinkled her nose. "Boring."

"Boring?" He'd expected another, racier ending.

"Yeah, what can I say? It was just, like he was still trying to do this snow job, telling me what a great lover he was, all his conquests. I felt like saying: Show me! Stop *talking* so much! It was just forced, I don't know . . . I didn't even know if I felt like seeing him the next night, but then I figured I'd really *make* it work." She looked intent, the way he imagined she looked trying to figure out why a computer system had broken down.

"How did you do that?" he asked, genuinely curious.

She looked a little embarrassed. "I don't know, I just—concentrated. And he was better, more relaxed. Suddenly it was great! It was funny, it was really good. . . . And when he said goodbye, he said, 'This was a little bit of heaven.'" She beamed, evidently genuinely touched by this tribute.

Misha had always wondered how men could get away with

16

lines like that. Probably you could get away with anything, if the woman was in the right mood. Anyway, Ardis looked pleased, her bright, dark eyes glowing with remembered pleasure. "It sounds," he began. "I guess I feel envious slightly . . . I mean, I, haven't—"

"But you aren't trying!" she exclaimed. She often, as with her husband, finished his sentences for him.

"True."

"Listen, I've got three women for you. . . . Will you try? Will you really call them? Brenda would *want* you to!"

"I know." That was too complex. He didn't want to think about what Brenda would have wanted. "So, who are they?"

"They're all terrific. It just depends on what you're looking for."

He laughed nervously. "I'm not—"

"God, you're terrible, Mish. . . . Of course you're looking! In your mind you've *got* to be, at least."

"Okay, in my mind I'm looking. . . . Tell me about them."

Ardis cleared her throat. "Well, one is the one I just hired. I told you about her, didn't I?"

"I don't think so."

"She's . . . Well, listen, she's probably late thirties. Is that too old?"

"No!"

"She's . . . well, she's not gorgeous. . . . She's kind of . . . How shall I put it? There was this girl Bren and I hated in high school: Shelley Wertus. She was a cheerleader and kind of an all-around jackass. Well, Martha looks like that, only older."

"In what sense? She goes around with pom-poms on her wrists?"

"She's just a little slow. Like, she asked me the same question about ten times today. I think she has a good heart. She was engaged, like, for ten thousand *years* to this guy in a wheelchair. I think he'd had polio or something. She took him everywhere. I mean, lugged this really heavy wheelchair—you had to fold it up and put it in the back of the car—she got back trouble lifting it. . . . And then he runs off with another woman!"

"Runs?" Misha asked. "How?"

Ardis brushed that aside. "Wheeled! I don't know! . . . No, he just met this other woman, some nurse, and they got married. When for years he'd said he couldn't marry her because he'd be too much of a burden. So the point is, she's a little depressed. You can tell, like, under the surface she has a lot to give, but you'd have to dig. She needs drawing out."

He sighed. "I'm not up to that."

Ardis laughed. "You wouldn't have to dig hard! Just . . . she has braces too. That's not really important, but I thought I should mention it since it's kind of rare at this age."

"On her legs?" He had imagined just the boyfriend as crippled.

"On her teeth! She just—They're not even that crooked, but her dentist said why not. It shouldn't take too long. I think maybe she has six months to go."

"Who're the other candidates?" he said wryly.

"Is it her braces? What? That the guy ran off? It wasn't her fault."

"I—I need something simple," he tried to explain. "Something—"

"*Nothing* is simple," she told him. "That's not the way things work. You take what's available. That's what life is all about."

He felt that basically she was right and certainly this philosophy, in work and love, had stood her in good stead for over forty years. "Just tell me about the other two," he said. "You said you had three lined up."

"They're not lined *up,*" she protested. "Okay, so . . . the second one is married. I don't know. You probably won't like that. That's not your kind of thing, is it?"

"I don't know *what* my kind of thing is. . . . What's the story with her?"

"She's pretty, I think . . . I guess, like, roughly my age, maybe a little younger. Is that too old?"

Misha laughed. "No! Dixie, age is irrelevant, I mean it." Dixie was her childhood nickname, one Brenda had always used.

"Men always say that, then they see one gray hair on the pillow and go into a coma. Okay, well, her name's Maxine, she has two girls about in college, and she just dug her way out of one of these

---

18

classic zig-zaggy things with some married guy. In fact, you know who it was? It was my former boss. That's how I know her, from my last job."

"What's a classic zig-zaggy thing?" he inquired.

"You know! Up, down, sideways. He loves his wife, he hates his wife, he's going to leave his wife, he's not going to leave his wife. Back, forth, till finally Max was ready to shoot both of them. He's one of those married-to-his-work types. I could have told her that three years ago."

"What about her husband?"

"What *about* him?"

"Well, does he condone these activities or is he in a state of blissful ignorance?"

She exploded. "Condone! What are you, a hanging judge? They've been married since birth, God knows what *he's* doing! Do you begrudge the poor kid a couple of minutes of pleasure a week?"

"Absolutely not," Misha said. "Everyone deserves a few minutes at least."

"With an attitude like this, you'll be a widower the rest of your life!"

"It could be."

"Mish, life doesn't come to you. *You* come to *it.*"

"I know."

"So, stop saying 'I know' and do something! Take a few chances. Look, what bothers me is it's such a *waste.* You're wonderful. You'd make millions of women happy. It's like, I don't know, buying a brand new car and then leaving it in the garage, not even driving it!"

"Definitely not brand new," he protested, flattered anyway.

She came closer to him. "You don't know . . . really. There are just not that many terrific men out there. I know. Believe me. I've looked. No matter *what* you're looking for. I'm not talking about marriage, grand passions, even for just a garden variety one-night stand. . . . You'd be amazed at how many—clumps there are."

"What makes you think I'm not one of them?"

"You're not!" She looked angry. "Bren *loved* you. Do you think she was a fool? That she couldn't have gotten anyone she wanted?"

Her flattery, wrongheaded or no, splashed over him wonderfully. He loved her for it. "Well, I—"

"Mish, I love you, okay? You're a wonderful person. . . . But Bren wouldn't want you to just sit around forever. We talked about it once, about what we'd do if either of us died? And we both agreed. I told her, 'Find someone for Simon. Get him someone good. I want him to be happy.' And she said the same to me about you. 'Make Mish happy.' "

At least death had spared Brenda the task of finding someone for Simon, something he could scarcely begin to imagine. He looked up at Ardis. The genuine warmth that she felt spread over him. Where did family feeling end and erotic craziness begin? He felt that on both sides they were so entangled that neither of them knew what to do. He couldn't, alas, be one of her many one-night stands, and what else *could* he be? "Who's the third?" was all he could bring himself to say, wanting her as she gazed at him with tear-filled black eyes.

"The third?"

"Woman? Girl?"

Ardis sighed, evidently glad to retreat from the intensity of the former moment. "Well, she's the daughter of my boss. She just dropped out of college for a few years and now she's doing something. I forget what. She plays the harp."

"Professionally?"

"No, I don't think so, just . . . She just plays it, I guess."

"How old is she?"

"I thought you said age didn't matter. . . . Twenty-eight probably, something around there."

"Too young."

"You said age doesn't matter!"

"Thirty's the cutoff point," he said. "Thirty-five, even."

She smiled. "I'll put her in cold storage for a few years. What's wrong with twenty-nine?"

"Too many hopes, fantasies, unrealistic expectations. I can't handle it. That's not what I want."

"So, what *do* you want?"

"Brenda, back."

Ardis was silent a second, looking down. When she looked up, her face was flushed. She was angry. "Look, Mish, what do you think? Do you think I *don't* want her back? Do you think there's been one fucking day since she died that I haven't thought of her? You were just married to her. You can marry someone else. She was my twin! She was, like, me! It's like you woke up one morning and half of you isn't there! Just gone. . . . You were close to your brother, but this is different. You just lost a wife. I feel like I've lost part of myself."

She started to cry, then turned quickly aside, as though ashamed of her tears. Misha stood up and put his arm on her shoulder. "I'm sorry, Dix . . . Maybe—"

"Maybe what?" Her voice was muffled.

He didn't know exactly what he wanted to say. What he meant was maybe he'd better try finding someone for himself, if he could. But maybe all of this had nothing to do with finding someone for him. Maybe it was just part of the flirtation between them which zig-zagged—a classic zig-zaggy thing!—from one inappropriate emotion to another. But they needed each other, if only to feel, while they were together, that in some way Brenda still existed, if only for the two of them. He knew, deep down, that Ardis would hate whomever he might find. Didn't she know that too? These women were clay pigeons for him to shoot down, just as he had been doing. "It was a nice dinner," he said awkwardly. "I—I like being here."

"I like having you here."

They smiled at each other. She hugged him and he stopped trying to stifle whatever existed between them and hugged her back. It was the only female body that he would have at such close range for a while, anyway. Unless a newly widowed Sophie zoomed back from Alaska to get his accounts and life back in order. Not likely.

They came for the bed at the end of the week. The truck was out in the yard. With them was another couple, teenagers also, a skinny girl with very short hair and a gangling boy in a straw hat. The three of them helped drag the mattress out the door while the pregnant girl sat on a rocking chair on his front porch and watched. They set it on the lawn for a minute before putting it in the truck. The short-haired girl lay down on it. "Hey, this is comfortable," she said. "This is a great bed!"

"It *is* comfortable," he said. "I've slept on it for seventeen years."

She stood on her head, turned a somersault. "Want to see me do a backflip?" she asked the two boys.

"Sure, go on, Von," the father-to-be said.

She was nimble, her body almost like a child's.

"You ought to join the circus," the other boy said.

She turned right side up again. "You're right . . . I should." She went over to Misha. "Listen, you got any other furniture you don't want?"

The boy in the straw hat came over behind her and clapped his hand over her mouth. "This isn't a garage sale, dope! He's just giving away the bed."

She yanked his hand away. "Will you let him talk for himself?"

Misha tried to think. "I have a TV. It's not in very good shape. It may not work at all, in fact."

"How much are you asking for it?"

"It's free."

"Free? How come?"

"I don't watch . . . and, like I said, it may not even work."

"We'll fix it . . ." She went over to the boy in the straw hat. "Hey, we got a free TV! What do you think of that?" She turned back to Misha. "Where is it?"

"I'll show you." He took her inside and showed her the TV, which was resting on the floor in the corner of the living room. She bent down to lift it. "It's heavy," he warned. "I'd help you, only I have a bad back."

"I'm strong." She grinned at him, an impish grin, flexing her muscles. "I used to be a ninety-eight-pound weakling, but now I'm a hundred and-three-pound weakling." But she carried the TV out to the truck, single-handed, her body bent like a pretzel to one side.

Misha went over to the pregnant girl, who was rocking slowly back and forth. "Would you like some lemonade?" he asked. Her face was pretty, he thought, not that far from childhood, the pouchy soft cheeks and round chin. She was wearing a blouse and cut-off shorts; her pale legs dangled like a rag doll's, not quite reaching the floor.

"Yeah, I'd like some," she said. "Thanks."

He brought out the large plastic container and a stack of paper cups, gave her a cup, and offered some to the three who had loaded the mattress and TV into the truck.

"Hey, a party!" the skinny girl said. "Do you have any cake?" she asked Misha.

The straw-hatted boy kicked her. "Ignore her, will you?" he said to Misha. "She's rude. Her mother never taught her any manners."

"Listen, it's my birthday in two weeks. Don't I deserve cake?"

"I don't have any," Misha admitted. He liked her. "How old will you be?"

"How old do you think?" she asked challengingly.

She looked very young, but he guessed she was older than she appeared. "Seventeen?"

She grinned with delight. "Right! See!" She turned to the other three. "He guessed right." To Misha she said, "People always think I look like some kind of kid. Just because I wear my hair short, I guess."

"*And* you don't have a figure," the boy in the hat said.

She tossed a glass of lemonade in his face. "Take that back!"

He laughed, wiping the lemonade from his eyes. "Okay, you're stacked. Loni Anderson lies awake at night, trembling, thinking: 'God, what if Yvonne Esposito hits Hollywood, I'll be out of a job.' "

"You know, you may not know this, but some men like the petite, delicate type."

"They do?"

"What do you think, mister?" the girl asked Misha. "Do you think I have a good figure?"

"Sure," he said, smiling.

"See!" She stuck her tongue out at her boyfriend.

"What's he going to say?"

"He has an honest face," she retorted. "I bet he never lies. Do you?"

"Rarely," Misha admitted.

The pregnant girl stretched out her cup. "I'm *so* thirsty," she apologized.

"Maybe it's the baby," the dark-haired boy said, the father-to-be. "Maybe *he's* thirsty."

"Will you quit that 'he'!" the skinny girl said. "What if it's a girl? What are you going to do, drown her?"

"It's going to be a boy," the dark-haired boy said firmly.

"Yeah? Well, right this very second it's probably lying there laughing its head off because *it* knows it's a girl. It's probably thinking: Boy, have I got dumb parents!"

"They don't think at that age," the boy said. "They just lie there, waiting to come out."

"Maybe they think," the pregnant girl said. "Nobody knows because nobody remembers."

"*I* think I remember," the skinny girl said. "No kidding. It was very peaceful and quiet, like floating, kind of."

Her boyfriend, the one she'd poured the lemonade on, poured a cup of lemonade over her. "This guy's going to think you're crazy." To Misha he said, "She *is* crazy, in case you're wondering."

"He's going to think we're wasting all his lemonade," the pregnant girl said, "after he gave us all this nice stuff."

Misha smiled. He was enjoying their antics. "That's okay."

The four of them stood up. The dark-haired boy shook his hand. "Thanks a lot for the bed," he said. "We really appreciate it."

"Now they can have a real sex life," the skinny girl said. "It's about time."

Her boyfriend lifted her up and pretended to be about to throw her into the truck. The pregnant girl stood watching them wistfully. "I don't really know anything about babies," she said. Misha couldn't tell if it was a remark addressed to him or just a thought that slipped out.

"No one really does till they have them," he reassured her. "It'll be okay."

"Do you think so?" That vulnerable, tremulous expression was, he feared, going to get her into an incredible amount of trouble.

"Sure," he lied.

She smiled awkwardly. "It's really nice of you, giving us your bed. We don't have that much money."

As though that weren't clear! "I'm glad to have it be of use," he said stiffly. He stood on the pavement as they drove off. From the truck window he saw the pregnant girl looking back at him. She waved.

Two

"So, when're you guys going to get married?" Vonni was sitting on the Ping-Pong table in Jed's father's basement, her legs hanging over the edge, a paddle in one hand. She'd just beaten Luther and Jed, maintaining her undefeated record.

Maddy, who was sitting in the one comfortable chair in the corner, felt her stomach clench. It was a question she couldn't answer. How could she? If it had been up to her, they'd have been married months ago. It was Jed's decision. All four of them knew that, but out of some unspoken courtesy Vonni and Luther never referred to it. "I—I don't know," she stammered.

Vonni and Luther had been married two months ago, the day they had graduated high school. They were in Jed's class; the three of them had been friends, "buddies" since third grade. Maddy had only transferred to Cayuga High when her parents had moved from Weedsport when she was in seventh grade; she was a year behind them at school. So it was different. Everything about Vonni and Luther was different. According to Jed, they'd always been friends, but in a purely asexual, kidding-around way: playing hooky from school, going fishing, hitch-hiking to Canada one summer without telling their parents. Sex had crept into their relationship on the sly somehow. And no one now, seeing them together, would have taken them for husband and wife. It wasn't just their age. Vonni still looked like a boy, with her sharp features, her short punky hairstyle. Maddy had never seen her in a dress. She'd said she'd gotten married in jeans and sneakers. "I mean, what's the big deal?" she said. "So, you're married? It's the same as always."

Now she said this for the dozenth time, obviously more to Jed than Maddy. "It sounds like this big deal. Marriage, you know, like: responsibilities, all that. Adult life. You've got to be grown up. . . . It's not *like* that! You just do it! Nothing changes. You can just fuck and your parents can't object."

But of course with them, with Jed and herself, it *would* be different. They would have the baby. He wouldn't be marrying just a person, he'd be marrying a person with a baby. And then—another difference!—Jed would never have even considered marrying her if she weren't pregnant. That was another unspoken fact that the four of them never dealt with. Vonni and Luther had been in love or whatever they *were* in since they were kids. They had no other friends; they were complete unto themselves. But Maddy had caught Jed on the rebound, when Garnet had tossed him aside. He'd fallen, almost the way someone in a faint might fall, into her surprised, willing embrace. She had spent the first five months with him in mortal terror that each day was the last. She couldn't believe he would want to have sex with her, that he considered her body worthy of even his briefly undivided attention. When she came home at night, after they'd done it in Luther's truck, she felt a halo of worthiness, not of sin, circling her. A good Catholic would have felt sinful, she was sure.

"Where'd we live?" Jed asked Luther. "*If* we did it?"

"I don't know. . . . Aren't you going to get a job?"

"I'm going to try."

Vonni looked over at Luther. "Did you tell him yet?"

"What?" Jed said, looking from one of them to the other.

Maddy felt herself hoping the news might be that Vonni was pregnant. Then it would be both of them, caught together, like the time she and her best friend had been sent home from school for giggling in assembly. They'd be pregnant together. It wouldn't seem so awful, so dumb of her. But she knew it was unlikely. Vonni claimed she hated kids, was never going to have them, not unless she could lay an egg and have someone else sit on it for nine months.

"We got a job," Luther said, almost reluctantly, obviously knowing Jed would be jealous.

"Where?"

"It's this, like, estate, kind of . . . outside Ithaca. This rich couple. They live in Texas. They got it from her mother, and they only use it summers. But they want someone on the grounds, you know, looking after things, making sure no one breaks in."

"We get free room and board," Vonni continued excitedly. "They won't even *be* there. . . . You should see it! Huge rooms! So many they don't even use some. They're just there." She grinned. "They think I'm Luth's brother."

Luther looked sheepish. "See, they really wanted a father and son because there's a lot of heavy work. That's what they advertised for. I knew we couldn't pull that off, so I said Von was my younger brother."

"He goes 'He's real strong. Watch him,' " Vonni said. " 'He can pick me up and carry me around the room.' So I have to pick him up and lug him all around the room while this guy watches. 'Impressive,' he goes. But we got the job."

"Will you live there, then?" Maddy asked.

She nodded. "Yeah, so what I was going to say is, if it's a matter of not having anyplace to go, you guys could come stay with us. There are, like, ten bedrooms. The baby could have three rooms."

But where to stay wasn't the real problem. It had been, when Maddy's mother and father had kicked her out. She always thought of it as a decision her mother had made. Her father was slow, quiet—he could've gone either way. But Maddy was her mother's seventh child, not her favorite. With the other six she'd stayed home, played with them, but by the time Maddy came she had had her job. She worked in the new ball-bearings factory the Japanese firm had set up in Auburn. She liked it. She liked going out for beer with her women friends at night, going bowling. In a funny way, she looked like Von, even at thirty-eight, even with seven kids "under her belt" as she put it. Maddy had thought she might be understanding about the baby, but she had screamed, "What're you—crazy? You want to live my life all over again? You want six kids by the time you're thirty?" She thought Maddy intended to have the baby, continue to live at home, and have her look after it while Maddy was in school. "You think I'm quitting my job, huh? So I can stay home another ten years? Forget it." Maddy's mother had never been impressed with Jed. "So, he's good-looking. Big deal. Does that pay the bills? You tell him if he comes around here one more time, I'll take that rifle down and blow his ears off!" There was a rifle Maddy's older brother, Carl, had once used for hunting hanging over the fireplace.

Jed had gotten the message. He hadn't come around; his ears were still intact. He knew Maddy's mother enough to know she was as likely to carry out her threat as not. The day Maddy graduated eleventh grade, she awoke to find her packed suitcase at the foot of the stairs and a note: "Have fun in your new life."

Who was she to turn to? Her brothers and sisters, most of them ten or fifteen years older than she was, were all married and scattered all over the place. The youngest next to her, Jarita, was an airline stewardess. She was the only one in the family, Maddy thought, who really loved her, who didn't boss her or tease her or beat her up when they had nothing better to do. But she was in San Francisco, which might have been as distant as China, as far as getting there went. And Jarita was always flying all over the place—to Europe even. She sent Maddy postcards from each city she visited. Maddy saved them carefully in a tin box and looked at them at night.

Jarita was the only one of her sisters who had escaped early marriage and instant parenthood. She had boyfriends whom she described to Maddy when she came home to visit, but about whom Maddy's mother, who admired and adored Jarita, knew nothing. "She just doesn't care for men," she said when Jarita had left, knowing nothing of the married pilot, the businessman in Paris, the Jewish doctor who'd almost had a heart attack on the way to Detroit, but whom Jarita had saved, really saved his *life!* They all wanted to marry her, Jarita said, but she was too busy having fun.

Maddy was afraid even Jarita would somehow share her mother's opinion. She had wanted Maddy to graduate high school and come to California to live with her. Maddy was sure she could never pass the stewardess test—you had to be smart *and* pretty. If you weighed more than 120, they fired you! But Jarita had said she could give her pointers, get her in through pull. "I have a friend who'd take care of it." It had always seemed to Maddy like a dream too incredible to be real, the two of them sharing an apartment, herself in a crisp blue uniform saving people's lives, flirting with pilots. It was a dream almost as unreal as the one of being Jed's wife.

"Does your father mind your staying here after the kid's born?" Vonni asked.

Jed shrugged.

His father was deaf, worked as a night watchman in the same factory where Maddy's mother assembled ball bearings.

"Maddy, what do *you* think?" Luther asked. "Want to get married? It's fun, nothing to be scared of."

Maddy brightened. "Yes, I'd like to," she said, though clearly it was no more Luther's business to propose for Jed than for her to accept before he'd asked.

"Great!" Luther said, as though all that had been missing was Maddy's consent. "It's settled, then? How about Saturday?" This time he did look at Jed.

"Sure, why not?" Jed grinned. "Saturday it is." He jumped up. "Want to play another round, Luth?"

"Do *what* Saturday?" Vonni said.

"Get married. . . . We'll go to the place you did."

"Saturday!" Vonni marched up and stared up at him, arms akimbo. "That's in two days!"

"So?"

"So, it's a ceremony, you jerk. What about her dress?"

"You got married in jeans," Jed reminded her.

"I'm different. Maddy wants to do it in a dress."

Maddy wondered how Vonni knew that; she'd never mentioned it to anyone, for fear that would show how deep down she really expected Jed to marry her someday. But the fact was that in the same tin box in which she saved Jarita's postcards, she'd saved thirty dollars from babysitting. She had told herself that, even if they were starving, she would save that money for a wedding dress.

"Yeah, but she's, like . . ." He gestured to indicate Maddy's protruding stomach. "Do they make dresses for women who—"

"Sure!" Vonni said, grabbing a paddle off the table. "Lots of them. . . . We'll go get one tomorrow, okay, Mad?"

"Sure," Maddy said. Had that been a proposal? Had he asked and she accepted? She wasn't sure, it had happened so fast. She was trembling with excitement, and impulsively hugged Vonni because she felt she had to hug someone.

Luther went over and shook Jed's hand. "Congratulations. You are now a man."

Jed guffawed, and then moved over to the Ping-Pong table and started to play. Watching them play, Maddy wondered if, after she and Vonni got the dress, she dared have a photo taken of herself and send it to the local paper. Maybe Garnet would see it! Jed's former girlfriend was rich, snooty. She'd once said if *she* got married, she'd have it announced in *The New York Times*. But maybe, seeing Maddy's photo, she'd have a pang. She and Jed had gone together eight months. And even if it was she who'd broken it off, supposedly because her parents thought she was too young to get serious about someone, she might, somewhere deep down, love Jed still. It was hard for Maddy to imagine anyone *not* loving Jed. Even if Garnet married someone rich, like her parents wanted her to, even then she would remember Jed, Maddy was sure, all her life, at eighty even!

The Ping-Pong balls clattered in the background. Against that staccato music Maddy dreamed. She dreamed of the dress because it was tangible, a real thing. Getting married to Jed, being his wife, was something her mind couldn't settle on. It seemed too enormous, too unlikely. But buying a dress would be different. She had planned it in her mind for months, looked furtively at bride's magazines in the smoke shop where they sometimes went after school for a Coke. When Jed or Vonni or Luther came over, Maddy would drop the magazine hastily, the way her older brothers used to when someone caught them reading *Playboy* or *Penthouse.*

It would be white. Not floor length—that would only be right if you were having a church wedding, like her three older sisters had had. Jarita claimed she would never have a church wedding. "I'm eloping, Mad," she said. "You can come. You can be my best lady. That's all. I don't want all Mom's drunken brothers heaving around and throwing up in the bushes." Actually, that had only happened once. When Doreen got married, Uncle Will had thrown up right over her shoes—she'd taken them off to dance. They were silk, made especially for the wedding, and she had to throw them away. But Maddy envisioned her dress made of something soft and white with lace, maybe in a big enough size so the waist wouldn't bind. She didn't want to feel pregnant when she got married, even if she was seven and a half months along. She wanted to feel like anyone else. Her boyfriend loved her and wanted to spend the rest of his life with her. That was all she wanted to think about when the judge, or whoever did it, made them say their vows. But she was glad Vonni was coming. Vonni could screen off the salesladies who might ask prying questions, she could help find dresses in the right size. It would be almost like having Jarita there, like having a sister.

When they were leaving, Vonni squeezed her hand. "So, I'll come by tomorrow, okay?"

"Okay." Maddy hoped her happiness wasn't too horribly evident. She was afraid it showed, the way she'd been afraid kids at school would be able to tell when she got her period or her mother could tell when she'd stopped being a virgin.

Luther glanced over at the mattress they'd gotten from that man. It was still in the corner of the basement. They'd slept on it there because it was cooler down here in the summer. It was August now, not quite as hot, but still sultry. "How's the bed?" he said, grinning at Jed.

"Pretty comfortable."

"Hey, you know what?" Vonni said suddenly, excited. "I just

got this great idea. I thought, like, maybe for your honeymoon, you guys could come stay at our place. We could fix it up, like a real hotel. . . . You want to?"

They didn't have any money to go anywhere else. Maddy had imagined their just returning to the basement. "That would be wonderful," she said. Vonni was so nice! She looked eagerly up at Jed. The whole day, which had begun calmly and uneventfully, was turning into the best and most thrilling day of Maddy's life.

"Sure, why not," he said.

"And I'm going to bake a real wedding cake with one of those, you know, things on top," Vonni rushed on.

"You want them to die on their wedding night?" Luther said.

She socked him. "I know how to do it," she insisted. "I did it once, in Home Ec. It's just like lots of layers, one on top of the other."

Maddy felt bubbly and lighthearted with excitement. After Vonnie and Luther left, she lay down on the mattress, thinking of the dress again. She hoped thirty dollars would be enough. For a regular dress it would be, but for brides they made everything expensive. Jed came over and lay down next to her. "So," he said.

"We don't have to," she said, knowing he wouldn't go back now. "If you don't want." She had never, even for a second, considered an abortion, but she had thought of maybe raising the baby by herself, how she didn't know. There was a girl in their class at school who'd done that, kept on with school even. But her grandmother had looked after the baby. One set of Maddy's grandparents were in Kansas and the other two were dead. That wasn't any help.

Jed slid his hand up her shirt. He claimed he liked the round feeling of her belly, the way her breasts were so big and soft, like pillows, he said, so much bigger than before. But she couldn't quite believe he meant it. She felt ugly, swollen. She didn't even try, when they made love, to come. It was hard enough anyway! And wasn't it dirty, somehow, to enjoy sex when there was a baby in you? Vonni said she'd read a book that said it was okay, that the baby wouldn't mind because he—she wouldn't even know. But how could they tell? Maybe the baby *did* know! Of course, if they hadn't done it once, there would be no baby, so the baby had no right to mind. These thoughts drowsed through Maddy's mind as Jed entered her and thrust vigorously back and forth. He never asked if she'd come—he never had asked, even before she was pregnant—so maybe he assumed she always did, or always didn't. But when it was over and he'd pulled out, he took her hand. Maddy thought maybe he was going to say he loved her. But he didn't. Anyway, getting married to someone was better than saying things about love. "Love doesn't pay the bills" was one of her mother's favorite sayings.

"So, listen, here's what we say if someone comes over," Vonni said as she and Maddy cruised up and down the aisles of the wedding-dress department of Rothschild's. *"I'm* getting married. You're, like, my married sister so you're going to get a whatever-they-call-it dress."

"Matron of honor," Maddy said. She knew all about weddings, from her brothers and sisters. "But the thing is, I want a real wedding dress."

"You'll get one, relax." Unceremoniously Vonni yanked off her wedding ring and slipped it on Maddy's finger. Maddy was shocked that she would do it so casually. She had thought it would be a bad omen if you just took it off like that, for no reason. "Okay, now you're married," Vonni said.

At that moment a stout, middle-aged woman approached them. "Can I help you girls?" she said with a smile.

"We're just looking," Vonni said breezily. She already had four dresses slung over her arm.

"This is the, uh, wedding department," the woman said, eyeing Vonni's jeans and polka-dot halter top suspiciously.

"Yeah, we know," Vonni said cheerfully, continuing to inspect the dresses. "I'm getting married tomorrow."

"Tomorrow?" The woman looked startled.

"My boyfriend and I've been engaged for five years," Vonni embroidered, "but my mother's been sick and now, all of a sudden, she's feeling better so we figured we'd better do it before she gets sick *again*. Because what she has is something that can just come back—like that!—without any warning."

The woman looked concerned. "Yes, my sister-in-law has that problem. . . . Well, are you in the right size area?" She looked Vonni up and down. "You look like you'd be a five, dear."

"Right, only we need to get a dress for my sister here—" She pointed to Maddy, who'd been standing, petrified, beside her. "She's expecting so we need something—" She gestured, indicating Maddy's shape.

The woman, rather than looking displeased, beamed warmly at Maddy. "An empire style, definitely," she said. "That way, it won't bind you around the waist." She went off and returned with several dresses. To Vonni she said, "If it's tomorrow we may not have time for alterations. Perhaps you'd better stick to waltz-length dresses rather than floor-length."

"Yeah, well, I want something I can wear later on," Vonni said. "Like to parties."

The woman nodded approvingly. "That's so practical, with prices what they are."

In the dressing room Maddy began anxiously inspecting the price tags. The cheapest dress was fifty dollars! One was two hundred! "What am I going to *do?*" she wailed.

Vonni lowered her voice. "Well, listen, one thing I once heard of . . . You can buy it, wear it, and then return it. You just have to make sure you don't spill anything on it."

"How *can* I buy it?" Maddy said desperately. "I only have thirty dollars."

"I'll get some from my mom," Vonni assured her. She pulled one of the wedding dresses on over her jeans and shirt. "That's just so in case what's her name comes in, it'll look real."

Vonni's daredevil self-assuredness was helpful, Maddy thought, though sometimes it scared her. You never knew what Vonni might do next. Like the time she'd sent a photo of herself, naked, to their gay science teacher with a note, "Do with me what you will." She'd told him to meet her behind the post office at midnight, but he never showed.

The saleslady looked in just as Maddy was struggling to get a dress over her head. The first two had been too tight. She looked at Vonni oddly. "Dear, I think you'll get the effect better if you take your jeans and sneakers off."

"That's okay," Vonni said. "Listen, we'll—we'll just come out when we're ready, okay?"

"If you like, there's a three-way mirror outside."

Maddy hated three-way mirrors. They always made you look fat. It was true that if you wanted to know what you really looked like to other people you ought to look in a three-way mirror. But it was so depressing! Especially from the back. And it had always seemed to Maddy that one of her breasts had a funny shape—it tilted off in one direction. Luckily Jed had never seemed to notice.

"That one's nice," Vonni said as Maddy gazed in the small dressing-room mirror. "I like that one." She leaned back, one leg crossed. She looked funny in the lace-encrusted wedding dress, her grungy Adidas sneakers sticking out.

"Yeah, I like this one too," Maddy said, staring at herself, entranced. She looked more the way she thought a bride should look than she would have thought possible. Her breasts looked full, but not lopsided.

"You look like a princess, kind of, in that one," Vonni observed. Suddenly she sighed. "God, you know one thing that's really started to bug me about being married?"

"What?" Maddy said worriedly, glancing at Vonni and then back at herself in the mirror.

"Sex!" Vonni said, so loudly Maddy was afraid the saleslady might come in and take the dresses away. Wasn't it true that only virgins were allowed to wear white dresses?

"What about it?" she whispered.

"I swear for the last three months, we've done it twice a *day,* rain or shine. Luth claims he can't sleep well if we don't do it at night. He says if we don't do it in the morning, he doesn't start the day right. I always thought marriage was supposed to make you *less* horny, not more! . . . And he always wants to do it with me on top. He's weird." She looked at Maddy with that keen, inquisitive look she had. "What position do you do it in mostly?"

Maddy was petrified the saleslady was right outside the door, listening to their conversation. "Just the regular way," she whispered.

"Why're you whispering?" Vonni said. "What do you mean, the regular way? With him on top?"

Maddy nodded.

"I never thought I was marrying a sex maniac," Vonni said wearily.

"I don't think Luther is a sex maniac," Maddy protested.

"Yeah? Try marrying him sometime."

That comment started Maddy on another worrisome train of thought. She knew that Jed and Vonni had once done it together. It had been two years ago, before she had moved to their school. Vonni and Luther had had a fight. Jed said he knew they'd make up, but he also wanted, as he put it, "to try Vonni out." Vonni wasn't sexy or even pretty, in Maddy's opinion, but she could look cute if she tried, which wasn't often. Once the four of them had gone to *The Rocky Horror Show* in Ithaca and Vonni had painted a strawberry decal on her cheek. She'd worn a tall black silk top hat and lots of eye shadow. Jed and Luther had sat at the back—they couldn't get four seats together—and some guy kept trying to pick Vonni up. She told him she had four brothers who were policemen and that she was gay and that she was just recovering from VD, but either he didn't believe her or he didn't care. In any case, he wrote his name and number on a piece of paper and insisted she take it. "How was it with Vonni?" Maddy had asked of Jed nervously. He'd just grinned. "She's lively." Of course, that was almost two years ago, and now Vonni had Luther and was married to him. But what worried Maddy was that once Jed had said it might be fun to try having sex together, the four of them, just in a friendly way. "I don't think I want to," Maddy had said. She was sure she would die if she saw Jed even touching someone else. It made her want to cry just to think of it.

Vonni looked at the price tag of the dress Maddy had on. "It's fifty."

"Did you bring any money?"

"Ten."

They pooled their money, but it wasn't enough. Out at the counter Vonni put down the dress Maddy wanted. To the saleslady she said, "These are really great, but I think my mother might be mad if I don't wear this dress that my grandmother wore that she's been saving in our attic . . . but my sister really loves this dress. Only we're not sure we have quite enough money because we had to spend a lot on this medicine for my mother just so she'd be well enough to come to the wedding? So, like, we wondered if we could come in Monday and pay the rest."

The saleslady looked flustered. She wrote out the price of the dress. With the tax, there was a difference of nine dollars and fifty-three cents. "Well," she said finally, "I don't see why not. *If* you can give me some means of identification."

Maddy panicked. Vonni dug around in her satchel and came out with her marriage license. "This is my sister's marriage license," she said, pointing to Maddy. "I carry it around for her so she doesn't lose it. She's in the phone book, I mean, her mother is . . ." She gave the name and address of her own mother.

The saleslady checked in the phone book and found Vonni's mother's name. "I hope everything goes well," she said, after wrapping the dress carefully in tissue paper. "You girls come back Monday and tell me all about it."

"We will," Vonni assured her.

When the shopping expedition was over, Maddy felt exhausted, mainly from the nervous excitement aroused in her by Vonni's wonderful overlapping lies. "You're such a good liar," she said, impressed. "I mean, I could never make things up like that."

Vonni took this as a compliment. "Yeah, I like making things up," she admitted.

"How come you carry your wedding license with you?"

"I don't know. . . . Hey, want to get a Coke? I'm starving!"

They arranged to meet the next morning at eleven. Vonni and Luther would come by in the truck. They decided not to tell Jed's father till it was over. Jed got dressed in a suit he'd had to buy once for a dance. He spent a long time in the bathroom while Maddy waited, in her wedding dress, seated on the mattress. What was he doing in there? What was he thinking? He was never that communicative, especially about his feelings. If only he was thinking happy thoughts about how wonderful their life together was going to be! If only he was feeling proud that they were going to have a baby! When she heard the toilet flush, she thought with alarm, Maybe he's throwing up. Maybe he doesn't want to go through with it.

But Jed came out of the bathroom, smiling. "Guess we might as well wait for them on the lawn," he said. He looked at her approvingly. "That's a nice dress."

He looked so handsome! Sometimes Maddy, looking at Jed, felt almost sick with a funny mixture of desire and wonder at the way he looked. His long dark eyelashes, the shiny thickness of his black hair, his eyebrows that tilted up at the ends, that dreamy, brooding expression he so often had. Even when she looked pretty, Maddy felt she looked ordinary. The only compliment people ever paid her about her looks was about her eyes, that they were big, that they had a nice expression. Or sometimes, if her hair was freshly washed, they said it was pretty too. I hope the baby looks like Jed, Maddy thought. Even if it's a girl. A girl version of Jed would be beautiful too, mysterious, intense.

There wasn't a long wait to get in to see the judge. Maybe not that many people got married in September on Saturdays. When Vonni and Luther got married, in June, she said they were lined up way out into the hall!

"There was this woman ahead of us," Vonni said, "who'd married the same guy four *times!* She said they'd be really happy, like, for six months and then they'd have terrible fights and get divorced . . . and then they'd start dating and get married and be happy and have fights *again.*"

"I'd never do that," Luther said. "Once is enough."

"Me too," said Maddy. She looked up at Jed, wanting him to concur, to swear, even if not legally, that he had no intention of ever marrying again. But he was staring off into space, not even listening.

They both repeated their vows softly, Maddy so softly that the judge said, "You'll have to speak up, my dear. Just a little louder, please." Then Jed slipped the ring on Maddy's finger. It had a little trouble going on because of the heat. It was Jed's mother's former wedding ring, which she'd left behind when she ran off with the other man. Maddy was afraid that wasn't a good omen, but Jed said it had also been his grandmother's ring and that his grandparents had been married sixty-three years. Looking at the ring, Maddy tried to imagine Jed and herself in sixty-three years. She would be seventy-eight, he would be eighty. Would they live that long, even? Would they be grandparents, maybe even great-grandparents?

When they got out of the building, Vonni threw rice at them. They went back to the truck. Vonni and Luther had fixed the back of the truck up in a special way. They'd put a big Just Married sign inside and laid down a shaggy white bathroom rug. And they had a six-pack of beer, all cold. "We can have champagne tonight," Vonni said. She was excited, almost more than Maddy was. Maybe in some way it was easier being excited about someone else's wedding. You weren't so nervous, anyway.

They drove through town and headed to Ithaca, where they were going to spend the night. On the way, gazing out the window, a sudden horrible thought struck Maddy. What if Jed wanted the four of them to have sex together *tonight?* On their wedding night? Was that why he had agreed to stay at Vonni and Luther's? Maddy knew she would do anything Jed wanted, anything that would make him happy, but she hoped so much that that thought hadn't occurred to him. Anyway, maybe it was something Luther wouldn't like. He liked her a lot, but as far as Maddy could tell he didn't like her in that way. Though it had made her feel good that after the ceremony he had kissed her and said, "Boy, you look gorgeous!"

The house Vonni and Luther were staying in was enormous. Maddy had thought maybe they were exaggerating, but it really did have as many rooms as Vonni had said. It had six acres of land, too, and a swimming pool, drained, several hundred feet from the house, with its own bathhouse.

There were beach chairs around the pool. Jed sprawled out on one, a beer can in one hand. "Hey, this is the life," he said. "Too bad we can't fill the pool."

"I know," Luther said.

Vonni was stretched out on the diving board, her head on the end over the pool. She looked over at Maddy. "So, how do you like married life, kid?"

Maddy looked at her watch. It had been her fourteenth-birthday present from Jarita. They'd been married an hour and fifteen minutes. "I think I like it," she said softly.

"How about you?" Luther said to Jed.

"Yeah, it's cool," Jed said, finishing his can of beer. Maddy wondered if he was getting drunk. She wasn't sure how many cans of beer you had to drink to get drunk. She didn't mind if he got a little drunk but she hoped he wouldn't drink too much. She didn't like beer that much, herself. It had such a bitter taste!

After they'd lain around the pool awhile, Jed and Luther drove into town to get some stuff to eat and Maddy fell asleep in the room Vonni had fixed up for them as their "bridal suite." It really was like a hotel in a way. The bed was enormous and at each corner it had wooden posts with knobs on the ends. There was a flowered rug, a little old but still pretty, and a big mirror over the bureau. There was just one picture, a landscape with two cows grazing under a tree.

When Maddy woke up, it was late afternoon. Jed was sleeping on the bed next to her. He rolled over and, as though still in his sleep, pulled over next to her. "Are you awake?" she whispered.

"Sort of," he mumbled. "Why don't you take your dress off, Mad, okay?"

Maddy had thought they wouldn't make love until that night. She knew it was silly since they'd been doing it practically every day, but she wanted to make it seem like a real wedding night. In her dress it was almost possible to pretend she wasn't pregnant, that the dress just had a full skirt. "Maybe we should wait till later," she said.

"We can do it later too," he reassured her.

"Well, okay." Carefully she removed the dress and draped it

over a chair in the corner of the room. The room was half darkened now. She was glad. She wanted him to think of her as she had looked in the dress, romantic, flowing, not pregnant and bulging the way she did without her clothes. Quickly she darted into bed, grateful that his eyes were still closed. Maybe he'd gone back to sleep! But he drew her to him and got right into position, after kissing her breasts for a while.

Maddy worried about her breasts. Now that she was pregnant, they were full and round, the way Jed liked. But afterward they would shrink down again. She had heard if you nursed your baby, they stayed big, for a while anyway, but eventually they would have to shrink. Of course, he knew what they were ordinarily like since she hadn't been pregnant when she met him, but maybe he had forgotten. If only a way could be discovered to make them stay big all the time! But at least the rest of her would be slimmer again. She had gained too much weight, even though it was a good thing to do for the baby. Once he was born, she would go on one of the many diets she'd been ripping out of magazines, maybe the one where they let you eat one dessert a day. She could never stick to the really strict ones that made you give up everything. Giving up everything was too hard.

It seemed lately, whenever they were about to make love, the baby woke up and started to kick. Maddy thought he was probably angry or indignant that they were doing it. Or maybe it was just uncomfortable for him. Jed always tried to be careful. He put his hands on the mattress on each side of her and lowered himself up and down, like someone doing pushups. But of course inevitably toward the end the baby would get jostled around. Patsy, Maddy's second-to-oldest sister, had once told her that her first baby had been born right after she and Fred had made love. The second after she came, her bag of water broke, she went into labor, and the baby was born two hours later! They practically didn't get to the hospital in time! Each time they did it now, even though the baby wasn't due for two months, Maddy was afraid that if she came, it would be like pushing some magic button. The baby would just come shooting out, like an angry bullet or who knew what. Maybe Jed's penis was like a feather, tickling the baby, and he would shoot out like a sneeze. Did his penis reach up that far? Maddy's knowledge of the inside of the female body was vague. She wished at times she'd listened harder in biology class. At least in the hospital, even if the baby shot out, the doctor was there to catch it. But what would they do if a thing like that happened while they were at home?

This time, anyway, it didn't. Jed moved up and down, his eyes closed, panting slightly. And then, at the end, just as he was coming, making that whimpering "uh uh" sound he always did, Vonni pounded loudly on the door. "Hey, are you guys hungry?" she yelled. "I'm fixing up dinner."

"We'll be down soon," Maddy called as Jed collapsed on top of her. What if Vonni hadn't knocked? What if she'd just walked in right in the middle?

Jed didn't seem to have noticed. He lay beside her quietly. "That was good," he said. "I needed that."

That made Maddy feel wonderful, that she had something he needed that she could give him. Her fears that he was going to propose they do it as a foursome receded to the point that she said, trying to joke, "What if Vonni had just walked in, right while we were doing it!"

"She could have joined in," Jed said, grinning.

Maddy's heart sank. "I think she loves Luther," she said tentatively.

"Oh sure," Jed said. "I know."

"Anyhow," Maddy rushed on, wanting to sweep this disturbing subject away forever. "I don't think Luther likes me that way, especially the way I look now."

"He likes you, Mad," Jed said, as though to reassure her. "He was telling me when we went to get the pizza, how he wishes Vonni had a figure like you do."

"It's just from being pregnant," Maddy said, knowing he meant her breasts. He couldn't wish Vonni had a big stomach like hers!

"Yeah, maybe. But I bet even when Vonni's pregnant she won't have that much."

Then why do you want to do it with them? Maddy wondered,

but decided against voicing this; she didn't really want to know.

"Yeah, Luth said when he was watching you, while we were getting married, he got hard, just standing there."

Maddy knew Jed meant this as a compliment. "Well—he's a nice person," she said, finally.

"Yeah, he's great. . . . It's funny, though, he says Vonni isn't as interested in sex as she used to be. He said it seemed like before they got married she wanted to do it all the time. She used to wake him up in the middle of the night, even! . . . And now she's, like, bored with it or something."

"Well . . ." Maddy didn't know what to say.

"What's the point of getting married, then?" Jed said. "If you're not going to fuck?"

Maddy could think of *millions* of reasons to get married besides that. Like wanting to care for someone and make them happy, and have a baby that would look just like them. She sat up. "I guess we better go down for supper," she said. "Vonni said everything's almost ready."

Vonni had done a wonderful job of setting up the long table. In the middle she'd put candles in silver candlesticks. She'd bought flowered napkins and had put a bunch of wild flowers in a vase. It seemed fancy since all they were having was pizza, but it made it seem more formal, like a real wedding dinner. There was champagne, which Luther managed to open without spilling too much. Jed said he'd just keep on with beer. "You can pour it in the wine glass," he said, holding his glass out to Vonni.

"It's your wedding!" Vonni said. "You can't have just beer."

"Dad says mixing drinks leads to trouble," Jed said.

"We all had beer before," Vonni said.

"Anyhow, I like beer," Jed said. "Champagne has a funny taste."

"Boy, you're really low brow," Vonni said. "Okay, suit yourself. There'll be more for us."

The pizza was really good. They'd gotten a special with just about everything on it: anchovies, green peppers, mushrooms, pepperoni. Vonni heaped her anchovies to one side and Luther reached over and took them. "The human garbage pail," Vonni said good-humoredly.

Then she brought in the cake. Maddy was truly impressed. Vonni had actually made a real wedding cake, from scratch. It was hardly lopsided at all. You couldn't have told it wasn't from a store. And on top there was a little bride and groom.

As they were eating it, Luther said, "Hey, guess who we ran into when we were getting the pizza? Miss Snotty Nose." That was his name for Garnet.

"What was she doing?" Vonni asked.

"Driving around in her car."

"Did she see you?" Maddy asked anxiously.

"Yeah, she came over. She *deigned* to talk to us."

"Did you tell her we got married?" Maddy pressed on, her heart thumping.

"Yeah, we told her."

"How did she act?" Maddy wished she would stop asking, wished she could act as though it didn't matter.

"Real cool, like, big deal, who cares."

"But underneath," Jed said, joking around, "she was devastated. . . . Remember how when she left, she almost hit that other car?"

"She's a lousy driver," Luther said. "That's all."

"Yeah, what'd you ever see in her, anyway?" Vonni said, cutting herself another slice of cake.

"Sex and money," Luther answered for him.

"I thought you never even *did* it," Vonni said. "I thought she was scared about her parents."

Maddy sat there, miserably. What a terrible conversation for them to be having on her wedding night!

"Her parents were—" Jed started. "I *hated* her parents!"

"Oh, she just made all that *up* about her parents," Vonni said heatedly. "*She* was the one who wanted a rich guy. She just blamed it on her parents."

"How do you know?" Jed said angrily. "You hardly even knew her."

"I could tell just by looking at her," Vonni shot back. "She wasn't even pretty! She was just a tease. If she didn't have that car and all that dough, you never would've looked at her."

"Hey!" Luther stood up. "Who cares about her, right? What difference does it make?"

There was a pause.

Maddy wished that, instead of asking, she had just let the conversation ease onto other topics. She felt that Garnet was the bad fairy, like in fairy tales, appearing on purpose to spoil things. She loved Vonni for attacking her. Never, in a million years, would she have had the nerve, though she thought Garnet was all those things and worse: mean, cold, fickle, dumb.

After dinner, they went into a gigantic room that Vonni said was the living room. They got stoned on some stuff Luther had, all but Maddy, who was afraid it might not be good for the baby.

"But it's all, like, formed already," Vonni tried to argue with her.

"Yeah," Luther said. "It's probably got two heads and seven toes already with that guy as the father."

"Still," Maddy said. She wanted the baby to be perfect, she didn't want to take a chance. She wanted it to be a boy or, if not a boy, a beautiful girl. But it was hard, being the only one who had some slight connection to reality. The three of them passed the joint back and forth till they were all laughing and horsing around about things that Maddy didn't think were funny at all, things that didn't even make sense!

"Hey, listen, I'm going to go to sleep," Vonni said, staggering up from the floor where she'd been sprawled out, resting on Luther's backside.

"Can I come up with you?" Luther said, pretending to beg. "Can I sleep with you, Vonni?"

"Only if you keep your hands to yourself," Vonni snapped.

Luther began moving across the floor on his knees, his hands in a praying position. "Hey, pretty please, couldn't we maybe, do it . . . just once? We don't have to ever do it again."

Vonni started giggling. "You are *such* a fool!" she said.

He jumped up. "She loves me!" he cried. "I can't take it. She loves me! We're going to do it! We're going to actually *do* it!"

Vonni socked him. "Shut *up!*" she said.

He scooped her up in his arms. "Okay, here goes. . . . A night of rampant sensuality."

"A night of *what?*" Vonni said, giggling again.

"Don't you remember? That's what Cortina said about that book we read?" Cortina had been their English teacher, senior year. He assigned really dirty books, claiming they were classics: *Women in Love, Lolita.*

Jed stood up, a little uncertainly. He took Maddy's hand. "I guess we should go up, too," he said.

"Carry her up," Vonni shouted as she and Luther proceeded up the long, winding staircase. "She's the bride."

"You want me to break my back?" Jed said.

"I'll carry her," Luther said. "How much do you weigh, Mad?"

"A hundred and twenty-eight," Maddy admitted, ashamed.

"You want me to carry you?" Luther said. "I'll do it."

"No," Maddy said, alarmed. "That's okay. I can walk."

In their bedroom the moonlight was streaming in, across the bed. Maddy wished the champagne had made her feel gay and cheerful, instead of sad and tired. But, catching a glimpse of herself in the dress, she thought, I look pretty, and felt better.

"Mad, the thing is, I'm kind of wiped out," Jed said. "I guess that stuff Luther got was pretty strong. Do you mind if we don't—"

"No, that's okay," Maddy said. "We did it before."

"Right." He grinned. "That was really good."

He fell asleep in one second, almost as soon as they got into bed. Maddy lay in his arms, staring out the window. She wished she had thought to buy some postcards. Well, she could buy some tomorrow. She began composing them in her mind. "Dear Mom, Jed and I got married. We are spending our honeymoon at a really nice place with a swimming pool. (It's drained but you can sit around it.) We have a room with a pretty old-fashioned bed. I'm going to save you a piece of wedding cake. Hope everything is fine at home. Love, Maddy." Would her mother want a piece of wedding cake? Maddy felt she would, or at least she felt her mother would be pleased, no matter what she might say, that Maddy had actually gotten married. Maddy was sure one reason her mother had pitched her out was she didn't think Jed would ever marry her. But now, once they were married, once the baby was born, they would forgive her. It wasn't fair, really. Patsy, her mother's next favorite daughter after Jarita, had been pregnant when *she* got married, and her mother hadn't minded at all. It was true Patsy had graduated high school, and Maddy knew that was another thing that bothered her mother—the fact that she'd dropped out without even finishing, the way her mother had done. But once it was over, ten years from now, who would know or care about that *or* that she'd been pregnant? The baby wouldn't know. Maddy had decided already not to tell him. It might make him feel sad, knowing his parents had had to get married. Whereas if they were happy, he would never even think of it.

She started another postcard in her mind: "Dear Jarita, Guess what? Jed and I got married! We are really happy. I don't know if Mom mentioned it, but I'm expecting a baby in a few months. I'm so excited. I wish you could come visit. Thanks for the cards from Portugal. It looks like a nice place. How are your boyfriends? Love, Maddy." The last time Jarita had visited, Maddy had already begun seeing Jed, but she wasn't pregnant yet. Or maybe she was pregnant but didn't know it. Jarita wouldn't mind, Maddy thought sleepily. That was the good thing about her, she found good reasons for things you'd done even when it didn't seem there were any. And she'd thought Jed was really handsome. "I bet you had to steal him away from a lot of girls!" she'd said, implying that catching Jed had taken some effort and skill on Maddy's part instead of just happening.

That was all the postcards Maddy was up to writing that night, even in her mind. She snuggled close to Jed, even though he was turned facing the other way, put her arms around him, and fell asleep.

Maddy had thought they would have trouble returning the dress, but they didn't, at all. The saleslady's face lit up when she saw them. "Well, how did it go, girls?" she asked.

Vonni looked sad. "We didn't do it," she said.

"You didn't get married?"

"No, see what happened was—remember how I said my mother was sick and all? Well, she got sick again, real suddenly, right when we were about to do it, and we had to take her to the hospital and so we thought it wouldn't be good."

"I'm so sorry, dear." The woman reached out to pat Vonni's arm.

"Yeah." Vonni continued to look convincingly sad. "And actually, I decided not to get married after all."

"Not at all?"

Vonni shook her head. "I decided I'm too young," she said.

There was a pause.

"Well," the saleslady said. "I wasn't going to say anything, but you *do* seem a little young, dear. How old *are* you?"

"Seventeen . . . so I decided I'd wait till I'm thirty." She pushed the box toward the woman. "So, could we get our money back?" She had helped Maddy wrap the dress very carefully, putting the tissue paper back. Thank heaven they hadn't spilled any anchovies on it!

The woman wrote up the exchange and actually forgot that they owed her nine dollars and fifty-three cents. She gave them nine dollars, the whole amount, in fact. "Hey, great!" Vonni said, giving Maddy back her thirty and dividing the nine. "Let's go out and splurge, okay? I feel like having a banana split."

It seemed to Maddy that it was more all right for them to keep the extra money if they spent it right away. But she had been trying lately to give up sweets, and said, "Only if *you* eat most of it."

"Never fear," Vonni said gaily.

She was as good as her word, scooping up big globs of ice cream with syrup and rooting around for the maraschino cherries that had sunk through heaps of whipped cream. Vonni was one of those irritating people who seemed to be able to eat as many fattening things as she liked and it never showed. After having her allotted spoonfuls, Maddy got up from the stool; it was uncomfortable sitting in a chair without a back. "I'll be back in a sec," she said.

She went over to the counter, still a little sad at having had to part from her wedding dress, though she could certainly see Vonni's point about it being better to have the money. "I'd like some razor blades," she asked the boy behind the counter. He was only a few years older than she was.

"What kind, hon? Is it for you?"

Maddy blushed. "No, it's for my husband," she said. Saying the word "husband" out loud like that made her heart start thumping loudly with excitement and fear. But the boy didn't seem to find it at all odd. He gave Maddy the kind of blades Jed used and smiled at her in a friendly way as she took the bag. "Stay cool," he advised her as she moved off.

Her first purchase as someone's wife! Her first banana split as someone's wife! Maddy wondered when you stopped thinking that way, when being married just became a boring fact that blended into the background of your life. Certainly for her it would take a long, long time, years maybe, possibly, she thought, even forever.

Three

"Advantage, Ms. Durante. She leads four-two, second set."

Jed was standing at the side of the court, watching as the other girl, whose last name was Gould, made a final attempt to retrieve the match. She had already lost the first set, six-four. Normally being a ball boy wouldn't have interested him, but now that he'd been doing it for three days, he was beginning to like it. The girls were in the Junior Division of the U.S. Lawn Tennis Association. They were taking part in a tournament for sixteen- to eighteen-year-olds, being staged at the women's college, Coolidge, where three weeks ago Jed had, to his own total amazement, landed a real job as assistant, one of five, to the Head of Buildings and Grounds.

It had been Luther who saw the ad in the local paper and suggested he try out. Why not, had been his attitude. That was how he and Vonni had gotten their job, just through the paper. They hadn't had any pull or anything, nor had they known anyone. Jed knew that on his side was the fact that he'd done construction work several summers; he knew a fair amount of plumbing from his father. It had all gone so easily! The guy who had interviewed him, Bill Hopper, whom everyone called Thornie for some reason, was tall and weedy with pitted skin, around thirty-something, probably. He had an easygoing manner that set Jed at his ease. "Okay, well, how's Monday? Can you start then?" he'd asked, after asking him a few questions. "Or is that too soon?" "That would be great," Jed said. He was so pleased to have the job, he realized he hadn't even asked about salary. It turned out to be nine thousand, but, Thornie said, maybe more if it worked out. Jed asked tentatively about housing. "My wife's expecting," he blurted out, "and we're living with my father, in Auburn." "No problem," Thornie said. "We'll find you a place. The college has lots of spare rooms. Enrollment's dropped quite a bit in recent years."

He had been as good as his word. True, their place was pretty small, just two rooms, a bedroom-living room and a kitchen, but it was half furnished already. It was attached to a larger house where a professor lived. In the old days it had evidently been the servant's quarters. Maddy was pleased. She liked the location of the college, right on the lake. He was glad because often lately she looked so tired and worried that he thought maybe that was the way she was going to be forever, not cheerful and bouncy, the way she'd been when they first met. Having babies changed things, Thornie told him. He had four of his own and had married young; that didn't strike him odd at all. He assured Jed that his wife, May, could get Maddy some odd jobs if she wanted to bring in a little extra cash.

It was a hot Indian summer mid-September day. Jed watched Gould serve. She was tall, tanned, with crinkly blond hair in a long braid that flopped from side to side as she charged around the court. She had a funny nose—it came almost straight down from her forehead—and straight black eyebrows. She looked a little like an Indian, he thought, not only in looks, but in manner—the fierceness with which she watched the ball, her graceful movements. Only she was losing. Jed had the feeling she was going to blow the match. Go to the net! he told her silently. That was the only way she won points, getting her opponent off guard. Durante was a small, chunky girl. She stayed back at the baseline and played a totally defensive game. Gould had some great shots. Her backhand, especially. She knelt down, took a deep swing, and really walloped the ball so it zinged across the net, often grazing it by just half an inch. And her serve wasn't bad either, though in this set she'd lost quite a few points by double faulting. She did that again. Jed ran to retrieve the two balls from the front of the court and handed them to her. She took them without looking at him. He wasn't sure she even saw him! Turning aside, he heard her mutter under her breath, "Fuck it, Capri, what's *wrong* with you? *Hit* it!"

She had been muttering to herself throughout the match. The other girl never said a word, never even changed expression. Sometimes Capri praised herself—"That's the way! Nice shot"—but more often it was exasperated, angry comments. "Shit . . . will you *place* it!" She was panting now, streaming with sweat, despite the headband across her forehead. It had been a long match, longer than the score indicated, many points taking minutes, the ball going back and forth twenty or thirty times. Jed could see how playing against Durante would be annoying. She never missed! Her returns weren't good, but she got the damn ball back from almost everywhere. It was like playing a machine. The volatility he sensed in Gould didn't seem to come to her aid. She was clearly unnerved by her opponent's cool, but unable to emulate or change the game to her own livelier style.

She lost the match.

Jed watched her go over, shake her opponent's hand, and then retreat into the shaded area where the players could relax before or after playing. The four all-purpose tennis courts were on a hill. Below, the lake, bright blue, flawless, stretched out, seemingly endless. Jed had heard it was over forty miles long and four miles wide, almost like an ocean. Some days it could get rough, with waves lapping onto the shore. Other days, like today, it was still as a penny. The Durante-Gould match was the last of the day. It had been the semi-finals. Tomorrow morning at ten the finals began, Durante against some other girl whose name he forgot.

He went over to the shaded area, glad to be out of the sun himself. On a small folding bridge table was a bowl of fruit, mainly oranges and plums, that someone had set out for the players. He brought the bowl over to Gould. "Want some?"

She was standing, her headband off, a towel over her shoulders, brooding. Her black eyes regarded him suspiciously. Jed felt a little like those slaves they'd studied about from Egypt who offered bowls of things to eat to queens. There was something imperious about her gaze, challenging. Without saying anything, she took a plum and bit into it, the juice spurting out onto her arm. Her skin was flushed bright pink.

"You should have come to the net more," he said finally.

"What?"

He cleared his throat. "I think maybe you would've won if you'd come to the net more."

"Yeah?" She grimaced, wrinkling her nose. "I know! . . . God, I *knew* that. But she was so steady! And I miss at the net. I'm not that consistent."

"You hit a few really good ones."

She grinned, pleased. "Did I?"

He was surprised she was so uncertain. "Sure. . . . She got scared when you came forward. You should have seen her face."

She sighed. "You're right. I tried that in the first set, but after I lost it, I got nervous."

"They called one against you that wasn't fair," he said.

She nodded grimly, looked over at the woman in the straw hat who'd acted as umpire. "I hate that lady! She was really unfair. She just decided she didn't like me. That really pissed me off—it's so unprofessional. . . . Hey, who are you, anyway? I thought this was a girls' college."

"I work here," he said briefly.

"What as?"

"Buildings and grounds."

"Huh . . . so, which am I? Buildings or grounds?"

"We do a lot of odd jobs, whatever's needed."

"You live on campus?"

He nodded.

Her face brightened. "Great! I didn't think I'd see a male face for nine *months.* They told us Ithaca is half an hour away and that's the big metropolis, quote unquote. You know, it's so *dumb!* My parents sent me here because they decided in all their immortal wisdom that I was boy crazy and I wouldn't concentrate on my studies unless I was in a less distracting environment. . . . Is that fair? I mean, here I work my *ass* off in high school—and it was a hard school: Trinity. I slave away, I get ninety-three in Geometry which I *hate,* I get an A minus in Biology which I can't *stand,* I get these terrific SAT scores *and* I get into Harvard. . . . And after one *year* they ship me off to this nothing place. . . . The girls are, like—I think the average IQ around here is about six. I mean, they're really the type who are planning to get married right out of college! In their twenties! Listen to this: one girl in my dorm has a hope chest. I didn't think those things really existed. She is actually sitting there sewing on these gigantic tablecloths, so if some fool decides to marry her, she'll have all this equipment. Jesus!"

She talked like a machine gun, with such intensity that he wondered why she hadn't won the match. "So, where do you live?" she finished up. "Where on campus?"

He mentioned the house.

"Do you have a roommate?"

Jed hesitated, strongly tempted to deny his now burdensome-seeming marital status. But he found himself saying, reluctantly, "I'm married."

The girl let out a hoot. "You're kidding! Come on, you're *my* age I bet, aren't you? Nineteen? Twenty? And you're *married?*"

Jed was pleased that she had taken him for a couple of years beyond his real age. He smiled and shrugged. "Yeah, I'm married."

"God, how come?" She stared at him intently, then suddenly put her hand up. "Okay, I get it. You went to high school together, right? You had sex once, maybe a couple of times, in the back seat of some vehicle. She gets pregnant right away because neither of you have ever thought of using anything. You beg and plead: 'Have an abortion!' She says she can't, it's a human life and all that stuff. You feel trapped, think of dumping her. . . . Then you figure, what the hell, do the honorable thing. So you let her drag you off to some judge and now here you are, saddled with some whiny brat who's driving you crazy, your sex life shot to hell . . ."

Jed stared at her, mesmerized. "What *are* you—psychic?" he said, half smiling.

She grinned. "Yeah. . . . Anything else you want to know?"

"Well, you're wrong about one thing," he said. "The baby isn't born yet."

"What month is she in? Your wife?"

"Seventh."

"Is she big as a house?"

He hesitated. "Pretty much."

She whistled, then held out her hand. "Hey listen, my name's Capri. . . . What's yours?"

"Jed." He took the hand she profferred, then released it quickly, as though it had been a more intimate exchange. "That's a funny name. Capri?"

"I know! . . . See, my parents just happened to be on their honeymoon, in Capri, Italy . . . and I was, so legend goes, conceived there. At least there's never anyone in my class with the same name. I don't like being ordinary."

Jed took a plum from the bowl and bit into it. It seemed to him he had progressed from slave to equal by the way she spoke to him. "So, what's going to happen to me in the next year, if you're psychic?" he said, feeling more sure of himself.

Capri stared at him carefully. "Let me see. . . . Well, it's news which is good and bad, like all news. The baby'll be a drag. It'll cry a lot, like all babies. You'll wonder why the hell you got into this . . . but then, lo and behold, you meet this fascinating other woman, someone you just can't resist. You struggle valiantly against your rising feelings of passion and lust. But . . . no use. You fall madly in love with her."

Jed laughed a little nervously. "What does she look like?"

"Good-looking, not in a conventional way, but definitely quality."

"And what about, what about my wife?" He found himself stammering, which he hadn't done since grade school.

"Your wife?" Capri shrugged. "She looks after the kid, she cooks you meals, she's a wife. What more can I tell you?"

The conversation had taken this alarming turn so rapidly that Jed decided to change the subject. He was used to girls coming on to him occasionally, flirting. When he'd been on the basketball team, lots of girls would come over to him after the game and it would drive Maddy crazy. But he'd never met anyone like *this* before! "Are you a professional tennis player?" he asked.

She smiled. "What—you don't like your future? Listen, you're going to love it. Into every life a little excitement and adventure must come. No, I'm not really a pro. I thought of it for a while, but my parents—despite their dumping me in this Godforsaken place—really want me to get a good education. I will! My father wants me to be a surgeon, like him. I just don't know. Cutting people up . . . they say women are better. We have more delicate reflexes, supposedly. Would you let me operate on you?"

"I don't know," he said. "I guess I'd prefer a man doctor, basically."

"Wonderful. . . . Could you tell me all your other macho prejudices before we go any further because I have, like, a very short tolerance for all that?"

"They're not prejudices," he protested. "They're real."

"Okay, let's change the subject," she said. "I don't feel up to a huge fight. . . . So *I* know where *you* live. . . . Want to know where *I* live?"

He nodded. She was wearing a white scoop-necked tennis shirt that clung to her body. Small breasts, but nice. Long legs, muscular but slim. Jed tried to keep his eyes above her collarbone.

"Well, basically during the week I live in one of the dorms. Jason Hall, you know that one? . . . Only weekends I sometimes go home: Cayuga Heights. See, what happened was my parents went through this classic mid-life crisis type thing and decided to move themselves up here. My father flies back and forth to New York where we lived before, and my mother is into this whole growing vegetables, weaving kick."

Jed had been staring at the small gold chain with a star on it that hung around her neck. He hadn't noticed it while she was playing, the chain was so fine. "What's that?" he asked.

"What's what?"

"That thing around your neck."

"It's a Jewish star."

"How come you're wearing it?"

"Because I'm Jewish, okay?"

Jed had never met a Jewish girl before. He remembered some boy at school who'd been on the basketball team with him saying that Jewish girls were short and dark and sometimes had moustaches like Italian girls. "How come you're blond?" he blurted out, hating himself for sounding stupid.

"Don't you like blondes?" Capri smiled in that teasing way. "I can dye it. What color do you like? Red?"

"I just thought. . . . Someone once said—I thought Jewish people had dark hair."

"Some do, some don't. . . . What else did you hear? Anything racy?"

Jed blushed. "No, not especially."

"Well, let me tell you," Capri said. "It's *all* true, everything you've heard. Jewish girls are incredibly sexy, incredibly smart, incredibly everything. See, it's a combination of things—drive, energy, this rich cultural heritage. That's why we're called the Chosen People. That's why we're going to rule the world in the next millennium."

Jed smiled. "Who's going to rule the world?"

"Me!" She struck a pose. "What do you think? Would I be good? I'm ruthless, but I'm also extremely compassionate. I think I might be terrific."

"You're the first Jewish girl I've met," he admitted.

"Good! I like being a first." She stared at him with that intent expression again. "You know, it's weird. In New York, where I come from, everyone's Jewish. I mean, not everyone actually *is*, but it *seems* like they are, kind of . . . and suddenly here *no* one is! Like, in my dorm the girls come up to me like they expect me to be some exotic specimen. I don't know *what* they expect me to do—hand out halvah or hang exotic things on my wall. . . . Listen to this: this one girl comes up to me and says if I want she'll drive me to some synagogue which is, like, nine million miles away. I've never even *been* to one! Or, like, they'll come up to me and start asking me about Israeli foreign policy or something idiotic like that. What do I care about Israeli foreign policy? Do you get what I mean?"

He nodded, though following her conversation was like riding on a rollercoaster. "I guess most people here are Protestant or Catholic."

"Which are you?"

"Protestant, Presbyterian, but my dad never went to church much. I guess I believe, in a way."

"What do you believe *in?*"

Jed was taken aback. "I don't know . . . I just meant I don't—well, I'm not an atheist or anything like that. But what I meant was it's not such a big thing to me as to, um, my, um, wife—" He stumbled over the word. "She's Catholic."

"Huh." Capri looked interested. "Does she do all that stuff with confession and everything?"

"She used to. . . . But I guess after we—" What he meant was after they started having sex, Maddy had felt uncomfortable going and had stopped. "What do they call you?" he asked, to change the subject.

"What does *who* call me?"

"I mean . . . do people call you Capri? Or do you have some kind of a nickname?"

"Call me whatever you feel like. . . . What do you *want* to call me?"

"Caps?"

"Okay, great, call me Caps. I'll just—"

At that moment the woman umpire came over and tapped Capri on the shoulder. "Dear, we're starting down now." She looked at Jed. "Thank you for your cooperation," she said formally.

"I enjoyed it," Jed said.

"Yes, some of these little girls are amazing, aren't they?" the woman said.

"I didn't see any little girls," Capri said. "Where were they?"

"The car is over there," the woman said stiffly. To Jed she added, "We'll see you tomorrow, for the finals, right?"

"Right," Jed said, trying to ignore Capri's smirking expression. She waved as she turned away. With her back to him, he could stare at her retreating figure as long and hard as he wanted without worry. She had a small ass, great legs. Shit.

Walking down the hill to his house, Jed suddenly realized that it was possible he was in big trouble. Or could be. Look, it's up to you. Nothing's happened. Nothing has to happen. He had known that something like this would happen eventually. How could you give up girls at seventeen? It was crazy, it didn't make sense. But he had thought it might be years. Instead he'd been married less than three months! And even when he'd imagined it, he had imagined himself pursuing some girl who would appear in some magical, mysterious way. That was the way it had always been. Even with Garnet, who, despite what Vonni and Luther and Maddy said, *hadn't* been a bitch. And it hadn't been her money that had been the main attraction. Maybe a little, but basically she'd hidden behind that, used her parents' apprehensions of him to justify her own fears of sex. Her hands were always so cold when she touched him! She was scared of all the usual things: that he wouldn't respect her, that she'd get pregnant, that he'd "use" her and then fall for someone else. And no matter how much he swore or tried to convince her, the same arguments would pop up like jumping jacks every time they were together. Till he gave up. It was never going to work. And noticed Maddy, who was there gazing at him as she'd been doing all year, quietly but persistently, with that dreamy blue-eyed stare.

This was different. Not just worse because he was married, but worse because, unless Capri was a tease, he didn't think he'd have to do much convincing, maybe none at all. You don't have to call her, he told himself all evening as Maddy fixed dinner. You don't have to do anything you don't want. Use will power.

Thornie had told him and the four guys who worked on the crew with him—Craig, Mickey, Hans, and Lee—that he would deck anyone who made remarks at any of the college girls. They were always passing by when the crew was doing outside work. Right now the crew was tearing up the sidewalks outside the library, using jackhammers to break it up. Then they loaded the chunks into a truck and took them to the local dump. Jed liked the fact that he was getting in good physical shape, although Thornie had told them the outside work would taper off once the weather got colder, around Thanksgiving. About the girls he said to them, "You can *think* whatever you want. . . . Just don't *say* anything. Got it, fellas?" He told them how once a college girl had complained about lewd remarks someone on the crew had made and it had turned out her father was on the Board of Trustees; there'd been a big stink.

"What can I do?" Craig said, shrugging. "I have a clean mind and a filthy mouth." Craig was the guy Jed liked best. He was stoned from morning till night.

"How can you do that and work?" Jed asked him. He was nervous enough about making mistakes, even with a clear head. The week before he'd had to wheel a wheelbarrow with almost a thousand pounds of wet concrete down a ramp through an open window; they were fixing the basement of the greenhouse. The wheelbarrow had tilted back and forth and Jed had felt sweat pouring off his neck and face. To drop all that concrete! To spill it, to lose his footing!

"I don't know. Why is it a problem?" Craig claimed dope made his nerves steadier. He'd once had a job, he said, doing construction on a skyscraper in Chicago. "Look, if you weren't stoned and you looked down two miles and thought about what might happen if you fell—forget it, man. Whereas I just thought: Hey, great view. It was like being in an airplane, only no airplane, just you."

Craig was the only guy on the crew Jed talked to about anything personal, to whom he confessed his frustrations about sex now that Maddy was so far along. Craig couldn't understand. "Boy, I think pregnant women are *real* sexy," he said. "You want me to help you out sometime?"

Jed knew he was just fooling around. Still he asked, "Sexy? How?"

"Oh, they're just so nice and round and soft." He looked dreamy. He was short and barrel-chested with a big fluffy black beard and friendly brown eyes. "I had a pregnant girlfriend once. Some guy's wife. He traveled a lot. It was great! Best sex I ever had. You just looked at her and she came!" He sucked in his breath, remembering.

Everyone was different in their tastes. Jed knew that already, but he still found it hard to imagine anyone actually preferring someone with a big belly sticking out in front of them. Anyhow, it wasn't just that. It was that Maddy seemed so fearful that she would go into labor every time they fucked, just because of some idiot story one of her idiot sisters had once told her. Or, right in the middle, she would say, "I can feel him . . . I think he's moving around. Can you feel him, Jed?"

The college girls would have been a problem, even if he didn't have a pregnant wife, just because of the barrier that lay between the crew and them, between the town and the college in general. It wasn't just that Thornie had called them out-of-bounds. It was that you sensed they all had boyfriends or maybe would only date other college guys, guys from their own social class. Not all of them were pretty, but some were real knockouts. Craig, obeying Thornie's injunction, said nothing as they passed, but to Jed he would mouth comments. Jed would lip-read them and comment back. "What an ass," Craig would mouth and Jed would mouth, "Which one?" The other guys didn't get what they were doing and thought they were crazy.

Every time a group of girls passed—they were usually in groups—Jed started if he saw a blonde. But none of them was Capri. And now that over two weeks had passed since he'd met her, now that the crazy sexual daze that he'd felt gripping him as he walked down the hill had passed, he felt better. Maybe she *was* a tease, he thought, almost hopefully. Maybe she didn't go to the college at all. Not all the girls in the tournament did, though the college held the tournament each year, hoping to attract students. See, you *do* have will power, he told himelf. What were you so worried about?

Then, one afternoon, driving to the IGA at the end of the day to get a few groceries for Maddy, he saw her. She was down at the end of the dock in a bathing suit, about to dive into the water. Jed stopped the truck and sat in it, watching her. She had to be crazy. The water was freezing. It had been freezing even in early September when he'd taken the job—way down in the sixties at least. If the sun stayed out for several days in a row, it warmed up a little, but no one swam in it now, as far as he knew. She dove in. Go, get your groceries! But it was dangerous for her to be swimming down there alone, without a lifeguard. What if she got a cramp? She could drown! It was his responsibility, as a member of the college staff, to go down and just wait around till she got out, just to make sure nothing bad happened.

Seeing his mission in a more altruistic light, Jed drove the truck down to the lakeside and parked it, and then walked out onto the dock. It was chilly at this time of day, four in the afternoon. A wind was blowing that you didn't feel when you were up on campus. Capri was swimming back and forth from the dock to a small wooden float that lay about thirty feet out. She swam intently, doing a smooth crawl, not seeing him. It was only when she stopped to rest, at the float, that she saw him and waved. She yelled something, but he couldn't hear. Then she started back. When she got to the ladder on the dock she called up, "Hey Jed, get me my robe, will you? It's in that house down there."

The casual way she used his name, her lack of surprise at seeing him, started his heart thumping. There was a small boathouse with a lot of old gear in it near the shore. Jed went back and found, near the doorway, a blue terrycloth robe. He brought it to her. She was standing, shivering, in a one-piece navy-blue tank suit. It was the first time he'd ever seen a girl in a bathing suit that wasn't a bikini. It looked good on her, though. Goose pimples were all over her arms; her skin looked almost blue. She grabbed the robe and rubbed herself up and down, jumping from foot to foot. "God, it's freezing!" she exclaimed.

"I know," he said. "You're crazy, going down here alone. You could have drowned."

She smiled. "Is that why you came down? To save me from drowning?"

"Well, I just worried that—"

"Haven't you been looking for me?"

"I just happened to be driving by."

She looked sad in a half-mocking way. "I'm crushed! Here I

thought you'd been spending all these sleepless nights, tossing and turning, obsessed with all these crazed erotic thoughts about me. You mean you haven't thought about me at *all?*"

"I've thought about you a little," he admitted.

"A little! That's not *good* enough! I wanted you to be spaced out, no other thought in your head. . . . Well, tell me this, were they R or X?"

"What?"

"Your thoughts . . . were they R or X rated? I'm assuming they weren't PG!"

"Both."

Capri smiled. "That's something, anyway."

They walked to the dock house. "You think I'm crazy?" she said. "I'm not. I'm a good swimmer. I try not to swim too much when I'm really into tennis, but I'm going to let the tennis taper off a little. Oh, I'll join the team and all, but . . . you know what I was thinking. It would be great to try and swim across the lake."

"It's four miles."

"So? I could work up to it. I could smear myself with grease like they do with the English Channel and you could come along in a boat next to me and fish me out if I started going under. Do you want to? In the spring, maybe?"

"Okay," Jed said.

She stepped into the boathouse; he followed her. On the floor was a very large red towel. It was so large it covered her almost completely. It made it look like she was wearing nothing underneath. "So, why don't you rub me dry, if you're so eager to serve a useful purpose?" she said.

He hesitated. "Where?"

"Anywhere. *You* choose." She wriggled around and a moment later her bathing suit fell to the floor next to the robe. She stepped over it, moving closer to him. "That'll make it a little easier," she said.

Jed just stood there, transfixed with longing and confusion.

Capri looked at him, frowning. "What's wrong? Don't you want me?" Her voice lost its snappy bravado and sounded genuinely uncertain.

"It's not that, I just—"

"Is it some great moral conflict because of your wife?"

"I—I don't know."

She smiled in a funny way, and then reached out and touched his shoulder. "Listen, worry about it later, okay? It's better to worry about things *after* they've happened."

First he rubbed her with the towel. He liked the feeling of the rough cloth coming between his hands and her body. There was even, in the back of his mind, a vague thought that he would *just* rub her dry. Maybe that was all she wanted! But the towel slipped and fell before he could catch it. They were in each other's arms, her cold naked body pressed against him. He saw the shore of safety drifting impossibly far away.

"Let's go in the boat," Capri said, pointing to the canoe in the back of the boathouse. "No one comes here, do they?"

"Not at this time of year, I don't think," he said thickly.

She scampered ahead of him, naked, the towel dragging behind her. "We can use it as a blanket." When they had cleared out the canoe, which was padded with old life preservers, Capri looked at him, puzzled. "Aren't you going to take your clothes off?"

"Sure, I guess," Jed said reluctantly.

"Do you usually fuck with your clothes *on?*" Bending over, she yanked a slightly bloody Tampax out of herself, then hurled it into a corner of the boathouse. "I have my period," she explained as he rapidly shed his clothes. "Is that okay? It's almost over."

Jed, naked now, lowered himself on top of her. "Sure, it's okay," he said. He couldn't tell if her body was as wonderful as it felt or if he had just forgotten what an unpregnant female body felt like. Maybe it was because of all the sports she did. Her belly was so flat, her legs so sinewy and strong as they gripped themselves around him! And it was the first time in his life he had ever felt someone wanting him as much as he wanted them. Even before Maddy had gotten pregnant, he'd felt that she lay there, slightly in a daze, grateful for his attentions, but not exactly carried away. He never even could tell if she came or not, but anyway, it didn't seem all that important to her. She'd once told him the part she liked best was lying in his arms afterward.

Capri moved with him, arching up so that he was as deeply inside her as he could be. Her hands clutched his shoulders so hard he was afraid she might make a mark, break the skin. "Oh God, that feels so good," she whimpered, sucking in her breath. She came convulsively, moaning, her wet hair flattened against the bottom of the canoe, half falling into her face. Jed fucked her hard, dazzled at the freedom of not having to worry that something might happen, that she might get hurt, that something might happen to the baby. He felt the way he thought Craig must have felt up on that skyscraper, too stoned to worry that he could fall a thousand feet and smash into the pavement below, just thinking: God, what a view!

When he'd unlocked himself from her, she smiled up at him. "So, what'd you think?" she said. "Was that okay?"

"It was good," he acknowledged.

"Oh God, I love men!" she said. "I love their way with words." She stroked his collarbone lightly with the tip of her finger. "Listen, I hope you realize you saved me from committing a serious crime."

"What do you mean?"

"I just get—I think this is typical, I read it somewhere. I just go *berserk* with horniness when I get my period. I thought I was going to have to *rape* my philosophy professor! Here's this poor guy, three kids, balding, you know, the usual thing. He thinks my insights into Hegel are so profound, I mean, I'm just regurgitating everything I learned last year. So, I go up to him after class to get my paper back and he's stammering on about what a delight it is to have someone of my caliber in his class, and I can see the poor guy is kind of trying desperately not to look at my breasts. . . . And you know I thought: what should I do? Should I put him out of his misery? I just wasn't *up* to it . . . I guess I knew you'd come along. I knew you'd find me."

"I *was* looking for you," he admitted, "in a way."

"Yeah," she said a little wistfully. "I knew you were." She looked up at him. "What do you think of my body? Some guys think I'm too much of a jock, a jockette. They don't like the muscles."

"I like them," he said.

She looked down at herself. "I do too . . . because, like, I used to be this classic pudgy Jewish kid, kind of sucking on her braids. A real dumpy mess, till junior high. And then I thought—hell, I can do better than that. So I did this whole physical fitness thing: jogging, lifting weights even. I just thought: just because I'm Jewish, why do I have to be flabby? And, like, for me it was really *hard*. Because I'm basically just a slob, a real sybarite. I really deserve the Nobel Prize for will power, giving up junk food, everything. My mom thought I was getting anorexic just because I lost fifteen pounds. I said, 'Mom, a hundred and fifteen is *not* anorexic.' "

"You don't look too muscular to me," he said. "I mean, you look in good shape, but—"

"*You* look in good shape," she said, looking him over appraisingly. "I guess it must be from doing all that construction work . . . I saw you the other day, outside the library."

"I didn't see you."

"I know . . . I purposely crossed over so you wouldn't. I thought you might, like, have a serious accident or something."

"We're not supposed to make lewd remarks at any of the college girls," Jed said, "or we'll get decked."

Capri frowned. "I always find lewd remarks sort of comforting, but I guess that's because I'm insecure." She ran her hand over his stomach. "I bet you're one of those horrible people that was never fat, even as a baby."

He grinned. "I was kind of skinny. My mother worried about me."

She smiled at him affectionately. "You know, this is an awful prejudice, but I think one reason I've always liked non-Jewish boys is they're just in better shape. I know it's the mind-body thing. I mean, Jews are just too busy *thinking* to care how they look. Or maybe they're too self-indulgent, I'm not sure which it is . . . but I think bodies do count, to *some* extent, don't you?"

Jed grinned. "Definitely."

"My breasts aren't that gigantic, but I guess you can't win them all."

"I like your body," he said

"Great! It's yours, whenever you want it."

That offer lay alarmingly in the air. Jed tried to push it aside, but he felt himself starting to get hard anyway.

"What's her name?" Capri asked.

"What?"

"Your wife. What's her name?"

"Maddy."

"Madeleine?"

"People just call her Maddy."

"What do *you* call her?"

"Just Maddy, like everyone." He was uncomfortable, even saying her name aloud. An image of her sitting at home, waiting for the groceries, flashed through his mind.

"Do you love her?"

Jed frowned. Various answers flew through his mind. It was less a matter lying or telling the truth than that he wasn't sure what the answer to that question was. "I guess . . . not enough, though," he found himself adding. "Not as much as she loves me, anyhow."

"Does she love you a lot?"

He nodded. "I don't know why exactly. . . . I'm not always that nice to her. She just does."

He was relieved that she said thoughtfully, "It's funny how it just happens that way. Like, last year there was this guy in one of my classes, Medieval Poetry, and he just fell madly in love with me. On the basis of nothing! He kept sending me these sonnets in the mail, sestinas, even, odes, madrigals. He had a friend set one to music! . . . And like, we'd hardly ever *spoken*. So finally one day I went to bed with him. I guess I thought that might cure him, like it would make me real and not some symbol. He'd see I was just a regular girl, no big deal . . . but he just got worse. I think maybe he had some psychological problem."

It was cold, lying in the canoe. Reality had begun to descend. It was dark out. Jed sat up and started putting on his clothes. "I was going to the IGA for some groceries, but I guess it's closed now."

Capri glanced at her watch. It was a digital watch. He saw the numbers flick from 5:45 to 5:46. "You've got time if you hurry," she said. She pulled on her jeans and yanked a big baggy white sweater over her head. "I guess maybe you should leave first," she said, "or don't you care what people think?"

"Yeah, I do care."

"Well . . . so." She seemed awkward suddenly, almost for the first time since he'd met her. "We'll figure something out . . . or do you want this to be just a one-shot thing? It's okay. I mean, I'd understand."

Jed cleared his throat. "I'd like to see you again."

Capri's face it up. "It was good for a first time, wasn't it? Usually it's so awkward and awful. But I thought we kind of—clicked."

He smiled. "Yeah, we kind of did." He wondered how many first times she had had. "Don't swim down here by yourself, though," he said as he was leaving. "Promise me, okay?"

"Sure." She kissed him. "I think you did save my life."

That night, lying in bed next to Maddy, who seemed to be sleeping, Jed decided he was entitled to see Capri until the baby was born, which was six weeks off. Maybe the baby would be late, which would give him eight weeks. God, some guys would've gone to prostitutes or massage parlors. He remembered that's what his Uncle Jim had said he'd done. He said he didn't have sex with them, he just had them jerk him off. "Because I feel like Emily is there in spirit," he said. "I close my eyes and I pretend it's her." He had smiled. "Some of those girls aren't bad." But doing that would cost money that he didn't have and here was a girl who really liked him, who was beautiful, who seemed to like sex.

He wondered if you could tell. He and Luther had once had an argument about that. Luther claimed you couldn't tell, that most girls got so good at pretending that there was no way anyone, even an expert, could tell if they were faking. He claimed deep down all of them were out for marriage and they just figured pretending to like sex was a way to get them there, like a means to an end. Jed sighed. Maybe he'd never met any of those girls. Neither Garnet nor Maddy had ever put on such a great show of liking sex. Garnet had been petrified and Maddy had been, mainly, quiet, affectionate, but hardly ever carried away. He sometimes wondered if he said to her, "I'll marry you, but we'll never have sex again," if maybe that would have made her just as happy.

He wondered if Capri minded that he hadn't gone to college. It sounded like all her other boyfriends had. She didn't *seem* to mind, but he couldn't tell. The thought of her going back and telling funny stories about him to her girlfriends made him angry. And he wondered: how many boyfriends had she had? What *was* boy crazy anyway? It was funny how they hardly ever said a boy was girl crazy, no matter how many girlfriends he had. But with girls it seemed they weren't allowed as many.

The next day, while he was on the job, she walked by. She was with two other girls. Craig nudged him. "The blonde," he mouthed. Jed pretended not to hear him, didn't even look up. After they had passed, Craig said aloud, "Hey, you missed something. That blonde winked at us."

"What blonde?" Jed said.

"Are you going blind? The one with the braid?"

"I guess I didn't notice."

"Boy, looking's free, looking's okay."

He felt good all day though, thinking about the wink, meant especially for him.

That Saturday Vonni and Luther came down to see their place. Jed and Maddy took them for a walk along the lake.

"Gee, it's such a pretty town," Vonni said. "It's so small. . . . You know what it reminds me of, Mad? Remember in 'General Hospital' that place called Beecher's Corners where Luke and Laura hid out that time, with Ma and Pa Whittaker?"

"Yeah, it *is* sort of like that," Maddy said. She and Vonni were walking side by side, Luther and Jed just ahead of them. They were passing the drugstore, one of the few buildings in town.

"Hey listen, would you guys wait one sec?" Vonni said. "I need to get some shampoo."

"I'll go with you," Maddy said, and both of them disappeared into the store.

Jed and Luther stood outside.

"So, it's going okay?" Luther asked.

"Yeah, I like it."

Across the road a group of college girls rode by on bicycles.

"Nice scenery," Luther said.

Jed grinned. "If we even say anything to them, we get decked."

Luther whistled. "You can think, though."

"Yeah." Jed looked at him. He would have liked to tell Luther about Capri, to ask his advice, but he was afraid to. He was afraid Luther would think it was wrong, especially with Maddy pregnant. Luther joked around a lot about girls, but the fact was he'd never done it with anyone but Vonni, and had never even tried.

"Maddy's really big," Luther said. "Maybe she'll have twins."

"Boy, I hope not."

That evening they all went down for beer to a little bar at the end of town called The Turning Point. Usually Jed liked that kind of evening. He'd missed Luther and Vonni and had been hoping they'd come visit. But now that they were here, he felt distracted. He tried following what they were saying, but kept losing track of the conversation. You have six weeks, he told himself. You better get moving. It was a peculiar situation to be in, to have someone who was so available, but who, in another way, wasn't. Where was he going to meet her that was really safe? It was such a small town. It wasn't even a town. It was called a village. Suddenly he jumped up. "I'll be back in a sec," he said.

Outside the men's room was a phone. He called the number she'd given him, which he'd memorized. Be there! Answer! he prayed. She didn't, but another girl in the dorm got her to the phone. Jed kept his voice low, even though the phone was down in the basement, far from the bar where Vonni, Luther, and Maddy were sitting and talking. "Uh, it's me," he said.

"You can't talk or what?" she said.

"Not that well."

"Okay, well, one thing I thought . . . How about Saturday? This girl in my dorm is going to lend me her car, and I thought we could drive down to Ithaca and maybe drop in on my folks. Or whatever. We could be back by dinner or so, earlier if you want."

"Your folks?" he stammered.

"Yeah, remember I said how they have this house outside

Ithaca? It's a great house. They have their own tennis court. We could play a little if you want. Mom used to be good. She's got all these trophies from college. And Daddy isn't bad. He's just kind of inconsistent."

Jed felt too rattled to think. He had thought of their going off in the woods somewhere, not going to meet her parents! "Um, I—"

"Is it too hard for you to get away?"

Maybe what she really had in mind was sex, but she didn't want to talk about it on the phone because of the other girls. "I don't have a tennis racket," he said.

"Oh, that's okay. . . . We've got lots of extras."

Someone was coming down the steps. Jed was petrified; it could be Maddy or Vonni. "What time?" he whispered.

"I can't hear you!"

"What time should we—"

"You know that building at the end of town on the lake side, with the kind of turret? Let's meet there at eleven."

"Okay, eleven."

Back upstairs, drinking beer, he prepared his excuse. He would say Thornie wanted him to get some equipment in Ithaca.

"Hey Jed," Vonni said. "You really must be working hard. You look zonked. . . . Do they work you real hard?"

"They really do," Maddy said seriously. "They tore up the whole road and Jed had to carry a thousand pounds of concrete."

Vonni reached over and squeezed Jed's forearm. "Hey, look at that! You can go in one of those magazines, *Playgirl* or something."

"Thornie says the outdoor work'll ease off around Thanksgiving."

"When the baby's due," Maddy said.

The baby. Six weeks. Up till now he'd been waiting, practically counting the days till the baby was born and Maddy would look and act normal again. Now, if by waving a magic wand he could have made her pregnancy go on for another six months, he would have done it in a second.

Her mother had her crinkly blond hair, but it was her father Capri looked like, Jed thought. He was tall and dark, with graying hair.

His black eyes had that same inquisitive, restless, examining expression. It made Jed nervous. "What do you do at the college?" Mrs. Gould asked. It was raining, so they couldn't play tennis, and they were sitting in the living room. "I thought it was all girls."

"Jed's coaching me in tennis," Capri said. "He thinks I should play net more."

"You should, darling," her mother said. "She's great at the net," she told Jed. "It's all nerves, really. My ace in the hole was my net game. Some of the girls were afraid they'd get hit in the face by the ball so they stayed back. . . . Of course the whole game was much less competitive in my era."

"Where did you go to college, Jed?" Dr. Gould said. "You look pretty young to be out already."

"I, uh, dropped out," Jed said. "Just for a year."

"I think that's so sensible!" Mrs. Gould exclaimed. "I wish so much *I'd* done that. You need time to think, to reflect, to decide where you're going. Don't you wish *you'd* done that, dear?" she asked her husband.

"Not really," he said. "I knew what I wanted to do."

"Yes, well, men are so—" She trailed off. "I suppose that's the secret to their success."

"Men are so what?" Capri said impatiently.

"Well, singleminded, I guess." She sipped her iced tea. "Unintrospective. Compared to women, I mean."

"Not any more, Mom," Capri said. "That's a stereotype, anyway."

"Which college were you attending?" Dr. Gould asked Jed.

Jed felt pinioned under his stare. "Uh—Radcliffe," he said.

They all looked surprised.

"I didn't know Radcliffe took men," Mrs. Gould said, looking puzzled. "Or do you mean Harvard?"

"Yeah, he means Harvard," Capri intervened swiftly. "It's kind of like a joke, Mom. The guys say they go to Radcliffe the way the girls say they go to Harvard."

"I see," Mrs. Gould said, still looking puzzled. "Or at least I think I do." She smiled appealingly at Jed. "I'm so bad about jokes. I just never get them! There's nothing so appalling as having to ask people to explain a joke."

"Yeah," Jed said, feeling extremely uncomfortable. Why hadn't he said Cornell or just Ithaca College? He wished her parents would leave. They'd said they had to go out shortly, for a lunch date.

"So, you knew each other?" Dr. Gould asked.

"What?" said Jed.

"You and Capri knew each other last year?"

"No, we didn't exactly know each other," Jed said desperately. He felt like there was a right answer and a wrong answer to all these questions and he had no idea what they were.

"We kind of saw each other on campus, but we weren't, like, in any classes together," Capri said.

"What an unusual coincidence that you should end up at Coolidge," Mrs. Gould said, smiling. "I think it's a marvelous school, don't you, Jed? Capri was afraid the girls wouldn't be that bright, but *I* think they are. They're just bright in a different way."

"Mom, he's not a student there," Capri said impatiently. "So how's he supposed to know what they're like? Take it from me— they're birdbrains."

"What *do* you do?" Dr. Gould said.

"I'm on Buildings and Grounds," Jed said.

"That sounds fascinating," Mrs. Gould said. "Don't you love the country up here? The lake!"

"Yeah, well, I come from up here," Jed said. His stomach was knotted into a ball.

"You do? Lucky you!" She turned to her husband. "Did you hear that, darling? Jed's family is from around here." Then she turned back to Jed. "Well, I must say I feel I've found my spiritual home up here. Sam says he still misses the city and all that, and I thought I would too. But you know I don't at *all!* Not one little bit."

Dr. Gould glanced at his watch. "I think we'd better go," he said to his wife.

"Oh, of course." She jumped up. "The Gufries get so livid if you keep them waiting. It's really her, I think. I don't think he cares so much." She smiled at Jed. "I'm so glad to have met you, Jed. You must come around here more often."

When they had left, Capri collapsed in a chair, like a rag doll, and rolled back her eyes. "Jesus, forgive me," she said. "I didn't know it was going to be the Spanish Inquisition."

"I got the feeling your father didn't like me that much," Jed said. With Maddy's parents it had been the other way around. Her father had always clapped him on the back genially and said, "How's it going, Jed?" Whereas her mother would narrow her eyes and tell him heavily weighted stories about teenage mothers who'd died in childbirth while he waited nervously for Maddy to come down and rescue him.

"Oh, he's just like that," Capri said, kicking off her sneakers. "It's just this classic double-standardish thing. Like, supposedly he's so 'terrified' about me and boys? . . . Well, how about *him?* How about this dopey doctor he's been fucking since I was in ninth grade? I met them once at the movies and he started going through this song and dance abut how they'd happened to 'run into each other.' Carmen! God, can you imagine fucking someone named Carmen? At least she's a doctor. If she'd been a nurse, I'd never have spoken to him again."

Jed looked at her. He wanted to ask something about sex, about when they were going to do it, but maybe that would be rude. It wasn't like they were dating in the regular way. "So, uh," he began.

"Listen, you want to see my room?" Capri said, jumping up. "It's kind of a mess, but—"

They started up the stairs, she first, he following. Capri was barefoot—she pranced nimbly, noiselessly up the carpeted steps. As they proceeded up the stairs, she started taking her clothes off. On the fifth step she pulled off her jeans, on the seventh she pulled her sweatshirt over her head. She wasn't wearing a bra. Finally, at the head of the stairs, she bent down to yank off her bikini underpants. Even then she didn't turn around to look at him, but continued down the hall, carrying her clothes in front of her. Then she flung open the door to her room. "So, what'd you think?" she said, turning around to face him.

There was that mischievous smile on her face. Jed reached out and grabbed her.

As they kissed, open-mouthed, he ran his hand down her shoulder blades and back to her round, small buttocks, stroking her rhythmically. It excited him to have her naked while he was still dressed. She slipped her hand under his shirt. "All the time they were there," she said into his collarbone, "I felt like we were in bed. That's all I could think about."

"Me too," he admitted.

She started helping him off with his jeans. "Wait, I can do it," he said quickly. Shucking his clothes, he watched her as she lay on the bed. Her eyes caressed his body, beckoning. Maddy always turned away when he undressed or looked frightened or perplexed, as though his having an erection was something unwelcome, scary. Capri reached her hand up to draw him down beside her. Her mouth circled his cock gently, like a liquid kiss, the tip of her tongue gliding up and down and around. With tantalizing slowness she moved up his body, sprinkling his stomach and nipples with light kisses. Her half-closed eyes widened and softened as he reached inside her. She was moist, trembling, the pungent smell of her body mingling with the cologne she wore.

"Enter me, okay?" she whispered. "I don't think I can wait. I just—"

He pushed inside her, forcing her back on the pillowless bed. He didn't bother slowing down, knowing that they would get there together or that it wouldn't matter. She tightened herself around him, her feet grazing his buttocks. Jed heard his own cry of release from somewhere far away, her own a softer echo. Then silence; the room, reality returning.

"Jesus, you're so good," she said, and then laughed, touching his hair, which was wet with sweat. "Maybe we were lovers in another life, do you think?"

"Sure," he said, not willing to let her go yet. They were just beginning.

Four

"Sure, I remember you," Misha said. "How's the mattress working out?"

"Okay," the boy said. He cleared his throat. "So, like I said, I was just wondering if you still might need someone just a couple of hours a week, maybe ten or something like that? . . . I got a job," he added proudly.

Misha reached out and shook his hand. "Mazeltov," he said.

The boy looked at him, puzzled. "What does that mean?"

"It's a Jewish expression. It means congratulations."

"Oh." The boy kept looking at him. "I have a friend who's Jewish," he said finally.

Misha smiled. "Good for you! . . . So what kind of job did you get?"

"I'm on Buildings and Grounds over at Coolidge."

"That women's college down by the lake? Nice location . . . Well, I'm glad you got something. With a kid on the way you need a regular job. Did she have it yet?"

"What?" the boy said.

"Did your wife have the baby yet?"

The boy shook his head. "It's supposed to come around Thanksgiving."

Misha thought a minute. "Well, listen, if ten hours a week is all you want or can handle, I think that might work. . . . You see that guy over there? The one in the blue shirt?"

"Yeah," the boy said.

"That's Homer. He does most of my body work. If it's okay with him, it's okay with me."

"I know a lot about cars," the boy said.

"I'm sure you do," Misha said. "*I* don't. I just sell them. But Homer knows everything. So tell him what you're after and let him decide. If he thinks he can use a little help, you're on."

Misha watched the boy walk off. He sat down in his chair. The other day, bending down to help Homer lift a tire, he'd felt a familiar streak of pain pass through his back. Uh oh. That had been twenty-four hours ago and this morning he'd been pleased that he'd been able to get out of bed and move around, pretty much as normally. But the pain was still there, and he knew from past experience that it could get worse with no warning. His intention was to take it easy all day, lift nothing heavier than a pencil.

He thought of the boy's face when he'd said "It's a Jewish expression." At that moment, he'd felt as though Wolf were there, shaking his head. That had been one of the reasons he'd been so eager to get Misha out of Auburn and to New York. "Jews are *not* rural people!" he would say. "What're you trying to prove? Do you see Jewish farmers? Can you see a Jew being dumb enough to spend his life yanking on a cow's tits? You're going to feel like an outsider all your life. Is that what you want? Like Mom and Pop?" But it had, Misha thought, been different for their parents. They had come from Germany early in the century, just married, come with that naive hopeful eagerness about America, maybe the last wave of immigrants that could feel that in quite such a pure way. They had settled in Auburn because they liked the country, the rolling fields, the farms, the lake. "It's like Europe," their mother used to say—for her that was the highest compliment. "We took one look at it and we said, 'This is it.' " "Okay, but that's *them*," Wolf would argue. "Their generation was all crazy. Is that the life you want? Helping out in some hardware store? Having your wife sell stationery supplies in a place so small they can't afford to fix the front door?"

Misha sighed. Why was he, ten years after Wolf's death, still having this argument with him? Maybe because he had always felt that Wolf was partly right. But it was comfortable, easier to stay than move, to let roots sink in rather than yank them out. There were times in his life when he could have gotten out, he thought in retrospect. If he hadn't met Brenda that vacation when he'd come home from college, if she hadn't herself been from Syracuse and liked this part of the country, maybe, like Wolf, he would have moved. She always felt Wolf exaggerated. "What's so wonderful about crime and pollution and mugging?" she would say. And to Misha, "He doesn't have kids. He doesn't know. For people without kids it's a whole other ball game."

But it was true. He had never really gotten over that feeling of being an outsider. Not that he and Brenda hadn't had friends, but it was something more subtle than prejudice, something about the way people spoke, the way they did things, the way they fixed up their houses. And it was the expression that always came over their faces when he said he was Jewish, a look of discomfort and then a quick eager comment to prove they weren't prejudiced. "I had a friend that was Jewish." "I had a Jewish teacher once." "I was reading this book the other day by this Jewish writer." Or once, when Seth brought a friend home from fifth grade who had looked at the Christmas tree in their living room and asked, hesitantly, "Is that a Jewish Christmas tree?"

There was hardly a day now that he didn't spend some time thinking of selling the store and moving. He still had part of the fifty thousand dollars Wolf had left him when he died. "Look, you're never going to have money," Wolf would say. "It's just—it's not *real* to you. You don't have the craving. It's like sex. There are people who crave it. That's different from wanting. Everyone wants. That doesn't get you anywhere. It's craving that counts." True, he didn't have the craving. He wanted some bottom-line comfort, a decent home, good food, but that was basically about all. He'd never had any special desire to travel. Hearing about Wolf's trips to France, to Greece, to Thailand was as real to him as going there himself; more real maybe. The way when as a kid he'd see a movie Wolf had described and think, "But it was better the way he described it."

The boy returned in about half an hour, saying it was okay

with Homer. "He says Thursday evenings and Saturdays are the best for him. Is that okay with you, mister?"

"Edelman," Misha said. "Misha Edelman. . . . What's your name, sonny?"

"Jed Parker."

Misha shook his hand. "Well, Mr. Parker, I'm glad to have you in my employ. That's a pretty heavy schedule you're on, isn't it?"

"Yeah, it is pretty heavy," the boy said, proudly and seriously, "but once the baby comes, I figured—"

"Right. You're a sensible man. . . . Your wife feeling okay? Not too tired?"

"She *is* kind of tired," the boy said. "She's real big too . . . I hope it's not twins!"

Misha smiled. "I'll keep my fingers crossed for you. So we'll see you Saturday, around ten?"

"Thanks, um, Mr. Edelman." He looked out into the yard. "You still got the Camaro?" he said.

Masha smiled. "Yeah, I still do."

"I think maybe you've got the price up too high," the boy suggested. "Six thousand's a lot."

"It *is* a lot."

They both stood gazing at it. On the boy's face was a look of wonder and appreciation. "Well," he said finally, breaking out of his reverie. "It sure is a beautiful car." He turned to leave. "See you Saturday."

It was funny. The first time he'd seen the boy, Misha had disliked him. This time he seemed like a nice kid, polite, eager. Maybe it had just been the heat. Or one of his moods that could descend without warning for no apparent reason. And what a position to be in: just out of high school, saddled with a wife and kid already. Maybe they have a great sex life. I hope for his sake they do.

He thought of the mattress. He had given it away impulsively, thinking maybe it would prompt him to do something about the house, rearrange things somehow. But instead all he'd done was move the sleep couch from the den into the bedroom. He kept it open all the time. It was pretty comfortable, actually. But it just made him feel like a guest in his own house, which wasn't much improvement on the way he'd felt sleeping in the bed he'd shared with Brenda.

He went over to Homer just before lunch and asked him if he thought the boy would be a help. Homer was always after him to get more help. "Yeah, sure, why not? He'll help."

He was not a man with whom it was easy to have a conversation, but he knew everything there was to know about cars and then some. Some of the cars he worked over so meticulously that they were, almost literally, as good as new, maybe better than they'd been at the start. And he hated selling any, which made them a wonderful team. His face would always fall when Misha said he'd sold a car he'd worked on a long time. "You sold the Olds?" he'd say, frowning. "Who'd you sell it to? Good people?" Misha was never exactly sure what "good people" meant. As far as he was concerned, it was people who had the cash to buy the damn thing. "Yeah, good people," he'd reply.

The next morning, trying to get out of bed, Misha let out a yelp of pain. It escaped from him inadvertently, as though someone had dropped a concrete slab on his big toe. The pain zinged in an arrow straight through him, down his spine and into his calves. A moment later he tried once again to move, this time very very slowly. No use. Misha sighed. Maybe he should have had the operation. Some guys claimed it was a real cure. "Sure you're never the same again," someone had told him once. "But you're never the same again anyway, right? The way you used to be. So, what's the difference?"

The only comforting thing was that he'd had these seizures often enough so they no longer scared him. The first few, when he could hardly move for several days, had given him panicked thoughts about permanent paralysis, of having to live with the pain as a constant thing. But usually after three days he could get up and move around. Then there'd be another two when he was okay if he didn't try to leave the house. And finally, after a week, he'd be just about back to normal with a few twinges. There was no cure. He tried to do back exercises every morning when he remembered, but it didn't prevent the attacks, though maybe it made them less frequent. He had a bottle of Valium that he knew was half full. If he took one every four hours, the pain seemed to recede, or maybe it just made him too sleepy and dazed to feel it as keenly.

He used the phone near the bed to call Homer, catching him before he left for work. Homer said he would handle everything. Which meant that if someone wandered in and spent half an hour waiting for service, Homer might ultimately ramble over and say, "Sorry, Boss's sick today. Try us later in the week," or "Come back next week, if you're around."

With a Valium in him, Misha spent a fairly pleasant morning in bed, listening to chamber music on the radio, reading Pushkin, drinking from a large carafe of grape juice and ginger ale that he placed on the floor beside the bed. He'd learned Russian in a crash course in the Army in the fifties. Though his parents spoke it at home, they'd never taught it to him or Wolf. He'd always liked the sound, the soft mellifluous vowels. All the necessary phrases had left his head entirely—"You are now in enemy territory"; "You have ten minutes to decamp"—but he still had a vague grasp on the essentials, as long as there was a dictionary close at hand. Mostly he read the same things over and over so that a dictionary was hardly necessary; he had the English translation tucked away in his head.

Sometime in the late morning he got up to go to the bathroom. As he was coming out, the phone started ringing. It was a comical position to be in, to know that there was no way on earth he could reach the phone, that it would take him at least ten minutes to cross the fifteen feet from the bathroom to the bed. The phone rang on and on, insistently. "Sorry," he said, shrugging. "I can't do it. Call back later." When he finally reached the bed again, the phone had stopped. He sank slowly against the pillows, exhausted.

It didn't ring again till midafternoon. He'd dozed off, taken another Valium, and been surprised to find, when he got up to rummage for some lunch in the kitchen, that the pain had abated slightly. When the phone rang a second time, he answered it on the first ring. "Hello?" His voice sounded a little sleepy and slurred to him.

"Mish?" It was Ardis. "Thank heaven I got you! I've been frantic! Where were you? I called before and there was no answer. Then I called your office and there was no answer there!"

"No, I'm sorry," he said. "I heard the phone before. I just couldn't get to it. It's my back. It collapsed again."

"Huh . . . badly?"

"The usual. . . . It'll pass."

"What's the usual?"

"Oh, I get these things from time to time. They come and go. It's nothing serious. I guess I've been forgetting to do my exercises as regularly as I should."

"So, you're bedridden?" She sounded concerned, which was comforting.

"Yup." He reached over to turn the radio down.

"I guess that rules out what I was calling about. . . . Remember the—my boss's daughter—"

"The harpist?"

"Well, she's not quite as young as I'd thought . . . thirty-three. And she said she'd love to meet you. So I was thinking of having you over for dinner tonight, but I guess I can set it up some other time. . . . What are you doing about food?"

"I have some things," he said vaguely.

"What do you mean—things?"

"Cans, that sort of thing."

"Cans! How about basics?"

Misha laughed. "What *are* basics, Dixie?"

She heaved an exasperated sigh. "Basics! You know. Bread, milk, butter, vegetables, meat . . ."

"I don't have any of those," he admitted.

There was a pause.

"Well, listen, how about this?" she said. "How about I'll come over after work and bring you some stuff? You've got to eat!"

"Wouldn't that be a lot of trouble?" he said, delighted.

"Why? I have to get some stuff for us. I'll just get extra. What do you want? Steak? Broccoli?"

"Steak and broccoli sound wonderful," Misha said.

"Okay, well, great . . . I'll get everything and I'll see you around six, depending on traffic."

For the remainder of the afternoon, Misha lay in bed, alternately reading, listening to the radio, and allowing himself to indulge in wistfully erotic daydreams about Ardis, steak, and broccoli. At five he got up and lumbered to the bathroom again, and managed to shave and wash in a perfunctory way. Should he change into fresh pajamas? Was this a "date"? He loved the idea of someone coming over to take care of him. Brenda claimed that his mother had fussed to excess over him and Wolf when they were kids, whenever they came down with the mildest ailment. It was true. Among his happier memories of childhood were of being sick, lying in front of the radio, feasting mindlessly on trays of soup, sandwiches, boxes of Ritz crackers, chocolate pudding inundated with blobs of freshly whipped cream.

Ardis arrived at six-twenty, opening the door with the key she still had. Once—he wondered why he'd forgotten until this moment—they'd lent her a key when they went on vacation so she could come here evenings with her boyfriend, the doctor with whom, five years ago, she was supposedly wildly in love. Brenda had met him once for a drink. Even for extramarital dalliances, Ardis had wanted sisterly approval. It had been awkward, Brenda had reported, having a drink with a man she didn't know, whose only connection with her was through her sister's bed. "If *that's* her idea of gorgeous, I don't know," she'd come home muttering. "You should have seen him! A beard, chain-smoking, a tic over his eye . . ."

Misha saw Ardis pass by the bedroom and head for the kitchen, her high heels clattering as she staggered through with two gigantic paper bags full of supplies. A minute later, still with her sheepskin coat on, she came breathlessly into the bedroom.

"What *is* this?" she demanded, looking around.

"What is what?"

"Where's the bed?"

"I gave it away."

"Yeah, but . . . this is the sleep couch, isn't it? Don't you have a regular bed?"

"It's comfortable." But he felt sheepish.

"Mish, did anyone ever tell you you're impossible?"

"Many people, many times."

"Going out to buy a bed is not that complicated! They're not that expensive!"

"I know, I know," he said, smiling.

"I know, I know," she mimicked, gazing at him in affectionate exasperation. Her expression softened. "So, listen, are you in terrible pain? How's it going?"

"It's a little better . . . as long as I take a Valium every four hours."

She came closer and picked up the bottle that he had placed near the bed. "These aren't supposed to be good for you," she said. "You can get addicted. I read about a woman who went crazy when she tried to kick the habit!"

"I just take them when I have trouble with my back," he lied. In fact, he took them a few times a week for insomnia too.

"Don't they make you sleepy?"

"Sure, but when you feel like this, that's a blessing."

She stood regarding him intently, and then took off her coat and draped it over the chair in the corner. "Okay, just lie there and relax. It'll take about half an hour."

He enjoyed the sound of her rattling around the kitchen, occasionally yelling out, "Where are your spices?" or coming to the doorway, a pan in her hand, saying, "Is this your biggest frying pan? What happened to the one I gave you for Christmas?" Delicious smells began drifting out, mouth-watering odors. Finally, Ardis came in carrying the bridge table and opened it near the bed. "So, which do you want, sweetie, beer or wine?"

"I don't think we have either." The casual "sweetie" zinged through him; it was Brenda's term of endearment also.

"I brought both. . . . Which do you *want?*"

"Which are *you* having?"

"What does it *matter* what I'm having? What do you *want?*"

"Wine," he said meekly.

She grinned. "I want wine too. . . . It's a good one, Bully Hill."

When everything was done, Ardis carried in two plates heaped with food, uncorked the wine, and pulled a chair opposite him. "I can't play the harp, but here I am!" she said. She clicked her glass against his, then drank thoughtfully. "Yum, good." Her lips were moist and reddened.

"You know, I think this is the best meal I've ever eaten," Misha said, taking a first mouthful.

"It can't be," she said. But looked pleased anyway. "When we were kids, Mom always used to cook us whatever we wanted on our birthday. Bren always picked lasagna or manicotti, and I always picked steak and artichokes with strawberry shortcake for dessert. Mom said, 'Dix, you better marry a rich guy.' But I never did."

"I feel ten times better already." He buttered a slice of the French bread. "Who needs a harpist? Anyway, wasn't she the one who was pretty young?"

"Mish!" Ardis' cheeks were flushed. "I told you she *isn't!* She's thirty something. Oh, fend for yourself. I'm giving up on you." She glanced at her watch. "Simon's going to bed now," she said. "It must be strange, having that kind of schedule, don't you think? I mean, eight in the evening for him is like two in the morning for us! But, you know, maybe it suits him. He's not that sociable a person." As though that might have failed to escape his notice! "He likes people once they're there, but if I never invited anyone over, I bet he'd never miss it. He might not even notice." She looked wonderingly surprised.

She was dressed for work in a navy-blue skirt and white blouse, looking more trim and businesslike than usual. Her typical party outfits tended to be more bohemian—embroidered Polish blouses, denim skirts with ruffles, anything in red. "How's work been?" he asked. Her presence, the good food, the wine made everything swim pleasantly around him.

86

"It's been okay, nothing special. . . . Oh, I had one good trip two weeks ago, to Toronto. They're using our system, but they ran into problems so I had to fly up and figure out what went wrong. What an ego trip! I get there, all these gray-suited men running around in circles, frantic. I hadn't slept all night, but I was really prepared. I got the whole thing straightened out by four in the afternoon. They called my boss, saying I was a miracle worker. God, I felt *so* great! It wasn't even that complicated." She sighed. "Then I went back to the hotel and collapsed in a heap."

"Alone?"

She looked indignant. "Sure, alone, why not?"

"No, I just thought—"

"Listen," she said angrily. "I'm fussy. I don't just . . . Sure, okay, I could have taken all ten of them back with me, but I was tired and I wasn't in the mood, and there was no one—There has to be a spark, you know. I mean, I don't just—"

"I'm sorry," he said. His spaced-out, fuzzy mood prompted him to say, "I guess I feel jealous at times of—"

"Of who?" She leaned forward. "Me? Them?"

"Them."

Ardis looked uncharacteristically awkward for a moment. "Well, it's not—" She stopped. "I don't love them," she murmured, leaning over her food. "I just do it."

Misha reached over and took her hand. "I wasn't being critical, Dixie. I admire it. I'd like to do that too. Want something, find it—"

She sat there quietly, leaving her hand in his, her eyes large and soft-looking in the dimming light. "Do you want *me,* is that it? Or what?"

"I just—"

"I thought it would be too complicated," she whispered, frowning. "I thought it would be like a taboo, almost."

"I don't know." Her hand, which he had seized on impulse, seemed to be his now. He stroked it gently, not knowing how to proceed.

Ardis' face moved closer to his. He could see the dark lashes that sprouted out at the sides of her eyes, the delicate vein near her ear. "Do you—do you think Bren would mind?" she asked tremulously. "What do you think? Tell me honestly."

"How can she?" His voice came out more curtly than he wanted or expected—that pain the Valium couldn't ward off.

"I don't want to do anything that would hurt her." She seemed to be having trouble speaking; tears glittered on her eyelashes.

"She's not here!" he cried, anger, sorrow, and desire yanking him in opposite directions. He closed his eyes a moment, trying to get control of his emotions, and then opened them again.

"So, do you think—" Before she had finished the sentence, they kissed, at first lightly, and then more lingeringly. Ardis tossed her jacket on the floor, and then sat back to unbutton her skirt, then her blouse.

Misha was glad that everything seemed to be happening in a fog, radiant and misty, like going to the movies without his glasses. Her slip was lacy, pink, revealing the tops of her breasts, the cleavage. "It's new," she said, looking at him for approval. "It was on sale. Do you like it?"

"I love it." He had thought, hoped, she would take everything off, but she lay down beside him in the slip, putting her arms around him, kissing him lightly.

"Can you move?" she said softly.

"A little."

"I'll do everything," she promised, wriggling out of her slip and bra. "Just tell me if it feels okay."

If he had had to stay in bed another month to pay for this, it was worth it, he decided. The fragrance of her hair, the softness of the skin between her legs, her round heavy breasts with silky nipples. She stroked and kissed him everywhere, but gently, as though the kisses were a medicine which would effect a cure. And he let it happen, caressing her back as far as he was able, touching her not only to return the pleasure she was giving him but to prevent her from floating away, out the window. When she eased herself down onto him, he opened his eyes one second and saw, suddenly, a tiny constellation of freckles near her left nipple, exactly the ones Brenda had had, but the pain that flew through him was so keen and quick that it mercifully eluded him and the intense pleasure that followed drowned out even that.

Afterward she lay in his arms, not looking at him, her eyes half closed, a dreamy expression on her face. "You know what I feel guilty about?" she said finally. "It's strange."

"What?"

"You know, Bren and I used to talk about men a lot. I'd tell her about my 'conquests' or whatever, and she used to look so wistful, so envious, even. I used to encourage her, 'Try it sometime,' I'd say. 'But I love Misha,' she'd say. 'How can I?' 'I love Simon,' I'd say. 'What does love have to do with it?' "

"Did you ever convince her?" he said wryly.

"Uh uh. You know what she said once? I always remembered this. She said, 'Death is enough of an ending. I don't want anything else that I know will end.' " She touched him. "I'm sorry though, Mish. Maybe I did it just to justify what *I* was doing."

"You're forgiven."

"It's a tribute to you, I guess, that she didn't want to, or anyhow didn't, no matter what she might have felt sometimes."

"I think people do what their personalities allow them to," Misha said. "Statements about morality are a glaze over that."

"Maybe . . . but I did—maybe it was just idealizing—I did envy your marriage. The way Bren used to say, 'We're best friends.' I never had that, not with any of my . . . I love Simon, I do truly, but it's not friendship. It's not what I had with Bren, even. He's been a good father, we get along, but . . ."

"She envied *you*," he reminded her. He remembered Brenda saying once, "She got the mistress genes, I got the wife genes."

"I know!" She smiled. "Are you okay?" she said in a suddenly concerned tone of voice. "I was so afraid I might be . . . I wasn't sure if you were in terrible pain, but too polite to say anything."

He laughed. "I was in terrible pleasure."

"Seriously. Tell me. . . . How do you feel now?"

"I feel wonderful." And in truth he had never been so expertly, yet tenderly administered to. He wondered if he could say anything like that without it seeming in some way an insult, or at any rate a reference to her other experiences.

"Mish, did you ever fool around?"

Misha hesitated. "No," he lied. Telling her, he thought, would be in some peculiar way half-equivalent to telling Brenda.

"I didn't think so. . . . You're not the type, I guess. You're loyal. I like that. Those are my favorite kind of men, the kind that don't cheat on their wives. I hate the others, you know, the ones that are always looking for a little action on the side." She seemed unaware of any irony in this. "Weren't you ever even tempted?" she pursued. "You're attractive. Women must have come on to you sometimes."

"Rarely," he admitted guardedly. "Sure, I was tempted."

"Were you ever by me?" She smiled mischievously.

"What do you think?"

She eased down again, her head on his chest. "I know I'm here for all kinds of crazy, complicated reasons, but part of it must be the taboo . . . I always thought you were the one man I could never have. I wouldn't have ever done that to Bren, even if you'd seemed more . . . accessible."

Misha smiled. "Didn't I *ever* seem accessible?"

"A couple of times, a little. . . . Remember that night Bren had that awful headache and you took her home and had to drive me back from the party, and that policeman stopped us?"

He remembered. It had been the dead of winter and a half-drunk cop had made them veer off the road, because, he claimed, Misha hadn't put his brights on going around a curve. Having gotten them stuck deep in ice, and caused a second car to veer off to avoid them, the cop drove off, saying he would call a tow truck. In fact, he never did. They waited almost an hour until another cop came by and pushed them out. But yes, he remembered—the icy cold and dark outside, the warmth in the car, Ardis sleepy and a little high from mulled wine, singing songs to cheer him up, and he, waiting for rescue, hoping he would have the self-control to hold on. "Yeah," he said. "That was a close one."

"You know, I'm glad you gave away the bed," Ardis said suddenly, looking around the room.

"Why?"

"Well, one, Bren. But two . . . I used to come here with Walter, remember?"

"I remember *about* him . . . I never met him."

"Yes, you did. . . . He was the doctor that looked after Daddy just before he died. Remember, when he had to have his leg amputated? I guess that was part of it. Walter seemed so soothing and kind and caring when Bren and I were such wrecks." She frowned. "I guess that was the only time I got into it kind of deep. I really thought of leaving Simon. Thank God I didn't!"

"Why thank God?"

"Well, he . . . Oh, I know Bren didn't like him. She didn't say so, but I could tell. He was a mess. What a marriage! His wife was this really spaced out . . . used to bring lovers home. But he put up with it, adored his kid. He was kind of a masochist, I guess. They had sex once a year! Except for me, that was it! What if I hadn't turned up? Maybe someone else would have. But the thing is, I thought: 'God, I'll be spending my whole *life* cheering him up, telling him he's great, a good doctor, a good lover.' It would have been exhausting. But still, when I drive past the hospital I feel a pang, kind of."

They lay in silence. Misha wondered: If by pressing a button he could cause Simon at this moment to die in his sleep of natural causes, would he? How would it be with Ardis permanently? Men had married their sisters-in-law—he'd heard of that. But he had the feeling that without her casual lovers she would be another person, maybe even one he wouldn't have liked as much.

"I wonder if I'll go on like this forever," she said, as though reading his thoughts. "It's funny. I thought at first forty would be some big cutoff point: no available men. I always tell my age. I hate lying about that. But they don't care! It's funny. . . . You read so much about how men go crazy if you're over thirty, but the ones I meet don't seem to care."

"You'll be terrific at sixty," he assured her.

Ardis laughed, then looked wistful. "And at sixty you'll be re-married with a new family, a new bunch of kids—"

Misha put up his hand. "Never. Not a new family. A new wife is all I can contemplate, even in my head."

"Things just happen," she insisted. "You meet somebody, you love her, she forgets to put in her diaphragm one night . . . What are you going to do, drag her off for an abortion?"

"I don't think I'd be up to it again, at my age, starting over—"

"I hope—" She stopped.

"What?"

"I don't know! . . . I guess I hope if you do remarry, you'll move somewhere far away. It'll be too painful otherwise."

"Darling, stop trying to marry me off," he said, kissing her, wanting her again. If she could sweetie him, he could darling her.

"Is that what I'm doing?" She let her tongue touch his lightly, playfully; the scent of the wine still lingered. "Is that what this is?"

After she left, having cleaned up, Misha was up till two in the morning, buffeted by various feelings. As she'd left, businesslike again in her blue suit, looking jaunty in her sheepskin coat and boots, she'd said, "So listen, if you ever need any basics—"

"I always need basics," he said.

"Poor helpless men," Ardis said, with fond mockery, head to one side. "What would you do without us?"

"I don't even want to think."

A taboo, once broken, ceases to be a taboo. Or at least becomes less of one. God had not—napping as usual!—struck either of them dead. And the sense of betraying Brenda, which he would have felt with any new person, was in some ways muted by its having been Ardis. "My other half," they had playfully called each other. Sometimes Brenda used to say, "Seeing Dixie is like seeing another me, leading another life, not me exactly, but still a little." He remembered her telling how once she'd entered a room and said, "Hi, Dixie," and then realized she was looking at her own reflection in the mirror.

Breaking taboos seemed to have a rejuvenating effect. In any case, the Saturday after his back attack, when he was feeling normal again, he went to Sears to buy a new bed. Maybe a new chair too! There was an entire section covered with beds of all kinds. Most of the buyers seemed to be young couples, hand in hand. He felt awkward, self-conscious, examining the beds.

A salesgirl came over, youngish, fairly pretty except for slightly coarse skin. Full lips and wildly curly blond hair. "What type of bed are you looking for, sir?"

Somehow the "sir," which seemed peculiarly polite, and her half-sexy manner made the whole enterprise take on a mildly salacious overtone. "Just a bed," he said quickly, to move past this. Probably it was all in his own head, anyway.

"What size? Single? Double? Queen? King?" She seemed impatient with his indecision.

"I'm not sure," Misha said. "Double, I guess."

He saw her glance at his wedding ring. "You're married?"

Probably in her life she had come across many married men without rings, never an unmarried one who wore one. What was it for? Warding off evil spirits? Sexy salesgirls? He suddenly felt idiotic. "I was," he stammered.

"So, how come you're still wearing your ring?" she questioned amiably.

"Habit."

"Huh." She looked at him inquisitively. "Yeah. I did that. I mean, I was never married but, like in my senior year, I went with this guy and he gave me his pin and I kept wearing it for a whole year after we broke up! It was like taking it off meant we weren't going together anymore. So, like, I know how you feel."

That was a relief. He wasn't sure himself how he *did* feel. "Well," he began.

"So, you want a double?" He wondered how much of her seemingly flirtatious manner was his imagination. He was sure other men could tell the serious flirts from the ones who did it automatically, just as a way of relating to men.

"Yes, I think a double would be good."

"How about a queen? We got a sale on queens."

"That might be a little large."

"No, it's not that much bigger." She showed him the measurements. "The king is the big one. . . . How big's your bedroom?"

"I don't know exactly," Misha said. "Medium size."

"Maybe you ought to get a queen," she said. "The price is practically the same and it makes it more comfortable if you roll over or if, like, you have a guest staying over with you."

He loved the word "guest." "Okay," he said. "I'll take a queen."

She looked amazed. "Don't you even want to try it out?"

"Well, I—"

"Listen, even in queens, we've got all kinds. Firm mattress, extra firm. You've *got* to try it out! You don't get a bed every day, right?"

"Right," he agreed.

She led him to the area where the queen-sized beds were displayed. They did look rather large. "This looks a little big," he said.

"Try it. Roll around a little. . . . Are you a restless sleeper?"

Misha shrugged. "A little."

"Well, then you *need* room. . . . Better too much than not enough, right? Look, these are good beds. I got one, and I'm just single, but I figured you never know."

"True."

"Aren't you going to try them out?"

"I think I need an extra-firm mattress," Misha said, clearing his throat. "I have a bad back."

She whistled, her eyes widened. "Oh, you're one of those! Boy, I get one of those every *day*, almost. I mean it. . . . Sure, you need extra firm. Otherwise you'll be a mess. Back trouble's serious."

"I know," Misha said.

"Do you do exercises?"

"Usually."

"You should get this book. If you do them every day, you'll never have trouble again."

"I think I have that book," he said. "I—"

"My girlfriend bought it and she's been fine, terrific, *better* than before." She looked at him with that touch of impatience again. "So, try the extra-firm one. See how it feels."

Misha sat down on it tentatively.

"Lie down!" she commanded. "Don't be shy . . . you want me to go away? I'll come back. You just lie around on all of them."

She walked off to wait on another customer. Misha, stretched flat on the extra-firm queen-size mattress, watched her trim perky behind twitching as she moved off. He lay down, closed his eyes, and tried to imagine himself at home. The mattress felt good. Better than the one he'd given away. She was right. It was worth trying it out.

". . . So, what'd you think?" She was standing in front of him again, pad in hand.

Misha opened his eyes with a start. He'd dozed off.

She grinned. "Comfortable, huh?"

"Yes, very . . . I'll take this one."

"You won't regret it. It's good. It'll last you years! Maybe you'll get married again, you never can tell."

"Maybe," he agreed.

"What happened? Did she walk out on you? I had three of those this week!"

Misha smiled. "No."

"It's painful to talk about, huh? . . . Listen, don't take it to heart. That's what I was telling this man yesterday. He goes, 'I'll never meet anyone. She was so gorgeous.' I go, 'Naw, wounds heal.' Want to know something? He's sitting there, kind of morose, and this lady, this woman comes over and they start talking and before you know it, they leave together! How do you like that? You can meet someone anywhere."

After she wrote up the slip, she handed him his receipt and said, "Hey, listen, here's my card." He glanced at it. Miss Dorothy Huck. "So, like, if you have any problems, just give me a call, okay?"

"I'll do that."

The ambiguous nature of their interchange left him confused. This generation was different. What to someone his age was a come-on, to them was just politeness. But he kept, for several hours, thinking of her pretty blue eyes and jaunty figure. Maybe she'd arrive with the mattress to help him test it out. Don't count on it.

Impulsively he drove over to Ardis' to announce his new purchase. The door was opened by her older daughter, Sheila, home from college. Sheila looked more like Simon, curly unbrushed-looking hair, sleepy greenish eyes, white skin. She hugged him, exclaiming, "Uncle Misha! Hey, great!"

He hadn't seen her in almost a year. "How's school?"

"Okay . . . I'm working my ass off."

"Still pre-med?"

"Yeah . . . it's a real grind, though. Listen, Mom's not here. She went out shopping. Want to have some coffee? I was just having breakfast."

It was two in the afternoon. "You must be on a funny schedule."

"I am! Crazy . . . Boy, it's so good to sleep late." She poured coffee for him. "So, how are you? Doing okay?"

"Sure," he said.

"Mom said you had some back trouble?"

"It's better now," Misha said, wondering how Ardis had conveyed that news.

"Poor thing! My roommate had that. She couldn't even *move* hardly for a week. Were you in awful pain?"

"For a couple of days." He felt an odd kind of embarrassment with her. She and Ardis seemed to get along, as far as he could tell, but he wondered how she would react to his more ambiguous status in the family. Of his two nieces, she was the one who Brenda felt had inherited Ardis' energy. Abby, the younger one, was more scattered, though with some of her mother's provocative sparkle. He remembered Abby, home late from a dance, interrupting a poker party, kibitzing, peeking over his shoulder, clouds of perfume diffusing into the room. When she finally went to bed, Brenda had gotten up and said firmly, "Let's open a couple of windows."

96

"How's—" He searched in his mind for the name of the boy she'd been going with for three years.

"Roger? Okay." She looked sad. "We're not seeing each other anymore, at least not in a romantic way."

"I'm sorry," he said, feeling that this sounded inadequate.

"Well, Mom thinks it's for the best, and she could be right. I mean, like now, I'm inundated with work. Who has time for sex, romance? And we were each other's firsts. Mom says never marry your first. . . . But it's also—I guess I haven't learned how not to take things like that seriously." She made a half-comic expression. "I mean, when I fall, I fall *hard*. Thunk! I wish I could be like Abby, bouncing from one person to another."

"What's wrong with taking things seriously?" he asked, touched by her youngness, her seriousness.

"Maybe in the end," she said, "but Mom says—"

At that moment Ardis banged open the back door leading into the kitchen, where they sat. She was carrying two large paper bags full of groceries. "What does Mom say?" she said.

Misha got up to help her. She pushed him away. "Are you crazy?" she said. "You're just out of bed!" She handed Sheila one of the bags, set the other down, and then sat, sighing, in a chair. "Tell me what Mom says."

"We were talking about Roger," Sheila said, shamefaced. "Or really about relationships in general . . . I was saying how I wish in a way I could be like Abby, juggling all kinds of different people. Remember the time she accepted *two* dates to the senior prom? And ended up going with both of them!"

"Well, life isn't like that," Ardis said firmly. "You've got to pick eventually."

Misha was surprised to hear this philosophy from her. Their glances met and they smiled.

"How's your back?" she asked, still smiling.

"I'm a new man."

"Good."

Sheila broke in, "Oh Mom, listen, I called Figaro's and made a reservation for five-thirty. I thought maybe I could take you and

Daddy out for dinner since it's your anniversary." To Misha she said shyly, "They've been married eighteen years!"

"I think you get double credit these days," Ardis said.

"It's true," Sheila said. "You know, I told my friends and they were like, 'Wow, eighteen years!' And I went, 'Yeah, *and* they're happy!' and they, like, never *heard* of it."

"What happened to verbs?" Ardis said. She looked at Misha. "Did you realize this is the first generation that's growing up without verbs?"

"I feel proud of you," Sheila said, kissing her mother.

Ardis sighed, pleased but with a conflicted expression on her face. "Thanks, hon."

To Misha Sheila said, "Do *you* want to come, Uncle Misha? Why don't you? I can change the reservation to four."

"Well, I—" He looked at Ardis, who revealed nothing by her expression. "Sure, I'd like to," he managed finally.

"It has to be early because of Daddy," Sheila said. She started leaving the room. "You can bring someone if you—" She stopped, and then blushed. "I'm sorry," she said. "Was that dumb?"

"I'll meet you there at five-thirty," Misha said. When she'd departed, he looked at Ardis and smiled. Her eyes caressed him, but she stayed where she was. "The main news of the week: I got a new bed," he announced. "Proud of me?"

"Definitely," she said. "Yeah, I heard Sears had a sale. What kind did you get?"

"Queen size . . . The salesgirl said it wouldn't hurt, in case I ever had a 'guest' staying over."

"Guest!" she exploded. "Did she invite *herself* over?"

Misha turned red. "No, she—"

"I thought usually by the time you've spent an hour discussing beds, there's usually an aura of—"

"No aura," he said, too quickly.

"Sure." She reached over and squeezed his hand. "I'm glad," she said. "It's a start, anyway."

"Toward what?" He was genuinely curious.

"Beginning again?" Her voice was wistful.

Five

It was the fifth week Maddy had come to Mrs. Grayson's to clean. May Hooper had gotten her these two cleaning jobs, both for retired members of the faculty. "It won't be hard work," she said, "and Thornie said you could use a little cash." Maddy had been glad. With Jed gone all day and even Saturdays and some evenings now, it was lonely just sitting by herself in their one-room apartment. She had no friends! May was nice, but she was in her thirties and busy. She had four young school-age children and also ran a beauty shop in the former post office.

Maddy heard the elderly woman come slowly and carefully downstairs. It was midmorning. Usually Maddy did the upstairs first. There were three bedrooms, but only one was really used. One was a guest bedroom and just needed dusting. The other was the one Mrs. Grayson's husband had slept in—it still had his bed and all his things in it. As Mrs. Grayson peeked into the room, she smiled. "How're things going?" she asked in her kindly way.

For some reason, though they really didn't look alike, Mrs. Grayson reminded Maddy of her great-grandmother, who had lived with them briefly when Maddy was a child. Her slow way of walking and that sweet, crinkly smile. Being here made her feel protected and good in some way she didn't totally understand. "They're fine," she said. "I'm done with the vacuuming."

"Oh good!" Mrs. Grayson said. "I always hated the vacuuming! I hate machines, don't you? Though they help, of course. What would we do without them?" She came into the room. She often wore the dress she had on today, a gray-and-black print, and over it a gray sweater. Maddy was glad Mrs. Grayson didn't change that often because she herself had only two maternity dresses that fit and she'd been wearing them every day for so long now that she couldn't remember ever having had *real* clothes, pretty clothes where she'd look at herself admiringly in the mirror.

It seemed to Maddy she'd been pregnant forever! She was even pregnant in her dreams, now. Though she knew it wasn't possible, she sometimes wondered if the baby was never going to come out. You'd think it would want to. You'd think it would be tired of sitting in there after all these months, doing nothing, just lolling around. It must be dark, claustrophobic, like being locked in a closet. Already the baby was a week overdue. Of course, the doctor said calculations about when babies were to be born were always just guesses. "They take their own sweet time," he said. "They follow their own inner clock."

May said she was lucky. Hers had all been early and so small that one of them couldn't even leave the hospital for a month. "You should have seen him," she'd said of her now-hulking son. "Tiny and red and wrinkled, like a nut. And now look at him!" It was true having to leave the baby in the hospital wouldn't be nice, but Maddy wondered if almost anything wouldn't be better than this. One odd thing was she wasn't even sure Mrs. Grayson knew she was pregnant. At least she never referred to it. That could be politeness, or it could be her eyesight, which she often said wasn't what it had been. And Maddy herself felt awkward just bringing it up, so she'd never mentioned it either.

"How about a cup of tea?" Mrs Grayson asked.

"Sure," Maddy said, relieved to stop vacuuming.

They sat down at the table and Mrs. Grayson brought in two cups of tea. "Now, dear," she said. "I've told you my memory is just dreadful now. Do you live here in Athena?"

"Yes, I do," Maddy said. She had, in fact, told Mrs. Grayson this before.

"And your family lives here too?"

"No, my family lives in Auburn," Maddy explained. "I live here with my husband."

"Your husband!" Mrs. Grayson looked surprised, though Maddy had mentioned being married before too. "What does he teach?"

"He doesn't teach," Maddy explained. "He works for the Buildings and Grounds department."

Mrs. Grayson and her husband had taught Art History, but she had been retired for twenty-five years. "Buildings and Grounds," she repeated thoughtfully. "Now I hope he wasn't one of those young men who came around here the other day insisting they had to blacktop my driveway."

"I don't know," Maddy said. "I don't think so."

"They came right up and said they had to. I said, 'Why, the driveway's fine, why does it need blacktopping?' 'We're doing it to all the driveways along this side of the road,' they said. 'All right, go ahead,' I said . . . and they proceeded to lop off an *entire* branch of the oak tree, spill that awful black stuff on my lawn, and then fling a bill in my face for twenty-five dollars! Now I'm retired and twenty-five dollars is a lot of money. 'Doesn't the college pay?' I asked. They used to, you know. They just shrugged."

"I don't think that was Jed," Maddy said, adding more sugar to her tea.

"Jed?"

"My husband's name is Jed."

"Why, I didn't know you were married, dear," Mrs. Grayson exclaimed. "You're so young!"

"Well, I haven't been married long," she said. She didn't want to say how long because of her advanced pregnancy.

"I should think not. . . . And you and your husband like it here?"

"Yes, we do," Maddy said, adding quietly, "We love the lake."

"Yes," Mrs. Grayson agreed. "It's such a wonderful lake, isn't it? My husband and I used to take walks every afternoon along the lake." She stirred her own tea thoughtfully. "How do you find the students?" she asked.

Maddy wasn't sure what she meant. She saw the college girls

passing every day, but she'd never talked to any of them. "They seem nice," she said.

"But how about their intellectual caliber?" Mrs. Grayson pursued.

"Pardon me?" Maddy said desperately.

"How do the students strike *you*, dear? You're closer to their age than I am."

"They seem," Maddy searched for the right word, "smart."

"In what sense?" Mrs Grayson said, squinting.

"I don't know," Maddy admitted.

"No, that's *it!*" Mrs Grayson exclaimed. *"I* don't either. They *seem* smart and yet if you hear them talking in the drug store, you really would wonder. Their vocabulary!"

They sat over tea awhile longer and then Mrs. Grayson got up to pay Maddy. She gave her the fifteen dollars she owed her and showed her to the door.

Maddy struggled into her coat. She'd bought it in a thrift shop at the end of town, near the IGA. The arms were much too long, but it could cover her and had a hood, which was the main thing. Oh, but she hated it so! When the baby was born, she was going to tear it up! Or maybe just use it as a blanket.

Walking home, Maddy passed a group of college girls going in the opposite direction. One of them was telling a story and the others were all looking at her and laughing. They looked gay, happy, not pregnant. Of course, really, when she thought about it, they weren't any prettier than the girls she had gone to high school with. Some had bad skin, some were too fat, some looked lonely or strange when you looked right into their faces. But, despite this, it seemed to Maddy they had some kind of aura, some special glow that set them apart. They would lead different lives from the girls she had known, she felt certain. They would marry handsome, rich men and have careers, not just jobs. If they had babies, they would have special nurses to take care of them who were trained, who knew all about babies. It was hard not to envy them, though Maddy tried.

The day after she went to Mrs. Grayson's, Maddy worked at

the home of her friend and next-door neighbor, Miss Saunders. Miss Saunders was even older than Mrs. Grayson. She was going to be ninety in six months, she said. Where Mrs. Grayson was small and round, Miss Saunders was tall with an aquiline nose and piercing eyes. Maddy was a little scared of her. She reminded her of a teacher she'd once had in sixth grade who, if you got something wrong, would crow with glee, "Now, aren't you ashamed of yourself!" Miss Saunders' house was easier to clean. It was just one level—a gigantic living room crowded with books and papers, a small bedroom, and a kitchen. It was hard to dust because Miss Saunders said she didn't want Maddy to rearrange her papers. "These may just look like piles to you," she said, "but there's a method in the madness." So Maddy worked her way carefully around them.

Unlike Mrs. Grayson, who more or less left her alone, Miss Saunders sometimes followed Maddy around, pointing out things that she'd forgotten to clean or that she hadn't cleaned properly. That made Maddy nervous. She was terribly afraid she might break something, maybe one of the Chinese vases Miss Saunders had on a ledge over her fireplace. What if it were terribly expensive?

Miss Saunders knew Maddy was pregnant. Somehow, though Maddy hadn't wanted to tell her, Miss Saunders had gotten out of her that she'd been married only a few months. It turned out that when Miss Saunders had taught at the college—she'd been an English professor—she had also had some connection with a home for unwed mothers. "Nothing to be ashamed of," she assured Maddy briskly. "Some of them went on to do splendidly with their lives. The sexual urge is something we must contend with and master. Otherwise where would we be?"

Maddy just shrugged. She was embarrassed to hear a woman who was almost ninety talking about sex. "My husband is very nice," she found herself saying, though Jed had not really been attacked in so many words.

"Oh, of course he is!" Miss Saunders said. "I haven't the smallest doubt of that. Why would you have selected him to be the father of your child otherwise? Genes are *very* important, my dear. Crucial. Every woman knows that instinctively when the time comes to select her mate."

Somehow Miss Saunders made it seem as though the dark, furtive, sometimes ecstatic grapplings in the back seat of the car had been determined by more conscious intent than Maddy had been aware of at the time. She didn't want to disillusion Miss Saunders so she said nothing. And she was not sure, even, exactly what a gene was.

This day the cleaning seemed to take even longer than usual. Everything did, lately. The baby kicked and fussed inside her for three solid hours, and Miss Saunders followed her around, chatting about various things that Maddy found it hard to understand. Finally it was time to leave. "How do you feel about fruitcake?" Miss Saunders said as Maddy was leaving.

"I like it," Maddy said, though she couldn't remember having had it very often.

"Well, then." Miss Saunders brought forth an aluminum-wrapped package. "Now every year Helen sends me this fruitcake. She knows I have dentures and I can't eat a bite. But every year there it appears. I've hinted till I'm blue in the face that she could just as well save her money, but it never does *any* good! . . . So, you take it home and share it with your husband. But don't tell Helen! It'll be our little secret."

Jed thought the fruitcake was good, though he said he thought both old ladies sounded a little cracked. He ate three slices hungrily for dessert. Maddy was glad of one recent development in their relationship. She had been afraid that when the doctor had said they should stop having sex, Jed would be mad. He hated rules and things people told him he had to do. But he just said, "Oh that's okay, Mad," and had hardly laid a hand on her since. A few times he'd hugged her in bed and she'd been afraid that was going to be an overture to something more passionate, but it hadn't. Maddy thought that was very understanding and kind of Jed, considering how much he liked sex. It showed he was thinking not only of her, but of the baby.

Another nice thing he'd offered to do was to take her to see her parents. Maddy had, in fact, written her mother a postcard after they'd settled in Athena. At first she'd thought her mother wasn't going to answer at all, but suddenly, about a week ago, she'd called. Evidently she'd gotten the number from Vonni's mother. She said she'd like it if Maddy and Jed came to visit over the weekend. That was convenient, since Jed had to go into Auburn on Saturday to work at the used-car lot. He said he'd drop her off there and then pick her up later.

In the car Maddy began thinking worriedly of seeing her mother again. She wished the baby had already been born. It would be so much better to appear with a cute, actual baby than to shuffle in looking eighteen months pregnant! But she had been so relieved that her mother had decided to "forgive" her that she decided to go right away.

"Oh, I knew she'd come around," Jed said as they were driving. "You're her daughter, aren't you?"

Jed didn't have any sisters and he hadn't seen his mother much since he was eleven. Maddy knew there was no point trying to explain how things were between her mother and herself. It seemed to her that there were two kinds of daughters she could have been that her mother would have liked, and she was neither of them. One was a docile, friendly, outgoing daughter like Doreen and Betsy, who always had lots of friends and never got into any trouble and did pretty well at school. Maddy knew that was the way her mother, who had been shy and funny-looking as a girl and had lived on a farm ten miles from town, would have liked to be. The other kind of daughter would have been like Jarita, who had taken the rebellious streak that her mother had channeled into motherhood and marriage and run wild with it. And yet not wild in a socially unacceptable way. No matter how many scrapes Jarita got into, she got out of them at the eleventh hour, and Maddy knew her mother, even when she screamed at Jarita, admired her for thumbing her nose at authority and taking life on her own terms. The trouble with herself, Maddy thought, was that she was neither. She wasn't as outgoing or conventionally pretty as Betsy or

Doreen, nor could she, in a million years, have had Jarita's flamboyant energy. She was just what her mother often called her: "an afterthought."

But still, she thought, to cheer herself up, she was married! She was sure her mother had never expected Jed to marry her. Maddy glanced at him. Deep down her mother would have to admit that Jed was handsome, handsomer by far than Doreen or Betsy's husbands. And now he even had a job. Two jobs, in fact.

Maddy's mother let them in, making a slightly mocking gesture of welcome as she ushered them into the house. She was wearing her dark green pantsuit, the one she went bowling in and considered too dressy for work. "Welcome," she said.

Jed reached out and shook her hand. "I'll pick you up around one," he said to Maddy, glancing in a not overly friendly way at Maddy's mother.

"Where are you off to?" her mother said in her wry, sarcastic tone.

"Jed has a part-time job at Edelman's," Maddy offered. "He works there Thursday evenings too." As soon as the door was closed, Maddy added, "And he has a regular job in Buildings and Grounds at Coolidge."

"So you wrote," Mrs. O'Connell said. "Well, good for him! Facing up to his responsibilities finally, anyway!" She took Maddy's coat and gave it a once over before hanging it up. "Where'd you get *this* thing?" she wanted to know.

"There's a White Elephant store in town," Maddy explained. "They have good things, though. Some of the college girls give their leftover clothes there that're hardly ever worn."

"College girls!" Mrs. O'Connell snorted.

Maddy moved into the living room. Her father was sitting in his usual chair. He was deaf and to make him understand what you said, you had to speak loudly and clearly in the direction of his left ear. Maddy bent down and kissed him. "Hi, Daddy," she said, pleased to be home again suddenly.

"No baby?" he said, smiling.

"Don't rush her!" warned Mrs. O'Connell. She looked at Maddy. "It looks like it must be pretty near now."

"Yes," Maddy said. "He's overdue, actually."

Mrs. O'Connell kept inspecting her daughter's figure. "You're not going to have twins, are you?" she said.

"I, I don't think so," Maddy stammered. "The doctor didn't say anything about twins."

"Doctors!" Mrs. O'Connell exclaimed, with the same derision with which she had uttered "college girls!" "Well, one thing, they certainly don't run on *our* side of the family."

"They don't on Jed's either," Maddy assured her.

"Some women never recover from twins," Mrs. O'Connell observed darkly. "There's a woman at the factory who says that to this *day* she is not the same person. Do you want to know something? The day those twins were born, she lost her sense of taste and it's *never* come back! Never! She could eat a turkey and it might as well be a scrambled egg. . . . That's what having twins lets you in for."

"How's Jed?" her father asked.

Maddy wasn't sure her father had seen Jed when he came. "He's working hard, Daddy," she said loudly, turning to him.

"Not too hard, I hope," he said.

"Why shouldn't he work hard?" Mrs O'Connell said, offended at this subversive suggestion. "He's young, he's strong." Suddenly she smiled at Maddy. When she smiled, her face was so pretty, so different that Maddy froze with pleasure. "Well, babies aren't so bad," she said.

"Yes, I—" Maddy began.

"What names have you picked?"

"Frank," Maddy said, "for Jed's father."

"And if it's a girl?"

She hesitated. "We haven't picked a girl's name yet."

"You haven't?" Mrs. O'Connell looked horrified. "That's bad luck, Maddy. You can't go into the hospital without a name! We'll pick one right now." She closed her eyes and concentrated, then opened them. "I've got it," she cried. "Minerva!"

Minerva sounded like a very fancy name to Maddy. "Why Minerva?" she asked.

"Minerva was the name of my grandmother," Mrs. O'Connell

said. "Always a lady! Raised twelve children, started her own business. . . . You need a name that will help your baby, Maddy, not just a pretty name."

"It's so long, though," Maddy said, knowing that if the baby was a girl, it would have to be Minerva. She didn't dare cross her mother about this.

"Long?" Her mother frowned. "I don't think so." To her husband in a much louder voice she said, "How does Minerva sound to you, dear?"

"Hmm?" said Mr. O'Connell.

"We were talking about what I should name the baby," Maddy said, bending close to her father's ear. "Do you like the name Minerva?"

"That's your grandmother's name, isn't it?" he said to his wife. "Sure . . . Minnie's a nice name."

Minnie was shorter, but the trouble was it made Maddy think of Minnie Mouse. Well, maybe the baby would be a boy and there wouldn't be any problems.

"Where's Jed?" her father asked. "Didn't he come with you?"

"He's working at Edelman's, the used-car place," Maddy said. "He works there in between times."

"That Jewish fellow? Yeah, he's got a good reputation," Mr. O'Connell said.

"He's nice," Maddy said. "He gave us a mattress free!"

Mrs. O'Connell looked suspicious. "What'd he do that for?"

"We needed one," Maddy said, "and he"— she decided not to put in about Mr. Edelman's wife having died—"was giving it away." After a minute she added, "It's comfortable."

There was a pause. Then Mrs. O'Connell said, "Marian says you have a nice little place down there." Marian was Vonni's mother.

"Yes," Maddy said. "It's small . . . but it's nice."

"Is there room for the baby?"

"He can sleep in the corner of the room," Maddy said. "There's a kind of alcove," she elaborated.

"And you're all set as far as equipment goes?" Mrs. O'Connell pursued.

Maddy shrugged. "Sort of."

"Well, what do you need?" her mother asked. "Do you have a crib?"

"No." Maddy had thought for a while they might keep the baby in the box from the hospital, till it got too big.

Mrs. O'Connell leapt to her feet. "I'll call Doreen. That husband of hers can drive the crib down to you over the weekend."

When her mother was being nice to her, Maddy felt the way she used to at school when a particularly handsome boy on whom she had a crush stopped to ask her something: delighted, but terrified that it might not last. "Won't she be needing it herself?" Doreen's youngest was three. She had five children.

Mrs. O'Connell sighed. "Well, I didn't mean to tell you this, hon, but I might as well. You know when Doreen was in the hospital having Timmy, the doctor tied her tubes! Didn't even ask her. Now that's against the law, you know. She could've sued him for all he was worth! But he told her, 'Mrs. Murphy, if you have another child, you'll die in childbirth and I don't want a murder on my conscience.' And Doreen said, 'Mom, he's right. He saved my life.' Something about her blood, I didn't quite understand. . . . So she won't be needing any more baby equipment ever!"

While her mother was on the phone arranging things, Maddy sat in the living room with her father. Because of his deafness, it was hard to have an ordinary conversation with him. Having to say things very loud made things sound silly, so she often didn't say anything. She remembered the times she'd liked best when she was a child were when the two of them would take a walk together, far from people, and she could yell everything out without fear of seeming foolish.

"You don't look old enough to be married," he said now, gazing at her affectionately. "Much less having a baby."

"I'll be sixteen soon," Maddy reminded him.

"Still . . . you're so small!"

Probably it was that, the fact that she was barely five feet two, as well as being the youngest in the family, that made her seem not old enough, Maddy thought. But the doctor had said size didn't matter at all in terms of having a baby. He said it had something to do with the bones around your hips and Maddy's were fine. She'd felt proud of that.

By the time Jed arrived to pick her up, her mother was in a good enough mood to greet him with, "How about a cup of coffee, Jed? You must be tired."

"That's okay," Jed said, seeming surprised himself at her friendly tone. He smiled at Maddy. "Are you feeling all right?"

"We've been treating her like a princess," Mrs. O'Connell assured him. "Have no fear about that."

It was true. Her mother had made her favorite lunch—cream of tomato soup with grilled-cheese-and-bacon sandwiches and seedless tangerines for dessert. Maddy hoped this magic spell would last after the baby arrived.

On the way home Maddy suddenly realized she was exhausted. She had been so nervous the whole time she had been with her parents that it had been like acting in a play, almost. Now, in the car, her eyes drooped shut and she fell sound asleep, drifting in and out of odd dreams about Jarita and herself going swimming on a beach in Portugal, babies in rows, crying . . . She opened her eyes with a start.

"Here we are," Jed said.

They were home again already! It seemed to Maddy they had only been in the car a minute. "I feel so sleepy," she said, yawning. "Maybe I'll lie down."

Back at the house she lay down, almost without waking up from the earlier nap in the car, and fell this time into a deep dreamless sleep that seemed to go on forever. When she woke up, it was pitch dark outside and Jed was bringing in some food from the kitchen. He'd set the table and everything, even warmed up the chicken from the night before and made Minute Rice and peas. Maddy felt that there had hardly ever been a day like this in her life, when so many nice things were done for her.

As they were eating, she asked, "When are we meeting Vonni and Luther?"

Vonni and Luther, whom they hadn't seen in over a month, were driving up from Ithaca and were meeting them at the town bar, The Turning Point, for a couple of beers.

Jed looked uncomfortable. "Mad, the thing is, while you were sleeping, Thornie came by and there's some kind of emergency at the college. Some pipe's burst in one of the art studios and he asked if I could go over and fix it."

"Tonight?"

"Yeah, otherwise everything'll get flooded."

"Oh." Maddy looked at him. "Then what should we do?"

"Well, I thought I'll drive you on down to The Turning Point and then, when the work's done, I'll come by again. It shouldn't take too long, maybe an hour or two."

Maddy was disappointed. She'd been looking forward to the evening mainly because Jed would be there. Not that she wasn't looking forward to seeing Vonni and Luther again too.

When they got to The Turning Point, Vonni and Luther were there already. It was very crowded and dark and noisy with rock music blaring in the background. Some college girls came here too with dates, as well as local people. Jed explained to Vonni and Luther about where he was going. "You keep an eye on Maddy," he said, patting her shoulder.

"Sure we will," Luther said.

Maddy looked at Vonni. She couldn't get over how thin she looked! Of course, why shouldn't she? She wasn't pregnant, she'd *always* been thin. She was wearing a hooded sweatshirt with question marks all over it, exactly like one Maddy had at home. They'd bought them together, in fact. That made Maddy think of all her clothes that she hadn't worn in so long. The maternity dress didn't even seem like a dress anymore. It seemed more like a uniform, something you just put on every day, whether you were in the mood or not. When she hadn't been pregnant, Maddy used to wear dresses because of all sorts of special reasons, because of the weather, or how she was feeling, or what had happened the day before or might happen on that day. Blue was for special days that she wanted to be good.

"I think I'm going to be pregnant forever," she confided gloomily to Vonni.

"No, babies are late lots of times," Vonni assured her. "Aren't they, Luth?"

111

"What?" Luther had to lean forward because of all the noise.

"Babies!" Vonni screamed. "Aren't they late lots of times?"

"Sure," Luther said in his relaxed way. "Lots of times . . . Want a beer, Maddy?"

One problem with drinking anything was that already Maddy had to go to the bathroom around twenty times a day. But on the other hand, sitting here with everyone else drinking wouldn't be much fun. She felt isolated enough anyway. "Okay," she agreed. When the large glass came, she drank two deep gulps, more because she was thirsty than anything else.

Luther stood up. "Mind if Von and me dance a little?" he asked Maddy.

"No, that's okay," Maddy said. "I'm fine."

But she felt like an old lady, sitting there, so fat and awkward, with no date. She looked down and began making a design on the tabletop with a spill of beer. Then she felt someone tap her shoulder. It was Jed's friend, Craig. He was one of the funniest-looking men Maddy had ever seen, but he had a friendly smile. "Where's your old man?" he asked.

"He had to work," Maddy explained. "A pipe burst in one of the art studios."

Craig frowned. "Oh," he said. He stood there, looking ill at ease. "Want to dance?" he said finally.

Maddy smiled tremulously, touched by his offer. "I can't!" she said, indicating her stomach.

He took her hand. "Sure you can."

"I can't dance fast," Maddy warned him.

"So, we'll dance slow." He put his arms around her, as though the music were completely different.

"This must be like dancing with an elephant," Maddy commented. He wasn't as tall as Jed, so she didn't have to look up as far to see his face. His beard touched her forehead lightly. It felt like moss.

"You look real pretty, Maddy," Craig said in a low voice.

The expression on his face was so genuine that Maddy just said, disbelievingly, "I do?"

He smiled. "You have real pretty eyes."

Maddy sighed. "Well . . . thank you," she said formally.

She had thought it would be terrible dancing, with everyone else gyrating wildly around them, but it wasn't. It was as though they were in a separate room in a separate place. And even though it was impossible for her to think of herself in anything like a sexual way, something about his warm, polite manner made her feel at least pretty, which was something she hadn't felt in a long time. Then suddenly she felt a splash of hot liquid cascade down her leg. Maddy felt mortified. The doctor had said this could happen, that you could even pee in your pants, and that it was good to wear a sanitary napkin. But Maddy hadn't wanted to. If only she hadn't drunk any beer!

"What's wrong?" Craig said. Evidently he hadn't noticed. She'd been afraid some might have wet his shoe.

"I just—" Maddy was trying to figure out how to explain to him when suddenly a terrible pain shot through her whole body, making her topple into his arms, like a tree falling.

"Are you okay?" he asked nervously, trying to support her.

Maddy opened her mouth to speak, but her throat was so dry that her voice came out in a squeak. "I'm having my baby," she whispered.

He looked terrified. "Right now?"

Maddy nodded and then, though she wanted so much not to, she burst into tears.

Everything that happened after that took place in a funny kind of staccato time. Craig got Vonni and Luther and the three of them made her sit down at the table again.

"Is it coming out?" Luther asked. "Right now?"

"No," Maddy sobbed, "but I better get to the hospital, quick."

"We'll take you in the truck," Luther said.

"I'll carry her," Craig said.

"Where's Jed?" Vonni said. "We better get him."

"I don't think there's time," Craig said. "Let's get going fast."

Maddy felt him lift her up and carry her outside in his arms. It was very cold. There was snow piled several feet deep all around the truck.

On the way to the hospital Maddy kept her eyes shut most of

the time. Somehow she felt that if her eyes were closed, the baby wouldn't be born till they got there. Vonni sat on one side of her and Craig sat on the other. Each of them held one of her hands and asked from time to time, "How are you doing, Mad?"

"Okay," she would say. "I'm doing fine."

Every time one of the pains came, Maddy was sure it was the baby, that he was finally going to shoot out, but it never was. When the pain went away, it was wonderful. Everything would seem clear and bright and still. Maddy thought intermittently of Jed. It didn't seem fair. There he was working and unable to even *be* there when his own baby was born. She hoped he would understand and forgive them for not having taken the time to get him. "Will you explain to him?" she asked Craig several times and he said, "Sure, Maddy, I'll explain."

At the hospital nurses came rushing out, but by then the pains were coming so fast, Maddy couldn't feel anything in between. She saw Vonni's face and then it vanished and a nurse was saying, "Should I give it to her now?" Someone sank a needle into her backside and even before it was drawn out, Maddy felt she was spinning down very fast into darkness.

When she woke up, she had a headache. She was in a strange room. It was dark and a nurse was walking by, carrying a folder. Maddy called out to her. The nurse came over to the bed.

"Did I have a baby?" Maddy asked.

"Of course you did," the nurse replied briskly. "How could you be here if you hadn't had a baby?"

"What did I have?" Maddy asked.

The nurse checked her chart. "A girl," she said.

"Is she okay?"

Finally the nurse's expression softened slightly. "You'll see her in the morning, dear."

Maddy had thought she wouldn't be able to fall asleep. It seemed to her she'd been sleeping almost steadily from the time she'd left her parents' house. Then she remembered being at The Turning Point and dancing with Craig. Had that been all right?

she wondered suddenly in retrospect. Dancing with someone who wasn't her husband while she was pregnant? Of course, he was Jed's friend and she didn't find him at all sexy, so she decided it had been all right.

The baby was ugly. Maddy felt her heart sink so when she first saw her that she prayed they had made a mistake and brought her someone else's baby. It had a few strands of black hair, but its face was all scrunched up and there was something funny about its—her—eyes. One focused straight ahead and the other wandered off to one side, as though it were looking for something. While the baby was nursing, Maddy checked the little plastic bracelet around its wrist. It said Parker. So it *was* her baby after all! But wasn't there some chance that there were two babies named Parker?

She felt guilty having such thoughts as the baby nuzzled against her breast, sucking hungrily. The baby seemed to feel she belonged to Maddy, to be having no second thoughts at all, far more definitely than Maddy felt she belonged to the baby. She waited for some serene, mystical feeling of pleasure to descend on her as the baby nursed, but couldn't and finally gave up on it. Drowsed and full, the baby fell asleep, her mouth never leaving Maddy's nipple, just widening away from it so she could breathe.

When Jed arived later in the morning, Maddy felt ashamed. They had taken the baby away. "Did you see her?" she asked.

"Yeah," he said. Then he came over and kissed her and gave her a bunch of flowers. "I'm real sorry I wasn't there," he said, looking so eager for *her* forgiveness that she felt relieved.

Maddy took the flowers. She wasn't sure what to do with them, so she just held them. "It happened so fast," she said, remembering.

"Yeah, Luth said he was scared he might not get there in time, especially when the car skidded off the road."

"It did?" Maddy said. She didn't remember that at all.

Jed went to look for a nurse who would give him a vase for the flowers. He returned with a different nurse from the one Maddy had spoken to during the night. This one was chunky and smiling, as short as Maddy. After putting the flowers in the vase, she said to Jed, "Okay, Daddy, time to see your baby."

"Oh, he saw her," Maddy said quickly.

"Well, he wants to hold her, doesn't he?" the nurse inquired. "He can even give her the bottle if he wants."

Jed looked a little uncertain. He didn't say either way what he wanted. But when the baby arrived, the nurse handed her to him. He took her stiffly and stood there.

"She won't bite," the nurse said, smiling. "Relax . . ." Then she handed Jed the bottle and showed him how to feed the baby. "They're not always that hungry in the beginning," she explained. "Just let her go at it till she's had enough."

Jed sat down in an armchair with the baby and started to feed her. Maddy felt touched at how awkward he looked. After the nurse had left, he looked up and said to Maddy, "I don't think I'm doing it right. Maybe you ought to . . ."

Maddy wasn't sure she knew the right way to do it either, but she took the baby and the bottle. She looked down at her, hoping she might have gotten better looking since the last time or that it might even be a different baby. But the baby looked exactly the same. In fact, there was one other thing about her Maddy hadn't even noticed before, and that was her ears. They stuck out like handles on each side of her head, big floppy ears that might have been cute on a puppy. The trouble was, Maddy knew where those ears came from. They were her father's ears. All her brothers had ears like that too, and even she had ears that stuck out a little, which was why she'd always worn her hair fluffed over them. Maybe once the baby's hair grew in, they wouldn't be so noticeable.

"What should we call her?" Jed asked.

"Is Minerva all right?" Maddy felt proud suddenly to have him there, looking so solid and handsome in his khaki jeans and blue sweater. "That's my great-grandmother's name."

"Sure, that's fine," Jed said.

Was he just agreeing because he was disappointed the baby

was a girl and he didn't even care what they called her? Maddy wanted to ask him how he felt, but she was afraid of hearing from him the same critical thoughts that were in her own head, so she said nothing.

But when Vonni and Luther came a little while later, Vonni just exclaimed right out, "Wow, look at those ears!"

Luther touched one of them. "She looks like one of the seven dwarves," he said.

Vonni socked him. "Boy, are you rude! She does not!" But after a moment more she said, "You know, when she's older you could tape them back, Maddy . . . or glue them or something."

"Glue them!" Luther said derisively. "With what? Elmer's Glue?"

"Sure," Vonni said. "Or, you know what, you could just have her wear a hat."

Maddy thought of mentioning that her own ears stuck out too, but she didn't want Jed to trace the origin of the baby's ears to her; she decided not to mention it. Vonni took the baby. She was starting to wake up. "I think she's cute," she said, peering down at her. "What're you going to name her?"

"Minerva," Maddy said. "Minnie for short."

"Minnie Mouse," Vonni said tenderly. "Hey, Minnie, I'm Vonni." A moment later she looked up with a worried expression. "I don't think she likes me. One of her eyes is looking at me and the other one is looking off in another direction!"

Luther looked. "She's just cross-eyed."

"She is not," Vonni said. "Cross-eyed is when they come together in the middle, like this." She crossed her own eyes and then uncrossed them. "No, you know what I think it is? . . . I think they told us this in Bio, that when they're born, sometimes their muscles are weak and it takes them a while to, you know, know how to do things, even to see right."

Maddy hoped this was true.

Vonni wiggled her finger in front of the baby's face. "Baby, come on . . . look at me with both eyes." A moment later she said, "I guess she doesn't want to." She handed the baby to Jed. "Where *were* you last night?" she said. "You picked a great time not to be there."

"I told you I had to work," Jed said angrily.

"A likely story," Vonni said, but good-humoredly. To Maddy she said with a sigh, "Mom says my dad was never there with any of us. She figured he would have passed out if he was. Maybe they would have had less kids if he'd of seen what it was like."

"It wasn't so bad," Maddy said. "I think they gave me a shot."

"That's what *I* want," Vonni said. "I want to be out from the first second."

"Me too," Luther said.

"You!" she exclaimed. She appealed to all of them. "Can you imagine *him* pregnant? Boy!"

The nurse came in and announced that visiting hours were over. Maddy was relieved. She felt tired and was glad that they took the baby away for a while also. She had the feeling it would take some time, both to get used to the idea that she was a mother and to get used to the baby herself. But eventually it would happen. Eventually a day would come when she would hardly be able to imagine life without the baby. Maddy felt sure of that.

Six

"I'll be back in five minutes, okay?" Craig said. He and Jed were in the library, moving a room full of book cartons from the basement.

"Sure," Jed said, yawning. The second Craig left, he sat down and leaned his head on one of the cartons. Two seconds later he was asleep. It was the baby. She never slept! Jed couldn't figure it out. She had to sleep sometime, maybe just never at night. Up till now he would have described himself as someone who slept pretty easily. He'd never had trouble falling asleep. He could sleep till noon, even when other people in the house were up. But with the baby it was different. Maybe it was her being in the same room. She was usually okay for about an hour after they went to bed. Then there would be a low droning kind of crying which Jed had trained himself to tune out. If Maddy got up right away, the sound would stop. But sometimes she wouldn't hear it or would lie there, hoping the baby would fall back asleep. Then it would pass on to a loud, demanding kind of yell, like a dog barking. Of course in some ways it was worse for Maddy, having to be up all night. But at least she could sleep sometimes during the day. She still worked at those old ladies' houses and she helped May Hooper in the beauty shop two days, but neither of those jobs was all day. Still, she was tired too. One morning, when he got up to go to work, Jed found

Maddy asleep in the rocking chair, with the baby, asleep also, in her arms. Often when he came home for dinner, he would find the two of them out cold.

How was he going to work this way? There were days when he felt like a sleepwalker, days when he'd fallen asleep literally standing on his feet. "Yeah, well, it'll pass," had been Thornie's comment. "The first couple of months are always rough." He spoke of it casually, the way someone who had lived through a war might describe a particularly grueling battle. But even though he was casual, that was more of a comfort to Jed than the other guys who were all single and to whom family life was something totally foreign, something other people did.

"Hey, Parker what's with you?" It was Craig, shoving him awake.

Jed shook his head. "Huh?"

"What's *with* you today?"

"I got about three hours sleep, that's what!" Jed snapped. "That fucking baby is driving me crazy."

"Yeah, well . . ."

There had been an awkwardness between them ever since the night Maddy had given birth. Jed knew that of the three of them—Craig, Luther, and Vonni—only Craig had known for an absolute fact that Jed hadn't been working that night. Craig knew Thornie never had them work at night. He knew the pipes in the art studios were in perfect shape. Whether he knew specifically where Jed had been—in the art studio fucking Capri—Jed wasn't sure. But it seemed to him there had been a kind of coolness on Craig's part ever since then.

It really got Jed pissed. What did he know? *He* could fuck anyone he damn well pleased and no one would care. *He* wasn't the one saddled with a wife and screaming kid. Okay, so maybe he'd had some pregnant girlfriend who was really hot. Let him try living with one some day.

Jed knew it was lack of sleep, but everything bugged him lately, grated on his nerves. Jokes everyone else laughed at didn't strike him as funny. At least if he had a sex life again with Maddy—

But Maddy was so tired all the time that she fell asleep the second she got into bed. Sometimes she went to bed right after dinner, at eight o'clock! Once, he'd felt so horny, he'd wondered if he couldn't just fuck her while she was asleep. He had the feeling she might not even wake up. But he hadn't.

He wished she'd lose some weight. She wasn't fat really, not even extremely plump, but her body felt baggy and soft to him. Her stomach was still like a pouch. She had said her doctor had told her to do exercises, but that she didn't have time. The trouble was that he wanted Capri, that it wasn't as easy as he'd imagined it would be to switch back. It wasn't just the weight or the baby. It was that Maddy was just like she'd always been. Sex just wasn't a major thing in her life. She did it, maybe sometimes she enjoyed it—he wasn't even sure about that—but he had the feeling that if they did it once a month, that would be fine with her. In high school just having someone to do it with, someone who was willing, who was pretty, who was nice, had seemed something of a miracle. But now it seemed a depressing kind of second best.

But he was being good. And he was going to keep on being! Luckily, Capri had gone away for Christmas vacation. The college was pretty deserted and would be till mid-January, when the girls came back. Jed thought of that interim period as training. If he could get her out of his mind now, by the time she returned it would be easy.

When he came home, Maddy and the baby were up. Maddy had just given the baby a bottle and she was lying in her crib, not crying, just gazing around the room. Jed looked in at her. Instantly she started wrinkling up her face, as though a rotten egg had fallen nearby. He walked quickly away. That was another thing. For some reason the baby didn't like him. It wasn't just his imagination. Every time she saw him, she always started to make dismayed faces or cry. If Maddy came over to her, she smiled or made soft cooing sounds. "She's just not used to you," Maddy said. "That's the way babies are."

121

The other thing that was bothering him about their sex life was that Maddy still wouldn't use any form of birth control. What didn't make any sense was that she didn't mind if Jed used condoms. In fact, she *wanted* him to. She said she didn't want to get pregnant again. But somehow it seemed to her less of a sin if *he* was the one to use something. Christ! He couldn't always remember to buy condoms, but when once he tried doing it without one on, she'd pulled away, more scared than indignant. He'd waited for her to fall asleep and had jerked off, angrily. Was that what marriage was all about? Jerking off after your wife was asleep? Anyway, he didn't like condoms. He never had, and doing it without them for six weeks—Capri was on the pill—was so much better that going back to it was especially annoying, even painful. It was also that to him Capri's being on the pill meant sex was important to her too. She wanted it to be enjoyable and easy, not some great task where you had to be prepared and equipped.

One night Maddy's parents came down and he and Maddy went to see a movie playing at the college, *The French Lieutenant's Woman*. It was a peculiar movie, he didn't follow some of it, but at times the woman in it reminded him of Capri. Her hair mainly. Capri's hair was lighter, but when she let it loose, it had that crinkly way of spreading out. And the woman in the movie had that same intent look, like she was looking through you, examining you. When the man tried to run away, not to see her anymore, Jed felt so close to him it was uncomfortable. He shifted in his seat and went out to the men's room.

Outside Maddy asked him if he'd liked the movie.

"It was okay," he said.

"She was sort of funny-looking," Maddy said. "I thought his fiancée was prettier . . . didn't you?"

"I don't know," Jed blurted out, afraid his feelings would show.

"And she was mean to him," Maddy went on. "His fiancée really loved him."

Jed wondered if maybe the guy wouldn't have been better off if he'd just taken off, left both of them. But he felt caught, couldn't. Damn.

The week the college started up again, Craig handed a note to Jed when he came to work. "Who's it from?" Jed asked, taking it reluctantly.

"Some girl," Craig said briefly.

Jed waited till he was alone to open it. It read: "Hi! So, how's life? Did she have it yet? Let's meet Saturday, okay? Call me . . . C."

He crumpled it up and threw it out. But that night he dreamed about her and woke up with an erection, grabbed Maddy and tried to pretend she was Capri. It didn't work, and it made him feel lousy. Still, he was determined to be firm and unyielding. Later in the week he was in the truck, loading some equipment, when he saw her, about twenty feet away. She was walking toward him, wearing her red duffle coat, the hood off, although it was snowing.

"Will you hurry up?" he said impatiently to Mickey, who was loading the truck with him.

Mickey looked at him with surprise. "Hey, man, relax. Where's the fire?"

"I'm cold," he said.

"So? . . . So am I. Okay, hop in."

Jed jumped in the truck and didn't look back. He felt like someone in a cowboys-and-Indians movie. Narrow escape. It was crazy, but what it reminded him of was that time at school when Maddy had told him she thought she was pregnant. Every time he saw her appearing around a bend, his stomach would clench up and he would want to run. But this was different. Part of him wanted to run and part of him wanted to do the opposite.

Friday there was another note. This time Craig just handed it to him with an ironic expression. Jed looked at him defiantly.

"She's beautiful," Craig said finally.

Despite himself, Jed felt proud. "Yeah," he said, smiling. He folded the note back and forth.

"Go on, open it. I won't look." Craig turned his back.

Jed ripped the note open. It was typewritten. There was a small hand that pointed to each sentence.

Shall I dye my hair red? Would that help? Listen: call, even if it's to say it's all over. I can take it. I just want to know what's going on.

She had added at the bottom a "P.S. I miss you!!!!"

She was right. He should at least call her, let her know what he'd decided and why. Actually, he'd meant to do that before the baby was born, but he thought maybe she knew or would guess that that was what he had in mind. They never talked about Maddy or even referred to his being married, so that when he was with her, he tended to almost forget it himself.

That evening he went to the local inn that had a pay phone and called her dorm. He was half hoping she might not be in. She was.

"Oh hi," she said, sounding so glad to hear his voice that his heart started racing. "I'm really glad you called."

"Yeah, well, I've been busy," he said.

"Did she have it?"

"What?"

"Did your wife have the baby?"

"Oh . . . yeah, she did."

"What was it?"

"A girl."

"Mazeltov!"

Jed laughed, pleased he knew what that meant.

"So, what about Saturday? Is it okay?"

He swallowed. "I—I don't know."

"What don't you know—if you're free or if you want to come?"

"I just—"

"Listen, Jed, why don't we just talk about it, okay? I mean, I can respect all your . . . whatever, moral things and all. My parents are in Guadeloupe for two weeks, so we could just sit around and talk. I'm going out Friday night, but if you wanted to just, like, drop in some time Saturday afternoon . . ."

Jed stared at the wall. He knew what would happen if he

"dropped in," and he was sure she did. "Sure, well, as long as you'd understand if we don't necessarily—"

"Oh yeah, I understand."

"Okay, I'll see you around two," he said.

"Wonderful." After a slight pause she said in a softer voice, "I missed you a lot."

Jed felt his stomach clench. "I missed you too." He hung up quickly before the conversation could go any further in that direction.

By Saturday he had almost talked himself into believing that nothing had to happen between them, that he was doing the right and honorable thing by facing her. It wasn't fair to just take up with a girl and then drop her, no matter what she was like. And the thing was—he couldn't help feeling proud about this—Capri liked him a lot. He knew that, even though they never talked about "love" or anything. He was glad that her parents wouldn't be there. The few other times he had come to their house, he had felt as uncomfortable as the first time. It was different from the way he used to feel uncomfortable with Garnet's parents, say. Garnet's mother, especially, thought Jed was beneath her daughter. They hadn't had money long; Garnet was their only daughter and it was important to them that she would marry "up." He felt they were scrutinizing him, hoping he would use the wrong fork at dinner or say something dumb. As a result, he was mainly silent, probably confirming their feeling that he was some kind of halfwit.

But Capri's parents, her mother especially, were casual and peculiar in ways he wasn't used to. Often her mother dressed just the way Capri did, in faded jeans, sandals, and a big floppy shirt. She seemed a little vague and dreamy. Once he'd come in and found her staring out into the back yard. "I'm just fascinated by that tree," she'd said the minute she saw him. "Would you come look at it, Jed? Tell me what you think." And they'd spent the ten minutes till Capri appeared discussing trees and whether they had thoughts and feelings and whether the shape of things determined the quality of their souls. Often he didn't have the vaguest idea what her mother was talking about, just as half of Capri's references to what she studied at school made no sense to him at all.

They both asked his opinion about things and listened carefully when he offered one. On both visits her father hadn't been there and Jed had been glad. Whenever he remembered the man's sharp, inquisitive stare he felt chilly. He had felt as though he were someone who had just robbed a bank being confronted by a policeman.

"Hi!" Capri was in jeans and a bright red velour top which came down just to the tops of her thighs. Her hair, which she usually wore unbraided only when they made love because he liked it that way, was loose except for being tied back with a red ribbon. Attached to the ribbon was a small Christmas tree decoration, a white felt unicorn trimmed with tinsel.

In the room behind her was a huge Christmas tree that grazed the ceiling, decorated with lights and little ornaments, mostly animals. Jed hadn't known Jews celebrated Christmas. He thought they did something else instead. Misinterpreting his stare at the tree, Capri said, "We still have it up. You won't believe this, but one year we kept it up till Easter! We had this wonderful tree. It didn't shed a single needle and it looked so pretty. I always hate it when people put them up just for a week and then toss them out on New Year's Day."

"It's pretty," he said. He and Maddy hadn't had room for a big tree, but he'd cut down a little one, which they'd put on a table in one corner of the room.

There was a fire going in the fireplace. Capri sat down cross-legged in front of the fire. "Sit!" she said ironically, noticing his hesitation.

He sat about two feet away from her, crouching, half ready to run.

"So, how's being a father?" she asked, with a half-smile.

Jed shrugged. "Not so great . . . I get about three hours sleep a night."

She looked sympathetic. "I guess it's just like that. . . . Though my parents always claim I was this perfect baby, never cried, slept through the night at two weeks. . . . It must be hard on your wife, though."

"Yeah," Jed said. Immediately he felt uncomfortable.

They stared at each other. He felt she was nervous too, which was a relief, but in another way it added to his own nervousness.

"We could just be friends," she said, "if that's what you want." What you want. What he wanted was her. He let his eyes drift over her crinkly golden hair and over the body he knew was concealed under the red top. "I don't know," he said, hating himself for being so inarticulate.

She looked into the fire. "Christmas vacation was awful," she said, abruptly changing the subject. "I went back to this high school reunion of my class and I don't know, the kids all seemed so . . . Either they'd changed or I'd changed or something. And I ran into this guy I'd really been crazy about my senior year, and he seemed . . . awful! Not even cute looking. A real nothing. So self-satisfied. He's at Princeton and he kept going on with all this junk about how well he's doing at school and how he's sure he'll get into the best law school and I thought: So what? . . . You know what I mean?"

"Sure," Jed said. Without knowing it was what he was going to do, he leaned forward and touched the ornament in her hair. "Is that a unicorn?" he said.

"Yeah." She smiled, right into his eyes, her expression softening, melting. "I love unicorns. I used to have this big thing about them when I was a kid. I used to imagine myself some kind of medieval princess and I'd have this unicorn for a pet."

The whole time she was talking, her eyes didn't leave his face. He knew what she was feeling as clearly as though he were inside her mind. He let his hand stroke her hair. "I like it when you wear it like that," he said softly.

"I know," Capri said. "That's why I wore it that way."

And then they were kissing and lying on top of each other on the rug in front of the fire and she was pulling off her top and her jeans and he was tossing his clothes into the corner of the room. Her skin felt cool and smooth, although they were so near the fire.

127

The light seemed to illuminate her hair, as though she were an angel in a Nativity play; the red ribbon fell off. But despite the urgency they both felt, they made love slowly, as though, having reached the decision that they would once again be lovers, they could afford to take their time and savor it. "Oh God, Jed," Capri whispered as he made his final thrust into her. The sound that came out of her, a sigh that was half like someone singing, dissolved into the air.

He lay on top of her a long time, not wanting to leave her body, knowing she didn't mind. It seemed to him that even their breathing was in unison. Finally he rolled over and lay on his back. They were so close to the fire that he felt the heat of the flames on his arms and neck. She ran her hand lightly over his stomach. "Your skin is so hot!" she said. "Like you have a fever." A moment later she smiled. "Wish me Happy Birthday. It was my birthday yesterday."

Jed smiled. "That's funny," he said. "It's mine tomorrow."

"How old are you?"

He hesitated. "I'll be eighteen."

"I'm twenty . . . Hey, I'm your first older woman quote unquote. Great!"

It was funny how her being twenty moved her in some way slightly further from him. She wasn't even a teenager anymore. "You don't look that old," he said, half kidding.

"Thanks a lot . . . Too old to be a *Playboy* centerfold." She wrinkled her nose. "I read that the cutoff for them is eighteen. After that we're no longer in full bloom. Devastating! Not that they'd ever have taken me anyway, with no boobs."

"I like your breasts."

She kissed him. "As far as they go, they're okay. . . . Listen, I once played a tournament final against this girl with"— she gestured—"and you should have seen her. Bounce, bounce . . . I don't care if you wear a sports bra or not, I wouldn't want to lug those things around the court. . . . You know, it's interesting, the older woman thing. Daddy's first affair was with an older woman. I think it's typical in some way. Like, he said—he was nineteen or something, still in college and she was twenty-eight, only she'd married young, maybe even twice, and was divorced . . . and like, he was kind of awkward with women and with her he didn't have to go through this whole bit of courting her, promising to marry her. They just did it. . . . It was the fifties so everything connected with sex was some kind of epic struggle. And I guess he knew he didn't want to get married right away but he didn't want to deflower a virgin or anything grisly like that. . . . Did *you* ever?"

"What?" Jed said. As always her words flowed over and around him without his trying to follow everything she said.

"Did you ever do it with a virgin?"

"That's all I ever did it with," Jed said. Then he corrected himself. "My wife was a virgin."

"My wife was a virgin," quoted Capri. "That sounds like one of those headlines in the *National Enquirer.*"

He was still thinking about what she'd said about her father. "I don't see how it's so different now."

"What do you mean?"

"You *still* have to go through a big thing to get most girls to do it. . . . You *still* have to pretend you love them and want to marry them."

"You do?" She looked amazed, as though she had never heard this before. "Did you with your wife?"

He looked sheepish. "Kind of . . . basically, I think girls just do it because they know guys want it. They'd just as soon . . . go bowling or something."

"No!" Capri exclaimed. "It's the exact other way around. Women are a *million* times more interested in sex than men."

"They are not!" Jed said. "You're crazy!"

"No! Listen, that's what civilization is all about." She sat up, looking all excited, her hair fanning out electrically in thin radiant strands. "See, men sensed right from the beginning, right from when people were in caves, even, that sex was really important to women. Not just important, but easier. Because, like, men have to worry about getting erections and it's this big complex thing . . . so what they did was, they created all these social structures to make sure women wouldn't get into sex. Like the double standard and stuff. Why do you think they didn't invent birth control until about fifty years ago? It was all because men were scared out of their wits that women would go sexually wild and just fuck all day long."

"That's a weird theory," Jed said.

"It's *true!*" Capri assured him. "Absolutely. Listen, it explains jut about everything that's ever happened on the face of the earth. Wars, factories, everything! . . . Did you ever take any Women's Studies courses in high school?"

"No," he said. "What's that? You mean, like Home Ec?"

"Home Ec! No! I mean, like Women in American History, the Philosophy of Feminist Thought, stuff like that."

"No . . . they didn't have stuff like that in my school."

"Well, they should've . . . but you don't have to worry. You've got me to explain everything to you." She looked smug.

Jed wrestled her onto her back. "Who says men have trouble having erections?" he said.

Capri started giggling. "Not you! Not teenagers . . . you know, middle-aged men."

He was inside her. "I never have any trouble," he said.

"Don't boast," she said, her eyes beginning to glaze over. "Oh boy, you don't, do you?"

While they were lying there after the second time, the doorbell rang. Their eyes met in terror. "Who is it?" Jed whispered.

"I don't know," Capri whispered back. "Listen, go up to my room, okay? Take the stairs around the kitchen."

Jed scooped up his clothes and ran around up the back stairs. It was cold in Capri's room. She'd left the window open. He looked out and saw a blue Buick parked outside. It wasn't one of her parents' cars. They had two. Feeling cold, he picked up a wool bathrobe that was lying on the floor and put it on. It almost fit him. Then he lay down on Capri's bed, which wasn't made, and waited. He figured he wouldn't go down. He'd wait for her to come up. There were a lot of her books piled up on one side of the bed. He looked at one of them. *Originals: American Women Artists* by

Eleanor Munroe. He wondered if they were for school or what. She must have been working on something because there was paper on the floor too, and some written-on sheets. For some reason he suddenly thought of Maddy. They'd never once done it in her room. Whenever he went over there, her mother made them leave the door wide open—for what good that had done.

Lying there, warmer now, Jed began to feel incredibly sleepy. He hadn't slept too badly the night before, but the tension of the afternoon and the ensuing days suddenly caught up with him. When he opened his eyes, Capri, dressed as she had been when he arrived, was leaning over him. "Coast's clear," she said.

"Who was it?"

"Some lady they know. . . . She didn't know they were away. Wanted to invite them to something."

"Did she . . . suspect anything?"

"No . . . I'm great at spur-of-the-moment improvisation." She sat on the bed next to him. "Did you sleep?" she asked tenderly.

"A little."

"You poor baby . . . you know," Capri looked solemn. "I think you deserve me, seriously."

"I do?"

"Yeah . . . I mean, face it: married to a virgin, a screaming kid in a one-room apartment, a father at eighteen . . . that's the pits."

"That's not the half of it," Jed said. He wanted to go on, but he felt uncomfortable telling her about Maddy refusing to use birth control and pulling away from him if he didn't have condoms.

"Does she like sex better now?" Capri pursued, though he hadn't said anything.

"Not that much."

She was silent, frowning, staring off into space. "Maybe you're not having enough foreplay. . . . For a lot of women that's a big thing. It isn't with me. I don't know why . . . *do* you?"

"Do I *what?*"

"Do you have lots of foreplay with her?"

"What's foreplay?" Jed said, laughing.

"I guess I better show you." Capri said, "just to give you the

---

131

idea." She kissed him all the way down to his cock and began sucking on it lightly. Then she lifted up her head. "There are many variations," she said. "The main thing is having lots of time. Not just rushing it."

He had never done it three times in one afternoon. "Is that lady going to come back?" he said now, reaching down between her legs, stroking her gently inside.

"What lady?" Capri said, stretching. "Umm . . . hey, you're getting the idea. That's it."

There was a moment at the end of the afternoon, as they lay entangled on her bed, that he thought: This is the best day of my life. He was surprised and totally unprepared for the feeling of sudden depression that gripped him the second he started the car to drive home. It was pitch black out and icy cold, down near zero. Snow had started to fall, but an icy snow, glittering on the window, made the windshield wipers scrape. He'd wanted to drive home fast, as fast as the car could go, but the icy roads made that too foolhardy. As it was, he skidded twice and had to bring the car back out of a ditch.

The heater in the car wasn't working; his hands—he'd forgotten gloves—felt cracked and cold. God, the car was a piece of shit. It had been ten years old when he bought it and for years, in high school, just having one had seemed enough, like having a girlfriend. Now he started remembering the red Camaro in Edelman's lot. It was such a beautiful car that sometimes, before he left, he just went over and stared at it, the way you'd stare at a painting that some museum had bought for a million dollars. One day Edelman had been sick and Homer had left early. Jed had debated taking the car out, just to try it, drive it around a little. But he had hesitated. Neither Edelman nor Homer was especially concerned about making money that he could see, but they were both careful. The kind who wouldn't give you a second chance. And he liked the job. Why fool around and wreck things?

A second chance. If only it hadn't been so easy with Capri! If only her parents didn't live in Ithaca and she was in the dorm and it was hard finding places to do it! If only she'd met some old boyfriend back in the city or decided that, now that he was a father, it wasn't right for her to continue seeing him. But her code of morality seemed pretty vague and fuzzy. Once she'd said of a gay friend, "Look, if they're happy, what difference does it make?" He wondered, not for the first time, what he was to her, what she thought when she thought of him. Great sex, something to get her through the year? Did she joke about him with her friends? She said no, claimed she wasn't that friendly with any of the girls, but that, in any case, she wouldn't have talked about him. "For your sake," she said. "I don't want to get you into trouble."

Sure. No, he knew what she meant. She wanted him, considered Maddy irrelevant, and left it to him to battle out any struggles of conscience. She'd never been married! It was just different. He remembered how once, after he'd broken up with Garnet and started seeing Maddy, Garnet had flirted with him one day at school and invited him over that evening. But the next day, seeing Maddy, her friendly, trusting face lighting up as he came toward her, he'd felt a much milder version of what he felt now.

It seemed to Jed he had two sides to his nature. One was the rebellious side that resented rules and being told what to do, especially by fools, but sometimes by anyone. He'd rather figure things out his own way than be given advice. Maybe that was because his mother had moved out so early in his life and his father had pretty much left him alone. There had been a few times in his life when the rebellious thing had gotten him into trouble. But whenever that happened, the other side of his personality, the desire to be good, not to rock the boat, struggled to the surface and he made amends. He couldn't even tell which side of himself he preferred. He got mad at his rebellious side because it seemed childish, like a kid having a tantrum. But when he brought it under control, he always felt a little angry, cowed. Sometimes he imagined it would be better to be just one or just the other. Totally wild, not giving a damn, or a real "nice guy" like Luther, who never seemed to even get the impulse to do anything wrong. The wild side of him never would've married Maddy. He just would've given her money for an abortion and told her that was that. And he wouldn't be letting even one thought mar the memory of the afternoon with Capri. He would just be looking back with pleasure and forward with anticipation.

Back home Maddy was fixing dinner. It smelled good—pork chops and sweet potatoes. He felt guilty as she looked up and said in a worried voice, "Oh, I was so scared about the snow. I wasn't sure the car would make it."

"Just barely," he said, kissing her.

She beamed. "The baby's been pretty good," she said. "She got fussy around four, but I fed her and now she's okay."

They still both called her "the baby" rather than by any name.

"Did you pick up the stuff?" she asked as she hung up his coat. He'd told her he needed to buy "supplies" for Thornie.

"Yeah, no problem." For some reason he added, "While I was down there, I decided to see a movie. That's why it took so long."

"Which one did you see?" She didn't ask at all suspiciously, didn't even look at him, just continued with cooking.

Jed's mind went blank. He should have at least checked what was playing. "Um . . . *The French Lieutenant's Woman.*"

"We saw that already!"

"Well . . . it was nearby."

"I thought you didn't like it that much."

"It was better the second time."

They had a quiet evening, the baby slept less fitfully than usual, and in the morning Jed woke up thinking: maybe he could give up Capri. Maybe he could think of the trip to Ithaca as a farewell. That thought lasted till about the middle of the next day, when it began dissolving, disintegrating, and finally vanished altogether, as though it had been a tangible object, a lump of snow becoming part of the earth.

The following Saturday Maddy went to Auburn to see her parents. The college had a bus that went in Saturday at eleven and her father had said he would drive her home at dinnertime. Jed asked if it was okay if he didn't go.

"Oh sure," Maddy said. "You've been working so hard."

He waited with her while she got on the bus. As a "special

134

favor" he'd agreed to look after the baby for the afternoon. The baby was okay till Maddy got on the bus. The second she disappeared, the baby started yelling her head off. "Oh Christ," Jed said. It was two o'clock. Maddy would be home, at best, by six.

Back in the apartment he unwrapped the baby from her snowsuit and put her in her crib. There was a half-finished bottle on the floor. He offered it to her, but she turned aside, her back to him, like someone pouting. Still, she didn't cry. That was something, anyway. So pout! Go right ahead. God, they really learned that early.

He ate an apple, looking out at the heavy snow falling, and without stopping to think about it, called Capri. She was in, studying.

"Want to come over?" he asked. He explained about Maddy being gone.

"Sure . . . is it safe?"

"Yeah, why not?"

"How about the couple who live next door?"

"Just come around the other side." He told her which door to knock on.

After he'd called her, he felt a moment of anxiety and then a defiant kind of pleasure. It took her half an hour to get there.

"What took you so long?" he asked, almost angrily, opening the door.

"Oh, my parents called right after you did . . . and I had to finish this chapter." She put her coat on the chair and looked around the room. "It's cute, kind of. . . . Is this the only room?"

He nodded.

Capri walked over to the crib. "Oh, the baby's here! How great! . . . I wanted to see her." She walked around to the other side of the crib. The baby was lying there, staring straight ahead, holding one of her own hands. "She doesn't look like you especially," Capri said. She bent down and touched the baby's hand. "Hi," she said softly. "I'm Capri."

"She's kind of funny-looking," Jed said.

"You mean her eye? What's wrong with it?"

"I don't know. . . . The doctor said she might need an operation later on or it might just go away."

"So? She's not Miss America. Big deal." She looked around further, finally stopping at the bed. "Looks comfortable."

"Yeah." But suddenly Jed wasn't sure if he had the courage to make love to her right there, especially with the baby watching.

"I was up till three," Capri said, stretching out, her arms under her head. "I feel zonked."

"How come?"

"Well, did I tell you about that guy I got into trouble with last year? Sam?"

Jed shook his head.

"It's a sort of weird story, but the thing is he was in one of my classes, Twentieth-Century Lit, and we were both kind of the best in the class. So we, like, showed off for each other and at the same time kind of competed for the teacher's attention. It turned out, I didn't know this, that the teacher was gay and he and Sam had kind of had something the year before. So this teacher had a real love-hate thing going for me. He liked me, but once Sam and I started dating, he started acting kind of strange. . . . He claimed he lost my term paper and he called my parents and said he thought they should know I was involved with an unstable boy. It was *so* vindictive! . . . So Sam got all spaced out and failed three of his courses and then Drier called his parents and put all the blame for that on *me!* He was sick, absolutely. Anyhow, Sam dropped out and we had to swear not to see each other. But this year he's back, doing okay, and he suddenly called, at one in the morning. We talked for two hours!"

"You know some weird people," Jed said. He felt jealous of their talking for two hours. What about?

"He thinks you're good for me," she said.

"What'd he say?"

"Just that I needed someone nonverbal and solid, with good values and stuff."

Jed laughed. Good values! But mainly he felt angry, both at the "nonverbal" and at her talking about him at all. Capri looked at him. "Are you mad?" she said.

"Yeah!" he exploded. "I don't talk about you to anyone."

"Well, it's different. . . . He's an old friend."

"I have old friends."

"What'd you mind—the nonverbal part? I didn't mean, I just meant—"

"I mind your doing it," he said angrily. "That's all."

"I won't do it again, okay?" she said meekly. But her meekness was different from Maddy's. It had some kind of anger just below the surface.

"Look, why don't you just go home?" Jed said suddenly.

"What?"

"I—I think this was kind of a mistake. . . . Someone might see you, the baby—"

"Who's going to see me? Are you expecting visitors?"

"I just . . . we can't do it with the baby here, not if she's awake."

"Why not? Primal scene? We can get under the covers."

"I can't do it with her watching," he said firmly.

"So, is sex the only thing we can do?" Capri said. "Is that, like, the only reason we see each other?"

He was silent. "Well, it's—"

She was angry now. "So, go fuck your wife, if you want sex," she said, glaring at him.

"I do. . . . Don't worry."

Capri had leaped up from the bed. "Some people—which may be amazing news to you—actually *talk* to each other. I mean, they actually consider that part of it important. Like, I know you'll never believe this, but some men find women interesting *people*, not just—organs!"

Jed hesitated. Her getting mad excited him, he didn't want her to go. "Okay, let's talk," he said softly. "What do you want to talk about?"

She just stared at him grimly, her mouth set.

They sat in silence. Jed, glancing over at the crib, saw that the baby had fallen asleep. He walked over to Capri and put his hand on her shoulder. "That's a nice sweater," he said. It was white with embroidered red snowflakes.

Without moving, she just stared at the floor, looking more melancholy than angry. "I think I'm an evil, horrible person," she said suddenly.

"No, you're not," he said. "In what way?"

"I mean, you're this child groom!" she said. "And you have this baby! It isn't like you've been married for nine thousand years and your wife drinks or picks up men at bars. . . . What am I *doing* here? Why do I get *into* these 'things'? Why can't I just have some regular boyfriend quote unquote like everyone else?"

He didn't know the answers to any of those questions.

"You know what I worry?" she said. "I worry that maybe what we have is the best there is, and here we have it now and we're just beginning, and maybe that's *it!* Maybe you just get it once."

He had an erection, but he was afraid if he made any move to her, she would bolt up and leave. "I don't know," he said.

Then suddenly she put her arms around him and kissed him passionately on the lips. "I love your mouth," she said, touching it. "You're so . . . beautiful."

"So're you." Jed put his hands under her sweater and let them ease up to her breasts. "I think the baby's asleep," he whispered.

"We can get under the covers anyway," Capri whispered back, pulling her sweater over her head.

But in bed with her his mood changed again. They started in quickly, afraid the baby might wake up. Capri never minded that. She prided herself on being able to "get going fast," as she put it. And normally Jed didn't mind it either. But this time, a few moments after he entered her, the phone started ringing. He stopped.

"Do you want to get it?" Capri whispered.

He hesitated. "They'll call back," he said, knowing it must be Maddy, maybe telling him she was setting out, maybe checking to see how the baby was. He began making love to Capri again. She had been on the verge of coming and did a moment later, as though the interruption had never occurred. Often she came before he did, he didn't care, but this time he was angry at her ability to block out the reality of where they were and his own inability. He couldn't come. Her arms were around him, but he felt she was lying there, bored, irritated with him. He was afraid the phone would start ringing again, that the baby would wake up. He was even afraid the baby was awake and was lying there, watching them.

"Do you want to stop for a while?" Capri whispered finally.

"I guess."

Jed withdrew, humiliated. What a dumb idea the whole thing had been! What was he trying to prove?

"I guess it's hard," Capri said, "doing it in the same bed that you usually—"

"It's not that," Jed said quickly.

"Was it the phone ringing?"

"I don't know."

Though it was totally not her fault, he felt angry with her, angry that she was so willing to find excuses for him as well as herself.

Capri glanced at her watch. "I guess I should go back," she said. "It's almost dinnertime."

"Okay." He watched her dress.

At the door she said, "I'm glad I had a chance to meet the baby." She said it formally, and then waved in the direction of the crib. "Bye, Minnie."

"So, I'll call you," he said flatly. He both wanted her gone and wished she could stay longer so the mood of the afternoon could be turned around.

He watched her walk off in the snow in her black boots, the red parka becoming smaller as she went down the hill. Then he made the bed, pulling the sheets and covers carefully and tucking them under. The phone rang again. This time he got it on the first ring. The moment it rang the baby woke up and started to cry. It was Maddy.

"Hi, Jed?"

"Oh hi," he said. "We just got in."

"From where?"

"Oh, I just took her out—down to the store."

"Did she mind the snow?"

"No."

Maddy explained that she was setting out, that she'd be home in half an hour. Jed glanced at his watch. Five-thirty. He would zoom down to the store before it closed and get something, anything, just to prove he'd been there. He grabbed the baby and put her in her snowsuit, put on his own coat, and drove the car downtown. The store was almost deserted. It rarely did a very booming business, since there were big chain supermarkets not that far from town. Spying a bunch of bananas, he took those, added a jar of applesauce and a box of cookies for good measure, and paid with a five he had in his pocket.

The baby seemed unperturbed by this whirlwind of activity. In the car he'd put her in a box they had in the back seat, covered her with a blanket up to her neck, and left the heater on so she wouldn't be too cold. Back at the house, unwrapping her, he became aware that she stank. He realized he hadn't changed her all afternoon. Ugh. Should he wait for Maddy to return and do it? He would have, but the stench was incredible in the warm room.

Holding his breath, Jed put the baby in her crib, the way he'd seen Maddy do, and took off her stretch suit. She was covered with shit! It had oozed all the way up her back, to her neck almost. The odd thing was it didn't seem to bother her at all. She lay there, regarding him with that peculiar stare, but unfretful. Meanwhile the shit was staining the crib sheet as well, liquid. Trying to breathe through his mouth, he put some newspapers under her and got a roll of paper towels from the kitchen. Then, after wiping her off, he sprinkled a lot of powder all over her bottom from a container Maddy kept near the crib. The baby's skin was red and irritated, but the white powder concealed that, maybe made it less painful. What was she thinking as she lay there, staring at him so fixedly? It seemed to Jed, though he knew this was impossible, that the baby knew everything that had happened that afternoon, even while she'd been asleep. He thought she knew he had called Capri, knew about their argument, knew he hadn't been able to come. All that knowledge was stored away somewhere in her brain, somewhere mysterious and unknown. He didn't like meeting her gaze; it unnerved him.

When he was done, having changed the sheet and dumped the stinking stretch suit and sheet in the bathtub to be dealt with by Maddy on her return, he let out a "whew" and washed his hands. He'd never known a baby that small could produce that much shit. God, what a mess. Let Maddy get home soon, he prayed.

Though the baby had been fairly quiet, the second Maddy turned the doorknob she let out a piercing yell, so loud that Maddy wasn't even able to ask Jed anything, nor he her. "What's wrong?" she cried, alarmed, rushing over to the baby.

"She was fine till now," Jed said guiltily. "I just changed her."

Somehow, with Maddy back, the baby seemed to recede into her usual minor part in his conscious life. He sat down and watched while Maddy gave her a bottle, carried her around the room talking to her softly, and then put her back in her crib. He was surprised at how Maddy talked to the baby as though she could understand. Did she think the baby did, or did she just do it? "It was snowing," Maddy said to the baby. "Did you like the snow, Minnie? How did it feel? . . . I was visiting my parents. They asked after you. They wished you could have come."

The first few times they had visited Maddy's parents, she had returned in tears because all her mother would talk about was the problem with the baby's eyes and how, if it didn't correct itself, it would take a terribly expensive operation, and where would they get the money? She would go on and on with an almost ghoulish delight about all the problems the baby would have, how she would be teased by other children, might be unable to learn to read. But evidently this time it had gone better. At least Maddy was in good spirits and talked on cheerfully about various things, her father's new Polaroid camera, the fact that her sister Jarita might be coming home for a visit.

Jed listened and did not listen. While she talked, bits of the afternoon's conversation with Capri kept shooting painfully through his head. "So she's not Miss America? Big deal. . . . He thinks you're good for me—someone nonverbal and solid with good values. . . . Some men find women interesting people, not just organs! . . . Maybe what we have is the best there is. Maybe you just get it once. . . . Do you want to stop for a while?"

After dinner they watched TV a little, on the small, not very good black-and-white set Luther and Vonni had given them. It was peaceful, and Jed both savored that and distrusted it. It seemed to him that Maddy's cheerfulness had a false premise, that though they were in the same room, married, they were in different worlds with different things that concerned them and were important to them. Probably that had always been true, but knowing it was like a static cutting through the quiet texture of everything. It bothered him.

Seven

The postcard was dated Feb. 12, and postmarked from Toronto. If it hadn't been that his daughter-in-law had retained her married name, Celia Edelman, Misha knew he would have been unable to remember who she was. Willed forgetfulness. Of course he knew who she was and knew, even, that she came originally from Toronto, but he had put her totally out of his mind with a completeness that had never even struck him until her postcard arrived. True, she had not died in the accident, had not even been in the car, but her only connection with his life was through his wife, son, and grandchild who no longer existed. Thus, by some carry-over, he had willed her, too, out of existence. It seemed easier. The card read:

Dear Mr. Edelman:
How have you been? I was wondering if you would like to have dinner on Feb. 20th. I'm going to be passing through Auburn. I hope you've been well. I'll call you that morning to see if it's okay.

Sincerely,
Celia
Edelman

Did he *want* to see her? No, not really. And yet he felt it wouldn't be fair to her to refuse. He must have some symbolic role in her life, her only tie with a past that in some ways had been more wiped out than his. Or was that true? She was young, still in her twenties. She'd been married only four years. Inevitably she would remarry, have other children. He was even, though it might have been uncharitable of him, surprised she had not remarried already. Why? You think it's that easy to replace someone? Or was it just that he had always wondered how happy she had been with Seth, but had never openly questioned it or even said anything to Brenda?

Brenda's only worry had been if Celia was "good enough" for Seth. He felt the opposite. Why had a girl who seemed fairly pretty, not a knockout but sweet-looking, with a lovely figure, and reasonably bright, married his son? Brenda claimed that Seth had "found himself" in the three years after graduating college. He had gotten a social-work degree in Syracuse and was working for a hospital. Okay, true, he hadn't become a dropout, but how different was he from the clinging, stuttering, asthmatic child he had been for over a decade? With Celia Seth had the same aggressive, bickering manner that he had had with all his girlfriends, the verbal baiting, the retreating into childish sulking if things didn't go his way. To Misha Celia, in her quietly down-to-earth way, dealt marvelously with Seth's moods, either ignoring them or going about her business. "Well, I guess it's time to take a walk!" she'd announced one afternoon when he'd been going at her for some piece of idiocy. She seemed to be someone who wanted to find practical "solutions" for things. Brenda felt she lacked Seth's "sensitivity" and awareness of people. *He* thought she was a dozen times more sensitive than his son would ever be.

Maybe they'd been happy together. If they had written announcing a divorce, it would not have surprised him, and yet he was afraid he had, for reasons he had never understood, some buried desire for his son to fail. He liked it when Celia told Seth off, maybe just because Brenda had coddled Seth so while he had mainly stood by and watched, wishing they had had more children so that her intense mothering feelings could have been diffused.

Ceila Edelman, nee Cowger, had, like himself, lived for two

and a half years to some extent with imaginary people in her head, had had to create a world from scratch. Interesting that she had gone home. He recalled her saying once that she hated Toronto and would never live there as an adult. Or was she just home for a visit? For the week after her card arrived, he found bits and pieces of memories lodged more securely in his mind than he'd realized, things she'd said or done; her way of peeling an orange, for instance, which had always struck him as singularly artistic. She would arrange the sections like petals in a perfect circle and pour honey in the exact center. Hadn't she once said she had wanted to be an artist, but had never had the training?

He was in his office, looking at the card once again, when there was a quiet knock on the door, so quiet he thought perhaps he hadn't heard it the first time. It was that little blond girl, Parker's wife. She stood there with her baby in a kind of sling in front of her, smiling uncertainly. "Um . . . hi," she said. "I'm Maddy. Is Jed here?"

"I think he's right over there," Misha said, pointing outside.

"I'm his wife," she pointed out unnecessarily.

"Yes, of course," he said. "I remember you."

"You gave us the mattress," she reminded him.

"How's that working out?"

She blushed. "Oh, it's fine. . . . And I had my baby."

"So I see."

"She's almost three months."

Misha went over to look at the baby, but it was hard to see much. She had a large wool hat on and was sleeping. "Well," he said, not knowing what to say, "he's over there, if you want him."

She retreated toward the garage. She looked prettier than she had that hot July day, but there was still something worried and uncertain about her. Pretty eyes. God, how could kids like that be parents? Crazy.

A few moments later she came back. "Um, I wondered," she said. "Could I use your phone?"

"Go right ahead."

She dialed a number and waited, but evidently there was no

answer. She put the receiver down and said to him, "I don't think they're there."

"Who were you trying to reach?"

"My mother." She frowned. "It's just . . . I have this dentist appointment and I was going to leave the baby with her. She must have forgotten."

"When's your appointment?"

She glanced at her watch. "Now."

"Well, putting off the dentist is always among the pleasanter things in life."

"The trouble is, I have to have some wisdom teeth pulled. They have to give me gas and everything. I'm just afraid—I don't know." She looked up at him pleadingly. "Listen, I know this is a terrible thing to ask, but do you think you could watch her till I get back? I thought Jed could, but he says he's in the middle of a job. . . . She'll probably just sleep. She has a good personality. I'll pay you—"

Misha smiled. "I'd love to look after her," he said. "I like babies."

"You do?" She looked amazed at this news.

"I'm even capable of changing a diaper," he said wryly.

Maddy sighed. "That's wonderful. I'll get back as soon as I can, I promise."

"Take your time," Misha said. "No hurry. . . . What's her name?"

Maddy took the baby out of the sling and handed her to him. "Minnie."

Misha held the baby, wondering what exactly to do with her, when Maddy came running back with a cardboard box and a plastic infant seat. There were several paper diapers and a prefixed bottle in the box. "I'll see you later!" she called, running off again, as though afraid he might change his mind.

When the door closed the second time, the baby's eyes opened abruptly, and she let out a howl. "Hey," Misha said. "Relax. She's coming back."

Something about the sound of his voice caught her attention.

She looked at him curiously. Was there something wrong with her eye? One eye stared right at him, but the other wandered to one side. "So, listen," Misha said. "What can I tell you? I'm an old hand with babies. I was a father, a grandfather. I have impeccable credentials. Do you want to see them or will you trust me?"

Suddenly the baby smiled. She had the most captivating smile Misha had ever seen, crooked, delighted, as though something very funny and improbable had happened. He smiled back at her. "Forget about your eye," he told her. "I bet they can fix it. And with a smile like that, you're going to do fine. Believe me. A smile comes first." The baby seemed to be pushing on one side of the woolen hat. Misha untied it. She had some black curly hair, not much, and two gigantic ears that popped out the second he took the hat off.

Who did she look like? There was something about her that was so familiar it was puzzling. "I know you've probably heard this line before," he told her, "but I have the feeling we've met somewhere. . . . Where do you hang out?"

The baby reached out and grabbed his nose.

"Hey! Take it easy. That's part of me. I know it looks just like a decoration. . . . You want something to play with? Let's see." He looked around the office and found the postcard Celia had sent. On one side was a brightly colored scene of a woman doing a folk dance. He gave it to the baby, who immediately tried to eat it. Misha turned it over to show her the dancing woman. "Now this is a card from someone named Celia. She has the same last name as mine. Edelman. Got that? . . . She used to have a baby, but something happened. It was an accident."

The baby looked at him carefully. It was strange, but Misha had the feeling she was understanding and following every word. Of course no one knew. Maybe they could. Or maybe they forgot everything. Or maybe a world without words was in some ways a more interesting and colorful place than it would later become. She had such an intent, shrewd expression, not calculating, but observant. Then she smiled again, and it came to him.

She looked like Wolf! Strange. His brother had never had children, so there was no telling what they might have looked like, but Misha felt certain this baby was the baby his brother would have had, if he had had one. "You're my kid," he used to say to Misha. For a second he wished so much Wolf were alive. He wanted to call him up and say, "You'll never believe this, but there's this baby in my office and she looks exactly like you." "Maybe she is mine," Wolf would joke. "I get around."

Through the window of his office he saw a couple walk into the lot. Uh oh. Business. He hesitated, and then carried the baby outside with him. It was a mild day for February, nearly sixty, hints of spring in the air. "Can I help you, folks?" he asked.

They looked middle-aged, slightly dour. "Do you take trade-ins?" the man asked curtly.

"Sure . . . what do you have?"

"We didn't bring her with us," the woman explained, "but she's in good shape."

"Seventy-eight Pontiac," the man said. "Sixty thousand miles on her. No major problems."

"What are you looking for?" Misha said. "By the way, this is my . . . grandchild. I'm babysitting for a couple of hours."

The woman beamed. "Well, isn't she a darling!" she exclaimed. "Look at her, Harold."

"There's something wrong with her eye," Harold said suspiciously.

"It's a weak muscle," Misha said.

"I'm sure that can be corrected by surgery," the woman said. "Don't you worry about it for a second. Remember Mildred Webb's son, dear? He had something like that, I don't remember exactly what . . . but now he's fine. Do it early, though. Because it's hard once they start school. You know how kids are. They can tease so!"

"We're planning to," Misha said. "Right, kid?"

The baby smiled.

"She's so sweet," the woman said. "You're so lucky! I'd give my right arm for a grandchild and I don't mean that as a whatever-you-call-it. I mean really! . . . But look at kids these days! Take our son, Nathaniel. Twenty-nine years old, he's been living with a girl for four years. 'When are you going to get married?' I ask. 'We're still making up our minds,' he says. Making up their minds! What's to make up? You *do* it, you just *do* it. By the time they make up their minds, they'll be too old." She shook her head. "But they don't think of that, these kids. One day they'll wake up and it'll be too late. It's just—"

"Hallie," her husband interrupted. "I'm sure this man is very busy."

"No, I understand," Misha said.

"I just hope you appreciate this baby, is all I wanted to say," Hallie went on. "Do you?"

"I do," Misha said firmly.

"Good!" She looked pleased.

What they wanted, in terms of a car anyway, was something smaller than what they had, a two-seater. "It doesn't have to be one of those jazzy numbers," Harold said. "Just something that'll get us there and won't put us in the poorhouse on gas."

Misha showed them a few models. The baby seemed content to be carried around the lot and looked appreciatively at the cars with them. In the end they decided to "think it over" and come back later in the day.

"How late you open?" Harold asked.

"Till six."

"Terrific. . . . We hear you're a pretty honest guy."

"Harold!" Hallie protested. "Of course he's honest."

"There's no of course about it these days," Harold said grimly. To Misha he said, "Am I right?"

"I'm afraid so," Misha said.

"Some of these guys, the car drives fine, then you're on the road a couple hundred miles and boom! The thing disintegrates on you."

After they'd left Misha went back to his office. He noticed there were some rusks in a plastic bag and took one out and gave it to the baby. She examined it carefully and began sucking on one end. "So, what do you think, baby? Want to go into the used car business?" Misha sighed. "You want to know something? Now I know this sounds crazy, but I hate cars. It isn't just the accident. I've never liked them. So I want to give you a piece of advice. I used to be a teacher. Okay, I wasn't earning much, but I liked it. I like history. I liked the kids. So my brother comes along and 'rescues' me. He's afraid I'll get stuck in some low-paying job all my life. He wants me to make it big like him in business. You know what I should have done? I should have said, 'Wolf, I know you have my best interests at heart, but scram. I can live my own life.'" The baby was watching him with undivided attention throughout this long speech. "If you think that's easy, you're wrong," he said. "It is damn hard to live your own life. People are always giving you advice, suggestions. Tell them to scram."

He wondered how he could entertain the baby till the mother returned. Did they play with toys at this age? She seemed perfectly content, sitting in his arms, listening to him hold forth. Then he had an idea. He got a magazine off the shelf with one hand. "I'm going to show you some pictures," he told her. "This is a place called Florida."

The baby placed one hand on the magazine. She seemed to be patting it or maybe she was pointing to something. "Okay, that's the ocean. You like it? It's really warm down there, beautiful climate. Never gets much below sixty. . . . See, what I had in mind was this. Why not sell the business and move down there, maybe try and get a teaching job? What's to hold me here? . . . What'd you think? Does it look like a nice place?" He turned the pages. There were photos of women swimming, flamingos. The baby seemed especially taken by the photo of the flamingos. She bent her head down so that her lips touched the page and tried with the tip of her tongue to taste the flamingo. "It's a nice bird," Misha agreed. "You could probably see one at the zoo, even if you never make it to Florida. What do you like about it? The color? Yeah, they're pretty birds. It's the tropics down there. Everything's exotic, different."

They went through the magazine twice. When they were finished, Misha noticed the baby was drooling all the way down her stretch suit. She began trying to suck on her sleeve. He took one of the small bottles out of the box, screwed on one of the disposable nipples in the bag, and fed her. She drank hungrily, draining the entire bottle in one sitting. He had forgotten, or maybe he had never known, what energy and passion babies put into eating. Eyes closed, she sucked with regular deep motions. Once she opened her eyes and looked up at him with a drowsy smile, like someone getting drunk, but enjoying it. Her lips curled into a smile around the edges of the nipple. When she was finished, he sat her up. She burped with a sudden loud noise. A little milk came up and dribbled down her collar.

Then she smiled at him again, that wonderful, crooked smile. "I know this is an odd thing to say," Misha said, "but you look exactly like my brother, Wolf. I don't know what it is, but you really do." She reached out and touched his cheek. Misha became aware that she was getting wet. He set her down in the box and changed her. She lay quietly, her legs apart, as he slid the new diaper under the old one. When again would a woman ever lie there so peacefully and acceptingly while a man had his way with her? She looked at him with an expression of such total trust and peacefulness that it gave him a pang. They had to lose that somewhere along the way.

Within the hour Maddy came back. She was breathless, as though she had run all the way. The entire bottom half of her face was swollen, which gave her a peculiar chipmunklike look. "Don't look at me," she said. "I look awful."

"How many teeth did he have to pull?"

"Four! He said it's better having them all out at once." The baby had fallen asleep and was lying, stomach down, in the box. "So, how was she?" Maddy asked anxiously. "Was it okay?"

"Fine . . . she helped me sell a few cars. She was terrific."

She hesitated, looking at him with a worried expression. "How much do I owe you?" she said finally.

"For what?"

"For babysitting."

Misha laughed. "I loved it. Any time."

"You're sure?" Maddy seemed to relax. "She can be funny with strangers. . . . Sometimes she just looks at them and howls her head off. . . . Like with my sister Doreen, who's had five kids, she just took one look at her and started yelling. And my sister felt so bad! And *I* felt so bad! You never know."

After she had left, Misha, looking back on the afternoon, wondered if he was truly crazy. He realized he'd been talking to the baby, not only as though they were old friends, but as though she understood everything he said. Maybe he had held so many conversations in his head with Wolf and Brenda over the last three years that he was losing some basic sense of distinction. He'd be talking to cars next! Partly, he thought, it was just that ease you feel with someone you know you'll never see again. And babies in some ways are like dogs—they look at you with such understanding that it's hard to believe they aren't following what you're saying. Still, better watch it, pal.

The following Wednesday Celia was due to arrive. He had wondered if she would actually call and was half hoping she might not. But at ten-thirty in the morning his office phone rang and it was she.

"Mr. Edelman?"

"Speaking."

"Um . . . this is Celia Edelman. I—I wrote you a card. Did you get it?"

"Sure. . . . Well, it was nice to hear from you after all this time."

"Can you?"

"Pardon me?"

"Can you have dinner tonight? I'm only going to be in town today."

Misha hesitated. It would have been as easy to make up an excuse as not. But he found himself saying, "Just tell me when and where."

They arranged to meet at one of the Italian restaurants in town, a quiet but pleasant one with home-made pasta. After hanging up, he called Ardis. Wednesday had become their day, the day she came over to his place and they had dinner together and spent the evening in bed. It was the highlight of his week; he minded giving it up.

"Something's come up," he explained. "An old friend, someone from college. He's only in town today."

"Huh . . . well, as long as you're not sneaking off with another woman!" She laughed at the unlikeliness of this.

"Don't worry. . . . How's tomorrow?"

"I can't."

Having counted on her being free, Misha felt a sharp pang of disappointment. "Why not? What're you doing?"

She laughed, but with slight irritation. "Sweetie, listen, I'm married, remember? So, like, Simon expects me here . . . Wednesday I've got set up, I mean I have an excuse all worked out, but I can't just . . . Do you know what I mean?"

Fuck Simon! Trying not to sound irritated himself, he said, "Well, how about . . . I'll be back by ten, I'm sure. Could you come over then?"

"For a quickie? No! What's the fun of that?"

"Isn't it more fun than nothing?"

"No! I don't like to *eat* in five minutes either. . . . If it can't be relaxed and leisurely, I'd rather just not do it." Her anger sparked through the phone at him.

"It's just . . . I've been looking forward to it all week," he said, trying not to sound plaintive.

"So have *I!*" She was clearly exasperated. "Look, who's cancelling, huh?"

"I'd rearrange it," Misha said, desperately wishing he could. "I just don't have his number."

There was a pause.

"Next time get his number," Ardis said.

"There won't *be* a next time. . . . It was foolish. I should've." There was nothing more to say, but he hated to hang up with this tension between them.

Ardis sighed. "I'm sorry if I sounded upset. It's just that I've been fantasizing about it all day. It means so much to me, being with you and—"

"To me too!"

"But we'll survive," she said, trying to sound cheerful, "and I'll see what I can do about later in the week. Maybe Friday. I'll call you back and let you know." She laughed. "I will leave no stone unturned."

"That's my girl."

He felt somewhat better at her admitting that their time alone together was important to her also. Yet he was still angry with himself for not getting Celia's number, and puzzled as to why he hadn't told Ardis who it was, had felt a lie was necessary. Surely there was nothing at all shameful about having dinner with your daughter-in-law, or your ex-daughter-in-law as the case might be. And yet oddly he had felt a husbandlike guilt simply because it was another woman. Absurd, in a way. It was as though Ardis stood both for herself, a woman he was involved with, and for Brenda, the two of them united into one person, watching over him carefully.

He arrived at the restaurant before Celia. He had never in his life been able to arrive other than early; when he tried to come late, he was on time. But he sat quietly, reading the newspaper, until she appeared. When he looked up and saw her approaching the table, Misha felt such an unexpected and terrible pang go through him that he was afraid he might pass out. She looked exactly the same. Why shouldn't she? Two and a half years wasn't long. Her light brown hair was short and naturally curly, almost like a boy's. She had a gaminelike, androgynous "cuteness" rather than anything approaching beauty: a dimple, a graceful, perky walk. She wore jeans or slacks a lot and they suited her. Brenda had always minded that she painted her nails, each one a perfect pale pink to match her lipstick. It was the fact of the perfect match, not just the painting itself, that Brenda claimed was lower-class in some way.

"I'm sorry I'm late," she said, sliding into the booth. She leaned over and kissed him in a friendly way. "Hi."

Misha was terribly afraid that she would notice his mood and take it personally. It was as though seeing her had in some horrible way brought back the whole thing. He thought: what if I can't get through this? His hands were shaking. When the waitress came and asked them if they wanted a drink, he ordered a scotch on the rocks, though he rarely drank anything other than an occasional glass of wine or beer. He wanted some kind of novocaine to get him through the next hour or two.

"So, how've you been?" he asked, taking a long gulp of the scotch. "You look well."

"Oh, I've been . . . I don't know! Up and down." Her eyes looked tearful, worried. "I had a really bad year, the first year . . . but now I'm okay, I think."

"Did you go home? I remember you came from Toronto."

She was sipping her whiskey sour, looking nervous. "The thing is, I sort of . . . I had kind of a nervous breakdown about six months after . . . I—I guess I couldn't handle it. I tried! I'd get up and try to do all the things I used to. I had a job, I tried to 'date,' but it was, like, I can't explain it exactly, but it was like some weird kind of gap between me and what was happening, like I was looking through the wrong end of a telescope. Do you know what I mean?"

"Yes."

"Then—God, I hate to burden you with this, but you asked." She was talking in a breathless way, her cheeks pink. "I was raped . . . It sounds melodramatic. It was this guy I was sort of dating. I didn't really like him, in fact, I kind of hated him, but I kept telling myself I should force myself to go out, and he seemed so eager. He was divorced. He kept telling me he knew how I felt. . . . So one night I went back to his place, which was dumb, I guess, but I didn't think. Or I didn't think he was the type who—" She stopped. "Well, anyway . . . the day after that, I just couldn't do anything. I mean, like I couldn't get out of bed and brush my teeth! So my doctor—I was seeing this doctor—he checked me into this mental hospital for about a month."

"I'm sorry," Misha said. The scotch was beginning to have an effect, partly blurring, partly in some way increasing the intensity of his mood.

She sat there, staring at him thoughtfully. "Now I'm fine!" she said, obviously making an effort to look cheerful.

"Good." He tried to match that effort.

"I've thought of you a lot. I wondered how you were getting along. I wanted to write, but I'm not that good at writing letters and then I thought . . . I guess part of me wanted to make a complete break. The doctor said that was what I did wrong, trying to break off the past instead of trying to understand it."

Misha remembered how Ardis had suggested he see a doctor in that first few months. He had refused, saying he could cope without it. "I had trouble too," he said, hearing his own voice from a slight distance, "but now things are good."

"Did you remarry?"

"No."

Perhaps he had spoken too harshly because Celia said quickly, "I didn't mean . . . You always seemed very happy with your wife. It's just sometimes men—my father remarried after my mother died and he's very happy."

"I'm fifty."

"So was he."

"*You* could have remarried," he countered.

"From a mental hospital?" She laughed bitterly. "Even going on a date was like some kind of monumental ordeal. I would have made someone a great wife!"

The waitress reappeared. They ordered and Misha asked for another scotch. He felt slightly better, but there were emotions hovering an inch from consciousness that frightened him.

"I'm sorry," Celia said softly. "Did I offend you saying that about remarriage?" She looked down at her drink. She was having a second one too. "I hope I'm not getting drunk. I guess I felt I might need it. It's like seeing you brought it all back . . . I didn't expect that."

"Yes, I know," Misha said. "I—" And then, just as the waitress appeared with their food, he broke down and started to weep. He was as amazed and horrified as if the waitress had wept upon setting the food in front of them. He covered his face with his hands, his shoulders shaking. He heard the waitress say, "Is he okay?" and heard Celia say, "Yes, it's fine. Please go away."

There was a luxury in tears as well as the relief that comes when the most embarrassing, unthinkable thing has happened and the world goes on. When he came to, Celia had moved into the bench next to him and had her hand on his shoulder. "Are you all right?" she asked gently.

Misha nodded.

"I'm so sorry," she said. "I wanted us just to have a relaxed, quiet dinner. You know, all the way over here I thought how I'd talk about all kinds of other things and then . . . it just came out."

"It's all right," Misha said. "Maybe one ought to"— he gestured—"let it all out occasionally."

She moved back to her side of the table and they had their dinner. After that it was, in some other way than what she had predicted, relaxed. They ate, sometimes talking and sometimes not. He wondered what the waitress had thought. Obviously the liquor, which he had hoped would anesthetize him, had also loosened some inner knot.

"I guess we're both the type who should never drink," Celia observed. "That happened the night I mentioned, with that guy. I wanted to feel attracted to him and I thought maybe if I had a couple of drinks, I might. But it doesn't work that way. I think drinking just makes you feel whatever you feel anyway—only more."

He remembered that first night with Ardis, the combined effect of the Valium and the wine and how that had gotten him past some barrier that would otherwise have been impassable. "Where are you going now?" he said. "Do you have a job?"

She nodded. "I'm a word processor."

"I thought that was a machine."

Celia laughed. "It is! Only, see, it can't do things just by itself. You have to, like, show it how. So, that's what I do. . . . Right now I guess I'm just basically a kind of glorified secretary, but I thought computers would be a good road to go. I have a friend who went into them and she's doing real well."

"Yes, I have a friend in that field too," Misha said. The waitress was taking away their plates. He was glad because, although his mood was calmer, he wasn't especially hungry and had barely touched his food.

"I think it's a good field for women," she went on, after ordering apple pie à la mode and coffee. "They don't care so much, as long as you're good."

"Yes, I think that's true." He was pleased to see her looking so much brighter and more cheerful than she had at the beginning of the meal. Maybe his breaking down had in some way made her feel less alone in her grief. At any rate, she ate with hearty appetite, scraping up every last drop of the pie and ice cream. "You're sure you don't want any?"

Misha shook his head.

"I'm just awful about dessert," she confided. "It's, like, the high point of the meal for me. All through the main course I'm thinking: Should I get pie, should I get cake?"

He smiled at her. "You don't look like you have to worry."

"I do . . . Seth used to kid me about my pot belly. I don't know. I just have one. I guess it's the way I'm built or something." But she seemed accepting about this.

Outside it had started to snow very lightly. "Oh, I'm so sick of winter!" Celia exclaimed, buttoning up her fur-trimmed blue coat. "Aren't you? That's why I decided to settle in Atlanta. I have a friend down there, from high school. She says it never gets below forty-five."

"Yes, I've thought of that," Misha said. "I've lived here so long, and still the winters seem to go on forever."

"They do!" she said. "Not just *seem* to."

He drove her back to her motel. It was a well-known one, on the lake, with a restaurant attached. He had been to the restaurant many times. They were known for a gigantic smorgasbord served every Sunday night.

"It's nice being on the lake," she said. "This morning I got up and took a walk along it before breakfast. . . . Would you like to see it?"

He wasn't sure what the "it" was—the lake, her room, or what. "Sure," he said, after a moment's hesitation.

Her room was neat. Except for the suitcase open on the chair, it was almost as though no one were staying in it. Along one wall of the room was a window, covered by drapes. Celia opened the door on the lake side of the room. They stood together, looking out at the moonlit lake. "I guess it didn't freeze this year," she said finally.

"No," Misha said. "It hasn't been that cold a winter." Standing so close to her, he was aware of some light scent she was wearing that seemed familiar. Perhaps she had always worn it.

They both turned away from the window simultaneously. Celia said, "I'm sorry I can't offer you anything to drink."

"I think we've probably both had enough," he said. Somehow this came out sounding more censorious than he had intended.

"Oh, that's right, I forgot." There was a sudden, awkward pause. She looked at him intently. Then she said, "Would you like some nuts?"

"Pardon me?" The awkwardness between them with its sexual overtones, the two of them in the small darkened bedroom, made whatever he said seem weighted.

She jumped up and began rummaging in her suitcase. "I went to this restaurant and for dessert they brought you this big bowl of nuts and fruit. I asked if you could take some home and they said sure." She took a plastic bag and dumped a pile of nuts on the bed, walnuts, Brazil nuts, and then sat down beside them.

Misha reached out and took a small handful.

"The only thing is, I don't have a nutcracker," she apologized.

"That's okay." He put them in his pocket.

There was a long pause.

"I guess I shouldn't have invited you back here," she said, not looking at him, but touching the nuts and arranging them on the bed. "I just thought . . . I don't know what. I guess I don't know how to act with men anymore!" She laughed nervously. "Or maybe I never did."

The look she gave him was so direct and so appealing that he found himself saying, "You're a lovely girl."

"Do you think so?" she said. "Do you really think I am?" She hesitated. "I don't know if my judgment about men is always that good. I want to trust them, but I guess it'll take awhile." She laughed again in that funny, abrupt way she had. "Being raped didn't help!"

"Did you prosecute him?"

"No . . . I should've, I know. They say you should. But I . . . I didn't want to believe it had happened. And I kept thinking maybe it was my fault." She gazed at him affectionately. "You're a very nice person," she informed him.

Misha smiled. "I'm not too sure of that."

"Did I seem terribly brazen?" she said hopefully. "Inviting you back here and all?"

"No."

"I'm trying to train myself to proposition men because I think you have to, you know. . . . I mean, it doesn't *pay* to be retiring. I was always so shy in high school. I think I'm getting a lot better." She stared at him, bemused. "It *is* a nice lake, though."

"Pardon me?" He wasn't sure what the connection was with their former conversation.

"I mean, I wanted you to see the lake. I didn't just want to lure you here."

"I was afraid I scared you," he admitted, "breaking down that way at dinner."

"No, I think we both—it's like we see each other and a lot of things come back."

"Yes."

Leaning back on the bed frame, her knees up, she looked very young again, like a schoolgirl. "Sometimes I felt your wife didn't like me," she said.

"Well, I think it was that she was so close to Seth," Misha said. "Too much so, maybe." He felt as though admitting that aloud were a betrayal.

"I think she thought I wasn't . . . educated enough," Celia went on, but thoughtfully rather than bitterly. "I'm not. He knew so much! We'd go to concerts and I'd just sit there, my mind would wander and he'd know everything about what was going on. . . . And with politics too. I don't remember facts that well. But I don't think I'm dumb."

"Definitely not," he assured her.

"In a way I was scared of all of you . . . you, your wife, Seth. The only one who didn't scare me was your wife's sister. I forget her name. She was always so friendly to me, lending me recipes and things. She was a really nice person."

"Yes," Misha said. "She is."

"Seth once told me she had, like, boyfriends? Even though she was married. But she never seemed like that type to me."

Misha didn't reply. Finally he said, "I guess I better be getting back."

She saw him to the door, padding in her bare feet. Even her toenails were painted that same pale pink. She kissed him goodbye on the cheek. "I'll send you a card from Atlanta," she said. "If you ever come down there—"

"Yes," he said, suddenly wondering if he ever would. "I hope everything works out for you, Celia."

At home, lying in bed, the whole funny tenor of the evening played itself back in his mind: looking at the lake, her tears, the nuts spread on the bed, her awkward, hesitant comments which so often seemed so uncannily accurate. He kept seeing Celia in his mind with Seth, the two of them arguing, talking, her feeding the baby, an evening when he and Brenda had come for dinner and Celia had burned the main course and they all had to go out. It was strange, seeing her now, to think she had been a mother, might by now have been the mother of several young children, taking them to school, making cookies.

When he spoke to Ardis the next day, she said she couldn't come by on Friday. "It's turning into a really hectic week," she said briskly.

He wondered if she had intuited that he had been with another woman, however innocently. How could she have, though? Wolf had claimed all wives had extrasensory perception when it came to things like that, that a little bell went off in their heads, even if you were three thousand miles away. Anyway, they weren't married! "I'm sorry," he said. "I missed you terribly."

Instead of responding to that, she asked, "How did your dinner go?"

"All right . . . he's not someone I basically feel that close to."

There was a pause.

"If you want to come by Sunday," she said, "Abby'll be here, but—well, whatever you feel like."

"I'd like to," he said. Maybe this was partly why he'd never gotten seriously involved with another woman during his marriage—if he was this guilty simply over a dinner with his former daughter-in-law.

Wolf thought guilt was an invention. "You want to know who should feel guilty?" he used to say. "The guys who come home and tell their wives all about it. What for? Just to ease their conscience. They should feel guilty. But the rest of it. . . . Look, what's the point of there being two sexes? It was done for a purpose. God, Nature, whoever monkeyed the whole thing into existence has to shoulder the blame."

There was no doubt that a part of himself he had basically forced underground for decades was pleased at his relationship with Ardis. Some kind of sexual pride. It was so different, being with a new woman, being seen differently, touched differently, responded to differently. He would have liked someone to tell about it, maybe boast indirectly, at any rate to talk to. Married, his sexual life had been so regular, so pleasant, that it had faded into the background, not unimportant, but not something he thought of very often. And the line that separated him from other women, even in his mind, had been, he saw now, more rigid than he'd realized. He had even censored thoughts, to the extent he had been able. And now suddenly, which he assumed was temporary, he saw all women sexually and wondered at the change. They all were both what they seemed, often proper, garrulous, impish, whatever . . . and then that other life, the way they were alone with someone in bed.

It was especially hard not to see Ardis' daughter, Abby, that way. She had always, even as a very young girl, had a kind of dreamy, natural provocativeness, sitting on his knee, fiddling with his hair, making him try on funny hats. He saw Ardis in her, the sudden playful gleam in her large dark eyes, the flamboyant style of dressing.

Sunday she was wearing a bright pink jogging suit and had her thick black hair in dozens of skinny black braids, each tied with a different-colored wool ribbon.

"Hon, that's a style for black women," Ardis said. "It just doesn't suit you."

"Bo Derek is black?" Abby said. "Hi, Uncle Mish. . . . What do you think? Do you like them?"

"Well, I—"

"You have beautiful hair," Ardis said. "You can't even tell this way."

"I do have beautiful hair," Abby said, laughing. She began undoing the braids. "Okay . . . see! Boy, what a dutiful daughter!"

Misha and Ardis sat and watched as she undid each braid and finally brushed out the released mass of black curls. Simon came into the room with a newspaper under his arm. "Where are the braids?" he said wryly.

"They hated them," she said, pretending to pout.

"She looks good in everything," Simon said. "Right?"

Abby kissed him. "Yeah, it's awful, isn't it? I look good in everything . . . except brown. I hate brown and gray. And I hate . . . Oh Mom, listen, did I tell you I got a B in Botany?"

"You did," Ardis said.

To Misha she said, "See, they have this stereotyped idea about me. I never study, all I do is think about boys . . . It's not true. I do think about boys, but I think about other things too."

"She's a smart girl," Simon said, patting her on the shoulder.

"I know I am, Daddy," Abby said, flirting with him.

Simon kept his hand on his daughter's shoulder a moment and then, with obvious reluctance, withdrew it. Misha, watching this, saw how hard it must be having a daughter like that. The complexities of being so intensely aware of her sexuality, but having to deny it constantly. He recalled a story Ardis had once told of how she had found Abby, at six, lying on the floor of her room clad in nothing but underpants. She had invited a little boy from her first-grade class over after school and was saying to him, "Pretend I'm an ice cream cone. Lick me all over." He was beginning to obey when the two mothers had intervened. After that, Ardis said, the mother of the little boy would never let him play at their house again, fearing that Abby was a "bad influence." Misha wondered if now, years later, the memory of that afternoon was tucked somewhere into that little boy's unconscious, replaying the scene so that the mothers would not appear. In her pink jogging suit it was easy to imagine Abby as an ice cream cone, a strawberry double.

"So, how's your business doing?" Abby said to Misha. "I hear it's hard with cars. Bill's father has a Chevrolet store in Rockland and he says business is really down."

"It's the economy," Simon remarked. "What can you expect?"

Misha wondered if Simon had always struck him as this irritating, or whether looking at him now as the cuckolded husband made him seem especially foolish and benighted. Misha couldn't believe what he felt was anything like jealousy; maybe it was amazement that someone as dynamic and alive as Ardis would choose to spend her life with someone like this, would want him as the father of her children. "I guess I *am* getting fed up with it," he admitted to Abby. "Maybe I'll sell the business and move to Miami."

"Oh, you've been saying that forever," Ardis said.

Misha was surprised at the sharpness of her tone, and also afraid the other two would read intimacy into her intensity. "Does that mean I'll never do it?" he said.

"Florida is so ghastly now," she went on. "I was at a conference there last year. It's all old people, all plastic."

"Remember Mac Grostein?" Simon said. "He had this scheme. He was going to go down to Florida and start a business growing flowers for funerals. He said someone dies down there every second, maybe more. . . . I wonder if he ever did it."

"That's morbid!" Abby exclaimed.

"He's probably a millionaire by now," Simon mused.

"I don't care," Abby said. "I think it's a sick idea."

She and Simon disappeared upstairs.

Misha looked at Ardis. It was strange in a way. For twenty years he and Brenda had made love once or twice a week and he could hardly recall a time when it had not been enjoyable and good for both of them. Enough so anyway that thoughts of other women had been in the background of his mind, not tormenting longings, just occasional desires that drifted in and out. When one of them had been sick or had to travel, he couldn't recall finding the temporary abstinence incredibly painful or hard to bear, although he had definitely looked forward to its cessation. But now, having grown used to the weekly encounters with Ardis, he found, to his surprise, that he missed it deeply.

"I was wondering," he said, speaking softly, "if maybe later tonight—"

He saw by her smile that she was enjoying his making the advances for a change. "Wednesday isn't so far off," she said teasingly.

Misha smiled in response. "Yes, it is," he said. "It's light-years away. . . . I'll be a different person by Wednesday."

She had moved so they were standing only a few inches apart. "I missed it too," she whispered. "All that evening I thought of you."

"So, what do you think about tonight?"

"Well, I shall do my best. For desperate situations desperate measures are in order."

Later, when she was with him, he thought how long ago it seemed that he had felt any connection with Brenda when Ardis was in bed with him. Maybe only that they were so different sexually and he felt that he, in some way, was a different kind of lover with her than he had been with Brenda. He wondered if it were possible, in marriage, to avoid that sense of being locked into a routine. It happened, whether you fought it or didn't. Or maybe it was that your wife saw you in so many different roles that your sexual identity was hardly your most important quality. She didn't look at you and think instantly "my lover," whether your sex life was good or bad. And where Ardis' sexual ease and inventiveness might have made him nervous if they had been married, now it seemed only a wonderful gift, something he had no desire to question.

"Shall I come Wednesday too?" she said as she left. "Or is that too soon?"

He wanted to say: come every day; but he only said, "I'll see you Wednesday," promising himself that in the future nothing would intervene on that day. Nothing, at the moment, had greater importance in his life.

Eight

The high point of the day, for all of them, was when they stopped work to watch "General Hospital." Actually, what was lucky was that they didn't have to stop work. On the other side of the former post office from May's Beauty Shop was a small thrift shop run by a widowed lady in her fifties, Mrs. Grace Jahr. Business was always slow for her, and to make the time pass, she had brought her TV into her shop. She watched it while waiting for her customers. It was a big color TV, a nineteen-inch one, set on a table with wheels. At three o'clock she and May would wheel the TV into the beauty shop and all of them, May, Maddy, Grace, and whoever was in the beauty shop having their hair done, would watch. Any comments made while the show was on were brief, clipped, like those of surgeons in the middle of an open-heart operation. "Can I have some Number Twos?" May might ask Maddy, or "Poke Mrs. Becker. I think she's been under long enough." Even the ladies under the dryers watched, the sound being turned up high enough to penetrate the drone and the cotton padding over their ears. Maddy had seen the show often in high school, although her mother disapproved of it. Mostly she had watched it at Vonni's house if school let out early.

Since Minnie's birth Maddy had worked three days a week at May's. It was a perfect job. May said she couldn't let Maddy do any of the complicated things, like cut hair or give permanents, since Maddy didn't have a degree from beauty school. But she let her do shampoos and sweep up and sometimes give manicures. Most of May's business came from the ladies of the town, women in their forties or fifties who had their hair set either once a week or for special occasions. The college girls came too, but only for trims or to have their hair blown dry. May thought they were stingy and didn't tip well. "Rich kids don't know what money is," she always said scornfully to Maddy when one of them had left.

Not all the college girls looked rich to Maddy. They certainly didn't all wear fancy clothes. May claimed that was because it was a girls' college. "They go all out on weekends," she said. "Who're they supposed to look pretty for during the week?" It seemed to Maddy that the girls studied hard. They brought heavy books with them and sometimes read those, rather than the magazines May kept in a rack for her other customers. The magazines were interesting to Maddy because they explained the private lives of some of the stars who were on TV. Sometimes the stars' lives were almost as complicated as the soap operas they were in. They seemed to constantly be having love affairs and getting remarried, often to people who were on the same show! It all sounded exciting and eventful to Maddy, far removed from what she knew as everyday life.

She had been lucky, not only in getting the job, but in the arrangement she had made about the baby. The woman who lived in the house adjoining theirs, Geraldine Farnum, had a two-year-old son who took a nap almost every morning about the time Minnie did. She had agreed to look in on Minnie every half hour to check if she was all right. She said she had to be home anyway because she was writing some long paper that would help her get a teaching job when her baby was older. When Maddy offered to pay her, she emphatically refused. "I'm right here," she said. "It does me good to take a break every once in a while." Most of the time everything was fine, but once she had called Maddy at the beauty shop to say the baby felt a little warm to her and she'd given her some aspirin. Another time she'd thought Minnie looked like she needed company and brought her into her own part of the house. "I hope you don't mind," she told Maddy. She had confessed to Maddy that she had secretly been hoping for a daughter and was still trying to accept not having had one, although her son was almost two. "You're so lucky!" she said, gazing at Minnie with such seemingly heartfelt pleasure that Maddy felt guilty. It had never occurred to her that someone could want a daughter more than a son, especially for their first child. "I guess your husband's pleased," she said to Geraldine.

"No, he wanted a girl too," Geraldine said mournfully. "We had a thousand girl's names picked out. . . . Well, we'll get a chance to use them someday, I guess."

To Maddy Geraldine looked old for the mother of such a young child. Her hair was partly gray, and she wore glasses. She reminded Maddy a little of a teacher she'd had in junior high who doubled as the school librarian. Geraldine had that same cheerful but worried expression, and even the habit of tucking her hair behind her ears. All morning, knowing Geraldine was looking in on the baby, Maddy felt relaxed, though she never quite rid herself of a feeling of guilt at not being there. She would rush home at lunchtime, breathlessly, and fling open the door. Most of the time the baby would be awake, lying there cooing, making her own soft sounds. They were like a private language, with its own idiosyncratic lilt and phrasing. Only once, Maddy had entered the room and found total silence. Knowing this undoubtedly meant the baby was asleep, Maddy nevertheless felt a grip of dread. She had read an article in a woman's magazine at the beauty shop about something called "crib death." Mothers would return to find their babies dead when there had been nothing wrong with them. It just happened! Her hands cold, Maddy ran over to the crib and peered at the baby's face. Her breathing was so quiet it was impossible to tell if she was alive or not. "Minnie?" Maddy said, her heart thumping. With a sigh, the baby turned and stretched one fist over her head. Maddy stood there, staring at her. The thought that came to her was the most terrible she had ever had and it frightened her much more than the thought of the baby's death. Some part of her had *wanted* the baby to be dead. Burying her face in her hands, Maddy wept.

She could not believe that thought. She could not accept that she was a person capable of such an evil thing. "Forgive me," she prayed to the baby who lay watching her tears with curiosity. "Please forgive me." It had been so long since Maddy had been to confession, and now she was almost glad because she would have never wanted anyone on earth to know of this thought. Even now that it was gone, she hoped that no one would ever know it had been in her head. Where had it come from?

It was true, the baby was still funny-looking and was still a girl, but Maddy could not believe that she had wished the baby dead for either of these things. Was it because of Jed? It was not that he hated the baby exactly, but ever since her birth, almost five months ago, something had changed between them. Maddy thought about this almost all the time and wished, more than anything, that there were someone she could talk to about it, ask about it. She would have asked Vonni, but Vonni and Luther visited rarely and usually Jed was around when they were there. And the trouble was, they didn't have a baby, so that what Maddy wanted to know didn't affect their lives. She wanted to know if what was happening with her and Jed was natural, something that happened with all couples, something that appeared but would then disappear. She could ask May, but May's four children were half grown. Would she even remember what it had been like, especially with the first one?

It was hard for Maddy to even explain to herself what she meant when she felt things had changed with Jed. When had he ever been different? He had always been quiet, rarely talking about his feelings, either for her or about anything. He had been as much of a mystery to her the day he married her as the day he had invited her on their first date or the night he had entered her body for the first time and she had felt amazement that he could want her that much, want her at all.

Yet it seemed to Maddy that something *had* changed, that Jed just wasn't there in some way. It reminded her of a movie they had once seen together, *The Invasion of the Body Snatchers*. Regular people would be invaded, their souls absorbed by mysterious beings from another planet. To the people who were married to them they would look the same, but in fact their bodies were now inhabited by someone else. But that had been science fiction! Who could have invaded Jed's soul and stolen it away? Maddy was not mystical; she didn't *believe* in things like that. Maybe she was just hypersensitive. It was only that she wanted him so much to be more affectionate, to tell her she was doing a good job as a mother since she doubted it so, to say occasionally that he loved the baby and was proud of her, that he was glad they were married, that he was happy in their life together. It might be—this was what Maddy hoped—that he was just working so hard that he didn't have time for all that. It was true, he had the two jobs and often had to work at night. But what bothered Maddy was not the jobs he took on, which she could see as his shouldering his responsibility for her and the baby, but the nights when he sat in their one-room apartment, a blank, brooding expression on his face, looking a thousand miles away. A few times he had leaped up and said he was going to take a walk, that he felt pent up. Maddy wished so much she had the courage to ask him what he was feeling or thinking at those times, but she never did. She just felt relieved when he returned, seeming calmer.

But she had decided, maybe because she didn't want to blame herself, that it was the arrival of the baby that had changed things. Not that the baby could be blamed either! She hadn't *asked* to be born. But it seemed to Maddy that before the baby had come things had been different. And it was because of that thought that Maddy watched "General Hospital" every day with such avid, almost anxious curiosity. She wanted to know what would happen to Heather.

Everyone else was more interested in Luke and Laura. Much of the conversation after the show was over each day was about them, whether they would get back together, whether Luke had really "raped" Laura. May contended that it hadn't been rape. "She loved him," she said. "She wanted it to happen. . . . That's not rape."

"Then why didn't he ask her nicely?" Grace Jahr wanted to know.

"She was married," May explained. "If he asked her, she'd of had to say no."

"It got their relationship off on the wrong foot," Grace said. She always knitted while she watched—mittens, pot holders, tea cosies that she sold in her store. She was the only one who didn't want Laura and Luke to get married. "She made her choice and she better stick to it," was her advice.

Maddy didn't exactly like Laura. She reminded her a little of her older sister, Doreen, and also of Garnet, the girl Jed had liked in high school. You could tell she knew she was pretty. She acted so innocent and sweet all the time, but she was really plotting to get Luke. Maddy hoped privately that she wouldn't get him, that Luke would come to his senses in time. But that didn't seem likely. Even now that they weren't speaking to each other, though by an odd coincidence they had ended up living in the same apartment building, still every time he saw her, his face got that gooey, melting expression; it was clear that he was still in love with her.

No one except Maddy seemed interested in Heather. "She's just crazy," May said dismissively, when an occasional episode made her the focus of the action.

Heather, who was married to Jeff, had given birth to a darling baby boy, Steven-Lars, and then, without even telling her husband, had sold the baby on the black market! Not for the money, just "because she was crazy." Though Maddy wasn't quite sure—she'd heard some story about how Heather might have needed the money. She hadn't seen all the episodes. But what did "crazy" mean? Maddy thought how often in her life she had heard people use the word crazy, to refer either to themselves or to someone else, but it was used in so many different contexts, it didn't seem to mean one particular thing. Her mother said of her best friend, Marion, "She gets crazy when she gets her period. I'm not going over there today"; or kids at school would say "Boy, was I in a crazy mood!" or "Wait till you hear the crazy thing Billy did yesterday!" What Maddy wanted to know was this: was craziness something you had in you, all the time, everyone, that one day could just come bursting out? Was that what had made Heather decide to sell her baby?

The trouble was, she hadn't been watching the show when that had happened and no one seemed to remember much about what had led Heather to the action, only that it had happened and that she now regretted it. What made her regret it most was that, by a really funny coincidence, Heather's best friend, Diana, had adopted Steven-Lars from the adoption agency. She didn't know it was Heather's baby and loved it like it was her own. She named it P.J. But when Heather saw Diana with the baby, she got wild with jealousy and decided to drive her crazy and get P.J. back.

Only it didn't work. Because when she came over one afternoon and put or rather dumped a lot of LSD in Diana's teacup, by mistake the teacups got shifted and she, Heather, drank the doctored tea and went crazy herself! *Really* crazy so that they had to put her in a mental hospital. For a long time she remained in a sort of catatonic state, not saying anything, which almost relieved Maddy because it kept her out of the way so she couldn't bother people. But it turned out she had been faking it. Heather was still smart, even though she was crazy. She began sneaking out of the hospital at night, dressed in the night nurse's uniform (she looked just like the night nurse) and scheming how to get revenge on Diana, whose husband, Peter, had died of a heart attack, leaving her alone except for P.J. In fact, supposedly Heather had caused his heart attack by telling him P.J. was really Steven-Lars when he was really sick. He had managed to tell Diana before he died. Now Heather was even madder at Diana, not just about the baby, but because she'd discovered Diana in bed with her own husband, Jeff. Heather didn't know that Jeff didn't "love" Diana. It was Anne he loved, but with a love that so far had been chaste. The night with Diana had "just happened." But now it seemed Heather was determined to kill Diana and even had a gun all loaded and ready to do it.

If there was a single question Maddy wanted to put to someone, it was: Did giving away your baby make you crazy? Or did giving it away prove that you were crazy? Did one horrible thing lead to another in some inevitable way? She wished so much she could take the story less seriously, the way some of the college girls did. Some of them laughed during "General Hospital," making fun of the actors and imitating them.

One opinion expressed by one of the college girls was that Diana was a "clunk" for acting so suspicious of Heather. She never did anything about it, just started moaning every time somebody mentioned her name. "People just will think *she's* crazy!" the girl had said. "She should just move or something!"

Maddy wasn't sure. She could see how Heather would scare Diana. What if Vonni had suddenly started trying to poison her and steal her baby because she had adopted hers by mistake? After all, Diana *had* been Heather's best friend. The next time Vonni and Luther came to visit, Jed took Luther up to campus and left Maddy alone with Vonni. The baby had just been fed and was lying in her crib. Vonni peeked in on her. "You know, I think she's getting cuter," she said. "Her ears don't look so big. Maybe they're shrinking . . . or maybe, like, her head is bigger so they don't look so big in comparison."

"I'm still worried about her eye," Maddy confided.

"Yeah," Vonni said. "Well, it could be operated on."

"But wouldn't that be really expensive?" Maddy asked.

"Yeah, I guess it would," Vonni said.

There was a pause.

Maddy had had so many imaginary conversations with Vonni about the baby and Jed and what was happening between them that now that she actually had her here, she didn't know how to begin. "Do you ever think of having a baby?" she said, trying to sound casual.

"Me?" Vonni laughed as though that was a truly crazy idea. "Can you imagine *me* as a mother?" It was true that sitting there in her denim work shirt, tight jeans, and work boots, Vonni hardly looked like a girl, even. Only her green nail polish, the red corduroy baseball hat tilted at a rakish angle over her short, dark hair, and the delicate small bones of her body would have given her away.

"I couldn't imagine me either," Maddy said.

"Well, but you did it," Vonni said.

Maddy had hoped she would say something more comforting, like "Anyone could tell you'd be a good mother," but she didn't. "I guess I'm not sure," she said, sighing and looking into the corner of the room.

"What about?" Vonni asked.

"The baby."

"You mean because of her looks?"

"No, just more . . . in general."

"Yeah, well, I guess it's hard," Vonni sympathized.

"I don't know if I love her enough," Maddy burst out.

"You seem to."

"Sometimes I feel like I'm just pretending."

"Maybe everybody does."

But that thought, though it let her off the hook, was almost more disturbing to Maddy. "I guess it's more Jed," she said.

"What about him?"

Maddy hesitated. "He seems, different, kind of, since the baby was born."

Vonni also hesitated. "Yeah, I know what you mean," she said.

The good and bad thing about talking to Vonni were the same, that she always said what she really felt rather than what she hoped you wanted to hear. "Does he seem different to *you?*" Maddy asked, her heart thumping painfully.

"Yeah," Vonni said. "I can't explain it exactly. . . . But we haven't seen you guys that much."

"How does he seem different?" Maddy asked, hoping some mystery was about to reach a solution that would illuminate everything.

"Well, like in school we all used to have a good time, horsing around and stuff. And now he seems more—serious, kind of . . . and Luther says he doesn't talk so much about things anymore."

"He was always a little like that," Maddy said.

"Right . . . I guess he's not really that different," Vonni said.

"I think he is, in a way," Maddy pursued.

"Like about what?"

Maddy tried to think how to describe it. "He doesn't seem to care about sex that much anymore."

Vonni looked amazed. "Really? Boy, you're lucky."

"I mean, we used to do it all the time and now we hardly ever do," Maddy said.

"Well, I guess he's working pretty hard," Vonni suggested.

"Still . . . I thought when I was pregnant it was because I

looked so awful, so fat, but now I'm practically the same weight I was before and it's the same."

"That shows he loves you," Vonni said emphatically.

"It does?"

"Yeah . . . when guys are *just* interested in sex, that's all they have on their mind, but when you love someone, you care about them in lots of ways, not just sex."

Maddy loved this explanation. "I guess that could be right," she said. But she felt compelled to press on. "Something's just different, I don't know what it is . . . I feel sometimes like he wishes he'd never married me, like he *hates* the baby."

Vonni just stared at Maddy with her dark intent eyes. "Oh," she said.

"Some nights he jumps up and goes out for a walk and it's like he can't stand being here." She was afraid suddenly she might cry. "It's my fault, Vonni. I *made* him marry me." And suddenly she did begin to cry, hunched over, ashamed, of her tears and of all the confused feelings inside her.

Vonni leaped up and began patting Maddy's shoulder. "No, you didn't," she said "He *wanted* to marry you. . . . He didn't want you to have an abortion, did he?"

"Yeah, I think he did," Maddy said. "But I just couldn't!" Her tears had receded a little. She looked up, red-eyed, at Vonni. "How do you tell Luther loves you?"

Vonni shrugged. "I don't know."

"Does he, like, tell you a lot?"

Vonni looked uncomfortable. "Luther's different," she said. "He's almost the opposite of Jed. He likes to talk about his feelings so much it drives me crazy! I wish he'd shut *up* once in awhile."

After that the conversation swung around to more general topics. It wasn't until later in the afternoon that Maddy mentioned her job at the beauty shop and watching "General Hospital" every day. "Lucky!" Vonni said. "I watch it sometimes, not every day, though."

Maddy swallowed. "What do you think about the part with Heather?"

"Boy, if I was Diana, I'd get out of town quick!" Vonni said.

"Do you think she's really going to kill her?"

"Yeah . . . don't you?"

"What do you think about the baby?"

"What do you mean?"

Maddy tried to think what she did mean. "Do you think Heather was crazy to give him away, especially when she was married and all?"

"She's just crazy, period," was Vonni's opinion.

"Some people do, I guess," Maddy said.

"What?"

"Give them away . . . for adoption, I mean."

"Like what's her name, that girl in our class, remember her?"

The girl Vonni was referring to, Lili Monrow, had been pregnant most of her senior year. But the school had let her attend classes anyway. She'd given birth just before final exams and had even come to the graduation dance. But if I had done that, Maddy thought, Jed never would have married me. Tentatively she voiced this thought aloud.

"Well, he might've," Vonni said.

"Do you think so?"

"Sure."

Maddy felt as though they had been circling slowly around some central truth that kept advancing and receding. Every time they came close to it, Maddy felt scared and felt, suddenly, that even if there *were* a "truth" she wasn't sure she wanted to know what it was. If only there were something between a scary truth and this ambiguous drifting fear that filtered through her life now like a fog!

That night, for almost the first time in her life, Maddy decided to initiate lovemaking with Jed. Wasn't that all right? If it was your own husband? She had read articles in magazines saying aggressive women made men impotent and she didn't want that to happen. But when they got into bed together she reached down and began touching his penis, which instantly began to harden. Then she didn't know what to do. She just held it, expecting him to make some move. Jed laughed. "It's not like the gearshift on a car, Maddy."

"What?" She was scared she was doing it wrong. Taking her courage as far as it would go, she crept down and tried putting it in her mouth. It seemed gigantic. She lay there, not knowing what to do, trying not to let him feel her teeth.

Jed rumpled her hair and then pulled her up to him. "What's got into you tonight?" he said.

"I thought we could try something new," Maddy said desperately. She'd read an article on that in a magazine too, how trying new things kept your marriage alive. "Did I do it all right?" she said.

He hesitated. "Sure."

"We can just do it the regular way."

So Jed climbed on top of her, pushed his penis into her, and began moving back and forth, and it was just like it had always been, right from the beginning. Maddy lay there, holding him, hoping he was happy, and wondering why sex was said by everyone to be such a basic, important thing. Sometimes she thought she was the only person in the world who didn't understand that. And then, just as Jed started to come, the baby began to cry. "Shit," he said, collapsing on top of her.

The next week, when Geraldine Farnum was giving Minnie back to Maddy, a thought struck Maddy. Maybe Geraldine would like her baby! She had said thousands of times how much she wanted a girl, how having a baby girl was the one thing that would make her life complete. She had had two miscarriages before Timmy, her son, was born, and two since. It had something to do with her uterus, but Maddy couldn't understand that. With Timmy she had stayed in bed for seven months and had to drink a glass of gin every night! That was what her doctor had recommended and it had worked, though Geraldine said she had never gotten to like the taste of gin.

Now, she and her husband were "trying" again. Maddy had never known anyone had to try that hard to get pregnant. It had always seemed to her something that just happened, whether you wanted it to or not. But Geraldine said no. She said unless you hit the exact twenty-four-hour period when you were fertile, you could do it "till the cows came home" and it wouldn't do a bit of good. What was hard, according to her, was determining when you were fertile. She kept a temperature chart and thermometer near her bed and every morning, she told Maddy, she took her temperature. The day it went up a little meant she was fertile. Sometimes she took it three times a day and the *second* it went up, she called her husband at the college and he came straight home and they did it right away! Once she called him while he was in the middle of teaching a class and he'd told the class there was an emergency at home and had rushed off in the middle of explaining how the French romantic poets had felt about death. That was how eager they were. "It doesn't make our sex life that spontaneous," Geraldine said wryly. "But what can you do?"

"Did you ever think of adopting a baby?" Maddy asked once.

"Oh sure. . . . That's what we'll do if all else fails. But it's so much nicer if it's your own. And babies are so hard to *get* nowadays! All these dopey teenage kids raising them on their own, not even getting married. It makes me so mad! They don't know a *thing* about babies, they can't even care for them. They just leave them at home with their mothers. . . . It shouldn't be allowed!" She was so angry Maddy felt taken aback, though she didn't think she really belonged in that category. But only, she had to admit to herself, because her mother would never have stayed home to look after Minnie if Jed hadn't married her. She'd had it with babies, she'd said.

Geraldine was friendly with a woman in town who'd adopted a black child, after having a white one of her own the regular way. "But that was political," Geraldine said. "I don't know if I believe in that. Though she's a darling little girl. . . . Would you?" she asked Maddy.

"What?"

"Do you think that makes sense, today's world being what it is, a white family raising a black child?"

"I don't know," Maddy said. She'd never even heard of it before.

"I think genes are important," Geraldine said. "I'd want to

know what kind of parents the baby had had . . . and I'm afraid Paul would want the baby to be Jewish, which would make it even harder. Jewish girls don't get knocked up that often."

Maddy hadn't known Geraldine's husband was Jewish. "Are you Jewish?" she asked.

Geraldine laughed. "No, just a garden-variety shiksa," she said. Seeing Maddy's puzzled expression she said, "That's what they call non-Jewish women. It's not used that flatteringly, usually, I'm afraid."

Maddy had been brought up to believe that Jews were usually rich, that they had businesses of their own and saved lots of money, like Mr. Edelman, whom Jed worked for. But Paul Farnum dressed almost like Luther, in jeans and a duffle coat and boots. Maybe he was only part Jewish. "Would *you* care if the baby was Jewish?" she asked.

"No! What difference does it make? As long as it's a healthy kid and the parents weren't strung out on drugs or something." She sighed. "You and I should count our blessings."

"Yes," Maddy said, though not certain exactly how Geraldine meant that.

"We have our health, one normal beautiful child, decent men whom we respect as husbands. What are we complaining about?"

Maddy hadn't thought they *were* complaining. But after a moment she said, "I'm not sure Minnie is that beautiful, though. . . . Her ears stick out so much."

Geraldine pulled her hair back. It was amazing. She had ears just like Minnie! "You just cover them, wear your hair long," she said. "It's no problem."

Geraldine's ears being so big delighted Maddy. That way, if she did adopt Minnie, people might think they were really mother and daughter. And she remembered how her mother kept saying that an adopted child on their block looked "uncannily" like his mother, that children and parents got to look alike, just like dogs and their owners. "If she wasn't a girl, I guess I wouldn't worry so much," she confided.

"What difference does it make?" Geraldine said.

"Well, for boys," Maddy explained. "For when she's older."

"Oh, that's all a lot of hooey!" Geraldine exclaimed. "Looks don't make any difference!"

"They don't?" Maddy had always thought they were the only thing that did.

"No, it makes me so mad the emphasis Hollywood puts on all that. Look at all the great courtesans of history, Cleopatra, Mme. de Staël. It was their personality that attracted men, not just big tits or upturned noses."

Maddy wasn't sure what a courtesan was, but she still found this information interesting and surprising. Though she did wonder if Geraldine felt that way because she wasn't that tremendously pretty herself. Naturally, she would never have said that, but Geraldine, amazingly, said a moment later, "Look at me! No one ever suggested I enter any beauty contests. But I have a gorgeous guy and we've been together fifteen years and my sister, Pammy, who's a real knockout, had a nervous breakdown last year because this married guy she'd been seeing, this real *creep*, deserted her."

One thing Maddy liked especially in talking to Geraldine was that, despite the almost twenty-year age gap between them, Geraldine spoke to her as an equal. She didn't try to boss her around or give her unwanted advice, the way Maddy's older sisters did. In fact, sometimes she asked Maddy's opinions about things and seemed genuinely interested in her replies. Now she asked, "When do you think *you'll* get started on another?"

"Another baby?" Maddy asked.

"Yeah." Geraldine poured herself another cup of coffee. She drank about ten cups a day, though she was trying to cut down.

"I don't know," Maddy said. Whether it was the age gap or not having known her that long, she didn't feel able to voice her anxieties about her marriage to Geraldine.

"Well, you're a baby still yourself," Geraldine said affectionately. "You've got all the time in the world. . . . My older sister, Julie, she's just a year older than me, and she had them real young, like you. Now they're in college, and I'm still fiddling with temperature charts! I'll probably be the oldest mother in Timmy's kindergarten class. But, you know, I don't think I'd have been ready when I was in my twenties. There was so much I wanted to do first! And Paul felt the same way. We really enjoyed those ten years, just playing."

Maddy had never met anyone who had married young and then waited that long to start a family. Maybe Vonni and Luther would be like that.

"But at my age, you'll have a whole new life ahead of you," Geraldine assured her warmly.

"Yes," Maddy said softly. A whole new life. But what would she do with it? It was different if you had a job or something you wanted to do. The thought scared her. At least babies gave you a sense of purpose, a reason for living.

At home that night she thought some more about the idea of offering Minnie to Geraldine. There were a lot of things about the idea Maddy liked. First, even if Vonni had wanted a baby, Maddy wasn't really sure deep down how good a mother she would have been. Whereas Geraldine seemed the most involved mother Maddy knew, always thinking about her child, worrying about him, even planning what he would be when he grew up! And that way Minnie would have a nice built-in older brother, but not too much older. Timmy seemed like a nice, quiet little boy. Maddy thought he would make a nice older brother, taking care of Minnie, showing her how to do things. And there could be no doubt that Geraldine wanted a girl and wanted a second child. Once Maddy had come home and found Geraldine in tears because her period had come. She had been sure, because it was two weeks late, that this time she was pregnant. The strangest thing of all was that evidently in the whole of her marriage Geraldine had never even used birth control, not because of her religion—her parents were Protestants—but because, having had such irregular periods as a girl, she didn't think pregnancy was a real danger.

Maddy wasn't sure how she would raise the issue with Geraldine. All she knew was that at first she would bring it up so vaguely that, if Geraldine didn't respond, she could change the subject and it wouldn't be embarrassing. She would start off talking in a general way about adoption, maybe.

On Tuesday, when Maddy came back after work, Geraldine was out shoveling snow. She waved gaily as Maddy came up the walk.

"Hey, guess what!" she said, hugging Maddy. "I'm pregnant!" And she dropped the shovel and did a little dance in the snow.

"Gee, that's wonderful," Maddy said weakly.

Geraldine's eyes were shining, her cheeks were bright red. She looked ecstatic. "I just found out today. The lab called an hour ago. . . . Gosh, I was so scared it would be another false alarm. Oh Maddy, I'm so happy!" As they were going into the house, she said, "Why don't you guys come over for supper tonight? I got this gigantic roast beef and champagne. And we've never really gotten our menfolk together. What do you say?"

"That would be nice," Maddy said.

She wasn't sure how Jed would feel about it, but when he came home, he said it was fine with him. He never worried the way Maddy did about whether people would like him or what to talk about. Maddy did worry about that a little. Geraldine was so friendly, she never worried about it with her, but Paul, her husband, was a professor. He'd even written a book! And he taught French. Maddy hoped maybe he and Jed could find something to talk about and she and Geraldine could talk about what they usually did. Getting dressed in her red wool jumper, her "best dress" from high school, she tried to smother her disappointment at Geraldine's getting pregnant. She wanted to feel pleased for her friend who had tried so hard, and she was determined not to let her real feelings show. But, despite these good intentions, she kept fantasizing that, when they opened the door, Geraldine would say it had been a mistake, that the lab had sent the wrong report. That had happened once to a girl in Maddy's school who had been told by a lab that she was pregnant, only to discover to her intense relief (she was unmarried) that the lab had mixed up her result with someone else's. Then, just as Geraldine was confessing her disappointment, Maddy would bring up the possibility of their adopting Minnie. She and Paul would be delighted . . . Stop! she told herself angrily. What a terrible person she was, even having fantasies like this.

Geraldine had said they could bring Minnie. Grimly, Maddy fed her, changed her, and took along an extra bottle and set of diapers, just in case. Lately the baby had been falling asleep pretty much at eight, but you couldn't tell in a strange place.

She glanced at Jed. He was dressed just in jeans and a plaid wool shirt, but he looked really handsome and she thought for a second that maybe everything she'd been feeling in the last few months was her imagination. One of her teachers at school had said she thought Maddy could "let her imagination run away with her."

The Farnums' part of the house was gigantic. It had been built in 1867 and all the rooms were enormous. There was a living room and a dining room, with eighteen-foot ceilings. Geraldine said at first it had seemed cold and spooky to her, but now she was used to it. Maddy couldn't help envying her all the room. She had often thought that if only they just had an extra room for the baby, she and Jed wouldn't have gotten off on the wrong track. He wouldn't have had to hear Minnie crying all the time. And the Farnums had nice furniture too, not all new, but pretty polished wood things and a long brown corduroy sofa with deep soft pillows.

Paul Farnum opened the champagne even before they started dinner. It was, Maddy realized, the first time she'd had champagne since she'd gotten married, the second time in her life.

"So, how do you folks like it here?" Paul asked, after they had drunk toasts to babies.

"It's okay," Jed said. "I like my job."

"I don't know," Paul said. "Sometimes it seems a little provincial to me. I get stir crazy around this time of winter."

"Paul's from New York," Geraldine put in.

"And I love it," he went on. He talked in a rushed, almost breathless tone. "People can knock New York all they like, but I'd rather live in a one-room apartment there than in a palace anywhere else."

"We came from Auburn," Maddy said, sipping her champagne.

Paul smiled at her. "Maddy, I must be the millionth person to say this to you, but you look around ten years old! And you're really the mother of a baby?"

"I'm sixteen," Maddy said, sitting up straight, wishing she'd remembered to wear eye shadow, which made her look older.

"Incredible . . . I guess the air must contribute to fertility up here. It seems like half the girls in my classes are knocked up or worried they are."

Maddy was really surprised at that.

"I think that's a *little* exaggerated, sweetie," Geraldine said.

"Look, more power to them," Paul said. "Half of them are gay, maybe more. What kind of social life can they have here in the boonies, especially in winter?" He grinned. "Not every professor can shack up with one of his students, and even if we all did, there aren't enough of us to go around, alas."

"*I* don't even think they're that pretty," Geraldine said crisply. "Do you, Maddy?"

"Some of them are," Maddy said.

"Oh sure, not all," Paul said. "But there's a blonde in one of my classes that's a work of art. If I were a painter, I'd do a portrait of her. . . . It's too bad I don't go for blondes."

Maddy wished Jed would say something. He was just sitting there, gazing off into space.

Paul refilled their glasses. "What do *you* think of blondes?" he asked Jed.

"I—I like them," Jed admitted.

"This one has dark eyes. It's really a striking combination. She has a kind of pre-Raphaelite look."

Geraldine got up. "It's lucky I'm not the jealous type," she remarked wryly. She went into the kitchen. Paul smiled at Maddy.

"Are *you?*" he said.

"What?" Maddy said. She was afraid she'd drunk the first glass of champagne too fast. Or maybe it was because she hadn't had anything to eat, but things were beginning to seem a little blurry.

"Are you the jealous type?"

She blushed. "I don't know."

"I think wives know if they have real cause to be jealous," he pursued. "There are lots of husbands like me who appreciate women, we like to look at them, savor them, admire them . . . but that's as far as it goes. Women *are* works of art, there's no doubt about it."

It seemed to Maddy she would be nervous married to someone like Paul, whether he ever did anything or not. And he talked so much, it made her feel even more ill at ease than Jed's silence.

"Les jeunes filles en fleur," Paul said, draining the bottle into his own glass. "That's what I think when I see them. Flowers, waiting to be picked." He looked dreamy and intense.

Maybe because she was a little bit drunk, Maddy began thinking of how Paul had to race home in the middle of classes to try to impregnate his wife. He must be proud that it had worked. At dinner he said, pouring red wine for all of them, "This time it's going to be a girl."

"Darling, don't jinx it," Geraldine said. "Whatever we have will be just fine."

"I've been dreaming of a daughter since the day we got married," Paul said. "Albertine . . . Big black eyes, long brown braids, just like the little girl next door I used to play with when I was a kid. . . . You know, I think those childhood fantasies have the most profound influence on your adult . . . don't you?" He looked at Maddy.

"What?" Maddy said. She was pleased in the abstract that he was asking her opinion, but nervous because she wasn't sure what to say.

"This little girl . . . every woman I've met I've compared to her. We never did anything. Never played doctor, none of that. I just used to sit there watching her color in her coloring book. She never went over the lines!"

"Just like me," Geraldine said, bringing in the roast beef. *"I* never go over the lines."

Paul laughed. "How about you, Maddy? Do *you* ever go over the lines?"

"No," Maddy said quickly, not sure what they were talking about.

"I didn't think so," Paul said. "You can look at a woman and tell the ones who scribbled in the margins and made cows green and skies purple. Those are the ones that are trouble, those are the ones to stay away from."

"Darling, shut up and carve, will you?" Geraldine said affectionately.

The thought ran through Maddy's mind that maybe if the Farnums didn't have a girl this time, she could still offer them Minnie. *She* had big black eyes!

"I bet you love having a daughter," Paul said to Jed.

"It's okay," Jed said.

"My brother just had twin girls," Paul went on. "Two at one shot! God, the lucky bastard."

The rest of the evening went on that way. Paul did most of the talking. Geraldine served and cleared and made occasional comments. Maddy spoke only when asked a direct question and Jed said almost nothing. When they went home, Paul hugged Maddy and kissed her on the lips. He had a winey, garlicky taste. "Listen, I'm glad you both finally came over!" he exclaimed. "Let's do it again . . . Gerry tells me what a great little mother you are and what a terrific friend for her. I can see what she means."

Although the trip home took only one minute, Minnie woke up. Maddy decided to feed and change her. That way she might sleep later in the morning. While she was doing this, Jed changed into his pajamas and got into bed.

"I guess I had too much to drink," he said sleepily.

"Did you like them?" Maddy asked, keeping her voice low, since one of their walls connected with the Farnums'.

"He talks an awful lot," Jed said and turned over.

That was true. Maybe it was because Paul was a teacher, Maddy thought. She had grown up with the idea that women talked and men didn't, though she had sometimes wondered if maybe men talked when they were alone with each other. But her father hardly talked—of course he was deaf now—and her brothers didn't say all that much. Then she remembered Vonni saying

Luther talked a lot about his feelings. She wondered what that would be like, tried to imagine it, and finally gave up. It seemed to her that, even though Jed's silences often disturbed her and made him more mysterious, it was the way things were meant to be. Though it would be interesting to be a man for one day, to be inside their heads and know what they thought about when they sat there so silently. Maddy imagined the thoughts of men as something totally different from the thoughts of women. She thought of them as fitting together in some magical, logical way, not wandering incoherently.

And she was jealous, she had to admit it, if only to herself, about how delighted Paul seemed at his wife's pregnancy. If only Jed could be that way! At least it had shown him that to some men a baby girl was something really valuable, important. She hoped, even though he hadn't said anything, that he had taken it all in.

The baby fell asleep and didn't even finish all of her bottle. Maddy changed her and turned her on her stomach. Usually she turned back during the night, but Maddy's mother said they slept better on their stomachs.

It had occurred to Maddy that, if she really wanted to give her baby away, she could go to an agency. There was one in Auburn. She knew that because several girls in town who had gotten pregnant while in high school had "given" their babies there. The agency even advertised in the local paper, sometimes showing photos of the babies or young children for whom they were trying to find homes. The ones in the paper usually had something wrong with them, though they always had "loving, friendly personalities." Maddy knew that, compared to these babies, Minnie would be extremely desirable. Except for her wandering eye, she really had no defects at all, and her ears didn't even show that much anymore, now that her hair was growing in.

But there was something so coldblooded and awful about giving your baby to an agency. Maddy thought it was a fine thing for someone else to do, but she couldn't imagine doing it herself. If the Farnums had taken Minnie, she would have known the baby would have a happy home, parents who would care for her. How could you ever be sure of that if it was the agency that picked the parents, not the mother herself? Maddy thought that was the wrong way to do it. If she were running such an agency, she would let the mother be the one to pick. That way the baby would end up at a home the mother liked, and her mind would be at rest. Maddy didn't trust something as impersonal as an agency. After all, one baby must be the same as another to them. Whereas she, Maddy, might notice lots of little things she didn't like in a couple claiming they wanted to be parents, and the agency might not even care!

But because she had been so uncertain, Geraldine's pregnancy was something of a relief to Maddy. Partly she kept hoping that Jed's mood would suddenly change, either in regard to Minnie or just in general. Sometimes she imagined a conversation they would have where he would offer an explanation for the way he had been acting that would totally set her mind at rest. That was always happening in "General Hospital." People had "secrets" that made them act oddly, and once they "confessed" what their secrets were, they felt so much better and were sorry they hadn't done it earlier. Maddy wasn't sure how to go about that with Jed. Some evenings when *he* sat staring off into space, she sat staring at *him*, thinking that she would give anything in the world to know where he was, mentally, at that moment. But she never dared ask.

One day, coming home from work, she was surprised to see Geraldine outside shoveling snow again. She had said that she was going to do no exercise of any kind for eight months and might even stay in bed half of each day, just to make sure she stayed pregnant. She attributed one of her miscarriages to having carried a heavy box of books up from the cellar of a house they used to live in. Coming closer, Maddy saw that Geraldine's face was grim, her eyes red. "I lost it," she said right away, digging the shovel viciously into the ground.

"What happened?" Maddy said.

"I have a crazy uterus," Geraldine said, laughing bitterly. "I don't know. I just woke up with cramps and an hour later—no baby."

Maddy just stood there. "I'm sorry," she said.

At that Geraldine flung her arms around Maddy, letting the shovel fall to the ground. "Oh, it's not fair!" she said. "I hate myself! I hate my body! What's wrong with me?" She hugged Maddy tightly, as though the physical closeness might assuage some of her pain. Maddy held her, trying to be comforting. "Do you want to have a cup of tea?" she said finally when they broke apart.

"I would love to have a cup of tea," Geraldine said.

She brought Timmy over and he played in the corner of the room while Minnie sat in her infant seat, babbling, chewing on her teething beads.

"You know what I've decided?" Geraldine said, sipping her tea.

Maddy shook her head.

"I'm just going to forget about the whole damn thing. I feel like I've been like some character out of Dostoyevsky. I've been obsessed by babies for the whole last decade, almost, of my life. I think about them, dream about them, read about them. I even write poems about them. . . . The point is, I have one kid, and maybe some day, when I'm forty-six, I'll have another. But I'm just going to burn all those fucking temperature charts and let our sex life go its own merry way and look for a teaching job and that's it!"

"That sounds like a good idea," Maddy said, admiring her vehemence.

"It's not fair to Paul," Geraldine said. "How would *your* husband like it if once a month you called him up and screamed, 'Get your ass home this second. We *have* to fuck.'? . . . Seriously, I think if anything would drive him to—doing something with another woman, it would've been this. One night we lay there and he said wistfully, 'Gerry, remember fucking? Just plain ordinary fucking where you do it because it's fun?'" Without seeming to do it on purpose, she gazed at Minnie. "She *is* a sweetheart," she said, sighing.

Maddy's heart was thumping. "Would you like her?" she said.

Geraldine looked puzzled. "What do you mean?"

"Would you like to have her?" Maddy went on, her voice shaking. "I mean, I could give her to you."

"*Give* her to me?" Geraldine asked, taken aback.

Maddy felt almost dizzy as she spoke. She felt terrible that Minnie was in the room while she said this. "I don't think I should have had a baby," she said. "We were too young and Jed didn't really want one. He didn't even want to marry me, really, and now it's so awful. I know he feels trapped."

"And you think without the baby your marriage would be happier?" Geraldine said.

Maddy nodded.

Geraldine reached out and squeezed her hand. "Oh, but honey, everyone's marriage goes through times like that. They pass . . ."

"Do they?" Maddy asked.

"Of course they do . . . Julie, my sister, says her husband never even *looked* at either of their kids till they were in high school practically. She did everything! But now he's proud as the dickens of both of them."

"Jed wanted a boy," Maddy said.

Geraldine sighed. "Isn't it ironic? It's so hard for me to imagine a husband wanting a boy. Paul just goes on and on about how daughters adore their fathers forevermore and that's what he wants: endless love. At least he's honest! . . . And you know, I really have thought at times: if he gets it at home, he won't go looking for it somewhere else."

"So, what do you think?" Maddy said. They seemed to be wandering away from her offer.

Geraldine smiled at her gently. "I couldn't take your baby, Maddy."

"You couldn't?"

"No . . . honey, how could I? You'd want her back, you know you would."

"No, I wouldn't," Maddy said. "Really. I've thought about it a lot. I wouldn't want her back."

"Well, you say that now, but you'd be seeing her every day, she'd be getting cuter and cuter. . . . One day you'd march over and say, 'Give her back,' and it would be too heartbreaking for both of us."

Suddenly Maddy wondered if she was right. And she realized for the first time that that was one point of an adoption agency, that you *couldn't* get your baby back, and also that you would never know where the baby was. If only Geraldine didn't live next door!

"You know," Geraldine said, "this is the kindest thing anyone ever did for me. I'll remember it all my life, really. You're such a wonderful person, Maddy."

Maddy felt an awful pang that Geraldine had taken her offer and transformed it into something altruistic and kind. Bending over, she started to cry. And Geraldine, seeing her, began to cry also. They sat there, letting the tears fall, not trying to control them. Finally Timmy ran over and yanked at Geraldine's arm. "Stop crying, Mommy!" he commanded. "Stop!"

Geraldine looked up and laughed. "Oh, I'm not crying," she said. "I'm just—" And she hugged Timmy and Maddy. "It's good," she said. "I feel so much better now. Oh, aren't we silly! We're just a bunch of fools!"

Nine

"Jed, could you stay a minute?" Thornie said. It was morning and the crew had just gathered to hear what their chores for the day were going to be.

"Sure," Jed said. He waited while the other guys trooped out. Thornie was sitting behind his desk, in his battered old office chair. The top of the desk was strewn with papers, envelopes, tools. He lifted up a screwdriver and tapped the telephone that sat at one corner of the desk.

"I got a call the other day," he said in his slow, drawling voice, "from a Dr. Gould. Does that name ring a bell with you?"

Jed's heart started beating painfully loudly. He just shrugged, hoping to stall for time.

"It seems this Dr. Gould has a daughter here at the college, a girl by the name of—" He stopped and looked at a piece of paper in front of him. "Carrie." He didn't pronounce it right, but Jed didn't correct him. "And this Dr. Gould says that it's his impression that you've been 'seeing' his daughter. In fact, he says you've been down to their house in Ithaca quite a few times. Is that true?"

Jed nodded. He was sure he was about to be fired.

"What exactly is the nature of your relationship with this girl?" Thornie had a kindly, quiet manner. If he had acted belligerent, Jed would have bristled, but he just looked at Jed, waiting patiently for him to explain himself.

Jed wondered if an excuse or lie was even possible. He sighed. "Well—" he began.

Thornie smiled. "Yeah, that's what I figured."

"What'd he call you about?" Jed blurted out, clenching his fists.

"Well, it seems you'd told him you were on the Building and Grounds crew over here and he wanted to know if that was true. I told him it was. I told him, also, though he didn't ask, that you were a good worker, honest, hardworking, never sick or late." He paused. "I didn't tell him one fact because I thought that fact might upset him, fathers being what they are. I didn't tell him you were married."

"Thank you," Jed said.

There was a long pause. Then Thornie said, "Jed, there's one thing about me that I think I mentioned to all of you early on. I'm not a yeller. I don't make scenes. I say something and that's it. Now I told you boys that I didn't care what kind of sex or love life you got yourselves involved in while you were working for me. People's private lives are their own. I'm no judge of anything like that. But I *did* tell you that any interactions with the college girls were strictly off limits. . . . Do you remember that?"

Jed nodded.

"Now, I'm a man and I know how hard that can be. Some of these girls are real beauties and some of them come on pretty strong. They can get lonely too. It's a long winter and all that. So I'm not putting the blame on you necessarily. I understand the temptation."

Jed thought he was going to burst. He felt like he was being roasted over hot coals. "Am I fired?" he cried.

"No, you're not fired," Thornie said. "But it's not because of the kindness of my heart. It's because you have a sweet wife, whom you may not appreciate at this moment in time, and a baby, and if I were to fire you, they would suffer. There's no need for that."

In a strange way Jed was almost disappointed. Part of him had been hoping he would be fired—not only because he felt he deserved punishment for what he had done, but because if he no longer worked at Coolidge, he wouldn't see Capri. He wasn't sure he had the will power to stop seeing her while she was around all the time. "That's real nice of you," he stammered.

"Jed, I'm not one to give advice when it's not called for," Thornie said, "but I'd like to say this. You married kind of young. So did I. You had a kid pretty early on. So did I. . . . You know, one thing I've learned is that when you get married, you basically don't know much about your wife and you don't even know much about yourself. I don't care *how* many years you've gone together. May and I knew each other since first grade! I don't care *how* intimate you've been before you get hitched. It's not the same. Marriage is something you learn how to do. No one's born knowing how to be a wife or born knowing how to be a husband . . . so if that wife of yours bothers you sometimes, remember she's just a kid herself. She'll learn. You've got to give her time. And you've got to give yourself time."

"Yeah," Jed said. "I know." Yet although he felt everything Thornie was saying was right, he also felt angry. How could anyone know about someone else's life? Had Thornie ever had with anyone what he had with Capri? Maybe if you'd never had it, you wouldn't miss it. But once you'd had it, how could you give it up?

"Now get on over to the Drivers' house," Thornie said. "And you can trust me, Jed. No one'll know about Dr. Gould's call except me. But if there's a next time—" He made a gesture of slitting his throat. "Understand?"

"Yeah," Jed said wryly. "I understand."

For the first half of the day, he felt relieved, almost lighthearted. It seemed to him that if he knew for a fact that he'd be fired if he saw Capri again, obviously he just wouldn't see her. He wasn't crazy! But then he thought, it's not a matter of not seeing her, it's a matter of not getting caught. By the end of the day all his anger about the situation had passed to her father. The bastard! What business was it of his? His daughter was twenty years old! Checking up on her like she was a baby. Jed felt he had hated Capri's father from the first day, with his short, intent questions. And there he was unfaithful to his own wife, the damn hypocrite!

He had arranged earlier in the week to see Capri that evening. They had discovered an ideal place to meet on campus. It was called the Alumni House, which was only used every several months when trustees or visiting speakers had to stay the night. It was a small house, old, but nicely kept up because of the stream of visitors. Jed had a key to it because all the crew had keys to all the campus buildings; he'd given Capri a copy. They went there only at night and always left separately by the back door. Capri brought sheets in a duffle bag and took them back with her. They'd been doing it for a couple of months now and no one had ever seen them.

This evening it was especially easy. He didn't even have to think of an excuse. Maddy was going to a movie at the college with Geraldine, and Geraldine had hired one of the college girls as a babysitter to stay with Minnie and Timmy. The movie ran from eight to ten. Jed sat restlessly in the room, watching Maddy get ready to go out. She was slimmer now and able to fit into most of her old clothes.

"Do I look okay?" she said.

"Sure, you look fine," he said, trying not to sound impatient.

Finally she left. He felt as though all the emotions of the day were still coursing through him: rage, fear, confusion. He almost didn't feel like seeing Capri, or at least wasn't sure he felt like making love to her. Quietly he let himself into the Alumni House. In order to be safe, he and Capri never turned on any of the lights. They both had flashlights. Following the light, he found her in bed. She was naked, her hair loose, reading one of her textbooks with a flashlight. The light illuminated her body and face in a strange, almost ghostly way. She looked up at him. "Hi," she said softly.

"Hi." But instead of taking his clothes off and joining her, he just stood there.

"Is anything wrong?"

"Yeah, there is," Jed said angrily. Until he heard his own voice, he hadn't even realized the mood he was in. He told Capri about what had happened that morning.

Capri sighed. "Oh Daddy!" she said. "He's impossible."

Somehow her tone, languid, almost affectionate, drove Jed over the edge. "He could have gotten me fired!" he said. "What's wrong with him?"

"Well, but you didn't get fired," she said, "so what's the problem?"

"Just because Thornie decided to be nice, just because I have a family."

"So? Aren't you lucky, then? Your nice little family protected you."

Jed grabbed her wrist. "Look, this may seem like nothing to you, but I have to support myself, a wife, and a kid—and that's important to me, doing right by them."

"I'm going to be sick," Capri said contemptuously. "All of a sudden bourgeois morality strikes and all that matters is your cozy little home. Is that it?"

"No, that's not it."

"I'm just like some little—" She waved at him, flapping her hands, as though the bedclothes were on fire. "Go to them! If they're all you care about."

"They're not all I care about," he said. "Just tell your damn father to get the hell out of my business."

Capri's hair often looked, as now, as though she had been plugged into a socket, each strand standing out on end. "He happens to love me. That's why he did it."

"I don't care why he did it," Jed said, furious. Her haughty, aloof manner made him feel like hitting her.

She looked up at him, hesitant. Then, in a much softer voice, she said, stretching out her hand, "Why don't you take your clothes off?"

He pushed her down and turned away. "Oh, go to hell," he said and slammed out of the house.

It was a mild evening. It was late March and the weather had been going back and forth from snow to heavy rain. The earth was sodden. Jed went down to the lake and began jogging along the path that ran by the no longer used railroad tracks. He wanted to run so hard and long that his mind blanked out. He didn't want to go home to Maddy feeling the way he did. God, maybe he should have hit her. But what good would that have done? He hated that in her, that way she moved from acting like the princess with her golden hair, languid, slightly arrogant, to putting her whole body and soul into making love with him, as though he were the center of her world and nothing else mattered. Which was true? And he felt a version of the same violent mixture of feelings. There were times when she seemed to be someone from a totally different world, everything that interested her, that she cared about having no connection at all to anything he knew or cared about. And other times he felt they were so close that they could have been brother and sister. He had told her things at those times that he had never told anyone and now, remembering this, he hated himself for it, hated himself most of all for admitting his true lack of feeling for Maddy and the baby.

Stupid. It had seemed, on that Indian summer day when he'd watched her play tennis and then had gone over to talk, dangerous but manageable. He'd never had any trouble handling girls, even when their actions and thoughts were mysterious to him. Somehow, he wasn't sure why, they always came around and did what he wanted. He'd never felt he couldn't, one way or another, manipulate them, even without their realizing what he was doing. So look, you fucked her a couple of times, maybe a few hundred times, what does it matter? It got you through the year. It wasn't unenjoyable. Her father tried to cause trouble, but didn't. You're home free. Just forget it, forget her.

He jogged for an hour. By the time he slowed down, circling back past the campus, he felt he had achieved what he wanted. He was exhausted and it seemed to him that if he went home, took a hot shower, he could get into bed and fall sound asleep. In the morning he would wake up and it would be over; he would never think of her again. But as he passed the Alumni House a thought struck him. Had she remembered to lock the door? If the house was found open, he could get into trouble. Someone might check into it. And she might have just torn out of there, not even bothering, not caring whether she got into trouble or not.

He opened the front door quietly. It had been locked again, but usually she left by the back door. There was no light; the house was in total darkness. Then he heard a sound coming from the living room. It was a gasping, hoarse, uneven sound that reminded him of something he had totally forgotten until that moment. Once he had gone hunting with his uncle and they had found a raccoon in a trap. In its efforts to get free, it had almost yanked its entire paw off. The paw was hanging by just a few sinews, but the animal, exhausted by pain, couldn't make the final move and just hung on, whimpering in that same staccato, panting way. Jed followed the sound.

Capri was sitting on the couch, naked, hunched over, her hair spread like a cape over her shoulders, weeping. "Caps?" he said hesitantly.

She looked up and then hunched down again, the sound continuing but more softly. He came over and sat beside her on the couch, putting a hand on her shoulder. Her skin was icy cold. Goose pimples ran down her arm as he stroked it. "Hey," he said. "What's wrong? Are you okay?"

Suddenly she flung herself into his arms with a passion that was almost asexual, hugging him to her as hard as she could. "I thought you wouldn't come back," she whispered. "I thought you were never coming back!"

Jed hugged her, stroking her back and shoulders, smoothing down her hair, trying to warm her. "Of course I was coming back," he said. "I just got upset. I—"

Her face was wet, but she seemed unaware of the tears. He thought how for an hour she had been sitting here, sobbing, in the darkness, cold, unaware of anything. "I love you so much!" she said into his chest. "I get scared sometimes. It's not your being married. I just don't want—I don't want to—" But she couldn't finish the sentence.

He carried her back into bed and reached for her, finding his way into her body from behind, feeling as though his whole body was warming her, protecting her, easing her out of the cold. She was kneeling, her hair spread over her back, silken, soft, and he stroked her breasts, pulling her as close to him as he could. Each time he thrust into her, she gave a cry that was half like the sounds she had been making when he had entered the cottage, moans that were almost like weeping. Yet he could tell by her body that she wanted him, by the way she moved to let him enter more deeply. Afterward they slept, both exhausted, unable to talk.

When he woke, she was lying with her arms under her head, staring at the ceiling. He reached out and touched her cheek.

"What should we do?" she said.

Jed shrugged. "I don't know."

"I can't not see you . . . I would if I could. Is that what you want? To stop now? Do you think it's too dangerous?"

"No, it'll be okay," he said, trying to convince himself as well as her. "We just better be more careful."

"Where will we go?"

"Maybe somewhere by the lake, once it's warmer."

"Does it ever get warm here?" She laughed.

"By May, usually."

"That's six weeks." She sat up. "I didn't want to get you into trouble," she said intently. "Truly. I didn't know Daddy was going to do that. He never told me anything."

"It didn't do any harm in the end," Jed said.

"It could've. . . . Oh, I know it's awful but sometimes at night I lie there, thinking of you lying there with your wife and I get so jealous! It's dumb. You don't even love her, she's just a wife. . . . But still, she gave birth to your child. It's like she has some hold on you, like you're welded together, and I feel so . . . ephemeral."

Even after all the emotional ups and downs of the evening Jed couldn't help feeling angry at the way she said so casually, "You don't even love her, she's just a wife." But it was his fault—he was the one who'd said that. It was just hearing his own words thrown back at him that way that bothered him.

Capri got dressed. "I'll leave first," she said, braiding her hair quickly and deftly. She looked different to him with her braid. It made her face more severe, more like an Indian. Then, with her coat on, she bent down and kissed him softly on the lips. "Bye," she whispered, and was gone.

Jed waited ten minutes and then got dressed. It was quarter to ten. He could still make it back in time.

But when he got back, Maddy was there already, evidently having walked in a few minutes before. She was sitting, still in her coat, holding the baby, who was screaming, its face bright red. By now the baby's lungs were strong enough so that its cries were like an adult's, not the insistent mewings of its first few months, but lusty, furious yells. The sound came at Jed like an ax hitting him right in the middle of his forehead. He had a splitting headache already. "God, what's wrong with her?" he said.

"She's teething," Maddy said apologetically.

"Oh Christ." He went into the bathroom, closed the door, and showered. When he got out, the baby was crying as loudly as ever. Jed felt his whole body shaking. "I just can't take this," he said to Maddy. "Is it going to go on all night?"

"I don't know."

"Listen—I'm going to go sleep at the college. I've got a key to one of the buildings. I'm sorry. This is driving me crazy. My head's ready to fall off."

"Okay," Maddy said. "Do you want to take a sleeping bag?"

He nodded, took the rolled-up bag, and left. As soon as he was a few feet from the house the baby's cries became dimmer. God, how could they make that much noise and be so small? He felt like he could understand for the first time in his life how people killed babies or at least beat them half to death. Not that he was afraid he ever would, but it was like they were crazed animals, nothing seemed to get through to them. Maybe it was just that tonight his nerves were so on edge that a whole night listening to that screaming, waiting for hours for it to calm down, was more than he knew he could stand. It was ironic, Capri thinking that the strongest thing that connected him to Maddy was the baby. It was the opposite. Except for duty, for feeling he had chosen this, he hadn't the slightest feeling for the child, no sense that it was connected to him at all. Maybe if it had been a boy, it would've been different. Or if it had looked like him, or even like Maddy. But it looked like nobody! Maybe it wasn't even their kid. You were always reading about babies getting mixed up at the hospital.

Back at the Alumni House, Jed let himself in the back way

again, stripped off his clothes, and fell into bed. He was glad he had brought the sleeping bag. He spread it out on top of the bed and crawled into it. It seemed to him that something of Capri lingered in the room, in the bed—some scent, some smell of sex. And at the same time the whole course of the evening played through his head: their fight, his jogging by the lake, the sound of her crying, their ardent but almost painful lovemaking. Without sorting anything out, he fell asleep and dreamed of nothing.

When he woke up, it was late, past ten o'clock. A pale winter sun streamed in from the living-room window. It seemed to Jed he had never slept better in his life. Yet he felt instantly guilty at the thought of Maddy. Had she been up all night with the baby? Enjoying the luxury of the quiet house, of being by himself, he lay in bed awhile. He felt calm, the events of the night before light-years away. And then he remembered Capri saying in that intense, gasping way, "I love you so much." She loved him! In the light of that, everything seemed different to Jed, everything. She had not just been fooling around with him, having fun for the year. Maybe it was even more serious to her than to him. And that thought delighted him, gave him a sense of pride that made him smile even though he was alone. All the rest was an act, just the way she was, the arrogance, the playful teasing. She was his on whatever terms he wanted for as long as he wanted. Forever? No, not forever.

He had always assumed that they would stop seeing each other at some point, and now he wondered if that had to be so. Not that he wanted to get married again, but was it that impossible that they could. . . . Look, how can you get married again, you jerk! You're married. I know. Married with a baby.

When he got back to the house, Maddy and the baby were asleep. He fixed himself some breakfast and ate it quietly at the table, watching Maddy. She was asleep, curled to one side, her hand pressed up against her mouth, almost as though she were sucking her thumb. At any rate there was something childlike about her position and the fluffy blond-brown hair that curled around her head. She was pretty. There was nothing wrong with her. Why couldn't he love her? He just didn't. He didn't know why. He thought she was a nice person, sometimes he liked being with her, but that was all. As he sat watching her, her eyes opened. "Oh Jed," she said. "When did you get back?"

"About half an hour ago." They both spoke softly so as not to wake the baby.

"Did you sleep okay?"

"Yeah. . . . How about you?"

"She quieted down around three. I think the tooth came through. Maybe it won't hurt her so much."

Maddy sat up and stretched. She looked pretty in her pink flannel nightgown that reached almost to the floor. He would have liked to want her the way he once had, but instead he felt only a kind of detached affection that made him sad.

The following week, shopping in Ithaca for Thornie, he ran into Capri's mother. He was coming out of the hardware store, and she was just putting a dime into a parking meter. Before he had a chance to turn away, she smiled at him. "Oh Jed, hi! You haven't been around in so long."

He suspected she knew nothing of what her husband had done. Still, Jed felt angry at her easy friendliness, which seemed a version of Capri's occasional arrogance. "I've been kind of busy," he said.

"Well, how about lunch?" she said. "Do you have time? I thought I might try this little place on the corner. It always looks so inviting."

"You mean now?"

She glanced at her watch. "It's twelve-thirty. I'm starved, aren't you? What do you say?"

"Okay," Jed said reluctantly. "Sure."

He wasn't sure why he was doing this. And yet he liked Capri's mother, even though she seemed sort of funny to him at times. She was wearing a straw hat and a big denim jacket with wooden buttons down the front, tan slacks, and sandals. "Do you work even on weekends?" she asked, looking at the bundles he had set down on the floor.

"Not usually," he said. "I just had to get this stuff for the guy I work for."

"I decided to take a self-imposed month off," she said. "I've gotten so much done this winter. I feel really proud of myself. I thought it would be hectic, with Sam flying back and forth, but you know, I like it. I hate to say it, but I *like* having him away a few days each week. It's so peaceful! I can be as selfish as I want, skip meals, work all night . . . and after all, we've been married forever. Why shouldn't we have our own lives?"

Jed didn't have to answer this because the waitress appeared. Mrs. Gould ordered a salad and a glass of white wine. Jed ordered a hamburger. "Nothing alcoholic?" she asked.

"I'll have a beer," he said.

The waitress listed the kinds of beer they had. She was a real cutie and knew it, a round but slim figure, very short skirt. As she listed the beers, she looked right at him, flirting. He hoped Mrs. Gould wouldn't notice. "Miller's," he said briefly.

"Miller's it is," she said, smiling and turning so he could see her butt twitching as she sauntered off to the kitchen.

"Isn't it amazing," Mrs. Gould said, looking after her in a thoughtful way. "Miniskirts coming back. I never thought they would. They say short skirts come back in times of economic prosperity, and that doesn't make sense about now, does it?"

"I guess not," Jed said.

"It's a style I just never felt comfortable in," she mused. "My legs are fine, but I felt, I don't know . . . Whenever I sat down, I was always dropping napkins over my knees. I think it's more attitude than anything else, basically."

The waitress brought their drinks.

"When I work, I never have wine at lunch, but today I'm just trying to catch up on all the trivia that's accumulated, you know, buying buttons and spices and what have you. . . . So, how are things going for you, Jed? Do you have any plans for next year?"

"Plans?" He wasn't sure how she meant that.

"Well, you said you'd dropped out of college. Do you think you'll go back in the fall?"

"I might," he said. "I haven't decided yet."

"What do you think you might do once you get out?"

"I might be an astronaut," Jed said, inventing on the spur of the moment.

"How fascinating! I think I'd like to too except you have to know so much science and math and I still count on my fingers. Also, I know this is silly, but what if you were up there and you pressed the wrong button and never came down? That would make me terribly nervous."

"Well, I guess they teach you all that stuff."

"My husband taught himself to fly," she mused. "Of course men seem to—oh, I shouldn't say this, Capri would kill me, but men *do* seem to be more adventurous, more able to take risks. . . . No, but Capri is right. She says that's all social conditioning, that women my age just weren't brought up to take risks and so we didn't . . . I bet Capri could learn to fly a plane if she put her mind to it."

Jed grinned. "I bet she could too," he said.

"Everything is so different now!" she exclaimed. "And I think it's wonderful. The freedom girls C's age have about sex, boys. When I think of all the moping around we did, waiting for the phone to ring. They just see someone they like and that's that. None of that coy idiocy."

Just at that moment the waitress approached their table with a large tray of food. She had the tray poised on one opened palm and just as she was attempting to slide it down on the table, she dropped it on the floor. All the food crashed down and spilled. "Oh, terrific, Ginny!" she said, hands on her hips. "Nice going." To Jed and Mrs. Gould she said, "Listen, I'm so sorry. I'm just the world's greatest klutz." She kneeled down on the floor and began gathering the food and broken glass together and putting it on the tray. Jed bent down to help her. A slice of avocado had fallen on her wrist and she leaned over, lapping it up. Her tongue darted out and scooped up the avocado. While she was doing this, her eyes stayed on Jed, sparkling with mischief. He wondered if she'd dropped the tray on purpose. Finally they got everything back. "I'll just be a minute," she said unregretfully. "I'm so sorry. Can I bring you another drink?"

"I think we're fine," Mrs. Gould said dryly. After the waitress had pranced off, she said, "Now *that's* what I mean."

"What?" Jed asked, trying not to watch the waitress's ass retreating jauntily in her denim skirt.

"The way she was flirting with you!" Mrs. Gould exclaimed. "No bones about it, just as bold as you please. The way that little tongue of hers came out, like she was lapping *you* up! Or was it my imagination?"

"No, I guess she *was* a little—" Jed began.

Mrs. Gould leaned forward. Her eyes were bright and glowing. "Now tell me, how do *you*, as a male, *feel* about all that? I mean, do you like it when women come on strong that way? Or does it offend your masculine whatever?"

"I guess it depends on the girl," Jed said.

"My husband claims he's so glad he's not single today. He says if sex were this easy and available, it wouldn't be any fun, that the whole *point* was battering down the girl's resistance, saying yes yes, while she said no no . . . but I feel *just* the opposite! I thought that was all such a drag! I envy Capri's generation so much! . . . And your generation too, of course."

"Your husband sounds sort of old-fashioned," Jed said, emboldened by her critical tone.

"Oh, he is, hopelessly! . . . And I think that's why he and C are at loggerheads so often. 'She's sowing her wild oats,' I tell him. 'You did. Why shouldn't she?' But he just won't see it that way, or refuses to." She looked flustered. "Oh, I didn't mean . . . I know how fond Capri is of you. I just meant in general I don't think she has to necessarily be engaged to . . . go all the way or whatever the current expression is. Do you?"

The waitress brought the food again, this time carrying the tray with both hands. "I hope you enjoy it," she said, smiling. "The good cook is on today."

"Well, that's a relief," Mrs. Gould said. "I wonder what the bad cook is like."

"Oh, he's not *bad,*" the waitress said. "He's just not *as* good." To Jed she said, "Want another beer?"

He shook his head.

She still had that provocative half smile. "Well, if you want anything else, just holler."

"We will," Mrs. Gould said to her, deadpan. To Jed she said, "I think you've made a conquest."

He had a mouthful of hamburger and just shrugged.

"Well, it's good Capri isn't here. She'd be *very* jealous!" She looked up at the waitress, who had retreated to the bar at the far end of the restaurant, where she was sitting on a stool. "Would she be your type?"

"I don't think I have a type that much," Jed said.

"Not even physically? Blond? Dark? Slim? Buxom?"

"Not especially."

"I was always attracted to men like Sam, those dark brooding eyes and that intense manner. Of course after twenty years it wears off a bit, but I still look at him sometimes at a party and think, 'You know, you didn't do badly, Marion.' "

"I think you're beautiful," Jed found himself saying. He had the feeling he was slightly drunk.

She blushed. "Do you? Thank you. . . . The fact is, and I say this without being idiotically self-deprecating, I really never looked that different. That is, I never had droves of men gasping helplessly at my feet but there was always the occasional person who for whatever odd reason . . . And you know, I wonder, really, what I should do about it."

"What do you mean?" Jed asked.

"Well, I suppose if I'm ever going to . . . Oh, I know you'll be discreet about this, Jed. I shouldn't have had that glass of wine, I guess. No, I just wonder. *Should* I charge off and have the requisite midlife affair with whoever? It would be so easy with Sam away half the week. And there are a few men who . . . wouldn't be averse. And yet? I just don't know. I don't know if I'm the type. Maybe sublimating it all into art is best, safest. . . . What if I fell in love?"

Jed had never had a conversation remotely like this with anyone the age of Capri's mother. He couldn't quite believe it was happening. And yet the longer the lunch went on, the less she seemed like Capri's mother or anyone's mother and the more he could imagine her with some other man. And, as with Capri, that way she had of confiding things so intensely and openly made him feel special. "Falling in love isn't so bad," he said, smiling.

"No, I guess not." She looked wistful. "But I think in your forties it's worse, somehow. I mean, it's like getting measles late in life. It could be fatal."

"I think you ought to do it," Jed said, imagining with pleasure how enraged Capri's father would be.

"Do you? You think I could handle it?" She waited gravely for his reply.

"Sure you could," he said. "You're sort of like Capri."

"Hmm." She looked pleased. "Maybe I am deep down, *very* deep down, but I don't think I quite have her bravado, her intellectual self-confidence."

They got up to pay. The waitress, putting the check down, said with a smile right at Jed, "Come back again soon!"

Mrs. Gould, without turning around, said, "He's taken, honey," and walked off. Jed laughed.

When they were outside, she shook his hand. "This was such fun! I hope I haven't interfered with your day or—"

"No, I just had to get this stuff."

"Oh, and Jed, listen, this is awkward, but could you not mention our conversation to Capri when you see her? Or maybe let's pretend we never had lunch at all. . . . Would that be okay?"

"No, I understand," Jed said. He grinned at her. "Have a good day."

She waved. "You too."

Driving home, he felt decidedly pleased with himself. Not that he expected her to rush right off and take his advice, but he could tell she had been listening. It would serve her husband right, the nosey bastard! I hope she takes three lovers and shoves them right in his face! . . . Then he thought of the waitress again. Why were there so many pretty girls in the world? Maybe it had been easier when Dr. and Mrs. Gould were young. Maybe if you knew it would be a long hard struggle to get a girl into bed, you'd never . . .

If only they put up more of a fight! But it seemed like, even with the shy, serious ones like Maddy, all you had to do was tell them how pretty they were and how much you liked them, and they kind of melted. He thought of the waitress's tongue lapping up the avocado and imagined her licking his body all over, quickly, softly, like a little cat. Watch the road and forget all that.

What was wrong with him? He had a wife, a sexy girlfriend . . . It was just that each one was different and you couldn't help wondering what that difference would be like. It was funny, though. He thought of his father. His mother had left home when he was eight, his father thirty-six. Yet for the last ten years he could hardly remember his father going out with a woman. He must have seen women at work, but on weekends he just read or watched TV. Once Jed had asked him if he ever thought of remarrying and he'd said, "Why? What for?" Jed had been only twelve at the time. The reply unnerved him. He wasn't quite sure himself why people married, but he assumed there was a reason. As he got older, he assumed sex was part of it, though he also assumed men liked someone to keep the house nice and cook decent meals. His father was a pretty good cook and a neat housekeeper, but what he did about sex was a mystery to Jed. Well, everyone was different. Maybe that's why his mother had left. Or maybe the one experience had made his father so bitter that he didn't feel like trying again. Yet he remembered once, looking for something in his father's desk, he'd found a bunch of love poems in his father's handwriting. They were a little vague, the way poems were, but they talked about breasts and dying falls and quivering thighs and moonlight on white skin. Maybe his father just had a good imagination!

When he got home, Maddy was over at the Farnums'. He found her playing cards with Paul and Geraldine. "We're teaching her how to play bridge," Paul said.

Maddy looked embarrassed. "I'm terrible," she said.

"No, you're not," Geraldine said. To her husband she said, "Paul, you're making it too complicated. You're scaring her with all these rules."

"I'm not scaring you, am I, Maddy?" Paul said.

Maddy shook her head. "I wish there wasn't the thing of the trump card," she said. "I think I sort of understand it except for that."

"Okay, well, end of lesson one," Paul said. "Sherry, anyone?"

"Darling, it's only three-thirty," Geraldine said.

Paul sighed. "Rules! My life is hemmed *in* by rules!" To Jed he said, "Is *your* life hemmed in by rules?"

"Sort of," Jed said. He felt uncomfortable with him, with the way he talked.

"Rules, babies, French poetry . . . what else *is* there in life?" To Geraldine he said, "Did I show you that translation?"

"What translation?"

To all of them he said, "I asked my class, my advanced class, to translate a poem by Eluard, and one girl did something astonishing. I couldn't believe it. She's a poet! Christ." He ran into the other room and returned with a paper. "Listen to this: Curfew." He read:

"What else could we do, for the doors were guarded,
What else could we do, for they had imprisoned us,
What else could we do, for the streets were forbidden us,
What else could we do, for the town was asleep?
What else could we do, for she hungered and thirsted,
What else could we do, for we were defenseless,
What else could we do, for night had descended,
What else could we do, for we were in love?"

"That's pretty," Maddy said when he was done. "Why is it all in questions?"

"Because life is a question," Paul said.

There was a pause.

Then Geraldine said, "Sometimes I find the French so exhausting. All that emotion about *l'amour, toujours l'amour*. It seems so adolescent, somehow."

Paul pretended to tear his hair out. "I've married a woman who is a philistine," he cried. "What am I going to do?" To Jed he said, "How did you like it?"

"I—I liked it," Jed said. He was petrified that something in his reaction would give him away.

"This girl comes up to me. Capri, her name is. Conceived on the shore of the Bay of Naples! She hands it in a week late. She looks at me with these black, mysterious eyes and says, 'I wanted to get it just right. I did thirty drafts.' Don't you love that name? Capri." He looked dreamy, in a trance.

"Does she have two sisters named Paris and Geneva?" Geraldine said. "Oh come on, give us some sherry. It's practically four."

Jed and Maddy went back to their apartment. Jed said he was feeling tired and wanted to lie down. He hadn't known he was tired, but when he lay down, he fell asleep. He woke up to find Maddy curled up beside him, her head on his chest. He thought she was sleeping too, but she just looked up at him. "The baby'll be up soon," she said.

"Yeah."

There was a long pause. Then Maddy said, "Maybe we should give her away."

"What?" Jed said. He still felt groggy.

"Maybe we should give the baby away," Maddy said.

"What do you mean? How could we?"

Maddy looked frightened as she spoke. "I was thinking we could give her to Geraldine and Paul, but she said no. . . . But we could go to an agency or something. Or like, put an ad in the paper."

"Why should we give her away?" Jed said, puzzled.

Maddy took a deep breath. "It's just, I've thought about this a lot, and I feel like maybe we were too young, maybe it's just too much . . . and she seems to bother you so much, yelling and all . . . I thought maybe we'd be happier without her. And maybe she'd be happier with some couple who really want a baby a whole lot and just couldn't have one for some reason."

"You mean, like give her up for adoption?" Jed said.

Maddy nodded.

He was silent. Freedom! My God, without the baby he would be free. He wouldn't have to stay with Maddy. They could go their own ways, live their own lives. The idea was so exciting to him that he felt ashamed. "I guess I need to think about it," he said.

"It seems like ever since she was born, we haven't . . . Things don't seem the same," Maddy said desperately. "Do you know what I mean?"

Jed's heart started thumping painfully. "Yeah, sort of."

"We never make love that much."

He had never thought she would notice about their sex life vanishing. "I've been working pretty hard," he said quickly.

"Oh, I know," Maddy said. "I know you have, Jed. I didn't mean— It's just I guess I'm not always sure if you're glad we're married."

Somehow this was a thousand times worse than his confrontation with Thornie. Maddy's plaintive, soft questions were like needles jabbing into his flesh. It stunned him. All he had worried about this year was getting caught, as he felt he had been with Thornie and Craig. It had never occurred to him that anything of what he was feeling might show on the outside, that Maddy, living with him, would notice any difference. And what *was* the difference, anyway? He was the same person, wasn't he? "Sure, I'm glad," he said, hoping he didn't sound as half-hearted as he felt.

"Girls, I guess, look forward to it since they're *born* practically!" Maddy mused. "But with boys it's different."

"I don't know," Jed said. "Maybe."

"I wasn't trying to trap you," she said.

"I know."

After a second she went on, "But I guess I did know if I wasn't pregnant, you wouldn't have wanted to marry me. . . . Only what I mean is, I didn't get pregnant on purpose."

"Yeah, I know you didn't." Beneath her rambling thoughts was a plea for reassurance that he wished he could meet without feeling like a total hypocrite. "Maybe you should've had the abortion," he said abruptly.

Once the words were out, he was afraid they sounded harsh, but Maddy just said quietly, "Maybe I should've."

In the silence that followed Jed thought they were both thinking the same thing. If she had had the abortion, they would not be here now. They would have broken up, she would have gazed at him wistfully in school, he would have ducked out, trying to avoid talking to her, and by graduation it would have been over, totally. . . . But then he would never have met Capri! "So, if we gave the baby away," Jed said, "how would we do it?"

"Like I said, through that agency in Auburn maybe . . . and they might find some couple with money who could fix her eye."

Jed wondered who would want such a funny-looking baby. "Do you think anyone will want her?" he asked.

"Oh sure," Maddy said. "Millions of people! Gerry was thinking of adopting once, and she said lots of people have to take babies with real defects, I mean who can't walk or talk."

"How come *they* didn't want her?"

"I guess they . . . want to wait. They'd rather have their own."

Jed thought the Farnums were a pretty strange couple. Their decisions about things seemed peculiar to him. "What would you do, once we gave her away?" he asked tentatively.

"What do you mean?"

"I mean, like, would you go on working at the beauty shop?"

Maddy was quiet a moment. "I thought maybe I could even try to get a degree at that beauty school May went to. It costs pretty much, but if I saved up, then I could get a real job, with her or somewhere else."

The image of Maddy working at a job that would pay her enough to live decently even without him was welcome to Jed. "That sounds like a good idea," he said.

Maddy sighed. "It's silly but I was scared you'd get mad at me," she confided.

"About what?"

"Oh, just about even the *idea* of giving the baby away. I was scared you'd think it showed I wasn't a good mother."

"I think you're a good mother," Jed said.

"Do you?"

"Sure."

"I wish we could have done it like Luther and Vonni," Maddy said. "Just lived together and been happy."

"We can still do that."

She smiled and then closed her eyes. Behind her eyelids Jed thought he saw daydreams of this future life, the two of them, nestled together. But surely she would be all right on her own too, wouldn't she? Guys liked her, she was pretty. Even if they split up, she could find some other guy. She'd probably get married again in a year! But he felt guilty cradling her in his arms.

That weekend after work he stopped in to see his father before driving back to Coolidge. His father was painting the front porch and had asked if Jed could come by and help him for an hour or two. He saw his father rarely now, about every month or two at most. When they were together, it was as though nothing had changed. His father acted toward him just as he always had, before Jed had gotten married or had a child—slightly distant, friendly, but at some remove that never disappeared.

They painted side by side, hardly talking. His father repainted the entire house, inside and out, every five years. Jed had no idea why. It was like his extensive vegetable garden. He did it because he'd always done it. "We might give our baby up for adoption," Jed said.

"Your baby?" His father looked horrified. "You can't do that, Jed! It's against the law."

"No, it's not," Jed said. "Anyhow, it's our baby."

"You can't sell a *person,*" his father sputtered, stirring a new can of paint. "That's slavery."

"We're not going to *sell* her!" Jed said, exasperated. "We're going to bring her to that agency."

"What agency?"

"There's one in Auburn. . . . They give babies away."

"To who?"

"To families."

His father shook his head. "You better look out or the two of you'll land in jail."

Sometimes Jed found his father so infuriating he could hardly stand talking to him. "Dad, will you tell me what's illegal about giving your own baby up for adoption?"

"You go see a lawyer," his father said. "They know all about that stuff."

"We will! We're *going* to."

His father was still shaking his head. "I never *heard* of anything like that. Why should you give her away? What's wrong with her?"

"There's nothing *wrong* with her," Jed said, trying to be patient. "We just think we're too young to be parents, that's all. We're not doing such a great job."

"Nobody does a great job," his father said. "You do it, that's all."

"I don't think I should've even gotten married," Jed admitted.

"Then why did you?"

"I don't know."

"You love her, don't you?"

Jed hesitated. He and his father had never discussed anything remotely personal, anything concerning women, sex, families. "No, I don't think I do," he said.

His father just kept staring at him. Finally he said, "That's bad . . . you shouldn't have married someone you didn't love."

"Yeah, I know . . . only she was pregnant."

"Why didn't she give it up for adoption *then?* You wouldn't have had to marry her."

"She didn't want to."

"Why not?"

Again Jed hesitated. "I guess she loved me."

Jed's father sighed. "Women—" he began. Then he stopped. "Your mother never loved *me,*" he said in that mournfully masochistic, laconic tone he had.

"Never?" Jed said, trying to joke because he didn't want his father's confidences.

"Never," his father said, almost as though he were boasting. "Not for one single solitary day. . . . Whenever we . . . had relations, she turned her back to me. Couldn't stand to look at me, I guess."

"So, why'd she marry you?"

"Didn't know what else to do with herself. . . . Oh, she had other offers. I don't know! Ask *her!*"

"*You* could've found somebody," Jed said. He realized he'd been repainting the same patch of wall over and over in a circle.

"For what?"

He hesitated. "Sex?"

His father shrugged. "I'm not like that," he said.

"Like what?" Jed said, wishing his father didn't anger him so much. He felt like dumping the can of paint over his head.

"Some men enjoy that aspect of life to the point where they're crazy! That's all they care about. . . . I'm not like that. If God'd given me a loving wife, I would have cherished and loved her. He didn't, and I abide by that."

God, what a phony bastard he could be! Jed hated it when his father referred to God. Mom, I hope you have a decent sex life with that guy you ran off with. Living with this guy would drive *anyone* bananas. "Anyway," he said dryly. "I just thought I'd tell you our plans."

"You'll dump the kid and then you'll dump the wife. Is *that* the plan?"

Finally Jed exploded. "No! Who's dumping anyone? What's wrong with you? We want the baby to have a good home, someone who can afford to take good care of her." What had shocked him was his father seeing his real intentions so accurately.

His father smiled, "Relax, boy. . . . It's your life. Just stay out of jail, that's all. And be happy."

Was that the sum total of his father's "philosophy of life"? Jed wondered. Stay out of jail and be happy? Shit. The man was crazy. "I'll try, Dad," he said. "Thanks for the advice."

Ten

Spring was going to come after all. Perhaps, Misha sometimes thought, that was the one advantage to living in such a cold climate—that when spring did come, you felt like getting out and doing some kind of dance to the sun god. If it were sunny every day, maybe you'd hardly notice after awhile. The first weekend in April, he decided to sit out in the yard and read. It wasn't really warm yet, just in the high fifties, but the sun felt wonderful, balmy, soft, caressing. He put on a heavy sweater, dragged out an old lawn chair from the garage, and sat in front of his house, directly in the sun, a blanket over his knees, a pile of old newspapers at his feet. From inside the house came the opening bars of *The Queen of Spades*. He had discovered opera about the time he'd learned Russian in the army and the two by Tchaikovsky were his favorites. He'd played them in the ensuing years so many times that the records were badly scratched. He really ought to replace them. He knew exactly where, on the first side, the needle would catch and replay the same line over and over until he lifted it gently to the next bar. Okay, it was schmaltzy, but so what? He loved Tchaikovsky and enjoyed letting the strange melancholy chords drift out into the quiet small-town street past him, over houses, yards, dogs, children playing.

Misha yawned. There was no reason he should feel sleepy—it was early afternoon—except perhaps the pleasure of the sun, and being tucked in the blanket. He opened a magazine, read a few lines of an article, and then let it drop to the ground. Without intending to, he dozed off. When his eyes blinked open again, two little boys raced by on bicycles, one of his neighbors was parking her car, and a young girl was walking slowly and sedately down the street. She was wearing a green-and-white-striped dress, sandals, and white knee socks. She looked almost as though she were dressed for going to church on Easter Sunday. But she walked slowly, looking up at the budding trees, as though, in her own way, she was savoring the lovely day just as he was. As she came closer, past his house, he saw it was Parker's wife, Maddy. He wasn't sure if she saw or recognized him. But then she turned into his yard, still walking in that measured way, a straw purse over one wrist.

"Hi there!" he called out.

"Hi." She walked closer and stood a few feet from him. "Isn't it a beautiful day?"

"Yes," Misha said. "It is. . . . Where's your baby?"

"I left her with my parents. They live just about two streets down from you. This is where I grew up."

So perhaps he had seen her as a child, playing on these streets. There was something familiar about her, but he thought it was more her manner, a certain small-town politeness and diffidence. "Have you lived here a long time?" she asked. She spoke awkwardly, making conversation.

"Twenty years."

She gazed at him thoughtfully. "That *is* a long time."

Misha became aware that, inside the house, the record was stuck. "Would you excuse me a minute?" he said. He leaped up, went inside, and moved the needle, turning the sound down. When he came back, she was standing in the same place. "Let me get you a chair," he said. "You'll be more comfortable. . . . Do you like opera?"

"I don't know," Maddy said.

"That's what I'm playing. . . . It's an old record, but I'm very fond of it. It's a Russian opera."

"Oh." She sat carefully in the chair he offered her, her arms resting on the arms of the chair. "I once tried to learn to play the piano," she said, "but I wasn't any good."

"You don't have to be good to like listening."

They sat in silence for a few minutes. "I guess I'm a coward," Maddy said, sighing.

"In what way?" he asked gently.

"Well, did you ever—was there ever anything you had to do, planned to do—it was your idea, even, but you kept putting it off and putting it off?"

Misha smiled. "Many times."

"Do you think that means you shouldn't do it?"

"Not necessarily."

"But how do you *know?*" The urgency of her tone caught at him.

"What is it you're trying to get yourself to do?"

She looked down at her lap. "It's about our baby," she said.

Misha smiled, remembering the afternoon he'd spent with the baby. "She's a great baby."

"Yes," Maddy repeated mechanically. "She's a great baby." Again she stopped. "Only we decided to give her away . . . I mean, like for adoption?"

Misha was puzzled. "Why?"

"We're not, we . . . I think we're too young." She seemed to choose from an array of confusing possibilities.

"You are both awfully young," he said. She seemed more so, even, than when he'd first seen her—the knee socks maybe, or the slim, barely formed figure that had returned after the child's birth.

"See, it was my fault," she said, leaning forward, her big blue eyes fixed on him. "I was scared to use anything, like birth control. I thought it was a sin. I was brought up Catholic and I thought you had to do it lots of times till it worked. And then I got pregnant and I made Jed marry me."

Misha had the sudden impression that this was like Confession for her, that he was the priest and she was coming for some kind of absolution. "How did you 'make' him marry you?" he asked wryly.

"Oh, I didn't *make* him, really!" she said, breathlessly. "But I didn't want to get an abortion and he felt guilty and these friends of ours were getting married and then my mother kicked me out of the house! . . . It was sort of a lot of things."

"He didn't have to marry you, sweetheart," Misha assured her. "Men frequently don't marry women they . . . get pregnant."

"I know," Maddy said sadly. "But I kept calling him over the phone and crying. I didn't know what to *do!* After my mother kicked me out, especially. So Jed said come live here, live with me and my dad. . . . See, his mother ran off with someone so it was just him and his dad in this big house. There was lots of room. It was like I would be a boarder, sort of. But then, once I was there, we started doing it more because we figured I couldn't get pregnant *again.* I mean, I couldn't get pregnant because I already *was,* so it was like why not? . . . And it went on and on like that!"

"Till you got married?" Misha asked.

"No, it just . . . maybe we could have lived like that forever! Jed's father didn't care. He was real nice about it. Maybe he didn't even *know* I was pregnant. Only I guess he must have known because I showed and all. What I mean is, he never said anything about it, or even asked if we were going to get married . . . and I didn't talk about it either. But deep down I kept hoping. That was what was in my heart."

Misha smiled at the quaintness of that expression. "And finally he proposed and you got married?" he said, trying to steer her meandering story into some kind of port.

"No!" she said in wonder. "We just . . . we were, like, sitting around with these friends, you met them, Luther and Vonni, and I forget what happened but Vonni said, 'When are you guys going to get married?' and Jed said, 'Tomorrow, I guess,' and we did! . . . But it was funny because it was like we never even discussed it! He never even, you know like in stories or on TV, he never even really asked me and I never even really said yes."

"I think it's often like that," Misha said, "in real life."

"Really?" She looked delighted at this news. "Was that how it was with you and your wife?"

Misha thought, trying to recapture that time so many years

ago. It was hazy, like a favorite movie seen too many years ago to recall the dialogue. "We'd been going together about a year," he said, "and I think it happened just sort of naturally. I think it was Brenda who brought it up, actually."

"Did you mind that?" Maddy asked seriously.

Misha smiled. "Why should I have minded?"

"Well, some men, I guess *they* want to do it."

"I'm not one of those men," Misha said.

"Oh." She seemed to be taking this knowledge in, turning it over in her mind. "And were you happy right away?" she burst out suddenly.

"What do you mean?" Misha said, frowning.

She cleared her throat. "I mean, like, was it hard being married compared to, like, just being in love? Was it different?"

"It was more relaxed," Misha said. "You see, sweetheart, things were different in our era. Sex outside marriage was very . . . fraught. My wife always felt guilty, scared. So it was nice not having that, just being able to . . ." He let his voice trail off, a stab of pain catching at him unawares, a fish hook in his heart.

"I think with us it was the baby," Maddy said.

"Pardon me?" He was still half caught in old memories.

"See, we only have one room. And she cried a lot in the beginning and Jed didn't get any sleep, and he had the two jobs and so . . . it *wasn't* like what you said. It *wasn't* relaxed. It was awful! . . . We didn't even do it any more! Isn't that funny? I mean, you'd think that would be the whole point of getting married."

"I don't think that's the whole point, exactly," Misha said gently. "Though it's pretty important."

"What do you think the whole point *is?*" Maddy wanted to know.

"Of marriage?" Misha frowned. "Oh, friendship, maybe, caring for someone, sharing your life, having someone accept you, despite knowing everything about you . . ."

She was staring at him intently as though what he was saying was very strange. "Well," she said, looking suddenly as though she might cry. "So, you think if, like, for a year or so, a couple don't do it that much that doesn't really even matter as long as they love each other?"

Misha sensed she was asking a lot of other questions beneath that question. "Yes," he said, aiming less for truth than for comfort.

"I think without the baby we'll be happy again," she went on after a moment, "and the baby will be happy too, and it'll all be okay." Her voice was trembling.

"But shouldn't you . . . Have you really thought it over?" Misha said. "It seems such a big step. Does Jed want to give her away too?"

Maddy nodded.

"I think you should think it over some more."

"No!" she cried, almost in alarm. "We did! We have! . . . We're just going to do it!"

There was a long pause. "Well," Misha said finally. "I hope it works out then. Any couple will be happy to get a baby like that. She's a spectacular kid."

Maddy beamed. "Is she?"

"Terrific. Smart . . . I mean it."

Her face at times reminded him of someone in a comic strip, the big round eyes, the almost comical ingenuousness of her expressions. "Would *you* like her?" she said brightly.

"What?"

"You can have her, if you want."

"Your baby?"

She nodded, happy. "She seemed to like you a lot, and you seem to like her."

Misha felt too stunned to reply. He was surprised to find his first reaction was, "But I'm fifty years old!"

"You are?" She looked surprised.

"Sure . . . I'm not a spring chicken, honey. I mean, I'd be seventy when she'd be ready for college, practically."

"Would you want her to go to college?" Maddy said, seeming very pleased.

"Well, sure, but . . . what I mean is, you need a young couple starting out. I'm not even married."

"You *might* get married," Maddy said. "My uncle did. He was like what you are, when your wife dies. He was one of those."

"A widower?"

She nodded. "And she's even nicer than my Aunt Helen! I mean, maybe that's not nice to say. I don't mean your wife wasn't nice . . . I just mean, you could meet someone just *as* nice."

"I could," Misha agreed, "but then again, I might not. There are no guarantees."

"So, you think it would be, like, too much work if you weren't married?" Maddy said. "Changing diapers and stuff?"

"Honey, hold on." Misha put up his hand. "You're talking about this so casually. . . . Are you seriously offering me permanent custody of your child?"

She nodded.

"Why me?"

Maddy shrugged. "I guess you seem like a nice person." And after a moment, as though afraid this was inadequate, she added, "And you did it before. You raised a kid so you know how. You're experienced."

Misha sighed. "I didn't really," he said. "It was my wife."

"But you, like, helped her, didn't you?"

"A bit."

"And you like babies?"

He struggled to get a grasp on the conversation. "Sure, I like babies. Who doesn't? . . . But raising a child is . . . it's more than just liking babies."

"It is?" She looked worried again.

"It's a tremendous responsibility," Misha said. "The child becomes the center of your life."

Maddy looked sad. "So, you mean, it's, like, too much?"

"I don't *know* what I mean!" he cried, caught between laughter and exasperation. Then, more calmly, "I just question, assuming you're making this offer seriously, that I would be the ideal parent."

Maddy was silent. She looked down at her lap. "Well, I just thought I'd ask," she said wryly, almost to herself.

"Tell me something. . . . Did you come by here especially, intending to ask me, or did the idea come to you while we were sitting here?"

"It just came to me," she admitted. "I mean, we'd decided about giving the baby away, but giving her to *you* just came to me."

"So, it was serendipity," Misha said, liking that idea.

"What?"

"A chance coming together of circumstances."

"You seemed to like her," she apologized. "But listen, it's okay. You don't have to . . ."

"I'm very flattered," Misha said. "Tremendously, in fact."

"Would you like to think it over?" Maddy said, her head tilted slightly to one side.

Misha laughed. "Yes, I would like to think it over. . . . How long do I have?"

"Would two weeks be enough?"

"I think so."

She kept looking at him. "*I* don't think you're so old," she said. "You don't *act* so old. I mean, not *old* old."

"It depends on the day."

"They say babies keep you young," she pointed out.

Misha was silent. How different was it from a man his age marrying a younger wife who wanted a new family? "Only it would have to be for keeps," he said.

"What do you mean?"

"Well, I couldn't. . . . Say, a year from now you popped up, saying 'Give her back' . . . I couldn't do that. You'd have to know this was it, forever."

"I know," Maddy said solemnly. "It would be forever." After a second she added, "It's not that we don't want babies. Maybe later we'll have them, once we're more . . . These neighbors of ours, the Farnums? They were married ten years before they had kids!"

"So were we, almost, well, maybe five or six. . . . But in our case it was because Brenda had a few miscarriages."

"So did Gerry . . . till she met this doctor who said drink a glass of gin every night, just while you're pregnant. I guess that sort of makes the baby drunk and it doesn't come out too soon? . . . She didn't like gin that much, though, Gerry, I mean."

Misha stood up and stretched. "I think I understand what you're saying. You're just not ready *now*. You want to be together, but you want time to really get to know each other, to enjoy each other's company."

Maddy nodded. She stood up too. "We don't *know* each other," she said, puzzled. "I don't even know what Jed's thinking most of the time!"

"Well . . ."

"He was in love with someone named Garnet," she confided, "in high school, only her parents were rich and didn't think he was good enough. I think sometimes maybe he's thinking about her."

Misha smiled. "Thoughts are mysterious. I guess one has to allow the other person that freedom."

Maddy shook his hand. "This was a good talk," she said, as though she were already, in her thoughts, at home, reflecting back on it.

"Yes, it was," Misha agreed.

Leaning over, she kissed him softly on the cheek. "Bye."

"Bye, Maddy."

What a funny girl! Was that what it would have been like with a daughter? That earnest, sweet, confiding tone? Probably more complicated if it was your own. He doubted she talked to her own parents that openly. Yet it was the fact that the baby was a girl that made the offer tempting, if he even allowed himself to admit he was in some way tempted. He had always thought that some of the problems he had had with Seth wouldn't have existed with a daughter. Easy to say, maybe just a way of letting himself off the hook. But he thought of Simon who, inarticulate and peculiar though he was, seemed doted upon to some extent by both his daughters. That would be nice, to be doted upon. With a woman his own age it would make him uncomfortable. He felt he would rather be known, understood, accepted . . . not elevated to some magic plane. For some reason there suddenly flew into his mind a conversation he'd had with Brenda once when they'd been playing Scrabble. She had pointed out that there was no opposite equivalent word for "uxorious," to dote excessively on your wife, meaning, she said, that men felt no amount of doting upon *them* could *ever* be excessive. He smiled. Sometimes he missed their Scrabble games, though she had usually won and he had felt at the time he was playing more for her sake than his.

Once Maddy had left, her whole visit seemed almost dreamlike, a version of the Annunciation, only instead of an angel, a teenage girl in knee socks, and instead of the Virgin Mary, a middle-aged man who sold used cars. In his mind he kept hearing Wolf. "It's the unexpected things that turn your life upside down that make it worthwhile." He had lived like that, enjoying the jolts and shocks of sudden change, but Misha had always felt he was the opposite, savoring familiarity, routine, the expected. And yet life had cheated him of even that, even the banal muted pleasures of a long marriage. And it left, as well as bitterness, a sense that whatever philosophy you had or followed or tried to follow, life would rip you up and toss you sky high anyway. So, why not a baby? If that was what he wanted. Whether it "made sense" or not. And who knew, any more, what sense was?

But just as he saw Wolf approving—"If that's what you want, go for it"—he saw Brenda shaking her head and sighing. "Honey, you don't know about babies. *I* did it all."

That had been the style of all the couples they knew: the wives took care of the children, the husbands worked. No one had questioned that pattern. But it was also that in their particular case Brenda had seemed so ardently and genuinely devoted to the baby that to have intervened, to have said "Let *me* do that," would have seemed—he felt this was genuine, no excuse—to be depriving her of her life's blood. Especially after the miscarriages! Why interfere when it was giving her such pleasure? It had never occurred to him, or to her, for that matter.

And yet what it had meant was that he had never had a relationship with his son, not really. They had never been friends, never had that closeness that he saw sometimes, rarely it was true, with fathers and sons who went into the same profession or shared some hobby. Seth had contempt for "business" and anything moneymaking, but a double contempt for him, Misha had always felt, for having entered a despised field and then not even having succeeded at it. And that contempt had rankled at him, though Brenda claimed he exaggerated it. When a day came at school for Seth to ask one of his parents to appear and describe his or her profession, Seth asked Brenda, who was teaching by then. It didn't even seem an intended slight. What would there be to say about cars?

Did it matter whose fault it had been? Certainly not now, after death. But even if he could have gone back in time to some age when Seth had been five or ten, Misha wondered what he could have done differently. Seth hated opera and classical music in general, preferring to lie in his room with rock stars screaming mindlessly in the background. What was the common bond that could have linked them? And yet some parents and children seemed to have it, based on something much more vague than shared interests, just love of some mysterious kind. Brenda and Ardis had seemed to feel that way about their mother, who was uneducated, simple, sweet, diabetic. He remembered how Ardis said she had once told her mother of one of her affairs. Her mother, plump, nearsighted, seventyish, had said finally, "But there isn't any physical aspect to this relationship, is there?" Ardis had nodded. Her mother had taken this information in and finally said, patting her daughter's hand, "I'm sure you have your reasons, dear." So there was that, too, which he had somehow missed, that link of fuzzy love, shared genes, who knew what.

He puttered around the house and finally, at seven, went out for dinner and a movie. The movie was second rate, but cleared his brain. When he returned home, the conversation with Maddy seemed many years away. He smiled, fondly remembering some of her turns of phrase—"That was what was in my heart," "You're not *old* old," "You could meet someone just *as* nice." Something almost lyrical in her ungrammatical exclamations, her abrupt turns of thought. And was the giving away of the baby to be a sacrifice to a marriage that should never have occurred in the first place? That was how it struck Misha. Maybe with other couples, even that young, it worked as some kind of solder, some binding. Not with Parker—too intense, restless, rebellious. It could only be a frustration. The image of himself as a fifty-year-old father seemed comfortably absurd, even being lightly tempted seemed some kind of spring fever. He went to bed, relaxed, at ease, knowing he would sleep well.

He had a strange dream. In it someome had a baby she couldn't keep, but it seemed more like Celia than Maddy, or some combination of the two. The reason was never clear, not even who the father was. But he came home and found the baby in an infant seat in the kitchen, with Brenda and Ardis playing with it. It seemed settled that he was going to stay home with the baby. The used-car lot had evidently been sold, or maybe didn't exist anymore. He started protesting, saying he was too old, knew nothing about babies, and they kept laughing and saying he would be fine. They were both flirting with him and yet it was as though there was some conspiratorial secret between them. Was the baby one of theirs? With whom? Which lover? "Take her," Brenda said, giving him the baby, who instantly clasped him around the neck in an almost erotic embrace, kissing his ears, hair . . .

He woke up with a start, trembling. It was three-thirty, cool, dark outside. Of all the possible kinds of dreams, he hated this the most, waking in the middle of the night, too close to morning to fall back asleep. Waking with that horrible jolt. He hated dreams, their eerie power, the way they tore mercilessly through your defenses, setting things up according to their own crazy patterns. Alone in bed, he felt frightened, almost sick. Was it dreaming of Brenda, which he hadn't done in a long time? She had been so real in the dream, and he knew that if it had been four years ago, he could have waked her up, they could have talked for an hour. Whether they would have made love or not, she would have lain in his arms, finding soothing explanations for the dream, unraveling it, taking away its power to terrify. He would have fallen asleep at dawn and awakened at ten to the smell of bacon, coffee. . . .

Maybe he should call Ardis. Misha looked at the clock. Almost four. Simon would be gone by now. No danger from that. But it was the middle of the night for her! She might have gone to bed late—she often did on Saturday night. And she's not your wife! In his mind he made the call, she rushed over, warm, sleepy, a raincoat on over her nightgown, tumbling into bed. A more erotic version of what the past with Brenda would have been like, but with all the same soothing elements, the same smell of bacon and coffee. He picked up the phone, dialed four digits, and then replaced it. Come on, she's asleep. Call her later in the morning. She can come over then, maybe.

Padding into the kitchen, he made himself a cup of hot chocolate and took a Valium. He thought of all the people whose jobs required them to get up every day at times like this. Wolf used to get up at four—he liked the quiet—and do most of his work before noon. Back in bed, Misha tossed for nearly an hour, and then, near six, fell into a dreamless sleep.

Luck was with him. Simon's mother, who lived in Syracuse, was ill. He was spending the afternoon and evening with her. Ardis said she could meet Misha at a restaurant. There was one they went to often—Marrietta's. They had wanted a place neither of them had been to with Simon or Brenda, which was hard to find. They had found one slightly out of town, hardly more than a diner really, but with good home-cooked food. They served sautéed milkweed pods, an odd delicacy he had gotten to like.

Ardis had been sick, she said. Nothing serious, a flu. She had taken a few days off from work and slept mainly. She looked a little pale and tired, though he might not have noticed it if she hadn't mentioned it. "I lost four pounds," she said. "Maybe it's worth being sick."

They always had the same waitress, who smiled at them in a kindly, conspiratorial way. Ardis said when she arrived first, the waitress had said, "Your friend is not here yet."

"How can she tell we're not married?" he asked. "We both wear rings."

Ardis laughed and then looked sad. "You're such a sweetie," was her reply.

Over coffee, he yawned. "Sorry," he said. "I woke up early

today." He told her about his nightmare, the desire to call her, reaching for the phone. "Well, I guess I'm glad you didn't," Ardis said. "I've been so zonked lately. I've been sleeping twelve, fourteen hours. Normally I wouldn't mind."

"It's hard, sometimes, sleeping alone in a bed," he admitted.

"I always have," she said. "We've had twin beds for ages . . . Simon is always afraid he'd wake me since he gets up so early."

Feeling better now, Misha told her about Maddy, and the offer. "She must have been kidding!" Ardis said. "You don't just give babies away like that!"

"No, evidently they've thought it over. . . . They feel they'd be better off alone, and for the baby's sake too."

She stroked his hand. "You, a father at fifty? I can't picture it somehow."

"*I* had trouble at first."

"At first?"

"There's something in it that appeals to me. Why not?"

Ardis frowned. "You're joking, right?"

"No."

She dropped his hand. "Mish, you know *nothing* about babies!"

"Nothing?"

"Nothing! Look, I know, I was there. Bren did all of it. . . . How many diapers did you change?" Before he could answer she said, "I'm not blaming you, I'm just saying you don't know any more than that fifteen-year-old kid. It would be crazy!"

"Nobody knows till they do it," he said defensively, taken aback by her vehemence. "Are women born knowing?"

"They're born—I don't know, with some instinct about it, some nurturing thing, hormonal maybe. Men just don't *have* that. They were too busy going out clubbing saber-tooth tigers or whatever."

"Do you really believe that?" Misha asked.

"Yes!"

"You feel men can never be competent as fathers?"

"I didn't *say* that! They can be great as *fathers,* not as mothers. The first five years belong to the mother."

"How about *Kramer vs. Kramer?*"

Ardis looked flushed. "That was garbage! I *hated* that movie! It didn't have *one* honest moment. . . . Where did he get sitters? They dodged every real-life issue. . . . Mish, listen, this is the story of my life! I really *did* do all that. I worked, I raised two kids. Am I asking the Nobel Prize for that?"

"What does *that* have to do with it?"

"If men make one round of French toast, change *one* bed, they feel like they should get a medal. . . . Women do those things every goddamn day of the week!"

He had never expected her to get so heated. "Listen, want to come back for a little while?" he said. The waitress had brought the check.

"I feel tired," she said irritably.

"So do I!" he said in the same tone.

Outside, in the car, she said, "I don't feel like fucking."

"Neither do I . . . I feel like *talking.*"

"We're just going to have an argument. I feel wrought up."

"Why?" Misha touched her shoulders. "I don't understand why you're so upset . . . I didn't even say I'd decided to do this!"

"That you would even consider it!"

He started the car. "Will you come back with me please?"

She sighed heavily. "Okay."

Inside the house, she collapsed on the bed. "I don't have one whit of energy," she said. She closed her eyes, and then opened them again. "Let's fuck, why not? It's less tiring than talking."

"I *want* to talk," Misha said wryly.

"We'll talk afterward." She held out her hand. He took it and sat down on the edge of the bed. Even as he undressed, he felt half not there, still in the various earlier moods of the day. But making love to her changed his mood—their argument seemed far away.

"You don't think I'd be a good father?" he asked into the quiet afterward.

"You're good at everything," she crooned, and that sleepy, satisfied glossing irritated him as much as her earlier fit of temper.

"I wasn't good with Seth."

"He was a difficult kid."

"I always thought with a girl it would be easier."

Ardis was silent, nestled against him, gazing at the ceiling.

"Maybe that's it," she said, "that it's a girl. Maybe I feel jealous."

"*Is* that it?" He was surprised. That hadn't occurred to him.

"Sure, a little. She'll adore you, you'll adore her . . ."

Misha thought. "Do you think it would be harder with a girl? I mean, raising her alone, without a wife?"

"Listen, one *second* after you get that kid, you will have a line six feet deep of women wanting to 'help' you raise her. You'll be beating them off with sticks!"

He laughed. "Why?"

"Because that's the ultimate lure. Poor lonely widower, alone with gooey baby girl. . . . Don't you ever watch TV?"

"Rarely."

"Look, women pick men up in laundromats! Some women find the sight of a forlorn man washing his own *socks* irresistible!"

Misha grinned. "No one's ever approached me in a laundromat."

"You're wearing a ring—still," she pointed out.

He looked down at it. "Do you think I shouldn't?"

"I think when you don't need it any more you'll take it off."

"Why am I wearing it?" He was genuinely curious.

"To pretend, to hold onto the past . . ." Her voice became melancholy. "Maybe I envy it too," she said. "The starting over thing. It was such a terrific time of my life, that baby bonding. . . . Now I just have to wait to be a grandma."

There was one of those pauses that he was used to between them. A pause in which they both contemplated the fact that, in reality, she could get divorced. Neither of them would suggest it or refer to it. "You really don't think men—" he began.

"They're so absorbed in their work, usually," Ardis said. "Bren and I talked about that so much, how women, no matter *how* absorbed they are—somehow it's in proportion. They still have emotional energy for other things. But men don't. I don't know why."

"*My* work isn't like that. It never has been."

"I know . . . maybe that is your appeal, partly, sweetie. You *don't* have that frenetic, rattled thing—"

"I thought women liked that."

"Maybe some do . . . or you can like someone despite it, or hope you can carry them beyond it. And you do for a while, maybe."

He wondered what past relationship she was musing on as she gazed off out the window. "What if one of your fixings up had worked?" he asked. "The harpist, whoever . . . and she had wanted a child?"

"True," Ardis said. "Maybe that would have been even worse. Like: which would you prefer, burning to death or freezing? Those were all failsafe fixups. I knew they'd never work."

He stroked her affectionately. "Look, it's a sexist world. At sixty I could have five daughters, five little harpists . . ."

"You could have a string quartet right in your home! Or even a small chamber orchestra. . . . Look, adopt the kid if you want. Or at least check it out. You need things that come to you, that's true."

"It was like a . . . I don't know what," he said. "I was just sitting there, dozing in the sun, and she appeared, like some vision."

"Okay." Ardis sat up. "No, I believe in visions, seriously . . . but just make sure the kid's okay. She could be retarded, some problem they aren't being up front about."

"I don't think so."

"I'm just saying check it out. Look, if you buy a dog, you take it to the vet first, just to be sure."

"I don't know anything about the legal aspect," he said. "Even if her husband agrees, they can't just leave it on my doorstep in a basket."

"You'll go to a lawyer. You'll find out how it's done. There're probably a bunch of rules, papers to sign." She went into the bathroom to wash up. "You've convinced me. Do it."

"How will I manage? Who will look after her during the day?"

Her voice came at him through the half-closed door. "How does anyone manage? How do women on welfare manage? How do women whose husbands walk out and they have sick triplets and never worked a day in their life manage? You'll manage!"

233

"How about what you said earlier?" He got up and put on his bathrobe, wanting to see her face as they talked. "How about the hormonal thing, that men don't have it?"

She was powdering her nose. "That's just a theory," she said.

"I'm afraid it's true," he said mournfully, watching her. "You convinced me."

"No." She kissed him. "It's just what women want to think—that only they can do it. I think there are two things women can do men can't—have babies and breast feed. And this kid is probably on bottles already."

He laughed. "Why didn't you say this before?"

"Because before I was on the other side. . . . Look, Mish, ask me tomorrow and I'll say something else. I have nine million opinions on the subject and they don't all jibe. Okay, maybe *most* men can't do as well as *most* women. But your're not most men. You're you. You'll be terrific. Father of the Year."

"You have me all confused," he grumbled.

Ardis looked contrite. "Poor sweetie . . . Will you be okay? Will you sleep all right tonight?"

"I always sleep well after you've been here."

"I'm here in spirit every night."

"Spirit is helpful, but . . ."

But the confusion he felt that night, tossing in bed, was a different kind. He was beginning to wonder if it mightn't be something he could handle, something possible. And then he worried that they had changed their minds. Maybe they had had a fight and now had made up, wanted the baby after all.

He wanted to try to be selfish—to consider mainly whether this thing, this uniting of his life with another living being, would make him happy. Or was it simpleminded even to think of "happiness" at this age? Really, he thought, he should be thinking of the baby. What would be good for her. But that was too ambiguous. Good compared to what? They didn't want her. Some other couple could be anything—good, bad. He could understand Maddy's feeling about not wanting to deliver the baby to a stranger, no matter how well chosen or researched by an agency. And the odd vulnerability of the baby struck him. No more so than any other baby, perhaps, but there she was, lying innocently in her crib while her life was being decided upon by such peculiar chance factors.

His age. He tried to think whether now, at fifty, he felt very different from the way he had felt twenty or ten years earlier. He was certainly more conscious of death, or mortality, and that was only partly because of the accident and Wolf's death. But he couldn't remember things he had been able to do when young that now seemed impossibly out of reach. He had never been good at sports, never stayed up late, never had inexhaustible bouts of sheer physical energy. Maybe, out of laziness, he had conserved some! Sometimes he felt tired more easily; the occasional bouts of back trouble gave him a sense he hadn't had earlier of his body being, in some sense, in decline. But sexually he felt—though maybe this was just the intensity of a new relationship—more alive than he had been before, more vigorous.

How about ten years from now? The kid'll be ten, still in grade school. But how could anyone tell what ten years would bring? He had no serious health problems, he didn't smoke or drink. As far as heredity went, his parents and grandparents had lived into their eighties. Maybe Wolf had, to some extent, burned himself out. He would have liked so much to have Wolf and Brenda back, just for one evening, to talk this over with them. Ardis had been so strange, leaping from one side to another—he would be terrible as a father, he would be wonderful. He knew all that was due to her involvement with him, that she couldn't see it objectively and was reluctant to "relinquish" him to another woman. And maybe it was also that, somewhere in her mind, she had imagined their present relationship going on forever, and knew the baby would change that. How, he wasn't sure, but it would make him a different person, make his life different. Right now all of his emotional life was centered on her in a way he felt wasn't totally healthy. He was merely a part of her emotional life; she was too much the focus of his. At times he felt like the male version of "the other woman," looking ahead ardently to their weekly comings together, savoring them in retrospect after they were over.

Wolf hadn't wanted a baby. Wouldn't he have thought this was crazy? And yet Misha remembered one of Wolf's girlfriends, acquired at some point during his second marriage, the one to Elsie. The girlfriend, Alkira, was Greek, a waitress at a small family-owned diner outside Syracuse, in her mid-twenties, with a baby son fathered by someone who had vanished several years earlier, a traveling businessman. Misha and Wolf used to go to the diner together Sunday nights. Alkira would bring them huge Greek salads—he always had indigestion afterward—giant rings of purple onion, hunks of feta cheese. She was tall, slim, with very thick black curly hair and a faint moustache, strong legs. You could imagine her on some sunny hilltop outside Athens with a clay pitcher balanced on her head, tending goats.

Wolf liked her being a mother and seemed to adore her baby son. The boy looked exactly like her, giant black eyes like olives, a dark smooth complexion, a certain serenity in his manner, a gravity almost. Wolf played with him, tossing him in the air. "Look at this kid!" he would exclaim to Misha, and Misha would wonder: if you like them so much, why not have one "the regular way," with your wife? But Wolf never wanted to do anything "the regular way." Ultimately the waitress went to business school. The only other thing Misha could remember about her was that Wolf said she had a life-size poster of Elvis Presley on the wall of her bedroom. Wolf always felt the singer was watching them with raunchy amusement while they were in bed together.

And then he thought of all the people they had known who had problems with their children, health problems, emotional problems. He thought of the woman next door to him who had had a fourth child at forty and whose husband had left her a year later. She screamed at the child so often and piercingly that Misha had several times thought of moving just to get away from the sound. It was like a chained dog. He wasn't sure at times if it was the mother or the baby, or if they were wailing in concert at the injustice of life, at their mutual hard lot, in rage at the way things had worked out.

The one thing that he genuinely felt was that, as a teacher, he had had rapport with his students. Of course, they weren't his own children, and he was teaching them a subject. But as he looked back, his interactions with them—and it had been a typical, inferior public school, not very bright kids, most not college bound—had been the high point of his professional life. It seemed to him that he was patient, that he was capable of kindness and devotion.

But more than anything, though he considered himself totally unsuperstitious, he could not help seeing the offer of the baby as life's way, clumsy and ill-timed though it was, of repaying him for the havoc the accident had wreaked on his life. Taking away and giving back. Once he had met a young widow who had lived on their street. Her husband had been a good deal older and died of a heart attack, leaving her six months pregnant. She had said something about liking the fact that her body was recreating life, even when emotionally she felt no desire to live. She liked being forced to become part of a natural cycle, she said, though had she known he would die, she would never have gotten pregnant.

At night, in bouts of insomnia, he roamed the house, considering how he would fix it up when the baby arrived. The extra bedroom now served no purpose. He could move out the books, give the desk away, repaint it. Of course, he would have to hire someone to look after her during the day. But, according to Ardis, that part wasn't hard. "Don't look for a Ph.D. in psychology," she warned. "Just a warm, friendly person." She even promised to help him interview potential babysitters, if he felt nervous about whom to pick.

"But is it fair?" he asked anxiously. "Adopting the kid and then leaving her all day with some overweight, bored woman who'll plunk her in front of a TV set?"

Ardis laughed. "What does overweight have to do with it? Natural mothers are all slim? They never watch TV? They're never bored? Listen, let me take you to a playground one afternoon. If you want to see a bunch of bored, schitzy, screaming messes—just spend one afternoon with a bunch of 'natural mothers.' I swear, if I were President, I'd pass a law that *no* woman was allowed to stay at home with her own kids. They all go crazy, they *all* drive their kids crazy—"

"All?" Her exaggerations still managed to put him in a good humor.

"Down to the last one."

"Brenda wasn't like that."

Ardis looked at him with a funny expression. "You don't know," she said enigmatically.

"What do you mean, I don't know? *What* don't I know? We were married twenty years!"

"I mean, you knew no more about her than any husband knows about his wife, even if they're married a hundred and *fifty* years! You knew what you wanted to know. She was a figment of your imagination."

He was aghast. "What are you trying to say? Wives know all about their husbands and husbands know *nothing* about their wives?"

Ardis wrinkled up her brow in a pose of comic bewilderment. "What *am* I trying to say? Okay, sure, yeah—no one, maybe, knows that much about who they're married to and that's just the way it is and has to be or whatever. . . . Two, yeah, I do think wives know more. Women observe more. Men rush around doing things."

Finally he exploded. "I consider myself extremely observant," he said curtly. "I think you're dead wrong. I think Brenda was a wonderful mother and loved doing it."

"Okay . . . you have a fantasy that makes you happy. Wrap yourself in it and stay warm for the next fifty years."

She went over and hugged him from behind. "You *are* extremely observant," she murmured, nibbling at his ear.

"Cut it *out!*" he said angrily, yanking away. "Stop manipulating me."

"I'm not."

"We had a happy marriage. . . . Leave that alone."

Ardis stiffened. "I will . . . but I'll tell you one thing, sweetie. Bren didn't want to be deified or cast in bronze. She wasn't like that. She'd laugh herself silly if she could hear you. She was wonderful as a real, flawed person . . . so don't make her into some kind of saint."

"I'm not." But he felt disastrously wrought up and wished they hadn't gotten into this useless, destructive argument.

The tension remained in the air. Ardis was breathing quickly, obviously trying to hold in whatever she was feeling. "I have a 'happy marriage' too, you know," she said, "so please don't think you're describing something totally beyond my ken."

"Do you?" He couldn't keep the sharp, sarcastic edge from his voice. He wanted to hurt her.

"Yeah, I do." She was flushed, her voice shaking. "There are nine million types of happy marriages, not just one! I could've left Simon for men who earn ten *times* what he does, men who are handsomer, better lovers, who know more about my work . . . but I stayed because I wanted to stay. *That's* the definition of a happy marriage, where both people know they can leave and *choose* to stay." She lifted her chin in the air, defiant, wounded.

"Why *do* you stay?" he pursued. "Just because he puts up with your fooling around with other men?"

"He doesn't put up with it! He knows nothing about it, nothing."

"How do you know?"

"How do I know anything? How do I know I'm standing here? I'm totally discreet about it and I always have been. I'm not doing it to hurt him."

"What are you doing it for, then?"

"Because sex is important to me and it isn't to him, okay? He could do it once a year, maybe, and be perfectly happy. I'm not like that. I don't think that makes either of us a monster."

"He's not a monster," Misha couldn't help saying dismissively. "He's a nonentity."

Ardis advanced on him, furious. "What do *you* know about him, will you tell me that? How many conversations have you *ever*, in all these years, had with him about anything?"

"Conversations! I've never heard him say more than four words at a time!"

"He's quiet. . . . Is that a crime? So, he's not a raconteur—"

Misha laughed. "A raconteur! Look, *I'm* not a raconteur, I—"

"I know! You're quiet too. I like that in men. I couldn't stand someone like me, jabbering on all the time. I admire people who only speak when they have something to say. What I don't get is, if you're like him, why are you attacking him?"

He could have retreated, but chose to hold his ground. "I want you to tell me one good thing about him, one reason you think you have a happy marriage, as you claim."

"Jesus, what a self-righteous bastard you are! *You* have the option on happy marriages, huh? You and Bren are up there among the rosy clouds and the rest of us—"

"Tell me *one* thing."

"Okay, I'll tell you a lot of things! . . . First, I think he's a kind, good, devoted person, and I haven't met nine million men of whom that can be said. Maybe I've been moving in the wrong circles or something. . . . And I think he's a wonderful father and he always has been, not just when they got old enough to be interesting, but all along. He got up at night and fed them, took care of them when they were sick, helped them when they needed help with homework, when I was too spaced out to do anything. He writes them every *week* at college."

Misha began feeling uneasy—he had not been this kind of paragon as a father—and also aware that he really didn't want a full and elaborated list of Simon's virtues. But he knew there was no turning back now. "But how about to you? As a husband? You say he can't get it up—"

"Why are you distorting everything? I love making love with him! He's fine. . . . It's just not that . . . frequent. There's probably something wrong with *me,* caring about it so much. Half the women my age I talk to are relieved if their husbands don't 'bother' them, as they put it. . . . Anyhow, is sex all there is to marriage? Is that all you and Bren had in common?"

Actually, as she was talking, it had run through his mind that his own marriage had been a milder version of hers, in reverse. He had cared more about sex than Brenda and, although it had sometimes been an intriguing challenge to carry her along when he was in a passionate mood, it had also—he felt guilty even thinking this—sometimes been a drag. "I think we—" he began hesitantly.

"Don't tell me!" she yelled. "You want to know things? Okay, here's something which is that all the years I've worked and scrambled and been too out of it to *talk* at the end of the day, Simon has never once berated me or said why are you like this, why do you care so much, why are you so ambitious? He's been supportive and good, boasts about me at parties. He isn't one of these fucking born-again feminist types that drive me up the wall."

"What's a born-again feminist?" Misha asked, smiling.

"One of those men that sit there waxing on about ERA and the importance of women's rights while their wife scurries around cooking, cleaning, putting the kids to bed . . . I mean, Simon put his money where his mouth was. He *did* it. He didn't just talk about it."

She didn't add that without the money she had earned, they could scarcely have lived decently, but Misha decided not to add that either. The anger had gone out of him, and her as well, he suspected. Exhausted, they stared at each other. Ardis came over to where he stood. She put her hand on his shoulder. "Mish, listen," she said, gazing at him tenderly. "I run off with you ten times a day in my mind. But I can't leave him. You see that, don't you? It would make a mockery of my whole life. I could never live with myself."

"No, I understand," he said, thinking how, in that feeling of family devotedness, no matter how differently it was expressed, she and Brenda were not that unalike, after all. He put his arms around her. "I love you," he said.

She kissed him gravely, softly on the lips. "I love you, and we both were, are, happily married *and* you'll be a terrific father. . . . Now will you call that kid and tell her you've decided?"

"Give me the phone."

She brought it to him.

Eleven

What surprised Maddy most was her mother's reaction. She had anticipated some version of the way her mother had acted upon learning Maddy was pregnant—disgust, attacks, sarcasm, vituperation. Instead, for no reason Maddy could fathom, her mother chose to see Maddy's deciding to give the baby up for adoption as a good deed, a self-sacrificing, altruistic act. She based part of this on the fact that Mr. Edelman was Jewish and therefore, she was sure, rich. Eyes gleaming, she described to Maddy the luxurious and wonderful life the baby would have: giant stuffed animals, beautiful dolls, her own gigantic room, a college education.

"He did talk about sending her to college," Maddy remembered, glad she could add some piece of evidence to this.

"Maddy, let me tell you something," her mother said. "I knew a Jewish lady once so I know what I'm talking about. There are two things they care about—money and education. They know how to make money and once they have it, they save it, they invest it. That's how come so many of them are bankers or teachers. This lady, she worked with Janie in the stationery store—every *night* she read a book! *Every* night! Just like someone else would read a magazine! Janie used to say to her, 'What about your eyes?' She'd say, 'What do I have eyes *for?*'"

Maddy wondered if her mother was right. She might be right about Jews in general—Maddy had never known any so she didn't know—but she wondered if Mr. Edelman was that rich. He lived in a house that looked very much like the one her parents lived in. It, like their house, needed a coat of paint, had a lawn that was uneven and in need of mowing. Certainly he didn't dress like a wealthy man. His clothes looked a little too big or rumpled, not especially elegant. But when she pointed that out to her mother, she was unfazed.

"That's just it!" she exclaimed. "They don't go for show. Some of them do, but most of them just save it. That's why they have so much. They don't drink it away like the Irish. They're smart. You look at what they have in the bank. *That's* what counts." And she chucked the baby under the chin. "I'm going to go see her when she's eighteen," she gloated, "and I bet she'll be the most beautiful, smartest grandchild I have."

"I thought you thought she was ugly," Maddy said. "Because of her eye and all."

"They'll operate. . . . Listen, Jews operate all the time. By the time she's fixed up, we won't even recognize her. Will we?" she said to Minnie.

It seemed a little unfair to Maddy that now that the baby was no longer hers, her mother was predicting such a glorious future for her. It was as though because Mr. Edelman seemed so eager to have her, the baby's value had risen abruptly, like a stock skyrocketing on the market.

"He's getting a bargain," Maddy's mother said. "If he went to some agency, he'd have to pay Lord knows what."

"But he wasn't planning on adopting a baby," Maddy said.

"Still," Mrs. O'Connell said. "If you were sneaky, you could make him fork over ten thousand dollars for a baby like this. I saw a program like that on TV. Some people will pay *millions,* they're so desperate."

"I don't want to sell her," Maddy said.

"I know you don't, honey . . . I'm just saying you could. I'm just saying he's a lucky man."

"You don't think he's too old?" Maddy said. "He's fifty."

"Fifty's not old," Mrs. O'Connell said. "Especially for a man. A

man of fifty—you can't even tell. Men age slower. It's some hormonal thing. But when they go—" She pointed thumbs down to
indicate a sudden and precipitous decline.

"Anyway, he might marry again," Maddy suggested, alarmed
at the gesture.

"Of course he'll marry again," Mrs. O'Connell exclaimed.
"Men always marry again. Look at your uncle! Look at your
brother!" Maddy's oldest brother had gotten divorced and, re-
cently, had remarried. "Men should never marry young. They
don't know what they're doing. When they decide late in life, they
know."

"But you and Daddy married young," Maddy pointed out.

"That's what I mean!" her mother exclaimed. "We didn't
know anything! We were babes in the woods."

Even though Mrs. O'Connell felt she and her husband hadn't
known what they were doing, they were still together after all these
years. Maybe it showed that people could start off on the wrong
foot and then reverse it somehow. And it did seem to Maddy that,
ever since they had finalized the agreement with Mr. Edelman, Jed
had seemed in a much better mood. A few times she had caught
him even singing or humming to himself around the house. They
still didn't make love a whole lot, not the way they had before
they'd been married, but when they did, Jed seemed very courtly
and tender, asking her if she had come, even kissing her sometimes
before he rolled over to go to sleep. Maddy was trying not to get
her hopes up too high, but it seemed suddenly that maybe everything would go all right. The beautiful warm spring weather put
her in that mood, hopeful, eager.

And she was glad that the baby was too young to know what
was about to happen. Maddy remembered how, when she was a
child, they had had a dog that developed cancer. Her father had
said dogs were lucky because all they suffered was the physical
pain of the illness, not the realization of their own mortality, which
was the real pain. And so the baby, not knowing her fate, babbled
happily, showing her new teeth. It was lucky, too, Maddy thought,
that the baby was suddenly at an age when she seemed to like
strangers. Two months earlier she had cried even at the sight of a

strange face. Now she waved gaily at strangers in supermarkets and allowed herself to be passed from person to person at family gatherings with a geniality that struck Maddy as almost promiscuous. Faces fascinated her, pretty ones, ugly ones. She patted people's faces, like a blind person trying to figure out their personalities from the shape of their nose or ears.

Her mother had once clipped out an Ann Landers column and attached it to the refrigerator. It had long since fallen off, but as Maddy remembered the gist of it had been reprimanding some woman who talked about her children as though they were her possessions. "They are with you for a certain length of time and during that time you love them and do your best with them," the article said. "But you do not own them. A time comes when you have to let them go, hoping that all the love you have poured into them will help them in their independent life." Maddy tried to convince herself that it was the same with her. She had had the baby only six months, not sixteen years, as some mothers did, but perhaps the same principle applied.

But would the baby remember her? And for how long? And in what way? Looking down at her, Maddy couldn't help wondering about that. She wanted the baby to remember her forever, in some way. And then she remembered a cat they had had to give away because her brother was allergic. When they had visited the family to whom they had given the cat several months later, he had ignored all of them and, instead of leaping instantly into their laps as he had at home, just curled up and slept on the edge of an armchair. Was he showing that he was angry at having been given away or did he just not remember who they were? And which was worse? The cat seemed happy, fat, relaxed. Maddy, eight at the time, had thought it was selfish to want the cat to miss them. He was happier not missing them. But she had stared at him for the whole visit, trying to catch his eye, as though, once she did, she could stare at him so hard that she would will him into remembrance.

The lawyer was a woman, Mrs. Liranzo. She was small and brown-haired, with glasses, between pretty and what Maddy's mother would have called "pleasant-looking." They had been sitting in her office for an hour while she had explained the conditions of the adoption. The baby would reside in the house of Misha Edelman for six months. During that time if either party changed their mind, it was still possible, if the lawyer agreed, to transfer her back again. A social worker would visit the home several times to determine how the baby was getting on. After that six months a final agreement would be signed whereby the baby would belong legally to Mr. Edelman.

"Is all of that clear to both of you?" Mrs. Liranzo said, looking from Maddy to Jed.

"Yes," Maddy said in a small clear voice. Jed just nodded and then added. "Sure."

Mrs. Liranzo turned to Mr. Edelman. "I understand you have arranged for a woman to care for Minerva while you are at work," she said.

"I have," said Mr. Edelman. He was wearing a blue suit and looked more like the prosperous businessman that Maddy's mother assumed him to be.

"This woman has cared for other children of a similar age?" Mrs. Liranzo asked.

"Yes, she's raised four of her own," Mr. Edelman said, "and she's worked as a housekeeper, looking after babies, for ten years." He smiled. "I interviewed thirty women. . . . She was tops."

"Thirty!" Mrs. Liranzo smiled. "That must have been exhausting."

"A friend helped me. . . . Someone with two of her own."

"Well!" Mrs. Liranzo looked at all three of them. "Everything seems quite in order, then. . . . Saturday is the day you've selected?"

Maddy nodded.

Mrs. Liranzo got to her feet. "I'm sure everything is going to work out beautifully," she said, "but, of course, if any of you have any problems or even just wish to talk, please feel free to call me at any time."

Maddy felt that remark was directed at her. Mrs. Liranzo

seemed to be smiling at her more than at the two men. Then she shook all of their hands and ushered them out of her office.

They stood outside in the spring sunshine, awkwardly.

"Well," Mr. Edelman said. "I'll expect you Saturday around two, then?"

Maddy nodded. On an impulse she asked, "What color did you paint her room?" She remembered he had said the week before that he was painting it.

"Light purple . . . lavender, I guess is what you call it. It looks nice."

Maddy liked lavender. It was more unusual than pink. She decided to dress Minnie in her lavender dress so she would match.

Somehow it was not as though they were giving the baby away. It was more as though she were going on a visit or to a party. The finality of it eluded Maddy, even when she tried to lie in bed thinking of it and wondering if she was doing the right thing. Jed didn't seem to have any mixed feelings about it at all. He had been amazed at first that Mr. Edelman would consider it, but now that it was definite, he had never once said, "Gee, I'm really going to miss her" or "Isn't it too bad to give her away just when she's getting sort of cute looking?" Maybe men didn't think that way. To them a baby was just a baby, even if it was theirs. Though Maddy, for the hundreth time, wondered if, had it been a boy, his feelings would have been different.

Vonni and Luther had said they would come Saturday morning with the truck and load in all of Minnie's equipment. Mr. Edelman had said not to bring a crib—he had bought a new one. So really it was just a matter of packing her clothes, the blanket she slept with that Maddy thought she seemed to like, and the extra bottles and diapers. Everything fit into two cardboard boxes that Jed had gotten at the IGA.

Minnie had had her morning nap, from nine to eleven. She seemed peppy and calm and looked, Maddy thought, attractive, in the lavender dress, though the sleeves pinched her chubby arms just slightly. Now that she was eating food three times a day, she'd put on a lot of weight. The doctor said that was good and that she wasn't over the range of normal weights for a baby her age. Her eye was still the same. Some of the time both eyes looked straight ahead, but sometimes, for no reason, one would slide to one side, as though there were something fascinating just out of reach of her range of vision.

Luther drove and Maddy sat next to him, the baby on her right in her traveling chair. Vonni and Jed sprawled in the back. The plan was that, after the baby was settled into her new home, they would drive back to Ithaca, have dinner in town, and later go to *Rocky Horror*. There was a feeling in the air, Maddy thought, as though it would be "just like old times," as though, without the baby, she and Jed could be welcomed back as a couple just the way they'd been a couple in high school. Maddy could tell that Jed was feeling jubilant at this. He joked around with Vonni and kept squeezing her arm and saying she had grown gigantic muscles because of all the hard physical labor she and Luther had been doing.

"It's true," Vonni said proudly. "I lift weights at night, too . . . I can even lift this guy—" She poked Luther.

"Yeah, she lifts me right over her head like a beach ball," Luther said. "I'm going to sign her up for the circus."

"Men like strong women," Vonni said. "That's what's in now— not little fluffy lumps."

"Let me feel that bicep again," Jed said, reaching for her.

Vonni let out a yelp. "That's not my bicep. . . . Now cut it out, Jed!"

"Hey, Maddy, keep an eye on those two, will you?" Luther said calmly. "Don't want things to get out of hand."

Maddy turned around. Vonni's eyes were sparkling with mischief, as they often did, and Jed had instantly assumed a pose of total innocence and formality. It was just a regular day to him! Maddy, turning back, wished so much there was some other person who could share her feeling of loss and sadness at giving the baby away. Ironically, even the baby couldn't share it, since she didn't know it was going to happen.

When they got to the house, Mr. Edelman was sitting out in the yard with a woman. They were talking, but got up as the truck pulled into the driveway. Maddy wondered who the woman was—the babysitter he'd hired, maybe? She was dressed in jeans and a white blouse, had curly black-brown hair and a friendly smile. Her breasts were large—Maddy saw Jed and Luther glance at them instantly as they got out of the truck.

"This is my sister-in-law, Ardis Marx," Mr. Edelman said. He introduced all of them to her.

Ardis came over and looked at the baby, whom Maddy was holding. "Aren't you a cutie?" she said. "Want to see your new room?"

The baby looked at her and neither smiled nor frowned. Ardis reached for her. Maddy was afraid the baby might cry, but she allowed herself to be carried into the house. Maddy followed. The room was really pretty. It was a very light lavender with a white shade at the window and a pot of flowers. In one corner was the crib—a really big one made of light-colored wood. There was a mobile over it with different-colored lambs hanging from it. "Not too original," Ardis said, "but it was the best I could find. . . . Do you like lambs, Minnie?"

Minne reached out and touched one of them. "I guess she does," Ardis said. She took the baby around the room, showing her everything. Maddy liked the way she handled her. She was relaxed and friendly.

"Are you going to take care of her while Mr. Edelman is at work?" she asked.

Ardis laughed. "Goodness no . . . I don't think I could go back to this stage. My girls are both in college. Anyway, I have a job."

"What do you do?" Maddy asked.

"I work for a computer firm in Syracuse."

Maddy was impressed. Computers always scared her, even the idea of them. "My brother does something with computers," she offered.

"Oh? What does he do?"

Maddy thought. Her brother had explained it once. "I can't remember," she said. She hesitated. "Did you meet the woman who's going to look after Minnie?" she asked.

"Oh sure," Ardis said. "I helped Mish pick her. He was all in a classic male quandary—what if he picked the wrong person? He's a real Jewish mother. . . . No, she's a terrific lady, adores babies, the kind who really prefers them when they're under five. I'm sure she'd love it if you came over sometime."

"I wasn't sure if I should," Maddy said.

Ardis frowned. "Yes, I see what you mean. . . . Well, but call anyway, just to see how things are going." She lowered her voice. "But you're so lucky about finding Misha. He's the most wonderful, loving man. He'll be a sensational father. I just know it."

"He had a family once," Maddy said, "only they were in an accident."

"Yes, I know. . . . His wife was my sister."

"Oh." Maddy felt awful. "I'm sorry."

Seeing the crib, Maddy remembered something she had not thought of for years, something she had completely forgotten. When she was one year old, her mother had had another baby, a girl. She had lived a year and a half and then died of pneumonia. Maddy shared a room with her—Daisy was her name—and because she was so young when the baby died, she wasn't allowed to go to the funeral and only vaguely understood when they told her the baby had gone away and wouldn't come back. The morning after the baby's death, she had waked up and looked at the crib, which was in the corner of the room. The room was the same size this room was and the crib was just in the corner like that. Maddy had gotten out of bed and looked in the crib; the baby wasn't there. She woke up her mother and her mother got angry and then started to cry and explained again about the baby not coming back. After that every morning for a month Maddy would wake up and go quietly over to the crib, expecting that the baby would be there; she never was. Finally they took the crib out of the room and gave it away, putting a bureau in its place. But for a year afterward, whenever Maddy looked at the bureau, she saw the crib in her mind. She even in some way thought the bureau *was* the crib and once opened all the drawers, as though expecting Daisy to be in one of them. She didn't remember now when she had stopped thinking about it. It was as though the memory of the baby had faded completely, but what came back to her now was that feeling, a scared, quiet feeling when she would look through the slats of the crib, expecting the baby to be there, and not find her.

Ardis turned away. She walked with the baby out to the yard where Misha was standing talking with Vonni, Luther, and Jed.

"How does she like the room?" Mr. Edelman asked.

"She loves it," Ardis said. She handed him the baby. "Okay, Daddy, there you go."

Misha looked awkward, but he held the baby, who, luckily, didn't cry, just reached out and grabbed a fistful of his hair. "Ouch," he said.

"Minnie, don't," Maddy reprimanded her, taking her hand away.

"Oh, that's okay," he said good-humoredly. "It doesn't hurt."

They all got back in the truck again. This time Vonni got in the front with Luther and Maddy got in the back with Jed. They waved at Ardis and Mr. Edelman, who stood in the yard. The baby watched them go, but didn't cry.

Maddy felt a hollow, strange, light feeling, unlike anything she'd ever felt. She realized part of her had wanted the baby to cry, to scream with rage at what was happening. But she didn't know what was happening. Would she ever know?

"Wow, that lady was *really* stacked," Luther said appreciatively. "Is she his girlfriend? Not bad for an old guy like that."

"She's his sister-in-law," Maddy said.

"Oh well, that doesn't mean anything," Luther said. "Incest is a big thing nowadays."

"You know, you two were really rude," Vonni said, "staring at her boobs that way. What do you think she thought?"

"Aw, she knows she has a good figure. . . . What's the point in having them if no one admires them?"

"I don't get what's so great about breasts," Vonni said. "What *is* it?"

"It's the shape," Jed said. "They're so soft and squishy and round."

"Yeah, but say, like instead of being where they are," Vonni said, "they were somewhere else completely different, like on your knees . . . or say one was on your knee and one was on the back of your neck. Would they still be just as terrific?"

"Boy, I hope I never meet a lady like *that!*" Jed said. "With one on her knee and one on her neck!"

"Yeah, but why wouldn't they be just as nice?" Vonni pursued. "They'd still be soft and squishy."

"Look, nature put them in the right place," Jed said. "Why argue with it?"

"Yeah," Luther said. "Like, Von, say some guy had a penis coming out of his bellybutton?"

"Ugh," Vonni said.

"She's not the one who's going to take care of the baby," Maddy said. She'd only been vaguely following their conversation.

"Who?" Vonni said.

"That lady, Ardis. . . . They hired someone else, but she said she was really nice."

"I think *he's* nice," Vonni said. "He's more like a grandfather, though. He's friendly."

"Do you think the baby will be happy?" Maddy asked.

There was a pause.

"Sure," Vonni said. "Why not?"

"Yeah, she'll be happy," Luther said.

"She didn't cry or anything when we left," Jed pointed out.

That was all any of them had to say on the subject. In the back of the truck was a very large pillow, like three pillows in one, flung to one side. Jed leaned back on it and took Maddy in his arms. She leaned against him, grateful for the physical warmth of his body. She knew she looked pretty today. She was wearing a new pair of light pink jeans and a pink-and-white-checkered gingham shirt, both recent acquisitions. Her hair was growing longer—it grazed her shoulders now—and she had brushed it to the side and fastened it with a gold barrette. It was as though, getting Minnie ready, she had felt she had to ready herself too, as though both of them were going to be given away.

Lying there, sleepily, Maddy thought of that morning. Minnie had waked up early, around six. She had not been noisy, had just lain in her bed making soft conversational sounds, but Maddy, who had slept restlessly all night, heard her and, getting up, took her into the bathroom to give her a bath. Minnie was at an age when she liked her bath. She splashed happily, pounding the water with her palms. The only tricky part was washing her hair. Maddy had learned to use just a little shampoo and then to trick Minnie into leaning back in her arms so that she could rinse the soap out without it getting into her eyes. Once Minnie had sat forward abruptly, the soapy water had gotten in her eyes, and she had screamed for a long time with rage and indignation. But now she allowed herself to be tilted back, while Maddy spoke to her softly and gently, saying, "See how much hair you have now, Minnie? See how nice and curly it's going to be? And you're going to have a purple ribbon to match your dress because you want to look special for Mr. Edelman." Even though Minnie couldn't understand anything Maddy was saying, Maddy explained everything that was going to happen to her that day. She explained why they had decided to give her away and how it had nothing to do with her not being a good baby. She described what a wonderful life Minnie would have with Mr. Edelman, what a kind, good man he was and how he would buy her beautiful toys and take good care of her. But Maddy could hardly talk. She felt it took all her will power to keep from breaking down and sobbing and hugging the wet, soapy baby as hard as she could. What if she was making a terrible mistake? Drying her off, Maddy hugged her close, wishing the baby could be inside her again, where no one could take her away, where they would be one forever. "Sometimes I'll come to visit you," Maddy told her, "but even if I don't, remember that I'll always be thinking about you. Always. For the rest of my life." The baby looked at her curiously. Maddy felt that somehow the message had gotten across.

Jed stroked her hair meditatively, as though he sensed she needed comforting, and she felt as though she were the baby and he were the mother, cuddling her, taking care of her. It was a good feeling. Then Vonni turned around. "Hey, none of that!" she said good-naturedly. To Luther she added, "The minute our backs are turned! You just can't trust kids these days."

"Give 'em an inch," Luther said. He was stopping for a light and looked around himself. "You know where that kind of thing gets you, don't you?"

Maddy and Jed laughed self-consciously; they knew.

Back at the house, they sat around awhile and then Jed and Luther drove into town to get the *Rocky Horror* tickets and some takeout Chinese food. Maddy went up to the room she and Jed had stayed in on their wedding night. Vonni said no one had been in it since then. "We don't even go into half the rooms," she said.

"Are you going to keep the job for next year too?" Maddy asked.

"No, I don't think so," Vonni said. "You know what I think I might do, Mad? I'm thinking of becoming a landscape gardener. I learned a lot, taking care of this guy's garden. There was someone who came over to do part of it and he taught me a lot. He said there's a school where you can get a real degree in all that."

"I should do something like that," Maddy said. "Maybe go to beauty school or something."

"Is that what you want to do?" Vonni said.

"Maybe," Maddy said.

"I couldn't stand a job where I'd be indoors all day," Vonni said. "Anyhow, do you really like cutting ladies' hair and all that?"

"I haven't really done it," Maddy admitted. "May won't let me because there's a law. You have to have a degree. . . . But I think I know how just from watching her." Suddenly she turned away. "I miss the baby," she said.

Vonni went over and patted her awkwardly on the shoulder. "You can always have another one . . . eventually," she said.

"Yeah," Maddy said. "I don't think Jed likes babies that much."

"I meant when you're older, like twenty-three or four."

That seemed impossibly far off to Maddy. Where would she be at twenty-three and what would she be doing?

They ate in the large dining room, sliding the paper containers of the Chinese food back and forth. "The Chinese have two good things," Luther said. "Food and girls."

"What do you know about Chinese girls?" Vonni asked suspiciously, gnawing on a barbecued spare rib.

He blushed. "Oh, just that woman who adds up what you have to pay. . . . She has such pretty long black hair. It's like silk."

"She wasn't that pretty," Jed said. "Some of the waitresses were, though."

"Boy, you two are really something," Vonni said. "Here we don't even notice other guys and you're gaping hornily at everyone who passes by."

"Oh, you notice," Luther said.

"I do not!"

"How about that guy who came around the other day to fix the porch?"

Vonni grinned. "Yeah, he was kind of cute, wasn't he? Guys with freckles are really cute."

"Freckles!" Luther snorted.

To get dressed for *Rocky Horror* Vonni really did herself up. She changed into bright purple shiny overalls, which hung so loosely on her skinny body that you could see right down to her breasts. With her Frye boots, a black cowboy hat, a lot of purple eyeshadow, and three tiny gold stars pasted on her forehead, she was a striking figure.

"What're the stars for?" Jed asked, touching one of them.

"Because I'm good," Vonni said haughtily.

He grinned. "At what?"

"Everything!"

Vonni offered to lend Maddy some makeup and clothes, but Maddy decided to go the way she was. She did borrow Vonni's mascara and eyeshadow, though, and put some pink lip gloss that smelled of strawberries on her lips. "Your hair is really pretty that way," Vonni said as Maddy brushed it. "Are you going to let it grow long?"

"Maybe," Maddy said. She liked the way her hair felt, silky and clean from having been washed that morning.

They got to the movie early and were able to get good seats, down toward the front. Maddy had seen the movie ten times. Sometimes she liked it and sometimes not, depending on her mood. Vonni thought Tim Curry was the sexiest man she'd ever seen. Maddy wasn't sure. Or at least he wasn't sexy in a way that made you wish you might some day meet someone like that in real life, like Timothy Hutton. Tim Curry was sexy in a scary way that made her nervous, even at the remove of the movie screen. Maddy always felt mixed about the story too. She knew you were supposed to make fun of Janet and Brad and yell "Vice!" (because Janet's last name was Weiss) and "Asshole!" when their names were mentioned, but, despite herself, Maddy felt sorry for them. She knew, too, that you weren't supposed to take anything in the movie seriously, but she did. She felt scared, just as Janet did, when they arrived at the haunted-looking castle in the rain with all those strange people. And when Eddie was killed and served up as a roast for dinner, Maddy always had to look away, though she knew it was just a regular roast and not a person.

This time, however, they all got stoned right from the beginning. Maddy remembered how on her wedding night everyone had been stoned but her and how left out she had felt at all the jokes that struck the three of them as hilarious. This time she took a deep puff every time the joint came to her, inhaling as much as she could. The trouble was that after about twenty minutes she felt so uncontrollably sleepy that she couldn't keep her eyes open. She would open them for a minute or two and then they would clamp shut again. It seemed to her she knew she was in a theater, watching a movie, but part of the time it was as though she were in the movie or dreaming part of it. Her head rested on Jed's shoulder, and she slept.

When she came to, she discovered to her intense embarrassment that her head was resting on Luther's shoulder. She couldn't remember how that had happened. She looked at him, confused. "I'm really sorry," she said.

He squeezed her hand. "That's okay," he said with a smile.

Driving back to the house, everything continued to seem strange and confused to Maddy. Though she knew it wasn't possible, she had the feeling that what was happening had already happened and she was just lying in bed remembering it. She stumbled out of the truck and into the living room. Vonni came in and lay down flat on her back, her arms outstretched over her head. "Wow, that stuff was strong," she said.

"But good," Jed said.

He and Luther just stood there, side by side, looking awkward.

"Okay, ladies," Luther said. "We have, like, this proposition we want to offer you."

"Only good for one night," Jed said.

"Oh boy," Vonni sighed. "What now?"

"You explain," Luther said to Jed.

Jed grinned. "Lost your nerve?"

"No, I just . . . Okay, well, listen, here's what we thought. . . . Seeing as how we're all good friends and stuff, we thought maybe just for tonight we might rearrange things in terms of . . ." He stopped, flustered. "Am I explaining it right?"

"We thought—" Jed began, but Vonni interrupted. "We get it . . . Boy, you two are something. Don't you ever think of anything besides sex?"

"Rarely," Jed said.

"So, how about it?" Luther said.

Terror-stricken, Maddy prayed they were joking or that Vonni would say they were total idiots and she wouldn't hear of such a thing.

"Well, just for one night," Vonni said. "That's it, and listen, I am completely zonked, so this is not going to be some huge orgy or anything you've been concocting. . . . Once, that's it, and then I'm going to sleep."

Jed laughed. "Orgy? Who's talking about orgies?"

She sat up and then went over to him. "Okay, here I am," she said, taking a gold star off her forehead and pasting it on his. "Do with me what you will." They started upstairs together, hand in hand.

Maddy, sitting on the floor, felt stunned. The image of Jed and Vonni walking up the stairs, hand in hand, kept replaying itself over and over in her mind. She wanted to run screaming up the stairs and tell them they couldn't do what she knew they were going to do. How could they? Her husband! Her best friend! And why was Luther just sitting there, ill at ease, but otherwise perfectly calm? Why wasn't he horrified too? "We don't have to do anything if you don't want," he said softly.

That remark reassured Maddy. Maybe it was what Jed was saying to Vonni too, admitting it had all been a joke. "I feel sort of funny," she said. "I think maybe I smoked too much of that stuff."

"I'll carry you upstairs," Luther said and, without waiting for her reply, scooped her up and carried her up the stairs and into the bedroom he shared with Vonni. There was a big bed in the center of the room, not made. Luther deposited Maddy on the bed.

"I need to go to the bathroom," she stammered.

In the bathroom all of Vonni's cosmetics were strewn around. Maddy saw the lip gloss she had put on earlier. She picked it up and sniffed it. Then suddenly, leaning against the sink, she began to choke. She tried to catch her breath, but couldn't. Panting like a dog, her mouth open, drooling, she leaned against the wall. She was so stoned that, even in her terror and nausea, nothing seemed quite real. The walls moved closer and then farther away. Maybe she was still in the movie! Soon she would wake up and find herself in the truck, riding home, her head on Jed's shoulder. Maddy wanted to move quickly to that point, to bring it closer, but how?

When she came back into the bedroom, Luther was lying naked on the bed, his arms under his head. His penis was sticking straight up in the air. Maddy looked at him carefully, then at his penis. She had read an article in one of the magazines at May's that you could tell about a man's whole personality by looking at his penis. Some of them looked mean, others friendly, others tender, others aggressive. She tried to remember what Jed's looked like but she couldn't. Maybe she'd never looked at it. Luther was taller and heavier than Jed. His hair was fuzzier and blonder.

"Do you want to lie down?" Luther asked tentatively, seeming disconcerted by her stare.

"What?" Maddy said. She was swaying back and forth slightly as the room spun on its own peculiar axis.

"Do you want to take your clothes off?"

Maddy collapsed on the bed, with her clothes on. She turned to Luther, who began to remove them slowly and carefully, like a parent undressing a child. When she was completely undressed, he looked at her with a blurry, adoring expression. "You're so beautiful, Maddy!" he said.

"Am I?" Maddy said, feeling, for the first time, nervous and almost aware of what was happening. But it was like giving the baby away. It was as though between what was happening and herself was a slight protective distance that made it like watching a movie, not that threatening. Luther began kissing her body from head to foot. He kissed her toes even! As he kissed her, he made murmuring sounds and kept talking all the time. This was so unlike Jed, who never talked at all, that Maddy was disconcerted, though fascinated. He praised all the parts of her body, said she was soft and silky and smelled wonderful and had marvelous nipples and gorgeous elbows. No one had ever noticed her elbows before! He even seemed to like her bellybutton and licked it carefully, as though there were honey in it, like an anteater. She saw the two of them and his words in balloons over his head, like someone in a cartoon strip.

"Does that feel good?" he kept asking. "Do you like that, Maddy?"

It did feel good, to the extent that she could concentrate on it, and yet it seemed funny at the same time and once she giggled and tried to stop because she was afraid he might be mad. "What's funny?" he said tenderly, touching her laughing mouth.

"I don't know," Maddy admitted.

"Do you want to do it?" he asked. "Are you ready?"

It seemed to Maddy that to not do it when he had labored so long and lovingly over each inch of her body would have been terrible, like not buying a pair of shoes when the shoe salesman had brought out twenty different pairs in every possible size and color. "Yes," she said. "I'm ready."

Even while they were doing it, Luther kept talking. He kept telling her she was wonderful and asking her if she was liking it. Maddy sensed that he didn't really require answers to most of these questions, they were more like a patter that was part of love-making for him.

And while he was moving inside her, the thought came floating through her head: Vonni and Jed are doing this too, right now. . . . But then the thought floated away again. It had no emotional content attached to it. Even when she finally came, it was a little as though it was someone else coming, someone else crying out, quivering, dissolving in pleasure. She felt she was Janet in the movie with Brad or with Frank or with Rocky, sometimes the scared, silly virgin, sometimes the abandoned, sexy harlot. Then she heard Luther cry and felt the two of them melt together in the final moment.

Lying in Luther's arms, Maddy felt calm and floating and serene. He was watching her intently with a worried expression. "Are you okay?" he said.

She wasn't sure what he meant. "Sure," she said.

"Did you, uh, like it?"

She nodded.

"I didn't seem too big to you?"

"In what way?" Maddy asked.

"Vonni sometimes says I'm too big."

"Oh," Maddy said. She tried to focus on the meaning of that sentence, but the words separated themselves and drifted apart before she could. Possibly Luther said something further, but she never knew what it was. The next time she thought anything it was six in the morning and she had just waked up.

The air coming in the window was mild, springlike. Getting out of bed, naked, Maddy went to the window and looked out at the green leafy landscape. The first thing she thought of was the baby. This was her first day without the baby, the baby's first day without her. Was she, right at this moment, waking up, looking around in the strange room, perhaps noticing the lambs on the mobile above her crib? First Maddy imagined the baby waking up and screaming with fear and anger at being in a strange place, screaming because Maddy wasn't there and she missed her so terribly. Mr. Edelman would rush in and try to comfort her, but the baby would remain inconsolable. But that image was too painful. Maddy changed it to another. The baby woke up, noticed the lambs, tried to touch one of them, and then, just as she was becoming aware she was hungry, Mr. Edelman, who had slept lightly, came in with a bottle. At first she was surprised to see him, but he changed her and gave her the bottle and she lay there, thinking of Maddy, but in a contented way.

"Maddy?" It was Luther. He was lying in bed under the sheet, watching her.

Maddy turned around. Seeing him, she remembered dimly what had happened the night before. But all she could remember were snatches of things—like Vonni pasting the gold star on Jed's forehead, Luther carrying her up the stairs, his licking the inside of her bellybutton. Had they made love? They must have, because she was aware of the smell of sex coming from her body, but, no matter how hard she tried, she couldn't remember anything about it. She felt self-conscious walking naked across the room with Luther watching her. She sat down on the edge of the bed.

He reached up and touched one of the heart-shaped gold earrings she had in her ears. "How do you feel?" he asked with a slightly worried look.

"I feel okay," Maddy said uncertainly. "Maybe I'll take a bath."

Lying in the warm bath, she felt better. Reality was closing in, but quietly, not with a rush, like novocaine wearing off after going to the dentist. She got dressed and, since Luther was waiting to take a shower, came down to the kitchen.

Vonni, in cutoff denim shorts and a wrinkled white T-shirt, barefoot, was cooking Sizzlean on a cast-iron griddle. She waved at Maddy as she came in. Jed was sitting at the kitchen table, busily eating cornflakes. "Hi," he said, looking at her and then quickly away.

"Hi," Maddy said. She realized she was hungry and waited while Vonni fried eggs and made toast. No one talked about what had happened, which was a relief to Maddy. It seemed easier not to think about it at all.

After breakfast they went down to the pool. Vonni and Luther had cleaned the pool and filled it because the couple who owned the house were coming back in June. It was a suddenly, unexpectedly warm day. Maddy put her fingers in the water. It was cold. But Jed and Luther took their clothes off and jumped in. They began splashing and ducking each other. Maddy lay down next to Vonni on the big double chaise longue. They spread a towel over themselves like a blanket.

"When are they going to grow up?" Vonni said, watching them.

The two boys got up on the diving board and began posing as though they were beauty queens. "Too bad you don't have your camera, Von," Luther said. "You could take our picture and send it in to *Playgirl.*"

"Sure, and they'd go out of business the next month," Vonni snapped.

"They don't appreciate us," Jed said, pretending to sob, heartbroken.

"Yeah, they do," Luther said. "They're just trying to conceal how horny they're getting looking at our gorgeous bodies."

Watching them, Maddy felt a sudden burst of hatred for both of them with their stupid horsing around. She hated Vonni almost as much, falling in with their jokes, as though nothing had happened, as though everything was the same as it always had been! It reminded her of how excluded she used to feel when she and Jed had first started going together and the three of them had so many in-jokes, so many memories from times when they had grown up together. She had felt she would always be an outsider, accepted by Vonni and Luther just because Jed had chosen her, but not really belonging. And now it seemed to her she had never belonged, not to Vonni or Luther or even to Jed. She hated all of them. Feeling guilty about the intensity of her feelings, she turned aside.

Vonni rolled over and sighed. Maddy opened her eyes. Vonni's face was about two inches away from hers. She could see traces of purple eyeshadow from the night before. "How was it with Jed?"

she asked in a whisper, the question feeling like a knife in her heart.

"It was . . ." Vonni didn't seem to know what word to use. "I guess it was a dumb idea," she finished, closing her eyes.

Maddy lay there, feeling the sun, waiting for the bubbles of anger and hatred to sink inside her. Half opening her eyes, she watched Jed and Luther, who were still fooling in the water, chasing from one end of the pool to the other. Oh, how she wished she could hurt Jed, really hurt him physically. She thought of how when she was young, her brothers, to tease her, used to hold her under water, grabbing her legs or sitting on her head. It had been so terrifying, feeling her lungs fill up, choking, afraid they wouldn't release her in time. And then that final moment when they did and she rose frantically to the surface, gasping for air. She imagined holding Jed under water like that. His face would turn purple, he would be unable to breathe, he would be afraid he was going to die, and still she would hold him under until the last moment, when she would let him go.

Then she felt Jed's hands on her shoulders. He began rubbing some sun-tan cream into her skin. For a second the feeling of his hands, the warm, sensual caress, was welcome. Then suddenly she jerked up, snatched the tube of cream out of his hands, and flung it into the bushes. "Stop that!" she screamed. "I don't want you to do that!"

Jed looked taken aback. "I just thought you might get burned," he said. "The sun's pretty strong."

"So what?" Maddy said in the same loud voice. "So I get burned! What do you care?"

"Maddy, I—"

"Go away!" she said. "Don't touch me . . . I'll kill you if you touch me again."

She knew the three of them were watching her in amazement and she didn't care. She felt shriveled into herself, hating herself as much as she hated them. Why had she gotten so stoned the night before? If she had been herself, she would never have gone along with their plan, their evil, dumb joke. But she had wanted to be stoned to still the pain of giving the baby away, she had wanted it as an anesthetic, and, in a way, it had worked. Except now she had nothing, no baby, no husband, no self, even.

The knowledge that her marriage was over came to Maddy with a cool, flat feeling, like the moment when a movie changes from color to black and white. It seemed as though the knowledge had been in her for a long time, somewhere beneath the surface, and suddenly had risen to the level of her consciousness. But her lack of surprise made her feel that she had known it before. It reminded her of the moment, as a child, when she had felt, for the first time, that she and everyone she knew would one day die, a knowledge that pierced through and vanished.

Eventually Jed and Luther got out of the pool and dressed. Vonni made sandwiches and they had a picnic lunch. After that Luther said he would drive them home.

Maddy sat between Luther and Jed on the drive home, hardly speaking, gazing out at the lake, which was so blue and clear that it was like the picture postcard they sold at the drugstore in town.

"What a gorgeous day," Luther said, driving with one arm over the seat, around Maddy, but not actually touching her.

"Yeah, I was really getting sick of winter," Jed said.

They talked about various things, while Maddy sat silently between them, aware in a dim way of their bodies touching her on either side, but recoiling. Her anger had cooled to a terrible dead feeling of desolation and despair. If the truck had caught fire and they had all burned to death, she felt she wouldn't have cared at all. "How come you're so quiet?" Luther asked.

"I don't know," Maddy said.

"She's thinking about the baby," Jed explained, and that surprised Maddy because she hadn't been, at that exact moment, and yet the knowledge of the baby's absence had been surrounding her all morning.

"You'll probably have ten kids by the time you're done," Luther said good-naturedly.

"Ten!" Jed said. "Bite your tongue!"

Luther pretended to bite his tongue.

When they were home, Jed helped Maddy out of the truck. Paul and Gerry were sitting outside, reading, their little boy playing next to them. "How do you like this day?" Paul called.

"It's great," Jed said.

"Come on out and join us," he said. "It's too nice to stay indoors."

"In a little while," Jed said.

They went into the quiet room, which looked unusually neat, the bed made. "I'm going to go for a walk," Jed said. "Want to come?"

"No, I'll stay here," Maddy said. She sat on the edge of the bed, watching him walk down the hill toward the lake.

Twelve

Spring and summer seemed to have come together, entwined. The weather darted from mild days in the fifties to days that veered over eighty with hot sun and cool breezes off the lake. It was easy now finding places to make love out-of-doors, away from the campus, safe places. Jed and Capri met outside town and walked to small beaches, enclosed and set back, along the lake. Sometimes they went into the woods, even though the lake was quiet—it was too early for motorboats or water-skiers.

"You were going to swim across," Jed reminded her.

"I know, but it's freezing! Have you tried it?"

He ran a hand down her stomach. "I thought you were such an Amazon," he teased.

"I'm out of training."

And, in fact, her body, which had been so tanned and muscular-looking when he first met her, was white and soft. "I tan fast," she said. "Anyhow I've always hated just lying in the sun, roasting, the way some girls do. Who cares what color you are?"

Once, just after they had finished making love, there was a noise down below and they saw one of Capri's professors, a woman, walking her two dogs, a Saint Bernard and an Irish setter. The setter was running wildly along the beach and zoomed into the woods. Seeing Capri and Jed, he perked up his ears and came over. In a friendly way he licked Capri's leg, allowed himself to be scratched behind the ears, and darted off.

"Albie!" the woman's voice came from below. "Albie, where are you?"

"Her husband just left her," Capri said. "He works in Rochester and he had a girlfriend there. She found out and kicked him out."

"How do you know?"

"Everyone knows."

"Harsh treatment," he joked.

"Why harsh? I'd do the same thing. . . . Not that anyone would ever be unfaithful to me." She grinned.

It was true, he couldn't imagine someone being, but, to tease her, he said, "Sure now, but how about when you're that age, forty something?"

"I'll be great at forty," Capri said, stretching back. "In my prime . . . and I'll have young lovers who'll admire me for my fantastic achievements."

"Which ones?"

"I don't know . . . I'll discover something amazing, a cure for cancer, maybe, or some new operation."

"You're really going to be a doctor?"

"Yeah, why not? I want to be rich . . . I'll do good at the same time, but I don't want to slog along at some nothing job and 'work my way up' and grovel around for promotions. That sounds sick."

Jed looked at her. Most of the time they were together, he thought of them as equals. Sexually they were equals. But when she spoke of her future with that calm, unruffled confidence it angered him. It rested on so many privileges she'd had without even knowing they were there.

"How come you told my mother you wanted to be an astronaut?" she asked.

He smiled, remembering that lunch. "I used to think about it when I was a kid. I guess really I'd rather design the equipment."

"Why don't you?"

"Go to college?"

"Sure."

No one he knew had gone to college, except Garnet. A year ago, he'd have said he couldn't, that he had to support Maddy and the baby. "I'm not that smart," he blurted out.

"Yes, you are," she said.

"How do you know?"

"I know! . . . Listen, I'm a supremely intolerant person. Most people's minds are mush. You know how to think. You ought to use it."

He was flattered, but wondered if this was just some way of her trying to bridge the gap between them, as though it were more justified for her to have wasted this much time with him because he was, after all, smart. They never discussed their future together. He assumed she would go away over the summer and be back in the fall. He knew he could keep his job as long as he wanted. But *was* that what he wanted? Fucking her on the side, even if he and Maddy weren't together?

He had told Capri about their giving the baby up for adoption. That was how he'd put it. He'd lied a little, saying they had brought the baby to an agency in Auburn and that she had been adopted by a young couple who hadn't been able to have children, but could afford to operate on the baby's eyes.

"That's nice of you," Capri said casually. After a moment she added, "I was pregnant once and thought of doing that, but then, I don't know, it seemed hard—lugging the kid around in your stomach for nine months just to give it up once it became a real person."

"So, what'd you do?"

"I had a miscarriage. . . . It was weird. That guy I told you about, Sam, we were screwing and I had these pains, I thought it was my period starting and then this thing came out of me, like this lump . . . and no more baby! I think the baby knew it had picked the wrong incubator."

Jed sighed. If only babies had the sense to know whom to pick! If only they did implant themselves only in women who wanted them, who were ready!

"Do you miss her?" Capri asked.

He was silent a moment. "No," he admitted.

268

In fact, if he had to compare it to anything, the silence at home was like living near a construction site and suddenly having the drilling stop. He woke up to birds singing. But he had the feeling Maddy thought about it more. Often when he woke up, no matter how early, she was already up, staring at the ceiling or sitting in the armchair in the corner, looking out the window. She seemed very quiet now, and thin, almost waiflike. And he wondered if handing her over to Luther that night had been such a great idea. Luther had been the one who brought it up and Jed had always liked Vonni. He had fun with her—she'd try anything, and her mocking way of pretending she was hating every minute of it was a reverse turn-on. The first time they did it, she'd worn the cowboy hat and sat on him, saying, "Okay, you have five minutes to make me come, and then I'm going to sleep." But when it went on longer than five, she hadn't seemed to mind.

He wondered if Capri would be jealous if she knew. She was so unpredictable in her reactions. Sometimes when they met, she would say, "I've been thinking about you all day, it must be spring fever . . . I just can't think of anything else!" Other times she'd bring her books and start studying five minutes after they were finished or ask him to quiz her on exam questions.

"You'll do well," he said. "What does it matter?"

"I want to show Daddy," she said. "I want to get all A's."

"Why do you care about him so much?" Jed still felt angry whenever he thought of her father.

"I shouldn't, you're right. . . . But winning his approval means something to me, still."

Whenever Jed saw Thornie, especially when he was with Maddy, he felt awkward. Thornie always smiled at the two of them benevolently. Jed knew he thought everything was fine between them, that whatever college girl Jed had gotten into trouble with was a figment of the past. Thornie and May invited them for dinner, and the two of them, it seemed to Jed, hovered around Maddy, telling her how pretty she'd gotten. Maybe they were just sorry for her for having given up the baby. Their eight-year-old daughter, Winnie, sat on Maddy's lap and let Maddy fix her hair in a special way. Maddy braided the hair carefully and slowly, and after that she and the child went down to the lake and skipped stones.

"Maddy talked about going to beauty school," May said, helping Jed to more potato salad. "That's a good idea. She's good with her hands."

"Yeah, I think she'd be good," he said without thinking.

"If you have a family or not, you need the wife working these days," Thornie said. "We couldn't hardly make it without what May brings in."

May laughed heartily. "He married me for my gorgeous figure, and now he's ended up with a business lady."

"Oh, I knew what I was getting," Thornie said, with laconic good humor.

Sitting in their back yard, with several half-grown children zooming back and forth, Jed thought this was the kind of family he'd dimly imagined he'd have, if he'd ever thought of having one. Yet he'd never thought it would be something hard to achieve. He'd always thought people got married, had kids, it worked out. Now he wondered if it was some talent he just didn't have, the way neither of his parents had either. And he couldn't help wondering, as he looked at May, who verged on stoutness but seemed self-confident and jolly, what was their sex life like? Was it all Thornie ever wanted or needed, just coming home for fifteen or twenty years, however long they'd been together, and climbing on top of the same woman? The noise from the kids, the endless responsibility of raising them—didn't that ever get to him? Didn't he have fantasies of just clearing out, starting over? Maybe not. Vonni and Luther would probably be together in fifteen years, even if it was hard to imagine them with four kids.

He looked at Maddy, down by the lake with the little girl. She was good with kids. Maybe he could've just lived through it, gotten her pregnant again, had someone like Capri on the side. . . . But that wasn't what he wanted. Yet what he did want seemed unclear.

Back at the house, when they were alone, he said, "We could drive down and see Vonni and Luther tomorrow."

"I'm going to visit my parents," Maddy said quickly.

"Oh . . . okay . . . listen, Mad, I'm sorry about that night when we—"

"It's okay," Maddy interrupted him. She was looking at the floor. "I know you've always liked Vonni."

"No, really, it was Luther's idea . . . I guess he's always kind of had this thing about you."

Maddy accepted this tribute impassively. "He's a nice person," she said finally.

Jed tried to imagine Maddy and Luther in bed together and what it had been like, but couldn't.

"I'm not sure if we did it, actually," she said, frowning. "I guess we must've, but I don't remember."

Jed looked at her, puzzled. That would have been strange—if, after Luther had gone through that whole deal setting it up, they hadn't even done it. And yet in some way Luther always seemed to put Maddy on a pedestal, maybe her being a mother, being slightly shy. "We didn't do it either," he was amazed to hear himself saying. "Vonni just wasn't in the mood."

Maddy looked up at him shyly, pleased. "I'm glad," she said. "I would have felt terrible if you'd done it, even just for a joke."

Jed felt awful. Why had he lied? How stupid! "She doesn't even have much of a figure," he felt forced to elaborate. "She's too skinny."

Later he wondered why, in almost every conversation they had, some degree of lying entered in, whether for good motives or bad.

"Jed, I wondered if I could talk to you a minute," Mr. Edelman said.

Every time an older man, especially one who was in an authority position, requested a private meeting with Jed, he knew he was in trouble. And yet, in this case, he couldn't, for the life of him, figure out what it could be—unless it was that Edelman had suddenly gotten sick of the baby and wanted to give it back. That seemed unlikely, if only because in the six weeks since Edelman had taken over the kid, he'd come in every Saturday, cornering Jed with glowing reports about how terrific she was, how smart, how beautiful, and how well everything was going. It was almost as though he wanted to convince Jed that it was all right, as though he thought Jed was lying awake at night worrying about whether the baby was doing well. Actually, all the conversations annoyed Jed. He didn't want to hear anything about it. He wanted, basically, to pretend the baby had never existed, had vanished in a cloud of smoke. Probably something of this had gotten across to Edelman, because lately he hadn't come over so much.

As they walked to the office, various possibilities raced through Jed's mind. The baby had been killed? They had taken her to the doctor and discovered she had some rare, weird disease that it would cost millions to cure and Edelman didn't think he could handle it?

Edelman closed the door to his office. It was a gray, warm day in mid-June. "I don't exactly know how to put this," he began.

Jed just looked at him, trying to look calm and unaccused.

"I guess you realized, Jed, or maybe you don't, what a difference having Minnie has meant in my life. It's been—well, it's changed everything for me. I feel like I'm not even the same person! And I'll always be grateful to you and your wife for having thought of me when you realized you wanted to offer her up for adoption."

"That's okay," Jed said uncomfortably, wondering where this was leading.

"Well, to make a long story short, I'd really like to somehow—well, not repay you because I don't think that's possible, but I wanted to offer you both some kind of gift, just to indicate how I feel, and I guess the only thing I could come up with was— How would you like one of the cars?"

"One of your cars?"

"Yeah . . . I thought maybe you could just pick out any one, whichever one you like best, and take it home. I've noticed yours looks a little the worse for wear." He smiled.

Jed felt there must be some catch to this that he hadn't heard. "You mean, free? Any car I want?"

"Right . . . I thought—you've always seemed to admire the

Camaro. I don't know if that's the ideal family car, but now that it's just the two of you—"

He had still, incredibly, not sold the Camaro, simply, Jed knew, because he wouldn't bring the price down from six thousand. Homer said, "It's worth eight. . . . It's in perfect shape. I won't let him take a penny less than six." It was like someone handing him six thousand dollars! For no reason! Christ, he would have paid to get the baby off his hands. He certainly hadn't expected a reward. Yet he felt touched at Edelman's gesture and wished he could express his gratitude without sounding mushy or dumb. "Wow, that's really nice of you," he blurted out.

"Look, a car is a car. . . . It's not a human being. It's not a fair exchange in any way. I realize that. But I wanted to make some gesture and this is the best I could come up with. But why don't you take a look at all of them and tonight, when you're going home, I'll give you the keys. You can keep it for a week and see how it drives, whether you like the feel of it. If it doesn't work out, bring it back next Saturday and you can pick another one, if you like."

Edelman stayed in his office while Jed, still dazed, walked out into the lot. He knew he would take the Camaro. He walked over to it slowly. He didn't look at it every time he came to work, but he was always aware of it. It was like a beautiful woman lying nude in the middle of the parking lot. Maybe the reason no one had bought it, apart from the price and the fact that most people wanted more sensible family-type cars, was that it was *too* classy-looking. It was like guys preferring to date a regularly pretty girl rather than someone who was a real knockout. Jed stood in front of it for a long time and finally, tentatively, reached out and touched it. Jesus.

On the way home, just getting into it, turning on the engine, settling back in the seat, he almost started to laugh. His heart was beating like a tom-tom. He had the feeling it must be a joke. The guy must be crazy. Giving away a six-thousand-dollar car because someone had given you a cross-eyed baby? Jed would have liked to drive fast, to take it along a stretch and let it go up to seventy or eighty, but then he thought: sure, crash it the first day you have it. Don't be dumb. So he drove carefully, keeping in the speed limit, except for one stretch just before the village where there was rarely any traffic. There he let it go up to sixty-five and then, as the village approached, he eased back down again. Driving into town, he felt conspicuous, absurd. He half wanted someone—Craig, Thornie—to see him and half didn't. Because it was such a gray, misty day, the red of the car seemed to gleam like a beacon. Slowly, he drove it up the driveway and parked it in front of the house. He leaped out.

Maddy was fixing dinner. "Hi," she said, half-turning.

Jed grabbed her arm. "Mad, come quick! You've got to see this!"

"See what?"

"Just come." He pulled her out the door.

She stood beside him, looking at the car. "Where did you get it?" She looked worried, as though afraid he might have stolen it.

"Edelman gave it to us as a present." He decided not to add anything about the baby.

"It's pretty," Maddy said. "Red is a nice color." But she seemed somehow unimpressed and turned to go back into the house. Jed followed her.

"I couldn't believe it," he said. "It's worth six thousand dollars! It's just a fantastic car."

"He doesn't want any money for it?" Maddy asked, going back to the hamburgers.

"No!"

"I guess it must be because you worked so hard for him and he couldn't pay you that much," she said. "Like a reward."

Jed wanted to tell her that had nothing to do with it, but he couldn't. He just sat near the window, staring out at the car, wishing some of his excitement was communicable to her. "Maybe we can take a drive after dinner," he suggested finally.

"Sure," Maddy said. "That would be nice."

But after dinner the rain started in harder and they never went for a drive. They waited until the weekend, when the sun came out. "Why don't we drive part way to Ithaca?" Jed suggested.

"All right," Maddy said. She got into the car and sat back carefully in the cushiony seat. She touched the material the seat was made of, smoothing it with her hand. "It's soft," she said admiringly.

But the drive was, somehow, a failure. Maddy sat quietly in her seat, gazing out at the lake, and Jed knew she could just as well have been at home or sitting in a bus. It didn't matter to her, it wasn't important. It was almost the way she was about sex. She was there because he had asked her to be. The car was important because he felt it was. And he felt disappointed that he could never really bring her closer to sharing what he felt.

"I got a letter from Jarita," Maddy said.

"Yeah?"

"She sent me a plane ticket. She wants me to come visit her."

"Are you going to?"

"I thought I might. . . . She has time off for a few weeks. She said she could show me the city."

"I've heard it's a nice place . . . Craig used to live there."

"I know . . . Jarita loves it now. She says she wouldn't move back east for anything." She paused to look at him. "Is that okay, if I go?"

"Sure," Jed said. "You deserve a vacation."

"I guess you'll be glad to get rid of me," she said with a funny, bitter laugh.

Ever since that night with the four of them, she had seemed more withdrawn. They never made love, even perfunctorily. When he touched her once, she shrank away. "No, not especially," he said.

"It's like we're not even married," she said desperately.

What did she mean? Had it ever seemed as though they were? Did she know about Capri? Jed had a sudden fear that she was going to say she had known all along. Then he thought: What does it matter? What if she knows? But for some reason he still didn't want her to know. "Well, I think it's—" he began.

"So, do you want to get divorced?" she said. She looked scared, either at her own boldness at bringing it up or for fear he would say yes.

Jed looked away. "Maybe we might as well," he said slowly, relieved she had been the one to bring it up.

"But then, why did we give the baby away?" Maddy cried.

"What's that got to do with it?"

"I gave her away so we'd be happy, like everyone else. I thought that was why you were acting so strange. . . . But you're still that way!"

"That's the way I am," he said, feeling desperate at the pain in her eyes and voice. "That's my personality."

"Then we shouldn't have gotten married!" She hunched over, as though struck down by this realization. "I—I thought we loved each other."

Jed couldn't, despite himself, force out a lie about loving her. "Maybe you could get the baby back," he suggested.

"Just by myself? Raise her by myself?"

"Some girls do."

"But didn't you love her a little, even?" Maddy said, sounding more puzzled than angry. "She was your baby! You were her father!"

"I didn't want to be anyone's father," he said. "Not now. Not at eighteen."

"That's selfish," Maddy said. "You don't love anybody."

"How do you know?"

She looked at him in amazement. After a moment she said, "Do you love somebody?"

In some way Jed wanted to tell her, if only to defend himself, but he said, "No, I don't love anybody."

"You love the car," she suggested ironically.

Jed smiled wryly, glad to veer off in any direction. "Yeah, it's a great car."

"I think cars are stupid," Maddy said, with such vehemence he was taken aback. "They're just big clumps of metal! Why do men love them? It's dumb!"

He shrugged.

"All they do is crash into things and kill people," she went on. "I *hate* cars!" The intensity of her anger was so extreme, for her, and so clearly directed at some unknown target that Jed didn't bother to reply. He just drove the two of them back to the house.

Maddy went inside and he stayed outside, looking at the Camaro. He felt too empty and depressed to even feel a vague exultation. In a way what he had wanted to happen was happening. He was being given back his freedom. The car was only a minor part of it. By the fall he would be free to do whatever he wanted, to screw around with a hundred girls, to move to another city, to go to college. And he knew that at some moment in the future he would wake up and savor that, enjoy it, even exult in it. But now, he felt far from exultation.

He thought, as he had often since she had made the remark, of Capri's claiming he was smart, that he should do something with his brains. Maybe he could! Maybe he would become an engineer, earn a lot of money someday, be a real part of the world Capri referred to so often and so casually. All this year it had always seemed something impossibly beyond his reach but now he wondered if that had to be true. Hell, he could marry her, even. Maybe not now, but in a couple of years. Her father would have a heart attack, but her mother liked him. He remembered her saying, "Maybe what we have you only get once." Their relationship was important to her too, though he knew she was too proud to ever hint at anything, ever ask him directly how he felt about her. She had final exams for a week, but after that they'd go for a drive and he would . . . Despite himself a small secret excitement began bubbling up in him.

The next week he drove the car everywhere. Craig couldn't believe he hadn't stolen it. "Come on, man, he *gave* you a car? A six-thousand-dollar car?"

"Sure, he likes me."

"You're going to get into big trouble. You know that, don't you?"

"Want to take a drive in it with me?"

"They'll throw me in jail with you."

Finally Jed explained the real story, how the car had been an exchange gift for the baby. But that didn't seem any more likely to Craig.

"You give him this *baby* and he gives you a six-thousand-dollar car? What is he—crazy?"

"Maybe."

"He's going to change his mind. He must've gotten drunk or something."

"I don't think so. . . . Look, do you want to drive with me or not? I have to go into Ithaca. Want to come?"

"Sure, why not?"

Driving with Craig was fun. Jed went as far over the speed limit as he thought he could get away with. "How do you like the way it drives?" he said.

Craig was slumped into the bucket seat, spaced out. "Listen, we've got to pick up two chicks. That's all we need. Then I'll know I've died and gone to heaven."

Jed thought of the waitress he had met when he was with Capri's mother and then thought maybe he should wait till Maddy was in San Francisco. "I know a good place we can have lunch," he couldn't resist saying. He parked as close to the front of the restaurant as he could.

The waitress wasn't there. Her replacement was pretty cute, but didn't come on half as strong. "Ginny?" she said. "She'll be in tomorrow. Are you a friend of hers?"

"Sort of," Jed said.

This one was tall and a little skinny, but she had nice legs. She didn't spill anything. "Will that be all?" she said as she brought their food.

"What else do you have to offer?" Craig said, tilting back in his chair.

"What did you have in mind?"

He grinned. "We thought you might want to come for a drive with us. My friend just got this new car." He pointed out the window.

The waitress glanced out at the car. "What'd—you steal it?"

"You want to go for a drive or not?"

"Okay. . . . Can my girlfriend come? I don't get off till four."

Craig looked at Jed.

"How about Ginny?" Jed said.

"What about her?"

"Could she come too?"

"She's not my friend." She looked uncertain. "My friend's nice."

"Sure, bring your friend," Craig said.

The friend, Martha, was short and round-faced with a million freckles and wiry red hair. She seemed most impressed with the car. "Hey, wow!" she said, her face lighting up. "You guys must be rich or something."

Craig pointed to Jed. "It's his."

"You must be college guys, right?" the tall waitress, Alice, asked. She got into the front seat next to Jed. The little redhead was next to Craig in the back.

"I'm in the engineering school," Jed ad-libbed.

"So was I!" said Martha, leaning forward. "I mean, I was an engineering major, but I dropped out for a year. It's a really tough program. . . . Are you too?" she asked Craig.

"No, I graduated," he said. "I work over at that women's college, Coolidge."

"I heard the girls there are real dummies," Martha said. "Just little rich girls who can't get into anyplace good."

"That's not true," Jed said. "They're smart."

"How do *you* know?" she pursued. *"He's* the one who teaches there."

"Hey, let's get some beer, okay?" Craig said.

He bought two six-packs and Jed drove to a semi-secluded place on the edge of the lake. Somehow he felt totally out of it; he didn't really care about either of the girls, and wondered if the outing hadn't been a mistake. He drank some beer and it relaxed him a little. Martha, despite her small size, put away three cans of beer. "I love beer," she explained, stretching. "And I love June. That's my favorite month."

"Me too," Craig said. "It's my birthday month."

"Oh, you're Gemini," Martha said. "Do you have a split personality?"

"Sure," Craig said. "Doesn't everybody?"

"Really, it's not the month," she said. "You have to know the exact *hour* you were born. My sister had a friend who could do your whole whatever you call it. She said she married the wrong person without even *knowing* it! But it turned out his sun wasn't in her moon or something."

"Is your sun in my moon?" Craig said, tickling her arm with a piece of grass.

"Time will tell." Then, without warning, she pulled her T-shirt over her head and lay back on the grass, naked from the waist up. Below she was wearing jeans and sneakers.

"Martha!" her friend said. "Someone'll see."

"No, we're pretty far from the road." She closed her eyes and smiled beatifically. "The sun feels great."

Jed glanced over at her. Her breasts were bigger than he'd have expected, but nothing about the scene was in any way a turn-on. He saw Craig looking at her uneasily, not knowing how to proceed. The gesture had been like one Vonni might make, not so much a tease as an almost tomboyish kind of desire to defy convention. He looked at the other girl. She was gazing off at the lake with a melancholy expression, her mouth pinched.

"What're you thinking about?" he asked.

"A poem."

"She writes poems," Martha said without opening her eyes. "She's really good. Tell them one, Allie."

"What're your poems about?" Jed asked.

"Love." She looked embarrassed.

"She won a contest once," Martha said. "Recite them one. Go on, Allie!"

"I don't feel in the mood," Alice said primly.

"Oh, go on," Craig said. "Do it. . . . We're all friends."

"No." She continued to sit rigidly, gazing out at the lake.

"*I* know a poem," Craig said. He got unsteadily to his feet. "Oh Captain! my Captain, our fearful trip is done, the ship . . ."

"Her poems are better than *that,*" Martha said.

"No, they're not," Alice said. "That's a classic."

Craig sat down again. "My dad used to make up dirty limericks," he said. "He was good."

"Tell us one," Martha urged.

"I can't remember . . . I'll make one up." He squinted.

> There once was a beauty named Alice
> Who usually lived in a palace
> She only could come
> To the tune of a drum
> Which—

"That's dumb," Alice interrupted. She looked offended.

"Yeah, I guess you're right," Craig agreed. He took another swig of beer.

"I bet you're not college guys," Alice said contemptuously.

"What *are* we, then?" Jed asked.

She shrugged. *"I* don't know."

"Actually, we're rapists and brigands," Craig said. "We just got out of the slam. We'd decided to live a good, clean life, but we saw this jazzy car and we just couldn't resist." He made a motion to indicate breaking in.

"You mean, you really stole it?" Alice gasped.

Craig grinned. "Let's just say we borrowed it."

"Hey, shut up," Jed said to him. To Alice he added, "It's *my* car. It was a present from a guy I know."

Alice had gotten to her feet. "I want to go home," she said.

"They're just kidding around," Martha said, tugging at her. Sitting up, she looked at Craig. "Aren't you?"

"Yeah . . . it really *is* his car." He reached out and touched one of her breasts.

She slapped his wrist. "Hey, come on! . . . This is a first date. I don't fool around with just anybody."

"Well, thanks for letting us look at them," Craig said. "They're real pretty."

She put her shirt on again. "I know."

They drove the girls back to where they lived. Alice lived about six blocks from Martha. They let her out first. She got out without saying anything, but Martha leaned forward and said to Craig, "Give me a call, okay? If you're ever in town."

"Sure thing," Craig said. He got in the front with Jed. "She wasn't so bad," he said when they were on the road.

Jed was still feeling strange. He didn't say anything.

"It's easy to get redheads into bed, especially the ones with freckles," Craig said. "They always make up their mind right away."

"I never did it with a redhead," Jed said.

"What do you like—blondes?"

"I don't know . . . anyone. I mean, the hair color doesn't matter that much."

"Do you still see that one—the one who gave you the note?"

Jed hesitated. "No."

"You were really playing with fire," Craig said, whistling. "If Thornie'd found out—" He made a motion of slicing his head off.

"I know," Jed said.

He'd arranged to meet Capri that Thursday, late in the afternoon. Her exams were over. She said she could borrow her parents' car. He didn't tell her about the Camaro. But she was there, waiting in hers, when he pulled up. "God, that's gorgeous," she said, walking all around, looking at it.

Jed felt pleased. "Yeah. It's in good shape too."

"Can we go for a ride in it?"

"Sure."

"Can I drive it?"

So far he hadn't let anyone drive it. He hesitated.

"I'm a good driver," she said. "I just want to see how it feels."

"Okay." He gave her the keys and got in the other side.

"It's too bad there isn't some place where we could go really fast," she said, turning on the motor. "How fast do you want me to let it go?"

"Better keep it under sixty," he said.

"I bet it could go a hundred," she said, going around a curve.

"Easily."

The fact that she alone, of everyone he knew, hadn't even thought of his having stolen it seemed typical. She'd just assumed he had six thousand dollars in cash to shell out on a car! But there was still a fantasy element to it that he couldn't help savoring—a beautiful blonde whom he was fucking, a gorgeous car, a flawless spring day. They drove back to the place where they had agreed to meet.

"We should do it in the car," Capri said, smiling. "It'd be perfect."

"I don't know," Jed said. "I don't think it would be that comfortable."

"Sure, let's." She took her clothes off and got in his lap, winding her legs around him. Their closeness to the road, her excitement about the car all made it worth the discomfort of his hardly being able to move. Afterward, she stayed there, with him still inside her, her head resting on his shoulder, their hearts racing in unison. "It has a nice smell," she said.

"So do you." He let his hand run down to her buttocks. Her skin felt damp, fragrant.

She pulled back and looked at him. "Jed?"

"Yeah?"

"I'm not coming back next year."

As she spoke, she loosened herself from him and climbed into the adjoining seat. Knees up, she sat on her shirt, hugging herself. Jed started getting dressed. "What do you mean?"

"I meant to tell you before," she said. "I just wasn't sure. See, Daddy said if my grades were really good, all A's, I could transfer back to Harvard, and they were. I really worked my ass off to show him I could do it. Not that there's a lot of competition here, but still . . ."

Jed didn't say anything.

"Are you angry?"

"Of course! Christ, what do you expect? You wait till three seconds before you're leaving. Why didn't you tell me earlier?"

She looked cowed. "I don't know. I've thought so many things.

Like maybe we were getting too involved. I mean, maybe it wasn't good for either of us, for your marriage or—"

"Forget about my marriage," he said curtly, noticing she was referring to everything in the past tense.

"Okay." After a second she said with a smile, "She's pretty."

"Who?"

"Maddy."

"How do you know?"

"I went into the beauty shop once. . . . She was there. She wasn't the way I'd imagined her, though."

"How did you imagine her?"

"I guess more . . . maternal, bigger somehow. She looks like a little girl."

"Yeah. . . . We're getting divorced."

"I'm sorry."

"It wasn't you. We shouldn't ever have gotten married."

"Well . . ." She looked at him with an uncertain expression. "I'm not leaving till the end of next week. I'm going to Europe for the summer, partly with Mommy and Daddy, but I think once I'm over there, I'll just take off." She grinned. "I'm going to Capri, to see my name place." After a second she added softly, "I wish you could come."

Suddenly he reached over and grabbed her by the wrist. "Let's get married," he said.

She looked horrified, then laughed. "Are you crazy?"

"Why is it crazy?"

"Look, you just got out of one insane mess. . . . Now you want to charge straight into another?"

"It would be different with us," he said. Yet he felt, even as he spoke, that he was clinging to her in some absurd way, wanting one thing to hang on to, one thing that would be solid.

"It wouldn't . . . We're just kids."

"But we get along so well. . . . You said that, that maybe we won't have this again with anyone."

"That's just sex."

Jed laughed bitterly. "Is that all?"

Capri touched his arm. "No, listen, I didn't mean that. . . . It isn't just that. I don't know what 'just sex' is anyway. It's not 'just'! Maybe it's the only important thing . . . but still, we have our whole lives ahead of us. We'll be different people in five years, in ten. You'd get to hate me, just like you did with Maddy. You'd feel trapped, I'd feel trapped . . ."

"Is just that I don't go to college?" he said. "That I'm not rich?"

She hesitated. "It's—it's a million things," she said evasively.

"What if I were some guy at Harvard?" He wanted to force her to be honest, even if the answer was painful.

"Jed, listen, it's true . . . I think that *would* be a problem, but that isn't the main thing. I'm not going to marry anyone, till I'm thirty, at least! It wouldn't be fair to the person. I want to really get established in my work . . . and I think you—you should figure out where you're going. I think you could do something with your life, if you really wanted."

Despite everything, he felt some kind of pride that she, unlike anyone he had ever known, truly believed he was capable of something. He sat back, staring at the green, flowering field all around them. "Let's meet in ten years," he said. "We can go on our honeymoon then."

"Okay . . . don't forget," Capri said. "I won't."

"I won't either."

She hugged him. "I love you," she said.

But he knew, driving home alone, that any fantasies he had of their future life together were just that—fantasies. She was going to lead another kind of life. He had been a way of getting through the year—no, maybe more. He wondered if they had never met, would his marriage have stayed intact? He couldn't tell. The thought of her going to the beauty shop especially to see Maddy made him uncomfortable, though in some strange way he wished he could have been there, invisible, watching it. Maddy not knowing, never having known.

That Sunday he drove Maddy to the airport. She had packed one large suitcase and was wearing a blue suit with a white blouse.

"I hope I have a good time," she said at the airport coffee shop where they had lunch before her plane left.

"Oh sure, you will," Jed said.

"Jarita said she might rent a car and we could drive down along the coast. She says it's really pretty."

"Down to L.A.?"

"Maybe not that far, but in that direction."

In some way he envied her. He would have liked to be getting on a plane and flying off some place he'd never been before. They talked about this and that, but there was an awkwardness to the conversation. Jed thought how, despite their having lived together a year, having shared in the experience of being parents, having made love hundreds of times—he knew very little about her.

"Will you take some time off?" Maddy asked. Her voice was tremulous, as though, beneath the surface, there were tears. He prayed she wouldn't cry.

"Maybe . . . I don't know where I'd go."

"You could fly out and visit . . . Jarita could put us both up."

So, she still wanted to be with him. They were still married; no matter how many guys her sister fixed her up with, she wouldn't look at any of them. He was still the only person she wanted. Why?

"Well, let's talk about it," he said, "once you get there."

He wished he could be two men at least: one rich enough to go to Italy with Capri and spend two months in Europe with her . . . and a husband who, like many others, would be looking forward to spending a vacation with his wife, time to relax, talk, be together. But he wasn't either of those men.

He walked with her to the place where they checked passengers through. Maddy set her purse down and turned to him. Jed took her in his arms. He held her tightly, feeling her tears against his cheek. "Have a good time," he whispered.

She nodded and then, so softly he almost couldn't hear, said, "I love you."

So, two women loved him and he didn't have either one! Terrific. But walking away from the airport, he couldn't help feeling some kind of relief. Even Maddy's face, her presence, was some kind of rebuke. He thought of going to Ithaca and tracking down Ginny, the waitress. Just fucking someone he didn't know for once, someone he would never see again. But then he thought of what a mess the encounter with the other two had been and decided to let it be.

When he returned to the house, Paul Farnum was reading outside. "Want a drink?" he said, pointing to a pitcher of something that was resting under the tree.

"Sure," Jed said, accepting a glass of whatever it was. Something strong.

"So, you're wifeless, I hear?" Paul said. "For a time, anyway."

"Yeah," Jed said.

"Gerry might go away for a week or two," Paul said. "I always think it's going to be so terrific, being on my own, but after two or three days, I just want her back again. I guess I'm a flop as a bachelor." He looked at Jed. "How about you?"

"What?" Jed said. He'd only been half listening.

"Are you going to do anything special with Maddy away?"

"No, nothing special." Jed felt uncomfortable.

"Your girlfriend's something," Paul said.

"What girlfriend?"

"Capri . . . I've seen you with her a couple of times. Maddy doesn't know, does she?"

Jed shook his head.

"She's trusting," Paul said. "A sweet, trusting girl. . . . But I guess at your age that can get—"

Jed got unsteadily to his feet. He realized he'd drunk a glass of practically straight gin. "Look, it's none of your fucking business!" he said and slammed into the house.

He knew his reaction was out of proportion to the remark, that some of the frustration of the past weeks had been building inside him without any outlet. Who was there to get angry at? Maddy? Capri? Himself? A moment later there was a knock at the door. It was Farnum.

"You don't appreciate your wife," he said solemnly. He was clearly drunk, or anyway halfway there.

"So?" Jed said. "What's it to you?"

"She deserves better treatment. . . . You apologize to her."

"She's not here. She's in California."

"You tell her what a wonderful girl she is."

Jed laughed. "Why don't you tell *your* wife what a wonderful girl *she* is, okay? Leave mine alone."

"Leave *mine* alone," Farnum echoed.

"Don't worry," Jed said. "I don't think you have any cause for worry."

"Why not?"

"Because she's ugly," Jed found himself saying.

"You jerk," Farnum said contemptuously. "You're just a dumb, teenage punk, you know that?"

Jed socked him. He was expecting Farnum to crumple up in a lifeless heap at his feet, but instead he squatted on the ground, panting, and then lunged at Jed, caught him in a wrestling grip, and threw him to the ground. The gin had slowed Jed's reactions down, and he was taken aback by the swiftness of the other man. He tried to get into a better position, but Farnum had his shoulders in a tight grip, like some small animal that seized your pants leg and wouldn't let go. Jed tried to yank loose so he could sock him again, when suddenly Gerry came out of the house.

"What in the world," she said. Then, seeing they weren't joking, she pulled at her husband's shoulder. "Paul, for heaven's sake! Are you crazy? Stop it!"

"He attacked you," Farnum said. "He attacked wives."

"Oh Lord." Gerry dragged him away. "So what? Who cares about wives?"

"You're a wife," Farnum said. "*You* care."

"Have you been drinking all afternoon?" She looked back at Jed. "Please forgive this. It's the heat and half a pitcher of martinis."

"I offered him a drink," Farnum was saying. "I told him he had a pretty girlfriend. I—"

Jed wished his wife hadn't come along. Even though Farnum had been in better shape than he'd expected, Jed was sure the alcohol would have done him in eventually. And a good fight would have been enjoyable. As it was, he felt slightly better, though his shoulder still ached from the grip the guy had put on it. Dumb bastard. And who else knew? Who else had seen them together? What does it matter? It's over! But he hated the thought of being watched without his knowing it.

Capri was leaving Sunday. She was driving with her parents to New York and then flying the following week to Paris. They had arranged to have their last date on the lake, rowing. The weather, now that it was late June, had settled into a string of perfect, hot summer days. They met at the boathouse where the canoes and rowboats were stored. Capri was wearing red shorts, a striped T-shirt, and a big straw hat. Inside the boathouse she patted the canoe where they had had their first encounter. "We should put a plaque up," she said with a grin.

"Yeah." It came back to him in flashes, her wriggling out of her suit, his rubbing her dry, the frantic excitement he had felt.

"Should we take a canoe or rowboat?"

"Rowboat."

They carried it out and slid it into the water. The lake was still deserted. It wasn't until July that the college posted a lifeguard on the dock during the day. A few boats were out. One person was water-skiing.

"She better not fall in," Capri said, looking up. "She'll freeze."

Jed rowed slowly and steadily out into the lake. He'd never been this far out before. When they were about midway, two miles on either side, he stopped. Capri unpacked the picnic lunch she'd brought and handed him a sandwich. She'd brought a bottle of wine too. They both drank straight from the bottle, passing it back and forth. It was warm and a little sweet, but good.

"Lake Como can't be prettier than this," Capri said.

"No," Jed said.

She was sitting facing him. "I've got a present for you."

"What is it?"

She took a box from inside the wicker picnic basket and

handed it to him. It was tied with red wool ribbon. Jed undid the ribbon. Inside was a long golden braid of human hair. He looked at it, puzzled, and then at Capri. She pulled off her straw hat. "Something to remember me by," she said.

She had cut off all her hair! Or rather on top it was still the same, but now it ended at her neck. It was like a boy's haircut, shorter than his even, though it still stood out in the same crinkly light curls around her head. "God," he said, stunned. Her long hair seemed so much a part of her, it was almost as though she'd cut her arm off and handed it to him.

"I guess it *was* a little drastic," she said. "But I wanted the whole braid, intact. . . . Don't look so horrified. It'll grow back."

"You still look pretty," he said, reaching out and touching her hair.

"I thought it would be easy for traveling. My hair grows fast." She took the hand he had put on her head and slowly kissed each fingertip. Then she turned around and sat, her body between his legs, her head tilted back, eyes closed, holding his hand against her breast. Usually he would have felt excited at that closeness, but maybe because of his mood, maybe because of the wine, he felt peaceful and detached, as though they had just made love and were resting afterward. He stroked her hair gently with his free hand, ruffling the curls.

Looking out over the lake, at the side opposite the college, he thought of how in the fall she had said she would swim across. One night, for no reason he could figure out, he'd had a scary dream. She was swimming and he was rowing along beside her, to make sure nothing happened. It was a dark, ominous day, the lake was choppy. Capri kept breathing with difficulty, spewing out water. He urged her to get back into the boat, but she refused, saying she could make it. At one point she went completely under and he, without thinking, dove in to get her. The water was freezing. He had to drag her up from the bottom and then pull her to shore. He had the feeling she might have drowned, her body was so heavy and cold; he felt petrified. He imagined himself appearing on the shore with her dead body in his arms. But when they reached the shore, she flung herself into his arms. "You saved me," she said. He recalled now that that was what she'd said the first time they'd made love, as they were parting. "Maybe you did save my life."

Jed looked out again at the opposite side of the lake. It was so clear that you could see houses, trees, all outlined sharply against the sky. He was glad she had never tried to swim across. It was further than it looked.

Thirteen

Sometimes, still, though she has had the job almost a year, Maddy feels like an impostor. Jarita has told her hundreds of times not to worry. Half the jobs in America, even more, she says, are gotten due to pull and influence. Once Jed wrote her that he wanted a divorce, once she decided to stay out in San Francisco, Maddy thought she would get a job as a waitress or a beautician. But Jarita fixed her up, redid her makeup, took her to her favorite beauty shop to have her hair styled—and lo and behold, Maddy looked, even to herself, at least eighteen, which was the minimum age for an airline ticket agent. Not that the woman interviewing her seemed to care. She didn't even bother checking for Maddy's high school diploma! "I did her a favor once," Jarita explained. "She was pregnant and didn't know where to go. I found a nice place and went with her, stayed with her that night. She's always remembered."

That impressed Maddy, that the woman at Personnel, who sat so calmly and efficiently behind her desk, had at one time been distraught, pregnant with the child of someone who didn't want to marry her. And yet there she was, composed, serene. "Wounds heal," Jarita was always saying, encouraging Maddy with tales of her own misadventures. "You should have *seen* me," she'd say. "I was a total basket case! I didn't get out of bed for two weeks!" And it was true, glancing at herself sometimes in an airport bathroom mirror, Maddy sees a pretty, nicely coifed young woman who could, perhaps, be almost twenty. Jarita showed her how to put brown shadow in the hollows of her cheeks that takes away the babyish roundness that Maddy thinks has always made her look so young for her age.

It is hard for her still to imagine that she is here, living with Jarita, sharing a beautiful apartment with her. Even during the two-week visit a year ago, she was afraid Jarita would find her boring, dumb, naive, but Jarita instantly began planning to get rid of her roommate, whom she said she couldn't stand. "We'll have so much fun together," she said. "We'll have a ball."

Half the month Jarita isn't even there. She travels all but two weeks of each month and in those extra weeks Maddy has the apartment to herself. Now it isn't so bad, but at the beginning the apartment, which has two bedrooms and a terrace, seemed gigantic to her. She huddled in her room, crossing off the days till Jarita would be back. Usually Jarita has layovers for a few days wherever she is traveling: New York, Hawaii, even London. When she comes back, it's exciting. She always buys presents for Maddy, perfume that she gets duty-free at the airport, dresses, books in foreign languages. Spreading them out on the floor, she tells Maddy about all her recent adventures, the men she's met, what it was like. To Maddy it's like the way "General Hospital" used to be before Luke and Laura got married. Jarita's adventures seem more exciting than "real life." All the men she knows, maybe because Maddy never meets most of them, sound intriguing, wonderful, terribly handsome.

Jarita distinguishes between what she calls her "flirtations," even though these may involve actually going to bed with someone, and her "serious lovers"—the pilot, the businessman, and the would-be movie director who works part time grooming show dogs. The pilot is married; she has known him six years. He is a "pal" but "mainly for sex." According to Jarita, he is happily married, but needs something more. "We have a lot of fun together" is how she puts it. The businessman is Jewish, not that Jarita would mind that, but he has a lot of psychological problems; he's been seeing a doctor for sixteen years. Jarita likes to talk to him because, in her spare time, she's taking courses in psychology and he knows all about that; his father was a psychiatrist. Partly he wishes he had been a psychiatrist, but instead he went into a business that manufactures women's lingerie. It's doing so well he can't afford to quit, though he says he hates it. He has given Jarita so many nightgowns and robes that, she says, she could spend the rest of her life in bed and not wear the same outfit twice. Some of the nightgowns are really campy—they have feathers at the hem or are made of peach-colored satin with deep V's in front and back. Now that he knows Jarita has a sister, the businessman gives Maddy nightgowns too. There are two she likes, baby-doll nightgowns trimmed with lace. One has flowers, one is pale blue.

But Maddy does not feel ready to accept any of the many fix-ups that Jarita would be happy to arrange for her. Steve, the would-be director, for instance, has a younger brother who has seen Maddy's photo and thinks she is a "dream boat." He, too, according to Jarita, made an early marriage, right out of high school, "so you two would have a lot in common." But the trouble is, even though the divorce is official now and has been for some time, Maddy still *feels* married. She has taken off her ring and put it in her jewelry box—it still gives her a pang to see it there, but she hasn't the heart to throw it away. She wonders often when that feeling, that she is married, will go away. She thinks one day it will simply disappear, but right now when she tells the men who flirt with her at the ticket counter that she "isn't available," she is telling what seems to her to be the truth.

One night she gets up and finds Jarita in the kitchen having a drink with a man Maddy has never seen before. He is tall and dark, a little on the beefy side. "This must be the baby sister," he says, his words slurred a little. "Hi, Baby Sister!"

"Hi," Maddy says softly. She feels embarrassed that all she is wearing is the flowered baby-doll nightgown. It is not see-through, but she has never been seen without all her clothes on by any men except the ones in her family, Jed, and, if you count that one time, Luther.

"Did we wake you up?" Jarita asks. She is wearing one of the businessman's gift robes, the long black lace one that, Maddy thinks, makes her look like a forties movie star, especially when, as now, she wears her long blond hair loose below her shoulders.

"No," Maddy says. "I just woke up . . . I felt thirsty." She goes and gets a glass of milk.

"Maybe Baby Sister would like to join us," the man says. "Maybe she'd like to keep us company."

Jarita looks at him sharply. "Cut the baby sister thing," she says. "One more word like that and—" She points to the door.

The man looks crushed. "I didn't mean anything. I have a younger sister too. She's just twelve. She plays on Little League. Do you play on Little League?"

Eventually Maddy takes her milk back to her bedroom. In the morning Jarita apologizes. "He wasn't even that great in bed," she says over breakfast.

Often at night Jarita talks about her sex life, comparing various lovers, past and present, their virtues and flaws. "What was it like with Jed?" she asks now.

"I don't know," Maddy says, meaning she has no point of comparison. This is true: the night with Luther is truly a blur. Anyway, she would never mention that to Jarita; she feels ashamed that it ever happened.

"How long did it take usually?"

"I guess five or ten minutes," Maddy says, trying to remember.

"Five or ten minutes! For the whole thing?" Jarita looks horrified. She sets down her spoonful of scrambled eggs. "Oh sweetie. We have to get you someone who knows what they're doing."

Is that not a long time? Maddy wonders. It's hard for her to imagine how it could take longer than that. "I don't want to meet anyone," she says.

"I know, hon," Jarita says tenderly. "I don't mean now. I mean when you're ready."

When will she be ready? Not that she dreams about Jed, or thinks of him all the time, the way she did the first few months. Now whole days, even a week, can go by without her thinking of him. But something will happen that will bring him into her mind again, and when this takes place, it is still painful, like an ache in her side.

One day, as she is typing out a ticket for someone, she looks up and sees Jed's friend, Craig. He is going to Hawaii, he says, for work.

"Well, gee, how've you been?" Maddy asks.

"Pretty good," Craig says. "I almost wouldn't have recognized you, Maddy. . . . Did you get a new haircut or something?"

"Yes." Maddy's heart starts beating harder, partly because she is afraid Craig will say something about her age that will be overheard, but partly because she wants to ask about Jed but doesn't dare. "How have you been?" she repeats nervously, typing.

"Oh fine . . . same as usual." As she hands him his ticket he says, uncomfortably, "I was real sorry to hear about you and Jed."

"Well . . ."

"I guess you were both pretty young."

"Yes."

Everyone says that—"You were too young"—and often it makes Maddy angry. It seems to her that their being young didn't have anything to do with it. But it is easier to accept this simple explanation than to search for the right one.

"I'm getting married myself," he says. Luckily, it is a slow part of the day. There is no one waiting behind him.

"That's nice," Maddy says. "What's her name?"

"Martha." He pulls out his wallet and shows Maddy a photo of a tiny red-haired girl with a lot of freckles. "She's going to be an engineer," he says proudly. "She's real smart."

"Why're you going to Hawaii?" Maddy asks.

"Her folks are out there. She went out ahead too. They say it's a real paradise. We'll see if we can get work." He puts the photo back.

After he is gone, Maddy has a brief, awful moment of wondering what girls Jed has seen since she left, whether he has gotten serious with any of them, whom he has fallen in love with, who has fallen in love with him. If they had kept the baby, even if they'd gotten divorced, she would still see him, hear from him. There would be that bond between them. But as it is . . .

The baby is a year and a half old now. Every month, on the day Minnie gets one month older, Maddy thinks of her age. She would so much like to know what she looks like now, what she is doing, if she is happy. Once she wrote to Mr. Edelman and he said things were fine. He enclosed a Polaroid photo of Minnie being held by his sister-in-law. It was a little blurry—Minnie had just had her first birthday then—but she looked cute, much bigger, with lots of black curls. Maddy put the photo in her wallet, and several times a day, often when she is alone, she takes it out and looks at it. She thinks maybe that at the moment she is looking at the photo, the baby can tell and is thinking of her too. She sent Mr. Edelman a photo of herself with her new haircut and asked him to give it to Minnie when she was a little older.

Often, when she is typing tickets, she sees babies the age of Minnie being carried by their mothers or playing on the benches at the back of the lounge. Sometimes they are crying and making a fuss and their mothers get impatient and slap them. Other times they stare at Maddy gravely.

Sometimes she thinks that, if she had it to do over, she would have an abortion. Having had the baby and then giving her away is something she knows will be with her always. For the first six months, she thought: I could get her back. Once she even decided definitely to do it, but after a day or two she wondered if it would be fair to the baby, who, by now, would be settled into her new life. And isn't it better, as Jarita suggested, to wait and meet a new person and then start a new family?

"You can have as many kids as you want," Jarita says. "Anyhow, you don't want to be like Betsy and Doreen, do you? Like some mindless old cow by the time you're thirty?"

Jarita speaks of their two older sisters with a casual contempt that both horrifies Maddy and secretly pleases her, since she has never liked either of them. Now during the day she carries around in her mind the image of herself ten years from now with this new family Jarita is sure she will have, a new husband, children. She wants the first one to be a girl and saves an article from a magazine that tells about a way of making love that will insure that the baby is born one sex or the other.

One weekend, when Jarita is away, the younger brother of her movie director friend calls. His name is Hayes. He says he would like to take Maddy out to dinner. For no special reason Maddy says she will go. He is a funny-looking man with a big nose and kindly blue eyes behind wire-rimmed glasses. He is wearing a shirt and a leather vest with fringes on it, but it looks unnatural, like a costume.

"Steve says you were married too," he says. "Did he tell you I was?"

Maddy nods. "I'm divorced now," she says.

"Me too . . . I have a little boy, though. He's almost four." On the table he spreads out photos of his child, playing, sitting on a swing.

"He's cute," Maddy says. She shows him the photo of Minnie.

"She doesn't look like you that much," he says. "You're prettier."

"She'll be pretty when she's older," Maddy assures him.

"Do you ever see her?"

"No."

He comes back to the apartment with her. Because he seems so ill at ease himself, Maddy feels more relaxed with him than she usually does with men. She offers him a drink, but he says he'd rather just have a glass of ginger ale. When they are sitting on the couch, he kisses her, but gently, as though afraid she'll mind. "Do you have a boyfriend?" he asks.

Maddy shakes her head.

"It's hard after . . ." He doesn't finish the sentence, but Maddy, in her mind, finishes it for him.

They kiss a little bit more, but he still seems not quite relaxed. "I guess I want to get married again," he muses, turning the glass around in his hand. "It sounds crazy. Right after Jane left, I thought: I'll never marry again, but now . . . I go to a psychiatrist and he said, 'Go to singles bars, play the field,' all that. I told him I couldn't. 'Go just once,' he said. 'What can you lose?' I just didn't feel like I could. . . . Do you know what I mean?"

"Yes," Maddy says.

She is relieved that he doesn't try to do more than kiss her. At the end of the evening he stands at the door, looking uncomfortable, and tells her he has enjoyed it and would like to see her again. Then he reaches out, hugs her tightly, and walks off.

In bed at night Maddy wonders what it would be like to be married to him. He is not good-looking like Jed. He didn't make her feel excited and nervous the way Jed did, but she feels glad she went out with him. She is always aware of being alone in the apartment—not scared, but aware of it. One solution, when she is lying in bed, is to take out one of a variety of mental slides she has in her head and play it in her mind until she falls asleep. This night she tries a new one. She imagines herself married to Hayes with three children, taking them to an amusement park. They go past all the rides, going on some, deciding others are too dangerous. He is carrying one of their children on his shoulders, the boy. The other two are girls, one a baby and the other a two-year-old who is in a stroller. After this slide has played itself out, Maddy turns to others that are more familiar. One is of herself and Jed in high school before they began making love together, when she started noticing that he was paying attention to her. She would get up each morning, dress carefully, and sometimes she would see him even before classes started. Other times he would saunter over to her at lunchtime and sit at her table. She would offer him one of her sandwiches, if she had something good, and would forget to eat herself, transfixed by the joy of sitting at the same table with him. And then, best of all, at the end of the day he might say casually that he would drop over that night (that was before Maddy's mother had threatened to shoot his ears off) and she could spend all the hours till after dinner dreaming about this, about what they would talk about, sitting in his car.

But the mental slide she likes best of all is the one about the baby. A month earlier Maddy's mother wrote saying she met Mr. Edelman on the street and he said he was thinking of moving with

Minnie to Miami because he felt the winters were too severe in Auburn. Maddy has never been to Miami or even to the beach, but she imagines it as an endless stretch of beautiful white sand and blue water with small frothy waves. In her fantasy Mr. Edelman walks down the beach, holding Minnie's hand, explaining things to her. Sometimes she collects sea shells and puts them in a tin pail. Other times she sits and makes sand castles, decorating them with seaweed. Maddy worries sometimes about the big waves, but Mr. Edelman is very careful. He never lets Minnie get too close to the water. He sits under a beach umbrella, watching her all the time. And the baby, feeling safe, cared for, places a shell on top of the sand house.

Even though she has never been to a place where it is always warm, Maddy is glad the baby is there. She knows she will be happy.

Jed is cruising down the main street of College Town, near Cornell, when he sees her. Even from the back, he knows it is she. Her hair is shorter, but the same color, reddish-brown. She is wearing a blue sundress—it is June—and high-heeled sandals. She has pretty legs and always wore high heels, even to school, even with jeans. Moving up slowly so he is right opposite her, he honks the horn. When he honks it the second time, she turns around. She is wearing sunglasses, big wraparound ones. At first her expression is just annoyed. Then she recognizes him. "Jed!" she exclaims. She comes over and stands near the car. "Goodness, you scared me."

She was always scared of everything, school, him, her parents, sex. It was half real and half play-acting, but it always had a certain appeal for him. "Get in," he says. "I'll take you for a drive."

"Okay." She gets into the car and then, taking her sunglasses off, gazes at him. "I never thought I'd see you again."

"I work at Coolidge. I've had the job two years now. Buildings and Grounds. . . . You still at college?" He can't remember which college she went to, some women's college her mother had gone to.

She looks embarrassed. "I dropped out for a year. I got sick. Mono . . . I was in bed three months. But I'll go back this fall."

"So, what've you been doing?"

"Helping my father at the store. It's kind of dull."

Her father had a chain of sporting-goods stores all around the state. "What do you do?"

"Oh, just selling . . . I hate it!" She laughed. "I'm terrible. I add things up wrong. He'd have fired me a million times if I wasn't his daughter." She is still gazing at him with that fixed stare, the same one that would stab right through him at school. She has the longest eyelashes he's ever seen, pale white skin with a blue vein near her ear that throbs slightly when she is excited or nervous. "How's Maddy?" she asks.

"Okay, I guess. . . . We're not together anymore."

"Oh." She looks taken aback. "I didn't know."

"Yeah, for about a year now. . . . She lives in San Francisco with her sister."

"I guess this is a terrible thing to say, but I always thought you could've done better."

"Like who?"

"I just meant you should've waited."

"Right . . . so, how're you? Any boyfriends?" He couldn't resist trying to get back at her a little.

"Not really . . . I went out a little my freshman year, but no one that . . . Mostly I just studied a lot. It was really hard. I almost failed French. I got all C's. I was scared they'd kick me out. It was a relief in a way to get sick."

So, she is still a virgin. Jed can't help getting a certain pleasure out of that.

She laughs in that soft way she has. "What was that look about?"

"Just remembering some of our . . . encounters."

"Was I awful?" she says with an urgency that takes him aback.

"What do you mean?"

"I mean, I was so . . . mixed up about what I wanted. I always felt so ashamed about the way I acted with you. It wasn't just my parents. I didn't know what I wanted. I really was scared." She sighs. "The worst part is I'd probably be the same now. I don't know if I've changed that much."

301

"You're still beautiful." But as she speaks, some of it comes back to him, the frustration of her seeming suddenly so tremulous and vulnerable, ready to do anything, and then the sudden panic at the last moment, the coldness at school, walking past him as though he weren't there, then a month later a sudden phone call: she had to see him.

"My mother was so sure you were after me for my money . . . I don't think you were, though. . . . Were you?"

Jed laughs. "Sure, that's all it was."

"Seriously."

"I was kind of mixed up myself then," he admits. "Yeah, maybe your money gave you some kind of . . . It made you seem different, the way you dressed, talked, all that. But it wasn't just that. You were sexy, even those dumb games you played. I just finally couldn't take it anymore."

"Do you have lots of girlfriends now?"

"Enough."

One thing he prides himself on is not having gone near any of the college girls. He's restricted his sexual encounters to girls in Ithaca or Auburn: the waitresses, a friend of Craig's girlfriend Martha, someone he picked up at a movie one night. He's had a few close calls with the college girls, but each time he's gotten away before anything could happen. Once he was at the IGA getting some groceries when the girl ahead of him didn't have enough money to buy some beer. They wouldn't let you charge beer. She was twenty-eight cents short. "Here." He handed it to her.

She was in a winter parka, her hood trimmed with fur, big brown eyes, pink cheeks. "Gee, thanks. . . . Listen, let me have your address. I'll pay you back."

"That's okay."

"Really, I want to."

But he wouldn't give it to her. A month or so later he passed her on the street and she came running after him, pressing the change into his hand. He took it and walked off.

Another time he was in the library reading a copy of *Popular Mechanics* when a girl came over and asked when he thought he'd be done. He said he'd just started reading. For the next half hour she sat in a chair opposite, staring at him. He wasn't sure if she was desperately eager for the magazine or just flirting with him. She was small with curly black hair and a snub nose, almost cute, but not quite. She wore a cowboy hat that reminded him of Vonni's. When he was done with the magazine, he went over and gave it to her. She took it and said, "It's a good magazine, isn't it?"

"Yeah."

"Do you go here?"

"What?"

"There's a boy in my class who says his father teaches here. He gets free tuition. I thought you might be one of those."

They talked awhile, but there, too, he didn't even ask her name or what dorm she was in.

He still thinks of going to college himself. A guy, someone who'd been on the crew, decided to go at night and work during the day. It takes longer that way, seven years, but you end up with the same degree. Maybe he'll do that. But so far it's just been daydreams.

He thinks of how different everything is in reality from the way it appears in your head. If someone had told him two or three years ago that he'd be cruising along in a red Camaro with Garnet looking at him with that wistful, fuckable expression, he would have thought he'd be out of his head with delight. Now she is just a girl, it's just a car, he is himself.

"Where do you want to drive?" he askes.

"I should get home by four."

"Should I drive you home?"

"No."

He decides to drive to Watkin's Glen. He turns off the main road.

"What happened with your baby?" Garnet asks. "Did you have it?"

"Yeah . . . we gave it up for adoption."

"So, you didn't even have to marry her. She just got pregnant on purpose. She knew you'd never have married her otherwise."

"So?"

"She trapped you. . . . You never really loved her, did you?"

303

Jed hesitates. "Yeah, I loved her." He isn't sure if he says this because in retrospect it seems true, or to get Garnet's goat.

He has been at the Glen other years for the sports car races. Maybe he'll go this year too. Today, because it's during the week, Wednesday, it's pretty deserted. They walk along the path, looking down the steep embankment to the water rushing below. Finally they come out onto the picnic grounds. Far off a family is having a picnic lunch, but they are tiny figures, just dots of color. Jed lies on the grass; Garnet sits, leaning against the tree.

As they had walked along the path, he could see down the front of her sundress to her small breasts. The dress hangs loosely on her—she looks thinner up close. "How long were you sick?" he asks.

"A long time. . . . Even after I was up and around, I'd get so exhausted, I'd feel like I was going to faint." She holds out the dress. "I lost twenty pounds. I've gained some of it back, though." She was always getting sick at school too, flu, colds. Maybe that partly explained her mother's constant hovering, as though she were a hothouse plant. "Did you remember your scarf, dear?" And he remembered times making out in his car when she would seem to be about to come apart, whether from nervousness or physical weakness he never knew. Once she'd started hyperventilating and almost passed out. Another time she had a bloody nose—streams of bright red blood that he'd tried to mop up with his T-shirt.

"Here you've been married, divorced, had a kid . . . and what have I done?" she asks rhetorically, stroking a blade of grass.

"What *have* you done?" he asks, smiling.

"I lost my virginity . . . God, I hate that phrase! I gave it away, I 'relinquished' it."

"Who'd you relinquish it *to?*"

She looks uncomfortable. "It wasn't love, it was . . . He was the manager of the store of my father's where I was working. He'd been divorced twice. In his forties, balding, in good shape, though. . . . We used to jog together at the end of the day. He liked teasing me. I guess I seemed like a kid to him, all my mistakes at work, his having to cover for me. It wasn't bad, doing it. I wanted to get it over with and I did. . . . How many girls've you done it with?"

Jed reflects. "I don't know . . . twelve, fifteen."

"Do they keep their eyes open?"

"Some, I guess."

"Will said that was what turned him on most, watching women go all crosseyed and berserk when they had orgasms. I guess I'd be embarrassed."

They are back in high school. Nothing has changed. She was always like this, talking about sex so much he would get excited, curious, halfway to the point of doing it, and then suddenly petrified. On an impulse Jed gets up and sits next to her, puts his arm around her light body. She is trembling, as she always did. "Should we do it?" she asks softly.

"Do you want to?" Knowing she isn't a virgin is something of a relief to him.

"Sure. . . . Anyway, to make up for all those times. I was such a tease."

"You weren't a tease," he tells her, kissing her neck, her ears.

She assures him she is on the pill, has been all year "just in case." A relief. He doesn't have any condoms and wouldn't risk another pregnant teenage girlfriend for anything in the world.

They keep most of their clothes on for fear someone may come along. And that, too, makes it seem like high school, that Garnet is fully clad except for her underpants, that someone may interrupt them—her parents? And nothing has changed. Her skin is cold, she breathes so quickly and intensely he starts being afraid she will faint, her eyes roll back and close, as though she is losing consciousness. Halfway through, Jed thinks, the hell with it, and fucks her as though she were any other girl. They aren't in high school; if she faints, she faints. He loses sight of her until after he comes, but knows, somehow, she didn't.

They lie side by side. "I guess we could've been doing this all through our senior year," she says thoughtfully.

Jed grins. "Yeah."

"I don't know . . . Sex is still confusing to me. I don't think I understand it."

"What's to understand?"

"Why it's so important, why it makes people act so strange."

He wonders whether, if they had done it all through senior year, she would ever have changed. Maybe he was better off with Maddy.

They walk back, hand in hand. He can see that in the eyes of an older married couple they pass, they appear to be young lovers. The envy of the older couple gleams out at them like a beacon. Garnet smiles at him, acknowledging it, half in irony.

He drives her home. She is quiet, her hands folded in her lap, her expression pensive. When they reach her house, her mother is out in front gardening. "I ran into Jed, Mommy," Garnet says. "Remember, we were in high school together?"

Hearing her call her mother "Mommy" makes her seem even younger to Jed. Her mother gives him the same suspicious look she used to three years ago. What have you done with my daughter? He feels more pleased at this moment for the not very satisfactory fuck in the Glen than he did while it was happening. "How have you been, Jed?" her mother asks, tight-lipped.

"I've been fine," Jed said.

"Jed's working over at Coolidge," Garnet fills in. "He's been there two years."

He knows her intent, in passing along this information, is to show her mother he is steady, has kept a job. As if her mother cared! He can see from the look in her eyes that her hopes of a prosperous and successful marriage for her daughter have not diminished one iota.

"Do you want to come in a minute?" Garnet says, deliberately defying her mother, even touching his arm.

"No, I can't. I have to get back," he says.

"I'll be around all summer," Garnet says softly. "Call me, okay?"

"Sure." He kisses her quickly, enjoying her mother's seething resentment in the background, and drives off.

He won't call her. Why? He doesn't really want to relive high school. Her father's money, their big house, seem irrelevant now. But, as after every sexual encounter he's had in the past year, he starts, while driving home, thinking of Capri. They haven't spoken or written since that day on the lake when she presented him with her braid of hair. Once he was in New York and thought of trying to look her up, and then realized she might be in Boston. When he imagines seeing her again, he imagines himself ten years older, an engineer with a good job. He comes to New York and has a minor injury of some kind, turns up at a hospital, and there she is, a doctor, coming out in her white coat to take care of him. She, in this daydream, looks the same. Her hair has grown in, the same long golden braid. She has had many lovers, but no one like him. As soon as she sees him, she gasps and runs over to him. . . .

He doesn't carry the daydream much beyond that. Crucial to it is his having the credentials, the engineering degree which he sees as a passport into her world. Someday, he knows, he will have that passport, whether or not she is there to notice or be impressed.

Occasionally, but very rarely, he wonders how Maddy is doing. He wishes her well. If he heard she was married, he would be pleased. Craig wrote a card saying he'd seen her working as an airline ticket agent, looking good. He likes that image of her, typing out tickets, her expression grave and concerned for fear of making mistakes. Probably she's going out with guys now, but he doubts anyone will get her into bed unless he comes with a marriage contract in one hand. Maddy.

He never thinks of the baby.

Sometimes, passing Edelman's car lot, he sees Homer and stops in to chat. But he only does this when Edelman isn't there. He doesn't want him rushing out with stories of how well the baby is doing. As far as Jed is concerned, it is easier to pretend she never existed. He has his own life to lead, to figure out.

Ardis has said she'll look after Minnie while the movers come to load the truck. Misha has been waiting an hour now, and they still haven't arrived. But the house is pretty much cleared out, everything either packed, sold, or given away. He had a garage sale to get rid of as much as he could, but a third of the stuff remained unsold. Finally, at the end of the day, he gave the rest away. Lugging it to Miami, where he imagines they will live in a smaller house, maybe even an apartment, doesn't make sense.

He roams through the house, trying to work up some nostalgia.

But it's hard, partly because it no longer looks like the house he lived in for twenty years. Some of the baby stuff Minnie outgrew he gave to the woman next door, who seemed grateful. He packed a few of her toys, the ones she seemed most attached to, and left a few with Ardis. "What for?" she joked. "I'm not going to need them for a while," meaning when she becomes a grandmother: Abby has written saying she's going to be married.

"Can't tell," he joked back. "You don't know what lies down the pike."

She has stopped trying to persuade him not to go, stopped deploring the horrors of Florida: the right-wing Cubans, the decrepit old people, the constant heat which, she claims, melts your brain. "You need a new start," she admits, acknowledging, if only indirectly, that if he stays, he will never get out of the relationship with her. It is too convenient, too satisfying. Even her not being fully available would probably suit him indefinitely, he has gotten so used to it. Once or twice he has the feeling she still, rarely, picks up men on her business trips, but he doesn't press her about it. It doesn't seem to have anything to do with their relationship. Maybe that's how Simon feels too, though he can't help feeling Simon would mind about him, if he knew. But what Simon knows or doesn't know, suspects or doesn't suspect, will always be a mystery to Misha. He's given up trying to figure it out.

About a month earlier he got a postcard from his former bookkeeper, Sophie. She is living in Kentucky. She didn't say whether she was married or not, or even what she was doing there. Just her address and a "drop in if you're ever down in this part of the country." Maybe, on the way to Miami, he'll veer west a little. It's not exactly on the way, but it doesn't much matter to him if he gets there a month earlier or later. He wonders if she is still chewing banana-flavored bubble gum.

He's been lucky about the lot. A guy from out of town came along and decided, for reasons best known to him, that it was a good investment. Homer decided to stay on. "Where would I go?" was his plaintive comment when Misha informed him of his imminent departure. He regards the move to Miami as folly for reasons slightly different from Ardis'. You stay where you are, change is bad, it's supposed to get cold in winter. Though Misha has explained that his intention is to try to get a teaching job, Homer regards this, too, as absurd. "You're a businessman, not a teacher. What do you want to teach for?"

Ardis thinks he just won't be able to get a job. "Have you read the papers lately? Teachers are jumping off cliffs, becoming photographer's assistants. . . ."

"So, I'll jump off a cliff or become a photographer's assistant." Statistics aside, he feels he will get a teaching job. Or maybe he is enjoying, for the first time in his life, not having to go to work every morning. Something will turn up. He doesn't really imagine he will join the ranks of the unemployed. "I can always come back here," he tells Ardis to comfort her.

"No, you won't. Once you go, you go."

He gave some of his old furniture to Abby for her new home. She and her husband are going to live in Syracuse. Ardis is pleased—she can visit them, bug them, as she puts it. "I'm going to be a ferocious mother-in-law," she says with relish.

He would like to see her as a mother-in-law, as a grandma, would like, even, to stay for the wedding, which is in August. But the house is sold, and the young couple who bought it want to move in right away. "You can fly back, maybe," Ardis suggests.

"Maybe." But he has never been fond of huge weddings. To his mind everyone should elope, as he and Brenda did.

It's clear to him, sitting here, that he is taking Wolf and Brenda with him. Somehow, he had thought they might stay behind, content to roam around in the minds of other people. But they seem determined to keep him permanent company, to offer unwanted suggestions and advice, to light on his shoulder in the midde of a conversation. He has stopped rebuking them or himself for their continued existence in his mind. Either he needs them or they need, in this way, to live on. He doesn't care which it is.

He knows Brenda would have liked the couple to whom he sold the house. The husband is a classics professor who is going to teach at Coolidge, but wants to live off campus. He is tall, lean, angular-looking. The wife is small, perky, Jewish, a violinist who wants to try to get a job in a small symphony. They have two-year-old twins, a boy and girl who look not at all alike, not even like brother and sister. The little girl is red-haired, flaming red, the boy dark like his mother. Misha can see how being a twin to someone of the opposite sex is totally different from the way Brenda and Ardis had felt about each other. But he knows Brenda would have played with them, talked to them, told them she was a twin. As it was he had said, "My wife was a twin," but they were too concerned about finding out about the neighborhood, schools, to care about that.

The person who was most openly upset about his departure was Mrs. Sebastian, who has been looking after Minnie during the week while he is at work. She has several grown children and looks after two others besides Minnie. He was amazed when, upon hearing the news, she burst into tears. "Leave her here with me!" she sobbed. "Don't take her away!" He wonders if Minnie will miss her as much as she, evidently, will miss Minnie. She has always seemed to enjoy going to Mrs. Sebastian's house but, when he comes to pick her up, she runs eagerly into his arms, never seeming reluctant to leave.

But who knows what she thinks or remembers, whether she even knows she ever had a life without him? When Maddy sent him the photo of herself, he showed it to Minnie, but she tried to bend it in two and he took it away. Ardis thinks she remembers nothing. She was glad when Maddy moved to California. "Why confuse her? You can tell her when she's older." Minnie calls him "Mee," a shortened version of Misha, or sometimes "Meesh," an imitation of what Ardis calls him. He is more comfortable with this than with "Daddy." He can't, despite his current immersion in diapers, bottles, and baby food, think of himself as "Daddy." Only sometimes, to tease him, Ardis calls him that.

He is glad that the baby is part of his life. Like Ardis, she appeared; he would not have sought her. That will, he suspects, always be true. But at least he can say of himself that he has had the ability to meet situations halfway, even if not to create them. When he takes Minnie out on weekends, if he is alone, people assume he is her grandfather. If he is with Ardis, they assume he has married a younger woman and started a new family. He wonders sometimes why this is true, since no one ever made that mistake when he and Brenda took Noah out. Was it just Brenda's letting her hair go gray? Does he, without knowing it, act differently with Ardis, or she, perhaps, act differently with him than Brenda did? One difference he is conscious of is that, when they are walking together, she always takes his arm, likes to touch him casually, though not in what seems to him a loverlike way; she just enjoys the physical contact.

Finally the movers arrive. A large truck pulls up and two stocky men get out and begin phlegmatically loading in the boxes and furniture. The moving company has a warehouse in Miami where they will store everything till he arrives. A week, two weeks, he told them it would take. He's not going to try to cover too many miles a day. The baby would find it tiring, though on shorter trips she's been fine, doesn't seem to mind the confinement of the baby seat. This spring he took her on weekends to a playground where there was a sprinkler. She seemed to like the water, so he's bought her a bathing suit. Maybe he'll try taking her into the pool at some of the motels where they'll stay.

At fifty-one he is finally going to see America! Part of it, anyway. He has never been south at all, except for a few trips to Washington. The adventure of it appeals to him, even the insecurity of not knowing where he will live or how he will support himself. Having a child to support could make the insecurity more anxiety-provoking, but somehow it doesn't. He likes the feeling that they are in this together, that his life involves someone other than himself.

"Be careful with that," he says to one of the movers. "Those are records."

"Rest easy," the man says.

Actually, it might have made more sense to leave the records here, the more ancient ones anyway, and buy fresh ones in Miami. But, when it came down to it, he couldn't bear to part with the scratched version of *The Queen of Spades* that had given him so much pleasure. Can he like a version as much that doesn't stop four times on the first side? Getting up and lifting the needle has become a part of the experience of listening to it for him, as though he were a part of the orchestra, helping them.

Minnie has a phonograph too now, a present from Ardis on her first birthday. It can play small thick plastic records, songs, nursery rhymes. She seems to like it, often brings him the records and waits while he puts them on. When he plays his own records, she usually ignores him, but sometimes comes and sits near the speaker, staring at it solemnly. He knows she must imagine there is someone inside singing; he thought that as a child.

"So, have we got everything?" one of the movers asks.

"I think so," Misha says.

"We're gonna store it for you, right?"

"Right."

"Okay. . . . Have a good trip."

"You too."

Misha watches them drive off. The house, emptied now except for the few things the Robertsons thought they might keep, looks even more forlorn. They are planning on having it repainted. In fact, the painter appeared the morning before to look the place over. "Looks like you haven't had a new paint job in a while," he commented.

Misha had never noticed, until everything was removed, how grimy many of the walls were. The only decent room is Minnie's, the one he and Ardis painted. He remembers that day: Ardis in jeans, spilling paint into her hair as she tried to do the ceiling with a roller. "How did Michelangelo manage with the Sistine Chapel?" she joked. At dinner the lavender streaks made her look like a punk rock singer. She said she could keep them in, for a new look.

When he arrives at her house, she is outside with Minnie, playing with her. They are rolling a red beach ball back and forth. The baby's aim is not that accurate. Ardis scampers into the bushes as the ball careens off to one side. Seeing Misha, she waves and tosses the ball to him. He catches it with one hand.

"Mee," Minnie says, running over, clutching at his pants leg. Her cheeks are smeared with mashed banana.

"I just gave her a little snack," Ardis says in explanation. She looks at him. "So, how'd it go? Everything packed up?"

He nods. "The house looked terrible when I left. . . . Did you ever notice how grungy it was?"

"Sort of. . . . Will they leave Minnie's room lavender?"

"I think they said they would."

He is glad Simon is not there. Even though this final parting is not the official one, though they have already had tears, passion, hugs, still something in his chest feels constricted. From her expression he knows she is feeling the same way.

"I got you a bunch of new maps," she says, going into the house to get them. "I wasn't sure if you had ones for all the states between here and Florida."

He hadn't. "Thanks." He looks at her; their glances catch, move away.

"How far do you think you'll get today?"

"Not very." It is past one already.

"I think she'll be good. . . . She's a good little traveler, aren't you, Minnie?"

"Good?" Minnie repeated.

"Bren and I always took turns getting carsick and fighting over the window seat," Ardis said. "But I think that's psychological. It comes when you get older."

"Right. . . . Well, should we get her buckled in?"

Ardis walks with Minnie to the car, and then stops. "Oh, listen, wait just a sec, did I show you the dress I got for the wedding? I got it the day before yesterday."

Misha shakes his head.

"Hold her a sec . . . I'll be right out." She returns, holding in front of her a low-cut yellow lacy dress with a full skirt. "I wish you could see me in it. It's so pretty!"

"I wish I could too. . . . Send me a picture."

"I will."

They put Minnie into her seat, then walk around to the other side of the car. "You know, I get down to Miami sometimes," Ardis says, "so maybe—"

"Sure." It amuses as well as pains him to think he could become one of her traveling companions: I know this guy in Miami. "Or I could just—come down for a visit or something, once you're settled. If you'd like."

The trembling in her voice pierces him; he finds he can't speak. Without saying anything further she steps into his arms. They hold each other tightly for a few moments. When she moves away, her eyes are bright. Biting her lip, she watches him get into the car. Minnie is looking at the two of them with curiosity.

Ardis laughs, her voice shaking slightly. "Here I thought you might run off with a younger woman," she says, "but this is ridiculous!"

Misha smiles, presses her hand, and then starts the car. He glances down and sees his now ringless index finger, a slight indentation in the flesh where the ring had been.

"Call me from the road?" she says anxiously. "Or when you get there?"

"I'll call tonight."

The baby reaches over and pounds on the horn. "Go!" she shouts gleefully.

Misha turns to Ardis. "Bossed around by women! What can I do?"

"It's your fate," she says tenderly, giving him a final quick kiss.

He watches her in the rearview mirror, standing there, arms crossed, in her red blouse and denim skirt, until he has to make a turn and she vanishes. Then he looks over at the baby. "So, kid," he says. "Are you ready? We've got a ways to go."

"Go," the baby repeats, thumping the front of her car seat.